Ivy Cottage

Rebecca Guy

☺☺☹☺☹☹

Also by Rebecca Guy

Ruin

Shattered

Haunted

Lost

About Author

Rebecca Guy was first introduced to all things paranormal at the tender age of ten when she received Hans Holzer's 'Ghosts–True Encounters with the World Beyond' from Father Christmas. She tortured herself with the stories late into every night, after which she was too terrified to sleep. Thanks Santa. The trauma started a love affair with all things horror and supernatural and she now like to write her own novels to torture herself and others with until they can't sleep. After all, sharing is caring. Rebecca was born and raised in Staffordshire. She still lives there with her three children and a beagle called Rosie.

f facebook.com/rebeccaguyauthor

⌾ instagram.com/rebeccaguyauthor

g goodreads.com/author/show/19771021.Rebecca_Guy

𝓟 pinterest.com/rebeccaguyauthor

Prologue

9 **99 CALL TRANSCRIPT EXCERPT**

Call handler (CH): Police, what's your emergency?

Caller: Oh, thank God, thank God. Please... (inaudible)... the pub.

CH: I didn't quite catch that, say again?

whimpering

Caller: White Road, town... (inaudible)... Masked... (inaudible)... Green Man.

CH: The Green Man pub?

Caller: Yes. Four men... They're inside, oh God. Please...

CH: A unit has been dispatched, sir. Are there people with you?

Caller: No. Yes. I'm out... (inaudible)... White Road.

*a yell, then 'leave him alone' in the background, a commotion is heard. *

CH: What's your name, sir? How many at the pub with you?

Heavy breathing

Caller: It's rammed. They're inside! They have guns! Please help!

Moaning, 'oh God no, please, please.'

CH: Sir? Can you tell me your name?

Screaming, a commotion, 'help us!'

CH: Sir?

Possible gunshot

Screams

Caller: He's hit! There's someone down! ... (inaudible)... No! Please... NO! Help us, Oh God, please help us!

Screams

Gunshots

LINE GOES DEAD

END OF TRANSCRIPT

One

T HE KEY TURNED EASILY in the lock, clicking the barrel over with a dull thud. Willow Townsend felt the cold metal under her fingers as the world seemed to tilt beneath her feet. Blood pulsed frantically in her ears and her vision doubled. She placed a hand on the doorjamb, closed her eyes, and began to count.

Breathe in for four, hold, out for six. In for four, hold, out for six.

It's okay. Breathe. Calm down. Stay present. Feel the wood under your hand. The paving under your feet, the smell of pine. Notice the breath in your chest, the beating of your heart...

Ah, well, maybe that was a bad one - her heart seemed to be racing a million miles an hour.

With a small huff she opened her eyes, and after a few more steadying breaths, the world seemed to come right again. She pushed a strand of mousy hair from her cheek where it had stuck with sweat.

Sweat.

Although it was a cool September day, and the temperature in the car had read just ten degrees.

She turned, pressing her back to the door, and released a long breath.

'Anxiety stems from thinking about the future, but I don't live in the future,' she whispered. 'What's here, right now?'

She inhaled the scent of the pine forest which wrapped the cottage and driveway with just enough open space to not feel claustrophobic, and just enough cosiness to feel like a hug. A gap in the trees gave way to a single-track tarmacked lane, which led down over the river Bree and into the village of Clover Nook below. Ahead, in the centre of the dusty stone and gravel packed drive, was her car, still cooling after the long journey.

'See, it's okay, the car is there, you can leave. There's always a choice. Always. You don't have to do this,' she whispered.

Although that wasn't strictly true. It was just a way of tricking herself out of the instinct to fight, or flee from, an old stone cottage in Central Scotland. A pretty cottage that she had rented on impulse after many urges from her concerned mum, and an understanding that things needed to change for her to feel okay again.

At least look around the place, even if you don't stay. The village is pretty and quiet. It would be a shame to run without even looking, especially as you've come so far... and you did promise Mum you would give it a go.

Willow chewed her lip as her mind began to settle into an uncomfortable compromise.

Clover Nook *had* been pretty in the sunshine. Along the single track lane she had passed a handful of grey stone houses with slate roofs, two small shops, a post office, community centre, and the Wild Pheasant pub. Just below her, at the bottom of the lane, was the only large house on this side of the village. A beautiful black and white building with a thatched roof, leaded windows, and large beams that trailed though it like a picture book cottage. On the outskirts of the village, there had been more houses dotted into the forest and hillside, but up here on this lane, she was alone. Ivy Cottage was the only house this side of the river, and that suited Willow just fine.

So, let's at least have a look around before you start back, eh?

As she felt herself backing down, there was a buzzing in her pocket, and her mouth stretched into a smile as she unlocked her phone. It was a message from Carlton.

Hope you're okay, babe. Missing you like hell. I don't understand this madness, but I do understand that you need to be given a chance to make your own mistakes. It's part of your healing. Anytime you need to, you can come home. There will always be a place for you here. Did I say I miss you?

Love always, C.

PS. don't forget we upped the Prozac to 40mg. If you struggle, it's okay to take 60mg, but no more. I have your prescription on file, just let me know when you need more, and I'll bring them to you. I know, I know, you're apparently hundreds of miles away, but... any excuse to see you.

Warmth spread through Willow. She missed him, too. Carlton had been her rock, the only one to have understood since the terror of that day, and he had been the right person to be with in more ways than one. Not only her long-term partner, but a psychiatrist by profession, he had taken care of her completely, inside and out. She was utterly grateful... but there was no way she would disclose her location. That would defeat the purpose of doing this at all, because he would make up all manner of excuses and end up staying here with her, or worse, taking her home.

She had promised Mum she would give this time alone, and she had promised herself. It was a promise she wanted to keep, no matter how much it hurt.

She messaged back, ignoring his urges to see her.

I'm good, missing you too. Just about to move in. Hopefully the year will go quickly, it seems such a long time right now!

Willow pocketed the phone, forcing herself not to immediately answer his reply. That was another thing she had to stop. She loved him, but she relied on him too much, and leaned on him for everything. She knew he didn't mind, but this was her time now, her own experiment in healing, because she'd discovered over the last four years that even a therapist didn't seem to hold all the answers.

Willow inhaled and blew out a long breath, pulling her attention back to the driveway. Now that her anxiety was subsiding, so was the impulse to get back in the car and flee.

And that's good, just go easy. No rush.

She turned to face the front door. The burgundy wood was sturdy and solid and adorned with nothing but a small round keyhole. It may have been stark and imposing, if the two large bay windows, with their colourful flower boxes, and a decorative free standing letterbox hadn't flanked it. As it was, the cottage was chocolate-box pretty, and the swathe of ivy enveloping the right-hand side only added to its appeal. She reached out a hand, felt her heart begin to thump, and paused.

Am I really going to do this?

Her hand was inches from the wood, and her breath caught in her throat. The door seemed to grow in size, like a strong sentinel, gatekeeper to all that is unknown, and all that is terrifying.

Stop it, Willow. It's just a bloody door. A normal door to a normal cottage.

Before she could think any further, she pushed the door open, grabbed her suitcase, and stepped inside.

She stood in a small porch area with a coat hook and a shoe stand to her left. Ahead was an entire wall of privacy glass, etched with thick swirls, and a central glass door. To capture the light in this small space, she supposed, but what she liked was that she could see shapes in the hallway beyond. The glass screen acting like a filter before she was exposed to the full 3D reality of the world inside.

Unlocking this second door - an added security measure that she liked - she stepped into a much wider hallway than she had expected. Plain brown carpet lined the floor, but it was a pleasant contrast to the freshly painted magnolia walls. A sideboard sat to her left, while a door to her right revealed a large storage cupboard. Beyond that, the cottage split in two.

To the right was a long corridor with three bedrooms, two smaller doubles at the back of the cottage, and one large bedroom with a bay window to the front. This room held a king-sized bed, flanked by a bookshelf and a small side table. Across the room by the window there was a dressing table, and to her right there was an enormous wardrobe, but even with the abundance of furniture, there was still space in here to perform her morning yoga routine.

Absolutely my room, Willow thought, feeling a tiny flicker of excitement light her stomach.

She left her suitcase in the bedroom and went back into the corridor. Past the bedrooms and back into the central hallway there was another glass door ahead. She pushed it open to reveal a bright living area, with a large bay window to the front and a smaller window to the side. A small dining table sat dead across from the door, flanked by four chairs. To its left, In front of the large bay, two small settees sat at right angles to each other by the fireplace. A blue rug divided the seating and the television, which sat on a stand in the corner.

Cosy, Willow thought, a smile lifting her mouth.

To her right, next to the dining table, a further glass door led to a small but functional kitchen at the back of the cottage. Above the sink was a window adorned with a red check blind, and next to it, another solid burgundy wooden door which led out to the back garden. To her left, after a stretch of worktop, was a further door, this one painted white. Inspection revealed the bathroom, which flanked the kitchen along the back of the house. Again, small but functional.

Shutting the bathroom door behind her, Willow walked back into the living area with a grin.

I like it. It's warm and cosy here. The place has a good flow, and a nice feel.

It was also a nice size for her alone, well protected, and secluded enough that the outside world wouldn't know she was here unless they ventured up the lane to Clover Nook woods. She had it on good authority from the owner that people didn't often trespass beyond the private lane sign at the driveway's end. The path into the woods took them away from the lane at the sign and up beside the cottage, but few people walked this side of the village. Access from the other side was much easier, and the walking more open with rising hills and incredible views.

It was more than enough for her to hide for a while. To be anonymous and invisible for as long as it took for her to understand who she was again and how to overcome her own paralysis of life.

I think I'm going to like it here.

She reassessed the small living room with a nod. She liked the low, uneven ceiling, and the neutral walls which seemed to give the room space it didn't have. Her eyes dropped to the fireplace, which was as ancient as it was charming, but she knew she'd never have to use it. The owner had renovated the cottage a few years ago. Oil-fired central heating had been added throughout, and the windows had all been replaced. The cottage would be more than warm enough.

Chocolate box, she thought, but without the hassle of being poky and chilly, as ancient houses often were.

Secure, as ancient houses often weren't.

Invisible, for as long as she needed to be.

'It couldn't be more perfect,' she whispered.

TWO

L ATER THAT AFTERNOON SHE cried - hard - as canned laughter emanated from the television in the background. She texted Carlton through her tears and told him she was doing fine, absolutely loving her new house. She even joked that she may not come home and that he could move in here with her.

To her relief, he stuck to her no calling rule and texted a reply that it wasn't possible - he had a client base in Bristol - and she should stop letting her emotions run away with her. Had she had her pills tonight?

Feeling her skin get hot, Willow sniffed as she put the phone on the settee and dragged her shoulder length mousy waves back into a ponytail. The hot flushes weren't frequent, but as with the anxiety at the door, she knew the signs. They appeared whenever she felt overwhelmed and out of control, and that was never a good thing. Carlton was adamant that she keep calm and keep on top of her medication after a hypoxia attack that had nearly landed her in hospital just a few months ago. As soon as her chest constricted, or she felt any symptoms, she was to stop, take her pills, and count her breaths until the feeling passed.

Waving a hand at her face, Willow picked up the packet of pills beside her, took one and washed it down with hot tea.

She wiped her tears and placed her head in her hands. She was tired. It had been a long day, not only physically, but battling the mental demons, too. At every turn, she seemed to be trying to squash a negative thought, which caused a negative feeling, which sent her on a spiral of anxiety and 'I can't' instead of her carefully rehearsed 'I can'.

Eager to get out of the mindset that was beginning to drag her down, Willow looked out of the large bay window. Outside the afternoon sun was lowering, but the sky was still blue, remnants of the beautiful end-of-summer day it had been.

I should get outside. A walk would lift my spirits.

Except that I'm tired. I can go out tomorrow. I've had such a long drive, and I can't be bothered...

'Be bothered,' she said, catching herself, 'stop making excuses. You are no longer Carlton's chastised, weeping Willow. From now on you are strong, adaptable, Willow, taking control of her life.'

Willow blew out her cheeks.

That'll be the day.

But without further thought, she swung her legs off the settee, slipped on her pumps, grabbed her coat, and made her feet move through the kitchen and out the back door. She triple-checked the lock before starting up the long lawn to the back gate and Clover Nook woods beyond.

The track from the gate was little used and overgrown, nettles and brambles snagging at her jeans and hoodie as she passed through. Just as she was thinking the front entrance may be a better option, the track opened up, and she stepped on to a small stony path which led both left and right.

Stopping to brush herself down and remove the bramble from her thigh, she checked both directions. Right led back past the hedge of the cottage garden, and so without too much thought, she turned left and began to walk.

Three

THE NOISES BEGAN NEXT to Willow as she hurried back to the cottage. A small rustle, a crunch, the sharp snap of a twig. Willow glanced left, her heartbeat rising as she squinted into the trees. She had been careless, the sunlight had long gone, and the moon was full, casting large pockets of foreboding darkness between the trees. She swallowed hard and hurried forward. She couldn't understand why she hadn't reached the cottage yet. It had taken under an hour to get out here and it was now taking far too long to get back.

Stupid, Willow, but the faster you walk, the faster you get back. It can't be far now.

She was focused on the path, keeping her attention on her stride to steady her breath, when there was another rustle alongside her in the foliage. The back of her neck prickled, and she came to a stop, her heart banging hard. The night was cool, but a bead of sweat ran down her forehead and into her eyes. She blinked against the sting, staying quiet, listening, trying to fight against the quickening of her breath.

There was nothing.

'That's the problem, Willow. It's quiet, that's all. There's nothing there. There's nothing ever there. You make it up, and scare yourself. Now breathe, you need to calm down.'

She put a hand out to lean against the thick trunk of a spruce and pulled in a breath as her heart thumped.

Calm down. Breathe.

In for four, hold, out for six.

As she blew out, Carlton's calm voice entered her mind.

'You hear things. You're waiting for them, babe. A footstep on the stairs, a voice in the other room. There's no one there. It's imagination. It's not surprising after all you've been through. Go easy on yourself. Breathe. In for four, hold it, out for six.'

'In for four, hold...' she whispered against the tree.

That had been the day she had heard someone upstairs. A fact she had been so sure of that she had called Carlton back from work to check the house. In his concern, he had ushered her into the car and gone into the house alone before coming out ten minutes later to tell her there was no one. He had then checked every room with her, until she had been calm enough to allow him to go back to work.

'...out for six.'

As her heart rate slowed, Willow took her hand from the tree and listened to the forest. There was nothing unusual.

'Nothing but the breeze. I'm hearing things, but it's okay. I know that now, and I'm understanding more quickly. It's in my head.'

The moon brightened as the clouds parted, and shadows elongated across the path.

I need to get back, she thought, beginning to walk again. After a few beats of steady rhythm, she began to calm.

Just my imagination, that's all.

Until a branch snapped loudly in the trees, and her stomach lurched as she swung her head left. Her heart pulsed in her ears as she stopped again and scoured the dark forest.

It's just an animal, either that or it's you, Willow. It's your imagination. Keep walking. It's fine.

But she wasn't so easily calmed this time.

Where is the damn cottage?

Swallowing hard, she turned, wondering if she had inadvertently taken the wrong path, but she couldn't have. There were no turns. No forks that she had taken. She had walked one straight path, and turned back on the same path.

One straight path, Willow, so why are you not back yet? Did you take a wrong turn somewhere? Did you go wrong?

Her stomach turned over, and heaving shallow breaths, she forced her legs to move forward. The path under her feet was the same as the one she had walked down. There was no mistake, there couldn't be. She hadn't turned from it once...

Her thoughts trailed off as the forest seemed to still. The air grew heavy and expectant, and gooseflesh puckered her skin. She slowed to a stop, her skin prickling under her clothes as a certainty hit her.

Someone, or something, was out there in the woods.

Next to her.

Watching her.

Tracking her.

'No. I don't like this. Please leave me alone.'

Her voice was loud in the stillness and a bird took flight in the trees above as she quickly snapped her mouth shut.

Evidence of madness. She would go under. Not only was she hearing things, but she was talking to them, too. Carlton had shushed her many times over the years.

Shhh, it's nothing, babe, just count to ten in your head. Distract your mind until the feeling is gone.

Thoughts of Carlton did nothing to calm her now. She wiped sweat from her brow with a shaking hand as her heart thundered against her ribs and her breaths became more ragged. Far from being placated by Carlton's familiar advice, the feeling that someone was hiding in the darkness only intensified, and a small whimper left her lips.

Watched, Willow. You're being watched. Who's there?

'No,' she muttered, 'I won't do this.'

She walked faster and began to count the steps in her head.

One, two, three, four...

The never-ending path stretching ahead, and impenetrable blackness on either side, were eating at the last of her resolve.

'Where is the damn cottage?'

There was a rustle of undergrowth beside her, closer now, and Willow flinched and began to jog as tears pricked her eyes.

'Leave me alone! Where's the bloody cottage?'

The rustle continued and fear propelled her forward even as her lungs seemed to shrink in her chest. Adrenaline fired her muscles despite the lack of oxygen, but as her speed increased, so did the thing at the side of her.

It was matching her now, beat for beat, forcing Willow to up her pace to a full-on sprint. She ran down the moonlit path, her arms and legs pumping hard, her lungs burning, and her eyes streaming. As the path stretched ahead into the darkness, the intense presence was all-encompassing, never leaving her side.

'LEAVE ME ALONE!' She screeched, stumbling as the path suddenly became uneven. Her arms flailed as her feet tried to keep her upright. She was aware of the thing in the trees almost on her as she slowed, but she was also aware of something else up ahead.

The cottage.

A break in the trees revealed the tall hedge of the cottage garden just ahead.

Relief and terror forced tears down Willow's face as she found her balance and ran. She was moving faster than she had ever run in her life, but the thing in the woods was too close now. It broke out of the undergrowth and there was the sound of running steps just behind. It was gaining on her... fast.

'It's too dark!' She screamed, and her hands clenched into fists. 'You're in my imagination. You can't have run all this way in there. It's too dark!'

The cottage hedge and gate were mere feet away, but Willow was suddenly sure that she wouldn't make it. This was the time. Her time. Whatever it was, it would kill her, right here on this path.

You should never have come here, never have left home, and now you won't ever go back.

Her heart thundered and her vision blurred as her limbs shook with fatigue.

'I can't get away. I won't get away. LEAVE ME ALONE!'

Tears streamed down her face as blind terror pushed her forward, and there was a pressure in her temples that she was sure would break her skull. The thing was almost on her now. So close she could almost feel it's breath on her neck, but Willow's legs were beginning to feel like heavy weights of lead. Then a darkness loomed next to her, a presence that she didn't dare to look at, and finally a force, knocking her feet from underneath her. She felt herself falling. Down, down, down, until she fell hard on the tiny path to the cottage gate.

She screamed, one hand stretched out to graze the wooden gate. She felt the sting of nettles and brambles as they closed around her, and then her head hit the ground and there was nothing.

An alarm was ringing. It began as a mere distraction, somewhere far off in the distance, but then grew louder and louder until it felt like it penetrated her entire being.

Willow groaned and dragged her eyes open. The lids were heavy, and her head felt groggy and sore. She had felt better after a heavy night out drinking with friends in the city.

Light streamed through a large window, and she blinked in confusion as flashes of the night before returned.

There was something in the woods. Chasing me. It knocked me down, didn't it?

Where am I?

Her chest gave a jolt, and she pushed herself up onto her elbow to look around the unfamiliar room.

'Where am I? Carlton? Carlton!'

There was no reply, and then, slowly, the unfamiliar room became familiar.

The cottage.

I'm in my new bedroom.

Not only that, but she was on the floor. Her pyjamas were wet down one leg, and the duvet was hanging off the side of the bed, along with half of the sheet. A smashed glass of water lay next to her, and her pill packets were scattered across the room. Her phone was nowhere to be seen.

'Shit,' she whispered, sitting up and scooting back against the bed. Her heart slammed against her ribs as she scoured the room, but everything else looked in place. Sunlight streamed through the window and the house was quiet and warm. Outside, birds chirped the dawn chorus, and her breathing slowed.

'It's okay, see? Calm down, it was just a dream. Just another dream.'

The vivid dreams had been a feature of her life for longer than Willow cared to remember, but they had dropped off over the last year and she didn't fancy their return. She rubbed her face with her hands and got to her feet, picking up the broken glass and her pills, and padding along the corridor to the kitchen.

She put coffee and sugar into a cup and switched the kettle on with a yawn, eyeing the back door.

Is it locked?

It was a dream, Willow.

But is it?

Humouring herself after the uneasy night, she checked the back door, and then checked on both front doors, too.

'Locked,' she said. 'Damn dream.'

Back in the kitchen, she stirred the coffee with one hand and twirled the packet of pills in the other.

40mg. One tablet twice a day.

Willow sighed. She had been taking 20mg for the last four years, but when she made the decision to leave for a year, the anxiety and nightmares had increased. In response, Carlton had increased the dosage of her medication.

'When did you have the pills yesterday?' she murmured, tapping a finger against the box.

She'd had the first one when she woke up, she remembered, but the other one she'd had after the crying fit yesterday afternoon. Just before the walk.

The walk she didn't remember returning from, although she had obviously made it home. Not only that, but she had locked the doors, undressed, and got into bed before the vivid dream had dumped her out of it.

'Well, at least I know not to have the second pill until I'm ready for bed in future. It obviously knocks me out.'

The alarm that had woken her began its pulsing melody again, and Willow realised it was her phone. She crossed to the kitchen toward the noise and put her coffee cup on the dining table where the phone lay.

Carlton's name lit the screen and Willow pursed her lips.

'No call policy, honey,' she said, cutting off the call and typing a message. His message came through as she was still typing.

Well, that hurts. I was only going to say good morning and ask how your first night had been.

He followed the comment with a sad face emoji, and she smiled as she fired her own message back to him.

Carlton, I love you and I want to talk to you more than anything, but you know not to call. Please. I mean it. I hate cutting you off like that. It hurts me too. The night was great, thanks. Slept like a log.

His reply was immediate.

Good. I was worried about you. I miss you, that's all.

Willow sighed and tapped her fingers on the table thinking of a way she could put this without hurting him, because she didn't want to hurt him, but this was something she would do whether he liked it or not - and she knew he didn't, he'd told her as much at every opportunity in the weeks before she left.

I miss you, too, but you can't call. I have to do this alone. Can you humour me?

I am, babe. I just don't see why I can't talk to my girl when she needs help. I can help you. I have helped you, haven't I? I just don't understand why you're doing this?

Willow sipped her coffee.

You have helped. I couldn't have done the last four years without you. But now I need to stand alone. I can't depend on you forever. I have to heal.

You are healing, and you can depend on me forever. I don't mind. I want you to.

Willow stared at his reply.

That's the problem though, isn't it? I depend on you too much for the answers, and you want me to. It's a no-win situation; Mum was right. It's been four years. Four. And I'm not a child. I want to work. I want to go out. I want to live and do all the things you tell me I'm not ready for. I want a life!

Tears filled her eyes as she messaged back.

I can't, it's not right. Let me try this, please?

I'm not stopping you, babe, but I'm going to say this. When you realise this isn't working, and that you're getting worse - which you will - come home. I'll be waiting for you. I won't message again, don't worry.

Willow felt her stomach lurch.

No, that isn't what I meant-

Her fingers stopped mid flow, and she bit her lip in thought. If she carried this on, he'd end up upset and she would call. She knew the ropes; it was a given. Just last week she would have done just that, but she was on a new path now. A path she wanted to stay on, at least while she was coping. She deleted what she started and tried again.

Thank you. I love you.

When he didn't reply, Willow slugged the rest of her coffee and went to get dressed. Carlton would be licking his wounds, but he would be fine. Like Mum had said, if he loved her, he would let her do this her own way. She had to be strong now, slay the demons, and the first demon to slay today would be the wood chaser.

Four

T HERE WERE TWO KNOCKS at the door before Suzanne's dark, disembodied head appeared around it.

'I've been trying to put a call through, Dr Mathers. It's Mrs West. She says the pills don't agree with her. Can we try something else? And does she need to see you?'

Carlton Mathers looked up from his phone. Mrs West always got his attention. She was one of his most prominent customers and making her happy, and her life easier, was exactly what both of them wanted.

'I can take the call if you're busy, it's just that you usually ask to speak with her?' Suzanne's dark eyebrows arched up into her cropped hair, and Carlton shook his head.

'Tell her I'll call her back in ten. I'll just check her file first. She may need to come in.'

He looked at the middle-aged secretary he had hired just three weeks after he started up on his own eight years ago. Loyal and smart. Sexy too. He didn't know what he would do without her.

Much like my weeping Willow.

Suzanne dipped her head and pulled it from the doorway.

'Oh, Suzie?' he called, and her face reappeared. 'Make a coffee, would you? I'm having one of those mornings.'

Suzanne smiled. 'Of course. Missing her already, eh?'

Carlton shrugged, and she pulled the door shut. He looked back down at his phone which showed Willow's last message.

Thank you. I love you.

It stung. It wasn't like her at all. One needy sentence from him would have her on her knees, but here she was shunning him, and it hurt like hell.

What if this year passes and she doesn't need me anymore? What then?

He worked his jaw as his fingers hovered over the phone. It wasn't in his nature to back down, but this situation seemed to call for it, at least until he knew how to handle it better.

I'm sorry. I love you, too.

He sent the message before he could change his mind. If she wanted time, she could have it. She was entitled to it, after all, and he knew the nature of her trauma would bring her back home eventually. She wouldn't cope alone, and she would realise that soon.

For now, he would just have to man up and bide his time.

Five

A FTER OATMEAL WITH BLUEBERRIES and Prozac for breakfast, Willow put on her shoes and coat and stepped out into the sunny September morning.

Birds sang, and the trees rustled above her as she stepped tentatively onto the stony path and looked around. Her shoulders relaxed as she realised how far the dream was from reality. The trees of last night were eerie and dense, twisted and menacing. Now, in the morning light, the woodland was bright, its tall, majestic trees towering protectively over everything underneath.

See? No demons.

Willow breathed a sigh of relief, turned left, and began to stride into the forest.

Sunlight dappled the path ahead, and shivering bright spots on the ground at her feet enticed her forward. There were no noises from the undergrowth, and as she passed the area she had turned back from yesterday evening, she felt a rush of pride.

You did it, you're out here alone, past yesterday's turning point, and striding onward. The best thing? Carlton isn't with you. You're doing this for yourself, by yourself!

And there wasn't a single flutter of panic or anxiety, she noted. For now, anyway.

As she strode on, she took a chance on a left turn that harboured a wide grassy path. She was enjoying the lush green springiness under her feet, the cool breeze on her cheeks, the smell of pine in her nose, and the sound of the birds in her ears, when her thoughts drifted to home.

Home, back in Bristol, where she would have been stuck in the house right now, watching daytime television while Carlton worked. Home, where she would have watched the windows for shadows and listened for footsteps and noises, even in broad daylight. Home, where she would have called Carlton a handful of times on a good day, and over sixty on her worst so far.

Pent up. Agitated. Anxious.

At home, there was nothing to do, nothing to take her mind off the anxiety. Up here there were things she had to do for herself. She had to *think* for herself, which was something she had given up long ago, and okay, she was terrified, and she had been spooked, but so far, she was having as many anxious free moments as those fraught with anxiety.

And really it's all thanks to Mum.

Mum, who had moved on despite the trauma, who had let it go and found peace. Watching her mum's recovery had made Willow wonder why she was so weak, why she couldn't be the same. What was stopping her from getting better? Mum had only one idea. She'd had to cope alone, while relying on professional help outside of her own life. Willow was living full time with the help. She was dependent, Mum had said, and it was doing her no good.

Since the attack that had taken her husband's life four years ago, Mum had sold the family home and moved into an expensive retirement village in Somerset. Somewhere she was always around others in a safe and secure environment. It had been her way. She couldn't have lived in the house after all that had happened, and so she had sold it. Took control and moved on.

Mum took control where you gave it away. Too scared to take it and face it, and Carlton was all too happy to help.

He did help. He did what he thought was right, but he's probably hindered you in the process.

Willow felt guilt circle her stomach.

Well, that's okay, I'm here now. It wasn't his fault.

She felt exertion pull at her calves and realised with surprise that she was back on dirt and walking sharply uphill.

Tranced out again. At least this time it was movement induced, not pill induced.

I suppose I–

Willow's thoughts cut off at a rustle in the undergrowth alongside her. Her heart banged and her chest tightened as an immediate veil of panic landed on her shoulders.

No. It's nothing, Willow. Keep walking, it's just a forest animal. Nothing to be scared of.

She forced her legs onward, trying to draw in air that seemed in short supply. The rustle continued in the foliage alongside her, keeping pace.

Just like it did in the dream–

Stop it, Willow. Just stop and it will go away. You're imagining things again.

She stopped, trying to heave air into lungs that seemed the size of a barbie doll's. The rustle stopped in the trees beside her, and then there was the sound of the birds, and the trees moving in the breeze, nothing more. She pulled in some easier breaths and was about to move on when the rustle began again. This time the bracken moved in the trees to her right, and she watched with mounting terror as the bracken swayed in formation. Something was heading toward her ... but above the bracken there was nothing to be seen, until...

Willow's breath caught in a scream as something black charged from the bushes, launching itself at her side in much the same way the dream 'thing' had done.

The scream let go as she toppled to her knees and covered the back of her head with her hands.

'Leave me alone, leave me alone, leave me alone,' she chanted as something slimy and wet flicked over her hands above her.

'For Christ's sake, Frodo, get off her! I'm sorry, so sorry. He's friendly, don't worry.'

Willow processed the accented words and looked up just enough to reveal four furry paws trotting around the front of her head.

'He's friendly, I promise. Frodo! Damn dog.'

The dog's legs trotted out of vision and Willow lifted her head to see a pair of white trainers and an outstretched hand.

'I'm sorry, let me help you up.'

Willow took the hand and clambered shakily to her feet.

'Oh Christ, you're shaking. I'm sorry, I'm so sorry!' The girl brushed Willow's arms with a brisk hand to remove the dirt. 'He's too friendly, I keep telling him.' She turned to the dog. 'Bad boy, Frodo!'

Willow took the time to slow her breath, noting that Frodo looked far too happy about being scolded. He sat, tongue hanging out in a grin, his tail wagging up path dust at his mistress's voice. He cocked his head on one side as she wagged a finger at him, and Willow couldn't help smiling as her breathing and heart rate finally slowed.

'It's fine,' she said, brushing dirt from her knees. 'I was in my own world, that's all. He made me jump.'

The girl looked at her, and Willow saw a pretty pixie face under tendrils of blonde hair which had fallen out of a loose ponytail. Her slender body was toned under the tight, breathable t-shirt and leggings.

'No,' she said. 'It's not fine. He's a bad boy.'

Willow made a fuss of Frodo, who lavished in the attention and gave her kisses that made her think when she got home, she may just get a dog.

'It's okay, really. He's beautiful. Is he a Labrador?' she said, running her hands over his sleek dark fur.

'He's nutty as a fruitcake is what he is, but aye, he's a Lab. He's a little boisterous, only eighteen months. He's not my dog, he belongs to my brother, but Evan works long hours, so I have him in the daytime. I work at home, see, and he's good company out here. I don't normally see a soul this end of the forest, it's far quieter than the Elm Lane end.'

'Yes, I've heard it's quiet here.'

'You've heard? Don't think I missed that, and don't think I missed the accent, either. You're not from around here, are you? I didn't think I recognised you, but then again, Evan says I'm a recluse, so what would I know? I don't miss many details though. It's part of my job!' The girl laughed, dimples appearing in her cheeks, and Willow smiled, her interest piqued.

'Your job? What do you do? It can't involve many people if you're a recluse.'

'I'm a writer,' she said. 'My butt is in a chair delivering word counts most of the day. This is my break. I walk daily, but I don't see many people out here, so I spend a lot of time alone. Evan says it's my downfall, and that I spend too much time in my imagination. I call it my livelihood, and I love it. So where are you from?'

'Bristol, in sunny England, but for the next year, I'll be living up here. I'm renting Ivy Cottage at the end of the lane.'

'Ah, so you're the new tenant! I've heard about you.'

Willow stepped back as Frodo whipped by with a long stick, which he turned to drop at their feet. She picked it up and threw it into the wood. The dog disappeared in a flash of black.

'You've heard about me?' she said.

Crikey, I've only been here a day. News travels fast.

'Oh yeah, like I said, I may not see many people, but I don't miss much. Last night at yoga a couple of the oldies were discussing 'the young lady who appears to have moved into the cottage all by herself.'

The girl squinted at her. 'What do you want with that ancient old place all by yourself?'

Willow laughed. 'It's quaint!'

'That's one word for it. I'm not sure many around here would agree.'

'What do you mean?'

The girl grinned and flapped her hand. 'Oh, never mind. Evan says I have an overactive imagination, and I know I have an even more overactive mouth. Forget I said anything. So, are you into yoga?'

Willow found herself thrown off track by the question. Her inquisitiveness about the cottage lost in the rapid conversation.

'Yoga? Er, well yes, as it happens, I love yoga. I usually practice every day, but I must admit time got away with me this morning. I haven't got round to it yet.'

A little scary dream got in the way more like. Then I had to take the pills which make me sleepy... such is life, eh?

Willow sighed as she looked at the path which led away up the hill.

'Well, it sounds like you need a good yoga session then, and I have the answer. It'll be a great way to introduce yourself to a few of the locals, too. I go three times a week to the community centre just down the road. Guess when my next session is?'

Willow looked back at her with a frown, stumped.

'I don't know.'

The girl slapped her arm playfully. 'Tonight, dingbat! And tonight is extra special too. You know why?'

How on earth would I know why?

Willow shook her head, flummoxed.

'It's hot yoga. Yoga, but in forty degrees.'

'Okay.' Willow raised her eyebrows.

'You ever done it before?'

'In forty degrees? It never gets that hot in England.'

'Well, it does in Clover Nook Community Centre on a Thursday night. It starts at seven. I'll let Tam know you're coming if you like.'

Willow blinked at the girl, who was still all dimples, like she had asked Willow to do nothing more than walk up the path with her.

'No!'

The girl's smile slipped. 'No?'

Willow checked herself, trying to calm her racing thoughts as she spoke.

Christ, she's only asked you to yoga.

'No. I mean, I can't. Not tonight.'

'Got a special date?'

Willow felt herself reel back, startled. 'A date? No, I'm already in a relationship, I'm just... Um...'

Bugger, what the hell are you doing, Willow, think.

'Washing your hair?'

'Could be,' Willow admitted.

'Okay, I get it. You don't like the thought of hot yoga. Let me sell it to you.'

There was a snap in the woods, and Willow's heart thumped, until Frodo reappeared with the stick. The girl threw it for him.

'Think of the most contortionist-y position you can get into, and then think of getting three times further, easily, with no pain. Can't touch your toes? You can tonight!'

Willow tried to bring her thoughts back to the girl, to focus on where the conversation was leading.

'What?' she said.

The girl laughed again. 'The heat loosens up the muscles so that you can stretch further into the asanas. Imagine doing yoga in a cold room and how much you have to warm up before you can even get into a strong warrior two? Now imagine a short warm up and you're doing it like a pro in seconds. It's amazing. Really. And you sweat buckets. It's like the most amazing detox. Not that your skin needs it mind.'

Willow was beginning to think it sounded like fun, but the thought of a downward dog in a room full of people she didn't know was sending her into a sweat - and that was before the heat had been turned up.

'I don't know,' she said, but the girl was already talking over her.

'You're new here, and it's such a great way to meet people. There are not many people you'll bump into out here, and the village will talk about you regardless. What do you say? Shall I tell Tam you'll be there?'

Willow paused, and the girl took it as a sign that she was coming round to the idea. She placed an arm on Willow's as she threw the stick again and Frodo raced off.

'Fantastic! I'll tell her. If you're worried about turning up alone, I can pick you up if you like? We can go together. Everything is provided, all you need is yourself.'

Willow was about to contest. She was feeling more than a little uncomfortable at now being picked up by a stranger, too, but the girl simply steamrollered on.

'Tell you what, give me your number. I'll message you first and then if your special date really is so special you can tell me later. It's hard to let someone down on the spot, isn't it?'

Willow grinned and nodded, handing her phone to the girl, who laughed as she entered her number. 'I mean, how crazy is this? I don't even know your name, and already we're off to yoga together.'

'Willow.'

'Ah, beautiful. Like the tree. Not the tree pose, of course, just the tree. Hi Willow, I'm Sophie.'

Sophie held out a hand. Willow took it with a smile, and Sophie squeezed reassuringly. 'I know I seem crazy, but I'm really not that bad. Give me a chance, eh? I'll soon have you hooked up with people around here, so much so, you won't want to go back to Bristol because you'll be having such a blast. What do you say... hot yoga?'

A grin spread across Willow's face, and a warmth flooded her chest.

Is this girl an angel? You wanted a life, Willow, and she's offering it to you on a plate. Are you going to take it?

'Okay,' she agreed with a nod, wondering if this whole exchange was a dream. Surely, in a few moments, she would wake up and Sophie would be gone.

'Brilliant!' Sophie said, holding her hand up for a high five that Willow returned. 'I have words to write, but I'll see you later, partner. Come on Frodo.'

Sophie turned left onto a lesser trodden path and the dog ran after her.

'I'll see you just after half six,' Sophie said over her shoulder with a smile and a wave, and then she disappeared into the trees. Come and gone as fast as a hurricane.

'Not if I see you first,' Willow muttered with a grin before starting back along the path toward the cottage.

As she made her way home, she realised two things.

The first was that she no longer felt afraid of the surrounding
woodland. The nerves had entirely gone with the presence of a
friendly face and chatter.

The second was that there was no way on God's earth she was
doing hot yoga tonight in a room full of strangers.

Six

I T TOOK WILLOW OVER an hour to get back, and she had used the time for some heavy self-reflection.

Did you come here to live life or to be afraid? Live life.

Did you come here to become more self-reliant or to hide? Self-reliant, whatever that takes.

Do you want to get to know people and make new friends? Yes.

All of this is a part of being here, of moving on and getting past old trauma, isn't it?

It was here that she stumbled a little.

But Carlton said that I wasn't ready.

Carlton isn't here.

But it's only been a day. I can give it a couple of weeks to settle in before throwing myself into this, can't I?

What's wrong with now?

I'm not ready...

Try it.

And so here she was, hours later, knees knocking, as she waited outside the front door for Sophie to arrive so that she could go to her first ever hot yoga session.

Not because she wanted to do hot yoga, but because she wanted to do what Carlton had said she wasn't ready for. It was as simple as finding out if she could.

That was all.

When she had thrown up her dinner five minutes ago, she had thought she couldn't. And now, standing here in her yoga gear, feeling faint, her heart banging in her chest, she thought she couldn't too. But here was Sophie, and suddenly there was no turning back.

'Hey stranger! Are you ready to see what your body can do?'

Sophie was dressed head to toe in grey Lycra with an obscure red and black pattern down each leg and across her chest. The pattern on her chest vanished as she pulled a hoodie over her head, which disappeared for a moment and then reappeared with a grin.

Willow swallowed the contents of her stomach and stretched her lips into a smile before forcing her legs to walk down the path to greet her new friend. She wondered if Sophie would notice her grey pallor, or the fact that she was shaking from head to toe, but if she did, she didn't say a word.

'Sure. When you said you were picking me up, I kind of thought you'd be in a car.'

'Don't own one. Clover Nook is two miles by three. Why the heck would I need a car? I work from my home office; all I need is that and the store and I'm good. We got snowed in last winter. A whole three feet of drifting snow. Best three weeks ever before it thawed!'

Willow fell into step with Sophie as they retreated down the lane, crossed the river at the bridge, and turned left into Clover Nook.

After driving through it in a state of anxiety yesterday, she hadn't taken the time to appreciate just how pretty the tiny village was. Most of the houses were smaller stone cottages with gardens full of late summer blooms, but the largest house in the village sat at the bottom of her lane, just left of the small stone bridge. Its thatched roof was perfectly kept, as were the huge freshly painted black beams and gleaming white walls. The only sense of old on this house was the structure which held the house up on its wonky frame, and one of the old lead windows upstairs, which bulged from its housing.

'McGracken house,' Sophie said, following Willow's eyeline. 'The oldest house in the village. It's a hostel now, the McGracken's still run it, been in their family for generations. Free beds, food, and drink. Heck, there's even free work if you want it!'

Sophie peeled off into laughter, and Willow frowned at the large house as they rounded the corner from the bridge and stepped onto a small pavement.

'Free work?'

'Aye, they let you stay for as long as you like, and eat from their table, but you help out in their yard. They're environmentalists, into sustainability. The house is off grid, you know.'

'Off grid?'

'They make their own electricity and gas comes from the methane in the cow dung from the field behind. They pump the water from the back hill over yonder.' Sophie pointed to a hill that rose behind the house and sank back down to the side of the woodland by her own little cottage. Beyond that, it rose again, something she hadn't noticed before. 'They're clever inventors, but, you know, we have all the mod-cons here. Why make life hard for yourself, eh?'

'It's for the good of the climate, I suppose, if they care enough.'

'Oh, aye. They care all right. Mr McGracken even instigated a few protests down in London last year about getting to net zero. Whatever that is.'

'Carbon emissions, I believe.'

Sophie cocked an eyebrow at Willow as they passed a post office, the Wild Pheasant pub, and a craft shop before coming to a building with a set of blue double doors. A white plaque on the wall above stated that this was Clover Nook Community Centre.

'You'll have to fill me in sometime. Honestly, I have no idea.'

Sophie pushed the left-hand door, and they entered a large square room adorned with silk covered tables and benches, and smelling of incense. A handful of people were taking off shoes and coats and stretching out legs and shoulders, and Willow felt the thudding of her heart beneath her T-shirt.

'Hi, Sophie.' The woman in front of a small desk in the corner smiled. 'Ah, this must be Willow, from Ivy Cottage. Is that right?'

Willow looked at the older lady, who wore a bright smile, a bright pink sports top, and black leggings. Her dark brown hair wore a streak of grey that ran from her right temple and ended in her tight bun, and wrinkles littered the corner of her eyes as she smiled. Willow wondered whether the streak of grey was intentional or natural, but a closer look showed further grey hidden amongst the dark.

Natural.

'...Getting on out there?'

Willow blinked, shocked from her thoughts, and back to the room where people suddenly seemed to be everywhere. She gulped, swallowing hard.

'What?' she croaked, feeling her chest tighten.

Not now, Willow, please. I need to do this. Can we just do this? If I want to be a new me, I have to do new things.

'I'm Tam,' the lady said with a smile. 'I said welcome to our group and our village, and asked how you were getting on out there.'

'Thank you,' Willow managed. Her heart seemed to be lodged in her throat. 'I'm good... um, it's good, so far.'

'Good to hear, pet, I hope you enjoy the class tonight. Don't worry about payment, the first one's free.'

Tam placed a hand on her shoulder. Willow froze, wondering if she would feel the tremors that had begun to shudder through her muscles.

Why didn't you bring your pills?

A whiff of Tam's flowery perfume reached her nose as the lady shouted out.

'Five minutes people, let's get into the room and onto the mats. Do any stretching you feel you need before we begin, and for heaven's sake, can we keep the door shut today? The room costs a fortune to heat, and this building lets it out as though it's free with plenty to spare. Use the toilet beforehand. It's that simple.'

Tam squeezed Willow's shoulder.

'Get your shoes and jumper off, pet, Sophie will show you in. I'll make sure there are two mats side by side for you both, don't be nervous.'

Willow nodded, the wedge in her throat almost blocking her airway.

Breathe, Willow, now is not the time to have an attack.

Willow sat down and focused on her breathing as Tam disappeared from the room, followed by a line of people who looked eager to get into the warmth now that they were a little less clothed.

'Told you she's nice. It's going to be fun. Are you okay?'

Willow took off her shoes and socks and placed her jumper next to them on the small bench. The smell of incense was beginning to make her feel sick.

'I'm fine,' she said. 'Or I will be once we get going. I just don't like crowds, that's all, and crowds of people I don't know make the anxiety worse.' She looked at Sophie, who gave her a sympathetic smile. 'I will be okay though,' she said, more for herself than her new friend.

'Aye, okay. Come on then. You should have said. I wouldn't have been so pushy. That's why you've been so quiet, eh?'

Willow grinned and couldn't help herself. 'I've been quiet because I can't get a word in.'

Sophie's mouth dropped open, her large brown eyes widening in surprise.

'Oh, I see. You're saying I'm a chatterbox, is that it?'

Willow stood up and then they were both laughing. Willow felt a flutter of affection for the small pixie-like girl in front of her.

'I have a feeling we're going to be great friends,' she said, hugging Sophie, who hugged her back firmly with a giggle.

The door to the yoga room opened and Tam's head appeared round the doorway.

'Ready, girls?'

Willow smiled and nodded as she followed Sophie into the room, followed by Tam.

The room was hot, but not stifling, although rubbing sweat out of her eyes every two minutes was getting annoying. Willow vowed next time she came - and there would be a next time - she would do like all the clever people around her. Bring a towel and a bottle of water. Sophie whispered an apology for not warning her she would need them while upside down in a straddle headstand. Willow, who was focusing on the pose, wobbled and fell as Sophie's apology caught her off guard. Sophie giggled, which set Willow off too, and they spent the rest of the class trying not to laugh each time they locked eyes.

The hour and a half went quickly, and after several poses that she hadn't done for a while, and even a go at new poses without face planting or falling over, Willow was glad to get to the final pose. Shavasana. The relax.

When Tam gently asked them to open their eyes if they wished to complete the practice, Willow was genuinely sorry to come out of her relaxed state.

'You look like you've been to sleep,' Sophie said.

Willow looked over at her new friend with a grin. 'I feel like I have... in a hot tub, right on the equator.'

'I hope you don't wear Lycra in the hot tub.'

Tam quietly shushed the group, reminding them that some people were still relaxing. Then she thanked them with the customary Namaste, before telling them to take as long as they liked to come round, and leaving the room with barely a squeak.

Willow blew a strand of fallen hair from her face as Sophie stretched her arms.

'What Tam didn't say is that you can take as long as you like... as long as you're out within five minutes.'

'And what if we're not?'

'She locks you in.'

Willow chuckled as Sophie laughed.

'Got to be better than sleeping at Ivy Cottage,' an older lady said from the corner, legs crossed and back straight, her eyes still closed. Willow turned to her.

'What do you mean?'

'Nothing,' Sophie said. 'Maud is having a bad day and likes to take it out on everyone else.'

Maud opened an eye but maintained her straight position.

'I'm not having a bad day, you rude girl. Ivy Cottage isn't right. There's something dark there.'

'Dark, my ass. The only thing dark is your sense of humour. Mel was one of my best friends. She lived at the cottage for six blissful years before she moved abroad.'

'A new house here was too close for her, that's why.'

Maud shuffled and finally opened her other eye. Willow held back a gasp as she saw that one of Maud's eyes was a cloudy blue and the other almost black, a striking combination against her aged olive skin and coarse grey hair.

'Bullshit,' Sophie said, making Willow jump. 'Mel got married to an Australian, that's why she moved abroad. Don't listen to a word she says, Willow.'

'Willow,' Maud said as Sophie pulled Willow to her feet and pushed her forward. 'It's nice to meet you, dearie. Keep your wits about you in that house. People have been driven insane by her-'

The door clicked shut behind them and cool air pressed around Willow.

'What-' she began, but Sophie cut her off, her friendly smile replaced by an angry frown.

'Ignore her. She's a witch.'

'That's not nice.'

'No, I really think she is. She apparently has the ability to *see* things, in her words. Honestly, nothing much comes of her predictions. Mel loved Ivy Cottage, don't you listen to a damn thing she says.'

'Maud causing trouble again?' Tam said, coming round the desk with a clean towel that she offered to Willow. Willow gratefully dried herself down before pulling her jumper and her shoes on over her wet gear.

'She's being vile,' Sophie said, putting on her own trainers.

'Ignore her, pet,' Tam said to Willow. 'Maud rented Ivy Cottage before it was put on the market six years ago. Mel brought it fair and square, but Maud never let her forget that she had been turfed out of her home. Bad egg, that's all.'

'Ah,' Willow said, drying her hair off as best as she could before redoing the bun at the back of her head. 'So, I'm in her house really, then.'

'You are absolutely not,' Sophie said. 'You're in Mel's house. And it's yours while you're renting it.'

Willow nodded, trying to calm the swirl in her stomach.

'Right, and the darkness?'

'There's no bloody darkness, Wills. She's trying to scare you. I've slept in that house a hundred times with no issues.'

Willow grinned and felt herself softening.

Wills. That was nice. Different. Maybe that was exactly what she needed to enable her to start over here. No more Weeping Willow. From now on she would be Wills, the strong, adaptable willow she should be.

'Let's go for a drink then,' Tam said with a smile. 'I'll get the first round.'

Willow's heart staggered to a halt. 'A drink?'

Sophie smiled and gave her arm a small squeeze.

'In the pub. We usually go for a drink after yoga. Sometimes it's just me and Tam, other times there's a few of us. You'll be fine.'

'I'm drenched in sweat,' Willow said, horrified. 'And I have no money.'

She avoided the real reason she didn't want to go inside the pub.

Crowds. People. No way out.

Yoga was quite enough for tonight. She had done it, and she was proud of herself. It would shock Carlton that she was here talking to people she didn't know, but that was enough for one night.

'Well, we're all in the same boat. Me and Tam sit in it this time every week to start the weekend off.'

'But it's Thursday,' Willow protested.

'It's not my fault they use the community centre for bridge club on a Friday evening,' Tam said, her brown eyes twinkling. 'Thursday is as good as it gets, I'm afraid. Ready?'

Willow paused. The only thing she was ready for was running out of the door and back to the cottage.

'Come on, pet,' Tam whispered into her ear. 'It'll do you good, and we'll take good care of you, I promise. Maybe you can tell us what's on your mind?'

Willow swallowed and wiped a fresh layer of sweat from her face with a shaky hand.

'I'm not taking no for an answer,' Tam said. 'One drink. That's all I'm asking. If you still want to go afterward, no problem, but ye gods, you haven't even had a sip of water for the last hour-and-a-half. I'm buying you a drink.'

Sophie nodded her head at Willow, who felt herself wither in defeat.

She didn't know which was worse; the anxiety, or trying to stand up to two such strong women.

Four minutes later, when the last stragglers had left, and Tam had locked the big blue doors, Willow entered the first pub she had stepped foot into for the last four years.

Seven

CARLTON CHECKED HIS PHONE for the fifth time in the last fifteen minutes. There were still no new calls or messages. Willow was disappearing into the unknown without him, and it wasn't something he liked.

He was used to being in control of her care, but while she was away, he had no idea what she was up to.

He looked at his message. The last communication they'd had.

I'm sorry, I love you too.

His hand clenched the phone. She hadn't replied. Not even a single emoji.

He slammed the phone face down on the desk, irritation working its way around his stomach, along with a new feeling. Fear.

What if, by setting herself free, she never came back?

He turned the phone over and unlocked the screen, his finger hovering over her name.

'Oh, no. Uh-uh.' Suzanne strode over to the desk and pulled the phone from his hands. 'Tell me you weren't thinking of breaking the silence?'

'Maybe,' he mumbled, the irritation falling away.

'She is entitled to space, hotshot. Leave her be. Where are you going now?'

Carlton looked up at her, confusion muddling his thoughts.

'Huh?'

'It's clocking off time. I've already done an hour over, and you've normally gone by now. There's nothing here that can't be done tomorrow, so we're leaving. Where are you going?'

'Home?' He rose from the chair with a sigh.

'Wrong,' Suzanne said. 'I'm taking you for a drink. You look like you need one. We'll go to the Wagon and Horses over the road, and you can loosen some of the tightness out of those wrinkles.'

Carlton raised his eyebrows, and she raised hers in return. A taunt.

Are you going to disagree?

It had been a long time since he had been for a drink inside a pub, and the Wagon and Horses had been his favourite five years ago. He checked his watch as Suzanne tapped a foot in the doorway, holding his jacket toward him with manicured red nails.

7.30pm.

Early when all you had to do was spend the evening at home alone.

'Well?' Suzanne was using her reflection in the door's glass to run a hand through her cropped hair and spike the ends to perfection.

'Okay,' he said with a nod. 'Just one drink, though. I have paperwork to catch up on at home.'

They jogged down the street, rain drumming around them as Suzanne's heels clicked on the tarmac. The road was always busy in the city centre, and more so in this weather. Carlton spied the pub and wondered how they would cross the road without detouring to the pedestrian crossing and getting drenched. The hiss of the traffic was constant, headlights illuminating the sheer force of the downpour and the rivers that ran in the gutters.

Maybe they should give this a miss.

'Suzie-'

'Now,' Suzanne said, and Carlton felt a sharp pull on his arm.

There was the harsh blast of a horn. Suzanne raised her hand in apology as she pulled Carlton across the road with her, up the stone steps, and in through the door of the pub.

'Whew,' she said, shaking out her wet hair with a laugh. 'Haven't seen rain like this for a long time!'

'I nearly never saw it again,' Carlton said, wiping water from his face.

'Don't be dramatic.' Suzanne grinned and walked through a door to the right into the bar. 'Whisky? Scotch? Or are you an ale man?'

'Ale,' Carlton said, flicking his hand to the Doom Bar pump on the bar. 'I'll get these though.'

'No chance. Is there anywhere to sit?'

Carlton turned to look, and everything suddenly seemed surreal. It was like his old life and this moment were coming together, as if the four years in between hadn't happened. As if he hadn't lost part of his life looking after his girlfriend after the attack.

It was strange.

Even stranger was the feeling when he scanned the room for a table.

The pub was modern and sleek. The walls were pale green, contrasting with grey, the wood pale and polished. Fake flowers lined every table top, and modern canvases lined the fresh walls. Everywhere he looked, people in suits were sitting with drinks, chatting, and laughing.

Carlton blinked, disjointed.

This place had been a real pub when he had last been inside. Old and dark. Somewhere for old men to hide. Now it had been transformed beyond recognition, the old men gone, replaced by younger workers and business people.

'They've done a great job, haven't they?' Suzanne said, catching his gaze. 'A fine dining bistro they call it now. Bet you don't recognise the place.'

'No. I feel like I've stepped into the twilight zone.'

Suzanne picked up the drinks with a laugh.

'Thank you, darlin', she said to the barman, and then she turned to Carlton. 'There's a table over there.'

She pointed, and Carlton let her lead the way to an intimate table for two in the corner.

They sat down, and Carlton felt himself relax as Suzie's company and the music soothed him as much as the beer soothed his throat. It was nice to be off guard, nice to be out with a good-looking woman just having a good time, like most normal couples did.

'Good to be out, huh?' Suzie said, reading his mind with a smile.

'It really is,' Carlton agreed, sipping his pint, as Suzanne picked up the menu and waved it at him.

'Got a ready meal in the freezer at home, or do you fancy dinner while we're here?'

Carlton cocked an eyebrow. 'Dinner out with my secretary. Why do I feel like this is planned?'

He almost took it back. The flirty connection had always been there, and they both knew it, but he also knew that she hadn't intended the intimacy of the table. It genuinely was the only space left.

Besides, they both knew that Willow was at the forefront of everything. She always had been.

Suzanne smiled back at him, taking a sip of wine, her lipstick leaving a red rim around the edge of the glass.

'I knew it would happen one day. I'm always prepared, like a girl scout, and here we are, so what do you say? Shall we do the deed?'

She wagged her eyebrows at him as she held up the menu, and they both laughed.

'Why not?' he said. 'What do they have?'

The evening passed quickly. It had been too long since Carlton had dined out, and far too long since he'd had a drink. His care for Willow had stopped him, but there was nothing wrong with a drink after work in future, was there? Good food and good company would give him more energy to deal with Willow afterward. A break, of sorts.

Carlton glanced at Suzanne who was babbling on about the idiot that had been her husband until three months ago, and how he was taking her for all she had.

'I may need a raise at this rate, or I won't be able to afford to live.'

Carlton smiled. 'You had a raise in January.'

'That was almost a year ago. Want another drink?'

Carlton finished his second pint and nodded, standing to grab the empty glasses.

'This is the plan, huh? Get me drunk enough to agree to a raise?'

Suzanne shrugged.

'Worth a try, eh?'

There was a tinkling tune that got louder as Suzanne took her phone from her pocket.

'Speak of the devil,' she muttered. 'I need to take this. I'll be right back.'

Carlton shrugged. He paid for more drinks and took them back to the table. There was warmth in his cheeks, and his legs were already a little unsteady. He would have to stop at this one while he could at least walk home or have enough of his faculties to get a taxi.

He sat down as his phone buzzed a message in his pocket.

Willow. Finally.

Warmth swirled in his chest, and he took a large swig of beer before fishing his phone out and opening it up.

Not Willow, after all.

His shoulders sank, and then rolled back in shock as he read the message.

Hey there, doc. Good to see you. I may need a few more pills. Mine have run out. You know what happens when I don't get my pills, don't you?

Carlton swallowed hard and his blood ran cold as he messaged back.

I can't see you. You are no longer my locality. Sorry.

He pressed send, put the phone in his pocket and looked down into his pint. He knew who the person was, of course, knew him well. He had dealt with the guy for many years before he had finally been moved out of Bristol.

Thank God.

He took a swig of beer as the chair pulled out opposite him. His fuzzy mind made his mouth smile at Suzanne, but when she spoke, her voice was too deep. Way too deep.

'I'm afraid that just won't do, doc,' it said. 'It won't do at all.'

The man smiled, and the pint slipped from Carlton's hand, landing on the table with a clunk that sent beer sloshing over his wrist.

Eight

I NEED MY PILLS. *I need my goddamn pills. Why the hell didn't I bring them out with me?*

Willow sat with her back to the corner where she could survey the whole pub, especially the door. The place was relatively empty. An older couple and their dog, and two men at the bar, who were propping up four pints between them.

Music tinkled from speakers on the walls, and Willow felt the familiarity of the beat somewhere deep down, but she just couldn't concentrate. She couldn't handle being here. The people looked harmless enough, but then they had that day, too, hadn't they?

Calm down, Willow, breathe.

In for four, hold, out for six.

The door is there. It's right there. You can choose to leave.

Sweat trickled down her back. Tam was at the bar, getting the drinks, laughing and joking with the men, who were obviously long-time residents. Sophie was caught up in a conversation with the older couple. Willow must have looked uncomfortable, because she was trying hard to get away, but the couple just kept right on talking even as Sophie edged from their table.

Another couple entered, and the door slammed with a sound like gunshot.

Willow jolted and gripped the table. The room seemed to get smaller, stiflingly hot, and the smell of beer and old wood clogged her nose and throat.

The new couple shouted a loud greeting to the bartender, who shouted something back. They were laughing now, the sound screeching in Willow's ears, and scratching at her brain.

She snapped. She had to get out. She couldn't *breathe.*

'Here we are.'

Tam appeared in front of her, placing down a water and two cokes. 'Last of the big drinkers,' she said, but Willow was too far gone. Her breath coming in ragged bursts, she looked at Tam.

'I'm... I'm sorry. I have to... to go.'

She stumbled around the tables and staggered outside, trying to drag in breaths of clean, cool air as the door slammed shut behind her. Her lungs were singing, her heart pounding, and she was shaking like a leaf as the world spun.

In for four, hold, out for six. Come on, Willow!

Don't pass out, you mustn't pass out...

With another bang of the door that made Willow's heart jolt, Tam appeared next to her.

'What the heck is up, pet?' she said. 'You look like you've seen a ghost?'

'No, I...'

Breathe! In for four, hold, out for six.

Tam's hand found her back and rubbed gently.

'That's it, pet. Keep it steady.' She followed Willow's rhythm. 'That's right. Breathe in, and breathe out. Breathe in, and breathe out.'

Willow was beginning to calm when Sophie opened the door and stepped out.

'What's going on?'

'Nothing,' Tam said. 'Just a little panic attack. We'll be in shortly, go stay with the drinks.'

Sophie nodded and went back inside, and Tam went back to soothing Willow, helping her to breathe, calming her back to mere anxiousness.

'Feeling better?' she said.

'Not completely, but better than I was, thank you.'

'No problem. Took me right back to my working days then, you did. I was a paramedic for twelve years before finding my calling as a mental health nurse. I worked in a care home for young adults with mental health conditions. We had a large house for those who couldn't look after themselves, you see, and a few serviced bungalows for those who could manage alone. The people in the bungalows could use the big house facilities if they wished to gather communally, and there were staff to keep an eye out for them, but I worked in the big house, looking after the needs of the halfway-ers, as we called them. Half able, always willing. Oh, we did have some laughs. There was one young man who-'

Tam broke off and placed a hand on her chest with a laugh. 'I'm sorry, pet, like you need to hear stories right now, eh? Look at me, rambling on. How are you feeling?'

Willow checked herself over mentally and discovered she was feeling pretty calm. She had come back from one of the worst hypoxia attacks that she'd had for years... and without the pills. Just a couple of months ago, Carlton had sedated her to get her breathing back to normal and her blood oxygen levels back up, just before she had ended up in hospital. A close call, he had said.

'I'm okay, now,' she said. 'I was actually enjoying the story. It took my mind off myself. You were a mental health nurse?'

Which explains why she hadn't freaked out and had calmed her with relative ease.

'I was. No longer, I'm afraid. The care home shut down, and I shut down with it. I couldn't believe the disregard for those beautiful people as they were shipped off to alternative places and torn apart from their friends. It was horrendous. Anyway, I'll continue the story if you come back inside? It's bloody cold out here, and we're still damp from the session. We'll catch a chill.'

Willow looked at the pub door and felt her heart stumble underneath her coat. She shook her head. 'I can't,' she whispered.

'Why not, pet? What do you think will happen?'

Willow continued to shake her head. It was illogical to think that anything would happen. There were only a handful of people in the place, she knew that, but she couldn't take that chance.

'I don't know. It's stupid. It's irrational. I just have such a fear of enclosed places filled with people.'

Tam raised her eyebrows.

'Hen, the place is empty, and you were in a yoga class in a small room with twice as many people just fifteen minutes ago. Don't give me that.'

'Okay, I mean the pub. I thought it was a fear of enclosed spaces, but maybe I just don't do enclosed spaces in pubs.'

'So, how can we work you through it?'

Willow frowned. 'What?'

'Well, you have a drink waiting inside, and I'm not standing out here. So how can we help you through it?'

Willow blinked and shook her head.

'I don't know. I can't be helped. I need my pills. They calm me.'

Tam laughed and rubbed Willow's arm.

'No such thing as can't be helped, and pills? No good for anything. Whatever this trauma is, pills won't help long term, they rarely do. They just prolong things, in my opinion.'

Willow shook her head. 'No. They help. They calm me down, and I can't go back in there until I have them. I could get hypoxia. Carlton already had to sedate me once, Tam. It's really dangerous.'

Tam looked at Willow with a concerned frown.

'The pills space you out, pet. Prozac, I presume?'

'Yes.'

'Right, Prozac sends the signal in the brain a different way, makes you feel all calm and sleepy. Like you couldn't give a toss, right?'

Willow nodded.

'It doesn't help, pet. Over a period it can help fire signals differently, but those things are also addictive. How long have you been taking them?'

'Four years.'

Tam stared at her, and then she raised her eyebrows. 'Right, and what dosage are you on?'

'Well, I was on 20mg. That had been helping a lot, but with the move here by myself I needed more, so I'm now on 40mg. I've only had one today, so I'm due another. That's why I had the attack in there.'

'40mg? Well, I have to say... I mean... Have you heard yourself?'

Willow drew her eyebrows together in confusion. 'I don't know what you mean.'

'You began with 20mg. You've been on them for four years and now you're up to 40mg. Tell me, how is that working out for you?'

Willow shook her head. She had to admit it did sound counterproductive when you put it like that. Like she had got worse over the last four years, not better.

'I don't know. I mean, my partner is a psychiatrist. He prescribes them for me, and he must know what he's doing. He owns one of the best private practices in Bristol!'

Tam nodded. 'He's also busy, right?'

'Yes, but-'

'Well, there you go. It's easier to keep you on the tablets while he spends his days working through other people's problems properly, eh?'

Anger stabbed Willow's gut.

'No. That's not it. Not at all. Yes, he's busy, but that doesn't mean he casts me aside.'

'No, no. I'm sure he doesn't. That was the wrong thing to say. I'm sorry.' Tam smiled with a shrug. 'Forgive me?'

Willow gave a small nod, but she was wary.

'Yes, I do, but without being rude, you don't understand the nature of my problems, and nor do you understand what it will take to get me through them. Carlton does the best for me because he loves me. He would never treat me like a second-rate patient to be pushed aside. My welfare comes first.'

Tam was nodding, her face remorseful, but said nothing.

'And so, I'd like to get back and get my pills. You know, maybe one day I'll be able to come inside, Tam, and I really want that, but at the moment I just can't.'

Tam was still nodding.

'Okay, I hear you, pet. How long are you renting Ivy Cottage for? And where is this partner now?'

'Until next September. He's at home, he has to work, and I... I needed the time alone. He loves me, of course, but sometimes he smothers me.'

'You have doubts, then?'

'About what?'

'His care?' She brought her hands up in front of her at Willow's expression. 'I'm not being judgmental, just asking a question, that's all. If you thought you were in the best place, why did you leave to come out here alone?'

Willow sighed. 'My mum. It was Mum who suggested that I take the year and see how I got on. I keep telling her we're obviously just not built the same, and she's stronger, but she said it would do me good. So here I am.'

'Sounds to me like your mum has doubts, too. She went through the same trauma as you?'

'Yes.'

'And how is she doing?'

'Fine. She's doing well now.'

'Any pills?'

Willow felt another stab of irritation and heaved a heavy sigh.

'No. No pills. She had them initially but was off them within five months.'

'Right. Okay, well, a year then. We have a year to help you and get you off the pills. For your mum.' She threw her hands up into the air. 'Fuck it, not for your mum. You've been too busy listening to everyone else and taking it as gospel. For you, Willow, for you. Shall we try?'

Willow stared as she let Tam's words sink in. Did she want to try? Did she want to be off the pills?

More than anything!

'Okay,' she whispered, 'yes. I'd like that. I'd just like my life back.'

Tam nodded and flicked her head down the darkening road.

'Go on then, get out of here while you can still see your way home. I'll see you at Yoga on Monday, right? Part of your therapy.'

Willow smiled.

'Of course, and there's no better therapy.'

Tam turned back to the pub with a nod and Willow felt a sudden flash of worry.

'Tam!' she called, louder than she needed to.

'Yes?'

'Why do you want to get me off the pills so badly? They do help. They really do.'

'If you say so, but I've seen a lot over the years. I'll refresh my knowledge and we'll go over some plans next time we meet.'

'I'd like that,' Willow said.

'Are you keeping in contact with this partner? Because he'll probably not like my way of trying things. Probably best you don't mention anything to him.'

'No, I told him I needed a break. He's been really good at leaving me alone so far.' Willow paused, and then carried on anyway. 'What do you have against him, Tam? You don't even know him. He is a good therapist, and I believe in him.'

'I know you do,' Tam said with a sad smile. 'But I'm not sure that any person with his level of knowledge should be telling you a simple - albeit scary - panic attack, is sending you out the back door of no return with hypoxia. Nor do I think you need sedating. I have seen far worse panic attacks than you have just had. Far worse. Think about it, that's all. Sometimes the people who love us can do the wrong things for the kindest reasons. You know, you said something interesting earlier. You said you had a fear of enclosed spaces, but when it came to it you identified the problem was the pub, not the space. Where did that come from? Think about what you've already done tonight that he probably said... what? You wouldn't cope with?'

Willow opened her mouth but couldn't counter the question. She was right. Carlton had said that she wasn't ready for any of these things.

Keep taking the pills, Willow.

Tam nodded.

'I thought so. Bye Willow, we'll speak soon, pet.'

Tam disappeared back inside, and Willow rubbed her arms and stared at the empty doorway, perplexed.

Who the hell is this woman? How does she know? And what does that even mean?

Nine

W ILLOW JOGGED DOWN THE quiet road. The light was fading fast, which wouldn't be a problem, except that she wasn't entirely sure where the end of her lane was.

By the time she recognised McGracken House, and the bridge over the river, it was almost pitch black, but it would be easy from here.

She slowed to a walk, the smell of damp bark, earth, and pine filling her nostrils. The cool air bit her cheeks and clung to the damp clothes under her hoodie. She shuddered as she pulled the hood over her head and stuffed her hands into the deep front pocket.

Halfway up the lane, the darkness intensified, and Willow glanced behind her. She could no longer see the lights behind the windows of McGracken House. There was no light from anything this far up. A flutter of something that sat between excitement and fear circled her stomach.

I'll have to get used to this kind of dark, I suppose. I won't need eye masks and blackout blinds here.

As if in rebuttal of her thoughts, the moon appeared from behind a cloud and the road was lit under her feet in the silvery glow.

Follow the silver tarmacked road, she thought with a grin. She turned to continue up the hill, but stopped in her tracks when she saw the cottage, bathed in the same ethereal silvery sheen as the road. Willow felt as though she were in some kind of dream as her breath caught.

Do I live here? Really?

She grinned, inhaled the fresh woodland air, and revelled in the sense of calm and peace that filled her. It was something that she hadn't felt in a long time.

At home she had always been anxious, cooped up inside, in a perpetual cycle of watching Carlton leave and waiting for him to come home. Going nowhere, doing nothing, and seeing no one had been one long anxious drain that had only seemed to make her feel worse as time went on. Why had Carlton stopped her from going out, anyway?

He didn't stop you. He just said that he wouldn't be there if anything happened, and hypoxia could kill.

Which only made me more anxious. Why didn't he let me at least try, maybe when he was around to call?

He didn't stop you. He was only taking care of you.

Willow felt a tremor of unease as she thought of Tam's advice earlier - 'I'm not sure that any person with his level of knowledge should be telling you a simple - albeit scary - panic attack is sending you out the back door of no return with hypoxia. Nor do I think you need sedating.'

She couldn't know how bad that attack was when he sedated me...

...or did she mean something else?

I'm not being sedated... am I?

Willow shook her head. No, of course not, but what about the hypoxia stuff, Willow? He used to tell you how dangerous that was all the time.

Tam's wrong. It wasn't just a panic attack. I don't have mild panic attacks; I have full-blown hypoxia inducing attacks.

All the time. Carlton told you all the time.

What is hypoxia anyway? You didn't even check.

I don't need to. Carlton loves me, and he has my best interests at heart. Always. He said so.

He told you ALL THE DAMN TIME.

Was he stopping you from going out?

Willow frowned and swallowed.

No. Everything was heightened tonight. On Monday, she would return to yoga and tell Tam she was wrong. She knew none of Willow's medical history. Hell, she didn't know her at all. They had only met three hours ago, and an hour of that was twisted into silent asanas in a forty-degree room.

With her resolve in place, Willow felt a little of the stress slip away, and the calm return. She followed the silvery road, and by the time she reached her car and the cottage, she was feeling relaxed and in control.

It was a strange feeling, but a good one.

With a smile, she unlocked the outer door and stepped inside. She placed her shoes and coat on the rack and turned to unlock the inner door.

In the dim light, a dark form caught her eye, passing across the glass and disappearing into the living area.

Willow froze with the key in the lock.

What the hell was that?

She squinted into the hallway through the swirls of the glass, forcing herself to look for movement, but finding none.

No, because it went into the living area. Is someone in the house?

Willow's heart jumped into her throat and a small whine left her lips as her eyes searched the empty hallway.

Yes, it's empty now, but did I see that? Did I? Or am I seeing things? I see things sometimes. I know that, it's fine.

But did you see that? Because that looked like a person, Willow.

No, it didn't.

She tried to pull in deep, calming breaths, but her lungs were like small pockets with barely enough room to get the air she needed inside.

It looked like a person. Dressed in black. You know it and I know it.

No, it didn't. If it was a person, why haven't they come back?

What if they're looting the front room? This place is isolated, great for thievery.

Gasping for air was making her dizzy, and indecision was root-ing her to the spot with fear.

You can't stay here forever, Willow. There's no one coming to save you. Get yourself together, decide what to do.

Willow stood a moment longer before the idea came to her. The 'person' had gone into the front room, so the best place to see them would be the front window. Luckily, she hadn't drawn the curtains before she left.

She stepped back out of the porch, her whole body trembling as she crept to the flower boxes underneath the front window of the living area. She peered inside, the bright moon giving her just enough light to make out the furniture. There was no movement. Nothing seemed to be out of place. Even her pumps were as she left them earlier, in the middle of the floor.

So maybe they went into the kitchen.

Willow clutched the stone windowsill as her vision blurred. An alarm was going off in her head as the dizziness and her wheezing breath reminded her of the danger that Carlton had always warned about.

Move. There's nothing else you can do, nowhere else to go.

Fear forced her onwards.

She moved to the side window and checked inside the room again. Her vision seemed to pulse along with her frantic heart-beat.

Nothing out of place. Why would someone come inside and not move a thing?

Willow continued on round the back of the house, scanning the garden for movement, and trying the back door, which remained locked. No one had come this way, and a look through the kitchen window showed the room was empty.

I think you imagined it. Same old story, seeing things that aren't there.

As worrying as that was, the thought eased her breathing a little, and she began to lose some of the sharp edge of fear. She moved onwards, circling the cottage. The rest of the windows along the back and round to the front window of her bedroom all revealed the same story.

Nothing.

No one, and nothing out of place.

You imagined it, Willow, it was in your head. How the hell are you going to cope here alone if you see shadows in every dark recess? You can't call Carlton every time you scare yourself now. You're on your own.

Her heart thumped again, and as the cold circled her body, she realised she was sweating in the frigid air. The world began to spin as she felt her grip on reality loosen. Her vision darkened as she gasped, trying to get enough oxygen to her brain.

There's no one inside. You need your pills, Willow, get the god-damn pills.

In the end, it was the fear of a lonely death, on this lonely lane, that moved her inside the house. The pills were still on the small table in the living room, she knew, because she had seen them through the window. She opened the packet with shaking hands and took one dry.

Her heart continued to thud frantically as she settled into a foetal position on the settee.

There's no one here. No one here. It's okay.

In for four, hold, out for six.

In for four, hold, out for six.

Oh, God, Carlton, I really wish you were here tonight.

With shaking hands, she pulled out her phone and looked at the unopened message she had received from him yesterday, back when she was feeling strong. Far from the argument she had been expecting after her insistence that he left her alone, he had simply replied,

I'm sorry. I love you too.

Tears filled her eyes.

See? He's not a monster, Willow. Why did you doubt him? Why did you let someone who doesn't know him sway your judgment? He loves you, he'd never hurt you.

The screen blurred in her vision, and she sniffed as her fingers hovered over the green call button.

Once won't hurt, will it? I need him. He'll tell me what to do.

He'll tell you to come home.

I'm strong enough for that. I just need to hear his voice.

She hitched a sob as she pressed to dial. The call rang out, but there was no reply.

No reply because he's respecting your wishes.

But I need to hear his voice!

Her shaking hand hovered over the call button for the second time, but the anxiety was coming back in waves, placing icy fingers around her neck. Fingers that squeezed and blocked her air.

She dropped the phone onto the floor as a wave of dizziness hit and she lay her head on the arm of the settee and closed her eyes.

In for four, hold, out for six.

In for four, hold, out for six.

As Willow struggled for breath on the settee, a dark figure slipped out of the kitchen and into the hall unnoticed.

Ten

'SO, WHAT ARE WE going to do about this situation, doc?'

Carlton tried to keep his composure, but his Adam's apple bobbed in his dry throat.

'There is no situation, Coop. I can't see you any more, I have no capacity.'

The man, Coop, sat back with a smile. A wedge of greasy blonde hair flopped over his cheekbone, while the back skimmed the collar of his leather jacket. He looked a little out of place with the suits in here, but two pints later, Coop was still unruffled as he refused to leave without Carlton's agreement.

'You have capacity. Cut the damn bullshit. My prescription takes a second to print out. I don't even have to fucking come in if you don't want to see me. Just get me the pills.'

'What happened to your new psychiatrist?'

Carlton refrained from asking why his dealer couldn't get hold of some for him because it was obvious. If Carlton wrote a prescription, Coop only had to pay a prescription charge, which was nominal compared to the dealer's price.

'I dumped him. He was a fucking dickhead. I mean, you're all fucking dickheads, really, aren't you?'

Coop smiled at a blonde who was passing with a couple of cocktails, and she bashfully grinned back.

'How are ya, darlin'?' he said, all teeth and charm.

'Fine,' she drawled, keeping her eyes on him a second too long as she passed. Then his smile disappeared, and his hard gaze was back on Carlton. Carlton looked into Coop's piercing blue eyes. A bad boy, with a penchant for leggy blondes, but a bad boy didn't even begin to scratch the surface with Coop. This one was bad to the bone.

Carlton thought about his odds of walking out of this place without having agreed to Coop's demands.

About as likely as Willow turning back up on the doorstep tomorrow with her suitcases, all fixed.

There had been no pressure enforced yet, but if he refused, Carlton knew just how much pressure this man could apply. He had felt it before, had almost been crushed under it. He pulled his gaze away and chewed at the inside of his cheek. Then he sighed.

'Just you,' Carlton finally said. There had to be some deal to make here. 'No one else. Do not bring your cronies around. I won't see them.'

Coop nodded slowly, a smile stretching across his face.

'Thanks doc, I knew you'd come through.'

'I haven't come through. There are a few rules this time. Number one, never come to the practice. I'll bring the prescription to you. Number two, I'll only agree to this for two months, and in that time, you'll get yourself a new psychiatrist. I can't be seen dealing with you. I could lose my license. Number three, don't bring others to my door. I'm at capacity. I mean it. Got it?'

Coop's grin widened.

'Always a stickler for the rules, eh, doc? Such a good boy you are. Where's the chick? You leave her at home with her nightmares?'

Carlton clenched his jaw, and his heart began to thump, anger and injustice firing through his veins.

'Don't you dare, Coop. Don't you fucking dare. Leave Willow out of this.'

'Willow? She's not worth pissing on. She's too much of a...' He trailed off, swinging a hand round in the air as he searched for the word, his brow furrowed. 'a 'not quite' kinda gal, isn't she?'

Carlton didn't reply. He stared at Coop across the table, anger coursing hot and livid through his veins.

In his pocket, his phone began to ring, but he barely noticed.

'Don't you think?' Coop continued. He held up a hand and counted on his fingers. 'I mean, she's not quite bright, not quite sane, not quite blonde, not quite attractive, not quite funny, not quite slim-'

Carlton felt his anger surge, bringing his whole being up and out of his chair to tower over the man sitting before him.

Coop didn't even flinch.

'Sit down, little brother,' he said. 'You could never deck me as a kid, even at a foot taller and seventy pounds heavier. Couldn't do it then and can't do it now.'

Carlton was still raging, adrenaline shooting a hand out to grab Coop by his leather collar.

'Take that back. You take that fucking back. All of this - all of her problems and all of mine - every bit of it is your fault. All of it. I could have had a normal life with two kids and a detached house by now. My life is getting back on track, Coop. Two months, and then get out of my life, and don't bother bringing those idiots round again either.'

Coop knocked Carlton's hand away, his face stern. He stood up, leaning across the table until they were almost nose to nose.

'I'll take as long as I fucking like. I'll be in your life for as long as I fucking like, and I'll bring round whoever the fuck I like, and do you know what? You'll treat them just like me. There will be none of this no capacity bullshit because we both know it's just that. Bullshit. Got it?'

'What on earth is going on here?'

Carlton turned to see Suzanne, red lipstick back in place. She stood tall on her stiletto's gazing from one of them to the other before rolling her eyes.

'Great. To what do we owe this pleasure?'

Coop gave her a grin that made Carlton feel sick.

'I'm back in town, Suzie. Glad to see me?'

Suzanne wrinkled her nose.

'All you brought last time was trouble, Coop.'

'And all I'm bringing this time is love,' he said smoothly. 'Guess I'll be seeing lots more of you around. You look hot out of the office, Suze, very sexy. After you've had a go with Carlton, come and see me. I'll show you what a real man can do.'

Suzanne's mouth dropped and Carlton was about to jump to her defense, but Coop beat them both to it. He placed a hand on Carlton's shoulder, giving it a hefty squeeze.

'Knocking off the fucking secretary, eh? Fuck me, little brother, you never fail to surprise me. I'm so impressed that I won't even say a word to Willow. She won't hear a peep. What did you do with her? Is she at home while you... work late?' He accentuated the words with air hyphens and laughed as Carlton blinked in confusion.

Coop winked. 'Have a great night. I'll be in touch.'

He readjusted his leather jacket, ran a hand through his hair, and walked out without a backward glance, leaving Carlton feeling like all of the air in the room had exited with him.

Eleven

WILLOW WOKE ON THE settee, still fully dressed, with a fuzzy head and a mouth full of fur. She blinked. The sunlight streaming through the front window made her eyes hurt and her head ache as she sat up.

The second morning waking up like she'd had a heavy night the night before.

I need to shake myself out of this funk, she thought, I'm not going to get anywhere drowning in anxiety and pills.

Go for a walk.

Willow considered the option. She had enjoyed the walk yesterday, and today would be full of nothingness if she sat around here.

Time to move on.

After a coffee anyway.

With a groan, she rose and took off her jumper before scratching at her itchy scalp. She remembered that she had come home after the pub and gone straight to sleep. No shower, and no getting out of her sweat-soaked clothes, and goodness knew she needed to do both now.

Throwing her clothes in the washing machine, she padded in her underwear to the small bathroom off the kitchen.

The shower was an electric model, set on the wall above the bathtub, which was adorned with a plastic shower curtain.

She pulled it across and turned the shower on.

The shower ran as Willow found fresh clothes and underwear, put them on the bed in the bedroom, and took her dressing gown and slippers into the bathroom. She hung the robe on the door and brushed her teeth in the sink opposite the shower, while looking into the largest mirror she had ever seen. Space enhancing, she supposed.

When the room got steamy, she stepped under the water, relishing the thought of being clean, relishing the thought of a new day, and a new chance to start over.

She closed her eyes, letting the hot water stream over her face and down her body.

Her anxiety attack at the pub, and the disagreement with Tam, who had imbued doubt about Carlton, had left her deflated and sickened.

I haven't felt that bad for ages. What the heck is wrong with me? I have to get myself together. I refuse to go backwards.

Bile rose in her throat at the thought of where she had been four years ago. Of the lack of control, and the lack of concern for her own life, the lack of wanting to do anything. Taking a shower back then hurt her skin. Back then, even getting out of bed hurt...

No.

Willow shook her head, freeing the images from her mind.

'No,' she whispered. 'I will never go back there. I won't allow it. I'm going forward now. Only forward.'

She washed and got out of the shower. Then she pressed a towel around her, drying herself before pulling on her dressing gown, and stuffing her feet into slippers.

She was folding the towel when she saw it, her breath catching in her throat.

A face.

In the fog of condensation that clouded the mirror was a face.

The sort of face a child draws, a round head with two dotted eyes and a wide smile.

A single word was written underneath.

HELLO.

Willow stared, the towel slipping from her hand.

Hello? Was that on there before?

She frowned, and then she chastised herself with a small laugh. Of course, it was there before. This was her first shower. The mirror hadn't had a chance to cloud over yet.

She bent to pick up the towel, her eyes not leaving the word.

Probably a message from the owner, albeit a creepy one. If she ever got a chance to meet with that person, she would tell them not to bother for the next tenant.

Willow reached to wipe the message away with a shudder, before brushing her hair quickly and exiting the room.

On edge, she scouted the small house, poking her head into the empty rooms, before getting dressed in the bedroom.

Something about the message was giving her chills.

Had there been someone in the house last night, after all?

There couldn't have been. The message was from the owner. Chill, Willow.

Willow pulled a soft cream jumper over her head, but as she smoothed it down over her T-shirt, she paused.

Oh, crap.

Her head swam as she realised what had been wrong with the mirror drawing.

When she had wiped it clean, drips of condensation had run down the mirror from the towel.

Those same fresh drips had streaked from three of the letters and where the circle joined at the bottom of the face.

Which could only mean one thing.

The message had been freshly written... while she had been in the shower.

Her stomach turned over with horror, and her heart began to pound.

I have to get out of here.

She quickly plaited her hair, pulled on her coat, and left the house with no coffee and no breakfast.

She no longer had an appetite, anyway.

The message came through forty minutes later as Willow powered down the path through the woods, the writing on the mirror pushed firmly to the back of her mind. The morning was cool, but a small sheen of sweat covered her face at the rhythm of her feet. She expected the message to be from Carlton, who was doing just a little too well at not contacting, especially after she had called last night, but instead it was Sophie.

Hey, it's all hands on deck at McGracken House if you fancy it? They've had a load of new sheds delivered which need painting. I'm taking a day off work today to help out. Shall I pick you up in an hour?

Willow's heart and mind went into overdrive as she considered the message. She chewed on her lip. Yoga and now shed painting? Twice in two days? Could she do that?

She could hear Carlton's voice in her head, hearing the same things he had said for the last four years.

'Say no. You need to rest to give your body time to adjust after the last attack. You'll just compound the issue. Stay in for the next few days. Look after yourself.'

Willow looked at the message again and hesitated to answer. Unsure.

Clenching her jaw, she pushed her phone into her pocket and continued along the path, which was now beginning to climb sharply. The dense evergreens on her right were a stark contrast to the sudden clearing that arrived at her left.

With a gasp of surprise, Willow cupped a hand to her brow and stared across the heather and gorse-streaked hills which rolled away into the distance.

Just below her was a small loch. Cool and glassy. A babbling stream wound through a grassy area, joined the loch, and then exited the other side as though it was just passing through. The entire area was clear of trees, except for one. Lush and green, the large tree spread itself wide, it's long branches brushing the ground in the breeze.

Is that a Willow?

Willow squinted into the sunlight.

It is! It's a Willow. A lonely Willow. A bit like me, really. How funny!

Her feet followed a small deer or sheep track down the side of the hill, through the bracken and heather, until she hit the boggy grass of the clearing.

From here, the world seemed bigger, warmer, and the sky seemed to stretch around her. She turned. A semi-circle of trees surrounded the top of the clearing. Close enough to feel protective, but far enough away to be non-intrusive and for the sunlight to fall into this sheltered, dipped glade. Today's brisk breeze barely reached her inside the bowl. It was like a small sun trap.

Willow moved to the tree, which seemed magical in its proximity.

The only one?

In fact, the only Willow she had seen in this woodland at all. How had this tree ended up here?

She pushed through the long branches into its cool inner circle and placed a hand on the cold bark.

'I bet you're not a weeping Willow, eh?' she smiled. 'I'd never weep another day if I could sit here forever.'

Under the Willow's branches she felt invisible, like she had a view of the outer world but was hidden enough not to be seen from the trees above.

She sat down at the base of the tree, where a few specks of warm dappled sunlight caught her body, and the stream babbled just beyond her feet.

She took out her phone and looked at Sophie's message as Carlton's objections immediately bombarded her thoughts.

Cocooned by the large steady tree, she felt safe. Held.

She silenced her mind, pushing Carlton out.

What do you want, Willow?

Not to go?

She chewed her lip.

Sure, that's a choice, but you wanted a new start. You wanted to see if you could do what he said you couldn't, remember?

He'd say you shouldn't do this.

But is he right? Will I break and make more of a fool of myself than I did last night?

The old willow would back out. Weeping Willow would sit inside, peering through the curtains, as the world went on without her.

But the new Willow? The one living alone, without Carlton to impose his medical words of wisdom and terror.

Was she going to bend or break?

'Only one way to find out,' she whispered, and under the security of the strong willow trunk she replied to Sophie's message.

Twelve

CARLTON OPENED HIS EYES to darkness, but that didn't mean it was early. They had installed the blackout blinds just after the attack to help Willow sleep.

She was doing a good job of it now, lying next to him, with a warmth he had missed from the bed for the last few nights.

He grinned, and then his eyes flew open with a start. When had she arrived home?

His heart swelled, and he found he didn't care. He grinned into the darkness and rolled toward her with a groan of pleasure. Under the covers, his hand found its way around her waist, and he pulled her close as she gave a groan of her own. He closed his eyes and inhaled the scent of her, although that wasn't so familiar, not Willow's usual scent.

She must have changed her shampoo.

He cuddled closer, his hand rolling down to a warm, bony hip, (*Has she lost weight?*) before travelling up to short hair that made Carlton frown in confusion.

Had she cut her hair, too? All of it?

It didn't matter.

He dropped his head down onto hers as she huddled closer, her own hand snaking around his waist. He felt himself stir, and then, with the force of a sledgehammer, he knew where he had smelled the scent before.

Every day. At work.

He froze, his mind tracing the bony hip, the short hair.

'Oh! Oh, no. Shit!'

He scooted backward, rolling away from her and out of the bed in one swift motion. He stood, seeing the shape in the bed rise in the darkness.

'Hey, hey, it's okay.' Her voice was croaky with sleep.

'Suzie?' he choked. 'What the-'

His heart was pounding, his body shaking. Was he even in his own apartment? What the hell had happened here?

The lamp came on and Suzie smiled at him as she sat up. A large T-shirt covering her frame. His.

He felt the bile rise into his throat along with the booze and the horror of what he had done, and he skidded into the bathroom just in time to get his head over the toilet.

It seemed his entire being was coming up and out, over and over, and then a hand placed itself gently on his back and rubbed.

'That'll be the booze. Heave it out, hotshot.'

At the sound of her voice, his stomach found some more to lose, and then he was done, sweating and shaking on the toilet rim.

It was Suzie who pulled him up and flushed the chain, handing him water in the cup from the basin, and making him rinse.

He blinked at her reflection behind him in the mirror. Bed mussed dark hair, his t-shirt hanging off one shoulder. He felt his stomach lurch and shook her hand away as she reached to stroke his hair.

'No. Please. Why are you in my bathroom, Suze? Why are you in my fucking *bed*?'

He felt annoyance ripple through him as she laughed and shook her head.

'My, my, you're really not used to the drink anymore, are you? You really have no idea what happened?'

Carlton clenched his jaw and shook his head. If he was being honest, he didn't even want to think about what had happened, let alone hear it.

'No. No. I can't do this, Suzie.' He mashed a hand to his forehead, scrubbing his palm to the spot where a headache was beginning to rage.

She laughed again as she pulled him away from the mirror, and out of the bathroom, toward the bed.

He snatched his hand from her grip with a guttural growl.

'No!'

Suzie turned back to him in the lamplight, her silhouette lowering itself to sit on the bed and pull something from underneath.

Carlton closed his eyes.

What the hell is going on?

Suzie stood again.

'Get back into bed, hotshot. I'm going to get you some coffee and pills. You look like shit, and you obviously have no clue what went on yesterday? Do you remember anything?'

'I remember you inviting me for a drink,' he said, angry at not recognising what she was doing, as much as at his response.

'Uh-huh,' she replied, rising as his brain tried to reason a list of possible combinations why she would be here in his bed. In the end, it came down to one.

'Did you... did you plan this?' he said, the breath leaving his lungs with the words, 'Did you?'

He swung to the door, but she was already gone, the landing light the only sign of her being there at all. He stood in the middle of his room as it seemed to swim around him.

'Fuck,' he murmured. He moved to the bed and sat down on the edge, elbows on his knees, hands over his face. 'What the fuck did you do, Carlton?'

He felt his stomach roll again, and he hiccupped, tasting bile. He bit his lip as his stomach bubbled, and frantically searched his mind for ways that Willow would never find out about this.

Fire Suzie, move house, move the practice, buy her silence...

Then she was back with two cups and a small packet, kicking the door shut behind her.

'Here,' she said, putting a cup and pills down on the bedside table next to him. He noticed she was wearing his slippers as she rounded the bed and sat on the other side. She flicked them off before getting inside and pulling the covers over herself. She patted the bed at the side of her.

'Come on. I'll explain everything you're missing.'

Carlton felt his stomach rolling. He licked his dry lips, not moving.

'I don't need to know, I just want...' he stopped, the words catching in his throat. 'I just want to know-'

'Did we have sex?' she said, cutting him off.

He snapped his head toward her to see she was shaking hers with a smile. A smile that said no? Or a smile that mocked him?

'No,' she confirmed. 'I promise you. Absolutely not.'

'No?' he said, almost breaking down with relief.

'No. There are things that went on last night that you certainly need to know.' His stomach lurched as she paused. 'But none of them are to do with... that.'

He nodded hopefully.

They hadn't done it. He hadn't crossed the line. He hadn't brought her back to bed - in a sense anyway - and she hadn't planned it either. Or maybe she had. She had never held back the flirting at work, but it had gone no further. Either way, he had held his own. He had stopped himself.

He sighed, getting up to fetch his dressing gown from the door, and sitting next to Suzie on top of the covers. Whether they'd had sex or not, she was still in his house and in his bed. His head was banging.

He opened the packet and swallowed two pills, taking a swig of strong coffee that burned his mouth.

'So, you want to know why I'm in your bed, right?'

Carlton felt the throb pull at his temples. He nodded.

'I suppose that would be a great start.'

'Do you remember walking home?'

Carlton squinted his aching eyes. 'Not really.'

'So, you don't remember the pub, either?'

He remembered the pub, he remembered how upmarket it had seemed. He remembered Suzie showing him the menu.

'Bits. I remember choosing my food. I think.'

'You don't remember Coop?'

Carlton swung to her with a frown. 'Coop? What does he...?'

And then it came back to him.

'Coop's back in town,' he said, rubbing a hand over his face.

Suzie nodded. 'You're in a whole heap of shit.'

'I'll handle him.'

'Not the point. You didn't handle him very well last night. In fact, you sank so much beer after he left that I practically carried you back here.'

'That would explain the sore head and the memory loss,' he said with a wry smile, taking another sip of coffee.

'Carlton, Coop is back,' she said, grabbing his arm. 'What if Willow had been here? Do you know what a close call this was? You need to deal with him. You need to send him away. I mean it, he can't have anything to do with the practice, and he can't be hanging around when Willow returns. No more 'helping' him. You can't. It's not safe.'

Carlton felt his anger flare.

'I understand the implications. I'm not stupid, Suzie. I can handle my own brother. More to the point, what the hell are you doing in my fucking bed?'

'You invited me to stay. You offered the bed. Nothing more happened except you crashed and snored for about three hours while I lay awake, trying not to touch you. Well, until you woke me this morning that is... I didn't realise where I was at first, sorry about that.'

Her eyes were serious. Carlton nodded.

'I'm sorry too. I was dreaming... I... I thought Willow was home. I didn't mean it. I offered you my bed?'

He searched his mind, trying to recollect whether that had been the case, although Suzie looked as serious as a sledgehammer heading for a wall.

'Yes. I was ready to go home, but you didn't want me out there with Coop's boys, if they were back. You insisted I stay.'

Carlton raised his eyebrows.

'But the bed? I have a sofa downstairs.' He looked at Suzie, who sighed long and loud.

'Okay,' he said, 'I'm sorry. This is all my fault. I don't know why I was so bothered about Coop's friends. He said they weren't back, didn't he? It must have been the beer. It's not your fault.'

Carlton finished his coffee and got up shakily from the bed.

'I don't know about you, but I need another one of these.'

Suzie nodded and scampered up with him, following him out of the room.

'Carlton?' she said, her whisper quiet feet padding the carpet behind him.

'Yeah,' he said, mulling over his actions from last night.

Why in the hell did you offer the bed? Why would you do that? You need to stop drinking before you've begun, kid.

He was at the foot of the stairs before Suzie spoke again.

'Carlton! There is a reason that you invited me to stay in your bed, not downstairs.'

Carlton wasn't sure he wanted to hear it. He put a hand on the living area door and opened it to darkness.

'Carlton?' Suzie whispered.

He reached for the switch and light flooded the room. The sight that greeted him nearly stopped his heart.

On the sofa, hands folded over his chest as though he were a vampire sleeping in a coffin, was Coop.

'Oh, fuck,' Carlton breathed.

'Precisely,' Suzie said quietly behind him.

Thirteen

M cGRACKEN HOUSE SAT PROUDLY on the edge of the village.
A timber archway perfectly flanked its solid black front
door, which sat symmetrically among the windows and huge
beams that ran through the walls. Flowers spilled across the
front, right up to a black wrought-iron fence that flanked the
tiny pavement. The sort of flowers that looked like they had
grown pretty and wild, but which had probably taken a lot of
organization and planning to achieve.

Sophie led them straight past the stunning front to double
wooden gates at the side. Today, one side was propped open,
and they stopped to let someone through before stepping inside.

Willow looked around in awe. Far from the small, cheery colour
of the property from the front, the back was sprawling. The
house was much larger than it appeared, and the gates headed
a driveway that led to various outbuildings, all built with the
same black and white timbers.

A large, open-sided barn, just ahead and to the right, housed
an old tractor and trailer, and bales of hay and straw were
stacked almost to the roof. Sophie explained that the smaller
outbuildings housed a variety of animals and pointed out the
paddocks behind the house to their left.

Ahead was a long sloping lawn dotted with mature trees and
well-tended flowerbeds, a summerhouse, and a large pond.

Sophie led Willow past the barn and through into a walled
garden which housed well-stocked and well-maintained fruit
and vegetables, and three large, sheeted tunnels. At the back
of the area were low boxes with glass tops and a large ornate
greenhouse that seemed full to bursting.

Through a door at the back of the wall, the land opened out again. In the field ahead, five bell tents were arranged on a semicircle of raised decking. They were strung together with bunting and fairy lights, and a large firepit sat before them, for communal gatherings, Willow supposed. A rough wooden archway leading to the decking declared that this was Heather Glade. It looked like a pretty glamping ground, but Sophie said no. Theses tents weren't for holidays.

If people didn't want to stay in the house, they were free to stop out here. Some people even pitched further out alone in their own tents. Nothing was out of the ordinary here.

Willow assessed the large tents through the rough wooden archway leading up to the decking, which declared that this was Heather Glade.

'What kind of people stay here?' she asked.

'All kinds. You name it, they've been. We've had people just passing through who stay on. They help out for a week or two and then go on their way. Some stay longer. There's one fella been here for around seven months now and he has no intention of leaving yet. There've been abused women, youth offenders, nomads, backpackers, depressives, people looking for a life break, people wanting to learn about sustainability. Lots of people pass through, and they all have one thing in common.'

'What's that?'

'They all say they leave better for having been here.'

'Well, that's good.'

'It's a healing place, therapeutic. There's no getting away from yourself here. Everyone has to pitch in and compromise. Working with the animals, and the ground? It's good for the soul, you know? It's a place for reflection.'

'Hmm,' Willow said. She was beginning to understand why Sophie had called her this morning. A healing place. Therapeutic.

How ironic.

'You'll see,' Sophie said, leading her back around the side of the walled garden to what looked like chaos.

There were people everywhere. Four were painting wood panels that sat against the wall in the cool sunshine. A further eight were hammering, banging, and screwing the panels together into large sheds.

On the edge of the activity, next to what appeared to be a drinks table, a young girl sat on a log playing soft folk tunes on a guitar. Next to her, a tall blonde lady in a long cotton dress was speaking to a man as her hand tapped against her thigh in beat with the music.

'It's like a different world,' Willow murmured.

'It really is,' Sophie agreed. 'Come on, I'll introduce you to Mrs McGracken.'

Willow smiled as they made their way over to the tall woman. After two awful nights that she put down to taking her second dose of Prozac later in the day, she had taken it all together today. She had thought it may serve her better if she was going to be out mixing with people in unfamiliar surroundings, and at the moment, it was doing its job well. She was nervous, but not overly panicky.

'Hello, Mrs McGracken,' she said, shaking the woman's smooth hand.

Mrs McGracken looked like a goddess, tall and willowy, with milky skin and pale blue eyes. Her blonde hair was tied in a loose plait that hung forward over her ankle length dress and a long cream cardigan that she held around herself with one hand. Her slim figure was deceiving. From afar she could have been any other thirty-year-old, but up close it was obvious that this woman was in her sixties at least, although the lines on her face were soft and dewy.

'Hello, Willow,' she said in a soft English accent. Her smile was warm and all-encompassing, and her eyes were bright. 'It's good to finally meet you.'

She had an air of royalty that almost made Willow want to curtsy before her. She stuck to a smile instead, although her cheeks reddened at the use of her name before she'd had a chance to offer it.

'It's a pleasure to meet you, too. You have a wonderful place, Mrs McGracken.'

'We, darling,' she said, showing straight white teeth. 'It is not mine. It is simply somewhere we are afforded to stay to enable us to help others. The others?' She swung her hand around the busy group. 'It is their home, too. Anybody who needs it. You included, my dear.'

'Oh, I'm okay. I'm at–'

'Ivy Cottage, yes, darling, but you're welcome here anytime. We have an open house and rooms for those wanting to stay and help. Most decide to stay awhile, but if they don't that's fine too. We're all on our own journey here. We take what we need. It's not about where we've been, it's about where we're going.'

Willow nodded, trying to make sense of what the lady had said, as an older man strode across the grass toward them. His tweed jacket and trousers, coupled with high boots, made him look like an eccentric professor. A thick grey mustache and a tweed cap that struggled to contain his wild hair completed the look. His Scottish accent was heavy and brusk.

'Helena, you're wanted on the phone.'

'Ah,' Mrs McGracken said with a warm smile. 'I'm sorry I have to cut you short. I'll let Sophie get you acquainted and show you where things are. Okay?'

Helena looked from Sophie to Willow, who were both nodding their heads. Then she placed a hand on each of their arms with a gentle squeeze. 'Thank you, girls.'

Pulling her cardigan closer, Helena walked back toward the house, meeting the man on the grass before they walked back to the house together.

'That's Mr McGracken. Mick.' Sophie said, pulling Willow toward the wall where the tins of paint and brushes lay on two long trestle tables.

'The paint is all different,' Willow said with a frown as she looked at the pastel shades of each can, but Sophie just laughed.

'Pick a colour, any you fancy. Helena loves colour. These sheds will line the back wall of the veg garden for tools and outdoor furniture and extra storage for the tents. She wanted them multicoloured.'

Picking a can each – Sophie a pale cream, and Willow a duck egg blue – they picked a couple of brushes and headed toward two unpainted panels that sat next to each other against the wall.

'Are these two panels okay to be painted these colours?' Willow said.

'Any colour is fine, as long as it ain't wood coloured,' the man next to them said. He wore jeans and a checked shirt, and a flat cap which his dark hair curled out from underneath. When he smiled, he was missing a good many of his teeth. Willow briefly wondered what his story was as she returned the smile.

Then she began to paint.

Under the rhythmic motion of the brush and the soft sounds of the guitar, the shouts and banging of the sheds being put together faded into the background, and time flew as one panel was replaced by another.

There were seven sheds in all and a seemingly endless supply of wood to be painted, but even the small blister that rose on Willow's thumb couldn't take away the stillness she felt watching the brown turn pale blue under her brush.

Even around all of these people, she felt calmer than she had been in a long time. There was no pressure to talk, and no one was taking any notice of the new girl on the end. All she found were warm smiles and good cheer.

Not having to talk gave her time to think. To think about how fast she had moved, how fast she was getting herself out, and whether it was the right thing to do. She thought about Carlton and his lack of attention that both pleased and aggravated the hell out of her at the same time. Thoughts of Carlton led to thoughts of Tam and what she had said about his treatment, especially him calling her supposed panic attacks hypoxia.

Was he right, or had he lied? And to what end? To keep her anxious, or to keep her inside?

She thought she may google the facts later and see who was right — Carlton or Tam.

Finally, her thoughts travelled to herself and how she was here in a small crowd of polite and friendly people working under the cool September sun. Last month she would never have put herself in this situation, and even if she had tried, Carlton would have said something to make her feel she shouldn't - or couldn't.

But here she was, doing it anyway.

When her thoughts stilled, she found herself simply painting, and then humming along as the girl strummed the guitar and began to sing Big Yellow Taxi.

Fourteen

L ATER THAT EVENING, FEELING better than she had in a long time, Willow sat on the settee in the living room and placed her mug of coffee on the small table. She switched on the television, pulled her feet up under her on the chair and reached for her phone.

There were no messages from Carlton. Nothing. Two from Sophie, one thanking her for a nice day, and the second asking if she wanted to join her back at McGracken House tomorrow - an obvious no-brainer that Willow replied to quickly. There was also one from her mum, asking if she was settling in okay. Willow fashioned a quick reply, making a note to call later, and then opened Google and began to search.

The results set her on edge. Carlton had deceived her. There was no other way to look at it.

Her symptoms, which were closely matched to panic attacks as Tam had said, could not land her in hospital easily. But Carlton had certainly said that, and implied they were much more serious, especially if she lost consciousness. Even if she blacked out - a point she had never reached yet - there was more chance of hurting herself from the fall than dying because she couldn't breathe. Often a blackout was just nature's way of stabilising the body and regulating oxygen levels in the blood. Hypoxia, on the other hand, was a very real condition, which could be deadly. That much was true. That she could get it from her panic attacks was almost unheard of. In fact, hypoxia and panic attacks were not linked at all.

Willow chewed her lip as her heart thumped.

So why would he say they were? What reason did he have to keep me thinking I may die each time I had a panic attack? Why would he tell me that these attacks were to be avoided at all costs? What was he getting from this?

She tugged at her bottom lip, thinking about what Tam had said about the pills. Should she stop taking them? Were they doing nothing? How did she even know that it was Prozac? If Carlton was lying about one thing, why not another?

Would he swap the pills? Surely not.

Her stomach swirled with uncertainty.

'Carlton, what the hell are you doing with my life? And why?' she whispered. 'What is this? There has to be a rational explanation, surely.'

There was a creak from the hallway and Willow swung her head to the open glass door where light shone in the corridor. The silence stretched. Blowing out a breath she didn't know she had held, she turned back to her phone. She found Carlton's contact and sat staring at the number.

Should I call him? It would be the easiest way to get answers.

She tapped her fingers on the side of the phone in thought.

There was another creak from the hallway, long and slow, like rusty hinges on an old door. The hair at the back of Willow's neck stood on end.

Calm down, the house is settling, that's all.

Except that the floor is concrete, and the wall is brick.

Unease ran through her, and she turned tentatively back to the doorway, wholly expecting to see someone standing there.

Panic fluttered in her chest.

I locked the door, didn't I?

A loud thud came from the direction of the bedrooms, and Willow shot off the settee with a small yell.

'Hello?' she called.

The house was quiet, pensive, and she took a few steps around the sofa toward the light of the corridor, which now looked ominous.

Willow balled her hands as she stared at the door, nails digging into her palms. Her chest hurt with tension, and her heart banged in her ears.

I can't go in there.

You have to.

No!

Her mind flicked to the mirror and the message in the bathroom.

Hello. And a smiley face.

Is someone here?

Her chest constricted until her lungs felt small and inflexible, like they were made of stone, not cells.

Why had she insisted that she do this alone? Why had her mother agreed that it would be good for her?

Willow wrapped her arms around herself, feeling the tremors that ran through her.

The house was silent, and the atmosphere thick, almost like an invisible barrier lay across the doorway to the corridor.

She swallowed hard.

The fact that Carlton seemed to have ignored her call, as well as feeding her misinformation about her diagnosis, was overshadowed by the longing to have him here now. By the knowledge that he would have been in those rooms instantly, and be back with his usual confidence and half-smile that said that there was absolutely no one there, never had been.

'It's in your head, babe. Have you taken your pills today?'

A flare of upset sat alongside the fear as the speck of distrust that had begun with Tam, and grown with Google, lodged in her chest.

Willow felt herself shake as she looked at the doorway, indecision routing her to the spot. The house was quiet, as though requiring a response before anything more happened, and frozen between the settee and the table, Willow felt a tear track down her cheek. She wiped it with a shaky hand.

Is this how it ends, Willow? Is this it? Are you going to quit already? And whatever Carlton is up to, he has no chance to explain from a distance. Once you're back, he can tell you any damn thing he likes. You're back under his control.

She blinked.

I wasn't under his control, was I?

As the quiet of the house enveloped her, a steely resolve crept up her spine, devouring some of her fear.

There's nothing here, you know that, don't you?

More tears fell. Tears of uncertainty, injustice, fear, love, and longing for her life to go back to the familiar. A life where she loved Carlton with all of her heart and knew that he would never hurt her.

Who says that he is?

Well, has he returned your call yet?

Willow felt more anger slide into her veins as she faced the long corridor.

Well, you either check this out, or you go running back home, which is probably exactly what he's waiting for.

'No,' she whispered. 'I won't go back. How could I trust him right now?'

The light in the hallway flickered, and cold air joined her in the living room. Not so much a breeze as a caress. She shivered as fear jolted back into her heart.

The door must be open. Not only that, but if the lights go out, you're screwed, Willow. Get in there and see what made the bang, stop this ridiculous need to lean on someone else. Maybe Carlton doses you up for that reason, to get you off his back.

A wave of shame landed in the pit of her stomach, and Willow pushed it down. She could feel sorry for herself later.

She forced her feet to move, and crossing the threshold into the hall, she saw the front doors were shut. Both of them.

She licked her lips and turned her attention to the corridor ahead of her. Three doors to three dark rooms.

So put the lights on. Don't think about it.

Moving to the first door, she reached out a trembling hand to the cool handle.

Ready? Five, four, three, two...

On one, she flung the door wide and hit the light switch.

The bedroom was warm, it's one bed and wardrobe sitting as they had yesterday. Still, she entered the room, quickly checking behind the door and under the bed before checking the wardrobe and curtains.

The fear almost ate her whole, but the strange thing was that this was different. Fear and resolve didn't equal panic attacks. For the last four years, she had been scared to let her heart beat too fast in case that had spiralled into what she had thought was hypoxia and potential death.

She hadn't questioned it. She had thought that Carlton had all the answers.

Another surge of anger sent her out of the door into the cool hallway and to the next spare room.

Same again?

With a nod, she counted backward from five and threw open the door, quickly stepping into the room and checking behind the door, in the wardrobe, under the bed.

Nothing and no one.

You're hearing things, Carlton's voice said.

'Things you put in my head?' she countered aloud.

With a frown, Willow turned to look at the last door along the corridor, her bedroom. The largest of the three rooms. More places to hide.

She swallowed hard, placing a hand onto the cold handle, and pushing it wide without even counting down. A gust of frigid air met her in the doorway with a force that almost pushed her backward.

Gritting her teeth against the fear that slammed through her body, she switched on the light.

Her breath clouded as her eyes scanned the room. The bed, dressing table, bookcase, drawers, wardrobe, windows which looked out into the night like soulless eyes.

Everything seemed in place, but the room felt wrong somehow, and the cold was unreal. The heating was on, the other bedrooms had been warm.

She rubbed her arms as her eyes fell onto a mass behind the door.

For a moment her heart seemed to flip right over, and then she gave a huff of relief so loud that she almost gave herself a heart attack in the quiet. She put a hand over her mouth to repress the nervous laughter that uncoiled from the pit of her stomach.

On the floor was the box that Carlton had given her as she left - a gift he had said. She hadn't seen what was inside yet, but she was certainly getting an eyeful now. The contents were scattered across the floor.

Leaflets, books, and DVD's.

She made her way to the pile, picking up the box and beginning to place the items back inside.

Books about anxiety and PTSD, leaflets outlining breathing techniques, a DVD about trauma and how it affects the brain. More and more and more of the same. Willow wrinkled her nose, an odd feeling stealing over her, like spiders crawling over her skin.

Was this protection, caring, or control?

She stared at the box and chewed on her lip.

You know what? I'm going to put this box away where I can't see it, and not open it until I get home, if I ever go home. I've done more without this crap in the last two days than I have in the last four years.

A small air of guilt sat in her chest.

You're being harsh, Willow, he's trying to help.

Willow cocked an eyebrow, her mouth a tight line. She didn't know whether she believed that anymore. She didn't know what she believed.

Then put the things away and see how you get on.

Willow didn't know where the tough voice in her head was coming from, but it felt better than the usual scared, whiny voice full of excuses.

Maybe it's time to put that voice away, too.

'Maybe it's time to put this shit away permanently,' she murmured, pushing the last of the paraphernalia into the box and closing the lid with a grin. She shoved the box inside the wardrobe before going back to the living room, leaving the bedroom door open, hoping to warm it before she went to bed.

She didn't notice that the bedroom window sat on the latch, and in the condensation that lay along the bottom edge of the glass where warm air met cold, was a smiley face and a new message.

HI.

Fifteen

S UBURBIA SUCKED, THIS APARTMENT sucked, and Cooper Mathers found himself at a bit of a loss as he met the new day.

He popped two slices of bread into the toaster and looked around.

The apartment was darker than a coffin, which had fucked up his sleep. He had woken at 3pm, alone. Carlton was at work, he supposed, and hadn't thought to wake him – or hadn't wanted to. He never did like to deal with things.

Pussy.

The toast popped. Coop buttered it and took it back into the living room, which had all the appeal of a clinical area - but grey. Grey walls, grey furniture, grey carpet. Even the fucking blanket he had pulled over him in the night was grey.

He mulled over his lack of plan as he chewed. Things definitely weren't going the way he had thought they would.

The original plan had been simple. He got out of jail (at fucking last) and paid the lovely Carlton and Willow a surprise visit. Happy families and all that.

For a short time, anyway.

Coop grinned.

Carlton had fucked it up, though, being at the pub when he had implied that he and Willow never went out anymore, and if Suzie was in the mix too... well, what did that even mean?

It wasn't like his brother was anything other than a predictable bore, so the pub had been a surprise. Suzie, even more so, and now Willow? Where the hell was she?

Curiouser and curiouser.

He felt a little off balance at how different things actually were now he was here.

Did someone tip Carlton off?

Coop frowned. He supposed he should have been annoyed, but intrigue won the emotional pull as he tried to understand.

Carlton was with Suzie.

Willow was gone?

The world was upside down.

It was almost funny... almost.

He sighed.

It wasn't too much of a problem, he thought, eating the last of the toast. He still had a few days before Radar caught up to him. A few days before the plan switched to phase two, when the fun began.

In the meantime, he would just have to stay here and work out what the hell his little brother was up to, and where Willow had gone.

He stood, brushing crumbs to the floor, and grabbed his leather jacket.

'Well, if I'm staying in this poxy joint for a few days, I'm going to need some beer, at the very least.'

Glad for something to do, he pulled on his coat and headed for the local shop.

Sixteen

T HE NEXT MORNING, WILLOW woke to streaming sunlight. She propped up on her elbows and looked around the room, which was calm and peaceful in the morning light. In fact, it was really light. She checked her watch and discovered it was 8.15am.

8.15am? She couldn't remember the last time she had slept so late and felt so rested.

She smiled, and then she remembered.

Google. The pills. Carlton.

Last night was the only time she hadn't had the pills in the afternoon. Yesterday, she had taken the whole 40mg together to get her through painting at McGracken House.

A small knot of unease pulled inside her stomach.

You really think he'd do this to you?

She swung her legs out of bed and frowned.

He'd only upped her dose a few days before she'd left to check she'd be okay. She thought the extra anxiety and sleeplessness were due to leaving, but now she wondered.

'How badly does he want me home?' she said into the room, narrowing her eyes. 'Is he trying to frighten me?'

Picking up her phone from the side table of the bed, she lit the screen. There were no messages, and no call back. He was doing as she had asked him.

Is that a good thing?

Knowing how bad she had been before she left, she had expected a little resistance to her wishes. She clicked to show his last message.

I'm sorry. I love you.

There had been nothing since. With a small frown, she clicked off the screen and put the phone down.

Letting the unease run her thoughts, which seemed more together than they had been for a while, she stepped out of bed. She opened the curtains, dressed, and padded to the kitchen, switching on the kettle. At the bathroom door, she hesitated.

Would there be another message?

Don't be silly, it was the steam that caused it. It's gone now.

Still, her heart banged as she pushed the door open slowly. It gave a small groan as the room came into view bit by bit. Shower, toilet, and finally mirror.

There were dried water droplets from the shower, and a long smear where she had rubbed the face away, but nothing more.

Releasing the breath that she'd been holding, she stepped inside and washed and brushed her teeth and hair. Then she made toast and coffee back in the kitchen.

She finished her breakfast at the dining table, facing out into the corridor, and wondering what the hell had felt so spooky about this house last night. Then she opened her phone and pulled up the google search, picking up where she had left off yesterday.

The pills sat on the edge of the table, but she hadn't yet taken one. She may. Just one. But not before she understood what she could do to help herself. Tam had said her episode at the pub was a panic attack - not even a bad one. It had felt pretty bad, but people had worse apparently, and Tam said that the pills weren't worth taking?

'So how in the hell do people cope with this without them?' she murmured.

Starting with the panic attacks, Willow googled everything she could. What caused them - Major life stress was listed - check. She was certainly eligible for them just with that one thing, although there were others she matched, too.

What symptoms they presented - dizziness, racing heart, feeling faint, sweating, chest pain, shortness of breath...

The next one made Willow stop in her tracks.

Fear of dying.

That was familiar. Every time she had an attack, she feared dying, but whose fault was that? Carlton fed her the line at every opportunity.

Have you taken your pills today, Willow?

Willow eyed the box on the end of the table, shook her head, and went back to the list. Around ninety-nine percent of the symptoms had applied to her at some point.

The biggest thing she had learned was that they weren't fatal. They would pass. And she could learn to deal with them.

The biggest thing was to stop trying to push through.

'Stop what you're doing and focus,' she said, narrowing her eyes as she read from the screen.

Not hard. They had stopped willow in her tracks more than once.

Breathe, slowly and steadily. Carlton had taught her that much right.

Re-focus your attention.

Splash water on your face if you are able.

A walk or light exercise can help.

Remind yourself that it will pass, and it is NOT dangerous, nor fatal.

Willow huffed an ironic laugh, but her thoughts were cut short at the small knock from the corridor. She looked up into the bright area, saw nothing, and then refocused on the screen.

Treatment, in the first instance, involved talking. Therapy. Not Pills.

It turned out there were a few steps before pills were considered.

But Carlton had me on them from the outset. Straight away. And we never discussed what had happened. In fact, I've never discussed it fully with anybody.

The bottom of this page told her 'suppressed feelings are always involved. If in doubt, talk it out.'

'Carlton is a psychiatrist, Willow, but he's never talked it out? He's never suggested you talk it out. In fact, when you wanted to talk, he shut it down. He said you have to move on from the past, not wallow in it. Remember?'

She nodded slowly to herself, a cold sweat hanging around her torso.

Further research told her that Prozac was used for extreme anxiety, but that it shouldn't be used for prolonged periods - was four years a prolonged period? She thought of her mum's five-month term, and how keen the doctor was to get her off them. Carlton had said that the doctor was negligent, but Mum had been just fine ever since - she had spoken about the ordeal, though. Therapy.

If in doubt, talk it out.

Willow put the phone down and rubbed her eyes with her hands.

There was so much to process, so much to think about. So much of her life had flipped right over in just two days.

And poor Carlton doesn't even get a chance to explain himself? Did he even tell you what he'd diagnosed you with?

'Trauma. That's all he said. I had been through a massive trauma but that I had to look forward, it would pass.'

There had been trauma. Her dad's life had been taken with it, and although the grief had eased with time, her reaction to enclosed spaces with crowds hadn't.

If Carlton had led her astray, for whatever reason, it had probably been to protect her. Even so, Mum had also been there on that fateful day, and she was now getting on with her life.

She wondered if Carlton had been holding her back, possibly on purpose. At this point, it seemed so, and Mum had seen it. She had been telling Willow to get out for a good many months - not away from Carlton; she had been careful about that - but away from everything she knew. She had kept her concern neutral.

Willow got up from the table and took her phone and cup into the kitchen to re-boil the kettle. As she waited, she fired off a message to her mum.

Morning, how are you? I slept in!! Can you believe it?

On a more serious note, I'm having concerns about Carlton. Can I ask why you encouraged me out here? Don't hold back, I want to hear it. Please.

She made coffee and was sitting back at the table before her mum replied, and the few lines she sent back were enough to force the air from her lungs.

I can, you're in charge of yourself now. You can listen to your body instead of your psychiatrist. The reason? I had concerns about Carlton, too. I didn't like what he was doing to you.

What he was doing to me?

The phone rang, and Willow answered.

'That was wrong of me to say,' Mum said. 'Ignore me, you just concentrate on getting better. If this works, I'm happy, Willow. It's about time you got your life back. I wasn't going to suggest this yet, it seemed too soon, but maybe you could find someone to talk to up there?'

Willow's heart was thumping fast.

'I will Mum, in fact, I think I've already found someone. She was the one who questioned my treatment.'

'Oh, well, that's good news!'

The relief in Mum's voice was evident, but she was being guarded, and Willow wanted the truth.

'So, what was it?'

'What was what, love?'

There was the sound of crockery and voices in the background.

'What was it that made you keep on at me to get away? I need to know.'

'Oh, Willow, you do push. It's silly really, and this is nothing to do with me, but I don't trust him. To be honest, your father never liked him, said he talked a load of crap, and that he was hiding things from you. I can't say I took to him either, although I wouldn't have gone as far as your father did. I always thought he was a good person. Your father always said manipulative, but I could never see it. I mean if you-'

Willow closed her eyes. She was still holding back to make her feel better.

'Mum. Please. Just tell me straight.'

There was a sigh, that clink of crockery, mumbling in the background, a shrill voice that asked 'sugar, Tone?' and a male, 'please.'

'Okay.' Mum said finally. 'I don't want you to be angry with me.'

'I won't. I already have my suspicions. Please.'

There was a chair scraping and laughter.

'It was after your father died, that's when I began to see it...' Mum paused and Willow held her breath. *See what*? 'I noticed little things. He would say things to you that weren't quite true, such as ... well, it's daft, really.'

'Tell me,' Willow said. Her heart was drumming in her ears. This was two people who had questioned Carlton's actions in the last twenty-four hours.

'It was a Sunday when you were visiting. I'd just moved into the village here, and you and Carlton came over, but it was Carlton who did most of the talking. I tried to include you in the conversation, but I was concerned. You were in a haze. I wasn't sure you heard anything I said. Carlton said it was normal for trauma patients and with the level of Prozac you were taking, but it just didn't sit right. He was preaching to the converted. I had been there. He seemed to forget that. Anyway, out of nowhere, you suddenly spoke, but you were slurring. It almost broke my heart to see you like that, but I jumped on what you asked.'

Willow swallowed. Her throat was dry. She had slurred?

'What did I ask?'

'You asked if I could take you to the sea. Just you and me. It was so simple it was heartbreaking. When Carlton said that you wouldn't manage the crowds, you argued. I argued, too. I'm your mother, for goodness' sake, and there are beaches that are not populated even in summer. I said I would find somewhere secluded, but he got angry and told me I didn't understand how serious your condition was. Eventually, he agreed to take you himself. He said at least if he was there, your condition could be controlled. I didn't like that word, but he said it was customary in his profession.

By this time, you were looking more alert and then he suddenly got up and pulled you to your feet, saying you had to be some-where. You told him you didn't want to go, but he laughed and said that you were meeting Kelly from school.'

Willow physically reeled back into the chair. She hadn't seen Kelly since they had stupidly argued over a dress, long before Dad had died, back when she actually cared about going out.

'I hadn't seen Kelly for years back then, Mum. I don't remember seeing her at all.'

'Willow, there was no visit. A few weeks later, I saw Kelly in town. She said she heard about the attack but hadn't seen you for years and asked how you were.'

Willow closed her eyes.

What the hell has been going on here? What has he been doing?

'The point is, he was so believable, Willow. It just rolled off his tongue. He was... *sincere*! But all the time he was *lying*. Oh, I know it was a little thing, but there was more than just that once. After I had spoken to Kelly, I checked out a few other things that didn't make sense, too. Small things. I thought about your father and his talk of manipulation, and obviously I had my treatment to compare to. I knew what had happened to me, and I knew that wasn't happening with you. Honey, you haven't even seen a doctor! There is no medical record of you taking Prozac for almost four years. He just dosed you up. I just... I don't know. I just thought if I could get you away from him, then you could have the space to think it through. I'm not saying he's a bad person, or that he isn't doing what he thinks is best. I'm not even saying what he has done is wrong. All I have to compare it with is where I am now, compared to you. Honey, you seem worse some days, and certainly no better. After four years! All I ever saw him do was dish pills into your hand, and I confess, I hated it. It didn't sit right. So, if you want the truth? The hard truth? I just don't trust him. I'm sorry, love. I just don't.'

Willow felt like she had been hit with a sledgehammer. Right in the chest. A chest that was constricting with a rushing force.

You wanted the truth.

Manipulation, dad had said. Why didn't she know he had thought that? Now Mum had said it too.

Manipulation. Lies.

Have you had your pills today, Willow?

But what does that mean? Carlton? My Carlton? And what for?

She rubbed a hand across her head.

'I'm sorry, love,' she heard her mum say.

'It's okay,' she whispered.

'It's not. I shouldn't have-'

'I needed it, Mum. I have the same concerns looking at it from up here...'

Manipulation.

'If I look back on the last four years, all I see is an enormous ball of fear. I can't even see right. It's like someone is holding a thick Perspex sheet in front of my face and asking me to see through it.'

Control.

'Mum? I can't even remember much. All I remember are feelings. Fear when he was gone, and relief when he was home. I can't...' she frowned and swallowed hard.

'I'm so sorry, love. I'm sorry. It's okay now, it will all be okay. Talk to this person, and keep thinking. I'm not going to tell you that you're right or wrong. I only know what I feel. You have to do what's right for you, and remember he should have his say about all of this too, although, when I remember those lies... I don't know. I'm not sure you'll get the truth.'

Wet splashes dropped onto the table, and Willow realised she was crying.

'Mum, why did you never tell me this?'

'Would you have listened?'

Willow shook her head.

'No.'

'No. You weren't ready. I didn't expect this call so soon, but I expected it within the year. All those things he had stopped you from doing? I knew you would do them alone, and I knew you would question things. You were always such an independent child. Fearless, and so headstrong, you never leaned on anyone. I saw him wear you down to complete dependency over the years after the attack. I didn't understand why, but I knew if you could get away for a while, you would find yourself and question it. That's all I wanted, was for you to question it. I know you got annoyed with my badgering over the last year, but I am so relieved you're there, and that you can see more clearly.'

'I can, Mum.'

'Good, all I want is my little girl back.'

'I'll get there, Mum. I'm determined to get well and sort this out.'

'And I know you will. I'm so proud of you for doing this. Ah, Phyllis is here. We're having brunch at the village cafe. I have to go. I love you, honey. Take care of yourself, and always pick up the phone when you need to. I keep telling you, it's good to talk.'

If in doubt, talk it out.

Willow smiled as she brushed away tears.

'Thanks Mum, I love you too. Enjoy your brunch.'

As they said their goodbyes, Willow realised she didn't even know who Phyllis was. She didn't know any of her mum's friends anymore. Growing up she had known them all, until Carlton anyway. That was the point she lost touch.

Carlton. The name was bittersweet. She wanted to believe he was only doing his best, but now she doubted his intentions, especially after the lies Mum had seen, too.

Well, she didn't have to confront him just yet. She had the year. She had already decided to talk to Tam, and Helena had been nice too. Sophie was due to 'pick her up' at 10.30am so that they could help with the sheds again.

Maybe it was the open air, but she had found yesterday comfortable, the atmosphere calm and friendly. She had a feeling McGracken House would keep dragging her back, and with the people there, that would probably help too.

Yes, up here she would heal. She would make sure of it. And while she was here, she would work out what Carlton's agenda really was before she decided whether she could trust him again.

She flicked to his last message, glanced at the stark words, the empty words, words so unlike Carlton, and then she switched the screen off.

Her entire world felt like it had been turned upside down. Everything felt wrong and uncomfortable. If she had a choice, she felt her head would go running back home and pretend she had never found out any of this. But her heart knew now, and Willow didn't know if there would be any going back from here unless Carlton had a damn good explanation for what he had done.

Seventeen

WHILE THE WEEKEND AND its revelations had certainly not been comfortable, Willow found that she'd had a good time, anyway. Sophie's constant chatter about everything from the weather and pigs to paint and shoes kept her mind occupied while she was out. Since Friday, she had spent most of the weekend out between her walks and visits to McGracken House. It was a shame that had to end today, but it did.

Sophie was back working, and the sheds were complete, standing proudly in a colourful pastel line across the back of the walled garden. She had even stayed over to help fill them and put shelves and glass in the huge shed that would be the potting shed. That one sat at the end of the row, just across from the large vegetable garden with its sheeted tunnels.

To be honest, she had been looking for a reason to go back, but couldn't find one. Which was ridiculous. Her chats with Helena had told her just how welcome she was, but dropping on the doorstep with no reason seemed too weird. Too *needy*.

So today she had walked in the drizzle to the forest clearing and sat under the Willow tree to clear her thoughts as she admired the surroundings. She watched the heavy grey sky and listened to the bubble of the stream on its way more forcefully downhill after the night's downpour. She had been back by lunch, hungry and soaked, and was now sitting with a cup of coffee, nursing one of the most intense headaches she'd ever experienced.

A look at her watch told her she had taken the paracetamol just an hour ago, when she had been doing more research.

'Should kick in soon,' she whispered, closing her eyes as she sat in the warm comfort of the cottage. Her thoughts turned to withdrawal, and she almost reached for her phone again.

No. I'll look when my head isn't screaming, she thought. Maybe.

Her hands shook as she sipped the coffee, thinking over the last few days. She had taken only one pill Saturday morning, and none both yesterday and today, but found she was feeling worse than ever.

The headache wouldn't shift, and she had been having hot flushes all day, but there was a positive. She'd experienced palpitations twice while out walking, but managed to control them with relative ease, using the instructions she had found online.

I stopped an attack almost before it began!

Me!

No Carlton. No pills. And certainly no death.

She smiled, the only celebration she could manage right now. She wanted nothing more than to curl up and go to sleep, but in just ten minutes Sophie was swinging by to pick her up for yoga.

It had been in her mind to cancel. She had done a session on her own this morning in the bedroom anyway, but then she had thought of the way Thursday's session had made her feel. Warm, limber, and calm. Even with all of those people around her, even on her first outing up here. The endorphins had worked wonders on her system, and besides, she wanted to speak to Tam. She wanted to understand more while things were fresh in her mind.

She sat with her head in her hands and closed her eyes, waiting for the pills to take effect as she waited for Sophie.

'So, what have you been up to today, Wills? Did you go to the House?'

'What for?' Willow was sitting cross-legged in the heat of the room, waiting for class to start. Around her, people were stretched out on the brightly coloured mats in quiet conversation. Some were lying prone in early relaxation, others were bent over their legs or stretching arms to the ceiling.

'Something to do?'

'We finished the sheds yesterday. I didn't want to go back and make a nuisance of myself. I went for a walk, tidied up the cottage a bit, then sat researching panic attacks.'

'As you do.' Sophie grinned. 'Find anything interesting?'

'Hmm, well, they're controllable without the pills. I know I'm supposed to have been through a massive trauma, and I'm not saying it wasn't, but the worst I've ever felt only seems to have been a mild attack. Which is strange.'

'Made worse by some husband saying you'll die...' Sophie trailed off as Willow's face fell. She sighed. 'I'm sorry. Tam told me. She's said nothing to anyone else. She was just concerned, that's all. Prozac can be addictive, and she doesn't know whether you're hooked.'

'He's not my husband and I'm not hooked,' Willow said, curling her lip.

Sophie shrugged. 'Isn't that what any addict would say?'

'I'm not an addict!' Willow said, far too loud. A few people looked her way. Maud's eerie eyes found hers across the room, and Willow tore hers away, looking back to Sophie. 'I'm not an addict,' she whispered. 'I haven't taken a single pill for a couple of days now.'

Sophie's eyes lit up in genuine delight and her mouth spread into a grin that Willow couldn't help mimicking. It was one of the lovely things about Sophie. Sometimes she could be brash, but at least she said what was on her mind. She was honest, which left Willow in no doubt where she stood. It was one less thing to worry about... especially now she had informed the rest of the village that she was possibly an addict.

'That's fabulous news!' Sophie grinned, taking hold of Willow's arm. 'What made you drop them?'

'This whole thing with Tam, and you, and then my mum. All of you really have shown me how much I trusted him. He's not a bad person, and I'm sure he was only doing what he thought was right, but it's been holding me back, I'm certain of it.'

'Look at you, up here, in a room full of people. No pills. None.' She squeezed Willow's arm.

'None.' Willow grinned back, her headache a minor thump now, and only a flutter of her heart that she attempted to breathe away.

'Will I ever find out what happened?'

Willow smiled at Sophie's forthrightness.

'Maybe one day.'

The door clicked open, and Tam came in, along with a waft of cool air, her pink leggings, grey crop top and grey streak all in place. As Willow's throat began to close and air became short, she had never been so glad of a distraction.

'Sorry about that ladies and gents, telephone call.' She smiled at Willow before moving her gaze to Sophie, and on around the room. 'Shall we begin?'

Willow was almost asleep when the poke came to her ribs.

'Come on, we're last. I told you, Tam will lock us in.'

Willow opened an eye reluctantly, tired, but happy and relaxed, although the headache was still sitting in the left side of her skull. Closing her eyes had seemed to dull it down, but back in the bright lights, it began to shriek.

'Urg,' she said, as Sophie pulled her up and a wave of dizziness hit her. 'Where's the toilet?'

'Out and left,' Sophie said with a bemused smile. 'I'll get changed and wait for you.'

Willow barely made the toilet before the vomit was in her mouth. She fell to her knees on the floor, ungracefully hurling up everything she had eaten, the spike of pain in her head like a hot poker.

She flushed and rose on rubbery legs, checking her stomach was stable before opening the door and letting out a small screech.

Maud stood by the basins. Her eerie gaze found Willow's in the mirror, and Willow placed a hand on her chest.

'Maud, I'm sorry, you scared me.'

'Aye,' Maud replied, her eyes squinting. 'You don't look so good.'

'I'm fine,' Willow said as she eyed the basins. Two. Side by side. Maud filled the one. The bitter taste still hung in her mouth. She needed to rinse, and she could do with washing her hands where she had clutched the toilet bowl. Trying to ignore her pattering heart, she walked to the empty basin. A whiff of something not altogether pleasant left Maud's skin. Like old bread that had been left to linger a few days, stale and musty.

Willow washed her hands and splashed her face with water. When she looked back up at the mirror, Maud was watching her, one milky eye, one dark, both sitting in a hooded socket which seemed to fold down to her cheekbones. Similarly, her cheeks seemed to descend to her jaw, creating loose jowls. This close, Willow could see the deep creases that lined her top lip and the odd coarse hair that sprouted from her chin.

'You don't look fine, if I may say. Trouble enough, I should think, with what goes in.'

Willow froze at the reference to the addict comment. 'Oh! No, Sophie was jibing. I reacted, that's all.'

Maud creased her loose lips into what Willow thought was a look of 'Whatever you say', glanced at the toilet and looked back to her.

'Have you seen her yet?'

Willow dabbed at her face with a paper towel. 'Who?'

'Ah, not yet, but she sees you.' Maud pressed her lips together and nodded slowly as Willow stared, the paper towel inches from her face. 'Oh aye, she sees you. Take care out there, Willow.'

Maud turned and left the room with an agility that her face belied, letting the door click shut behind her. Willow's head pounded along with her heart, and her hands shook as she dried the rest of her face.

She's just an old lady with a grudge. Don't let her get to you.

She sees you?

Willow looked back into the reflection of her own brown eyes. She hadn't been in the shower since that day, but the memory of the smiley face and the cheery hello made her blood run cold.

It was from the owner. Simple.

Now get out before Sophie and Tam think you've been eaten by the toilet.

***

They sat in the cool of the community centre with two teas and a coffee from the machine in the corner. Sophie had also taken a chocolate bar from the vending machine for good measure.

Tam had locked the door behind Maud, who had been the last to go, wishing Willow a peaceful night and hoping she felt better soon. Icy fingers had crawled through Willow's hair at the lady's smile.

'Are you not feeling well, pet?' Tam said, sipping at her tea.

'I'm fine. I just... well, I threw up. Maud was in the toilets when I finished, but I feel great now. I'm good.'

Tam pursed her lips and gave her a pitying look that put Willow on edge.

'I'm great,' she reinforced.

'I believe you,' Tam said. 'Millions wouldn't with the pallor of your skin right now.'

Willow let her breath go. It wasn't like she had anything to hide from Tam. Sophie smiled and knocked Willow's arm.

'Tell her. Go on.'

'Tell me what?'

Willow smiled. 'I didn't take my pills today. In fact, I haven't had one since Saturday morning.'

Instead of the whoop of delight she had expected from Tam, her mouth fell open, her eyes flashing concern.

'Oh, but... Willow, no. No, you mustn't just come off them. It doesn't work like that, pet. Christ, you must feel awful. No pills at all?'

She placed a hand on Willow's head, just as her mother had done when she was a sick child.

'None. I'm fine.'

'Clearly not. What was your dosage? 40mg? And for a few years, you said?'

'No,' Willow interjected. '20mg. Carlton had increased it to 40mg, but I only took that much for a couple of weeks. They were giving me nightmares. I couldn't sleep. I only took twenty yesterday and the day before.'

'Right, and each day for four years before that?'

'I guess.'

'You shouldn't just come off medication like that, you should-'

'I'm fine,' Willow said, although her head still thumped and her hands shook. Tam took them in hers.

'You're cold.'

'It's freezing in here after being in that room.'

Tam nodded and pressed a hand to her face again. 'You don't seem too bad, considering. How have you been feeling? What symptoms?'

Willow frowned. What symptoms could be attributed to coming off a pill that was addictive? As opposed to the symptoms she felt each day? Where to draw the line?

'Um, well. I slept well and woke fine. Since then, I guess a headache that won't go away. I'm shaky, and I've just been sick. That's all.'

Tam raised her eyebrows.

'That's all? There's no need for any of that.'

'I go through that on an almost daily basis anyway, without being sick, of course.'

'Any panic attacks today, and I mean even slight palpitations — anything.'

Tam gripped her wrist, placing two fingers on her pulse. Willow suppressed a sigh.

'Two on my walk in the woods, which I controlled. One before I came here, and I suppose some palpitations in the bathroom with Maud.'

'Anyone would get palpitations in the bathroom with Maud,' Sophie snorted.

Tam shot her a stern look and Sophie bit her lip, looking away.

'No need, Soph,' Tam said, turning back to Willow. 'That's all?'

Willow thought about it, but there had been nothing else out of the ordinary today. She nodded.

'You're lucky. You shouldn't come off these things cold turkey. It can be dangerous.'

'I'm okay,' Willow pressed.

'Yes, you are, but the first few days are always the worst. There may be more to come as your body gets the drug out of your system. Your brain state may even alter after so long on a chemical pill.'

Willow felt her defences crawl up.

'You told me I didn't need them. I questioned a lot and decided I didn't. That's all there is to it. People come off heroin cold turkey. This is just Prozac. Prescribed Prozac. I'm not an addict.'

Tam nodded and let her gaze fall.

'Okay, and yes, you're right, but that doesn't mean there isn't a better way of doing it. Coming off slowly, reducing the amount is safer-'

Willow slapped a hand on the table.

'I'm not touching those goddamn pills ever again!' she said, glowering. Tam recoiled, and Sophie stared. 'If I didn't need them then, I certainly don't need them now. I controlled the two attacks today just fine. I researched what to do. If I'm sick, it won't last forever. I've just completed an hour-and-a-half forty-degree yoga session, for Christ's sake, and the entire village now thinks I'm an addict. I'm not a bloody addict!'

Willow was breathing heavily, as though she had just sprinted the mile to the community centre. Her cheeks felt flushed, and the room was spinning slowly, causing the nausea to return. Tam caught her hands again, with a nod.

'Okay. Okay, I'm sorry. Yes, you do seem to be handling it well, so far. I just didn't expect this so quickly, I mean, we only chatted last Thursday. I had a whole mental plan drawn up that I was going to speak to you about today. I didn't expect that you would have jumped the first forty hurdles before I'd even begun. You've shocked me, that's all.'

Willow felt her anger subside, leaving her feeling more tired than she had felt for the last four years.

'I'm sorry too, I didn't realise. I really, really, don't want to take any more of those pills, though. Especially before I ask Carlton exactly what they were for, and why. I just... I get a bad feeling.'

'Okay,' Tam said, 'I don't think there's anything bad about caring though, and lots of people are on way more of a dose than you are... were. If you really don't want to take them again, we're going to have to manage the attacks, the withdrawal, and the symptoms together. I have a plan though, if you're ready to hear it.'

Willow smiled and nodded. Any plan she was involved in was far better than being spoon fed pills for reasons unbeknown to her.

'That would be great, thanks Tam.'

Eighteen

'**W**HEN ARE YOU LEAVING?**' Carlton said, trying to be casual as he brought two beers in from the kitchen after work. It was bad enough that Coop had slept on his couch for two nights and was still here this evening, but he also knew there wasn't a way to force his older brother from anywhere he wanted to be.

'Cheers, bro,' Coop said, clinking the bottles as he took one from Carlton's hand. He swigged three large gulps before bringing the bottle from his lips with an audible 'ahhh'. 'Well, I was thinking about sticking around a while, actually.' He pushed his hand onto the fabric of the grey sofa. 'It's not much of a bed, but it'll do for a while, you know? Thought you may have upgraded to a two-bed by now. Are you moving up in life or going steady?' He moved his hand across the front of his body, palm face down.

Carlton sat on the chair opposite, which was a smaller replica of the larger two-seater Coop was sitting on. The room didn't hold much else but the television.

These apartments were spread over two floors which gave the illusion of space from the outside with their 'house' like appeal and neat front doors, but in reality, there was a small lounge and kitchen diner, (apparently, although the most they had managed to fit into the kitchen had been a couple of bar stools aside an extra length of worktop which called itself a breakfast bar). The kitchen was barely big enough to swing a cat, the lounge with its window looking out onto the side street, much the same. Upstairs was a large bedroom - only because this design was also used for the two-bed apartments, where there probably wasn't room to swing a few more cats - and a functional bathroom. That was it. Period. But for Carlton and Willow, it was home. Cozy, neat, and good at its job.

'We don't need to move. This place is great for work. I can even walk when I want to.'

Not that he did often, but that was beside the point. He took another sip of beer, prepared to continue, but Coop beat him to it.

'Oooh. Walking to work, look at you! Last of the climate freaks. What about the chick?'

'What about her?' Carlton aimed for nonchalance but felt his jaw clench at the mention of Willow, especially from Coop's lips.

'She working?'

'Why would you need to know?'

'I don't,' Coop said with a sneer. 'She's just not here, and she's always here. It's kind of 'in your face' fucking obvious, bro. So where is she?'

'Doing better. She's gone away for a while.'

A shadow passed over Coop's face and a frown twitched his eyebrows.

'She's doing better, eh? So, she's upgraded to leaving the house. What a shocker. Away where?'

'I don't know.'

Coop narrowed his eyes, assessing him while he took another gulp of beer. Then his face lit up, and he clicked his fingers at Carlton with a wide smile that lit up his sharp eyes.

'Ah-ha!' he said, thrusting the beer bottle toward Carlton, fore-finger pointing at him. Beer sloshed in the bottle and Carlton tried not to react as some spilled from the side and dripped onto the grey carpet. Dark grey, luckily.

Coop hooted a laugh. 'I knew it! I fucking knew it. You are shagging her, aren't you? Your chick found out and fucking left. Fuck me. Who would have seen that coming?'

Carlton felt his stomach jump up into his chest. He had to get off talk of Willow. If Coop was back in town for her, he was glad he didn't know where she was.

'She's on a small holiday, Coop. She'll be back, and I'm not sleeping with Suzie.'

'So, what you mean is, she hasn't found out yet? But now she's taking a holiday, so you can fuck in peace?'

Carlton worked his jaw and stared into the bottle at his beer.

'Just stating the obvious. If it's supposed to be a secret, you're not doing a great job of hiding it, bro. She spent the night here two days ago. Just because you were sloshed to shit doesn't mean I was. Could you get it up? I mean, you were totalled. Absolutely fucking totalled.'

'I didn't get anything up.'

'Shame,' Coop said with a flick of his head. 'Not really surprised, though.'

Carlton felt his anger rise. His teeth had been clenched together for so long that his jaw ached, sending a shooting pain through his temples.

'For the last time. I am not sleeping with Suzie, and Willow is away for a few days. Speaking of which, I don't need you here when she arrives home. You can't sleep here. You need to find somewhere else to go.'

Coop finished his beer with a roll of his eyes.

'I don't have anywhere, you know that.'

'Find somewhere. I can't have you here.'

'Well, I could.' He swung his eyes around the room in fake appraisal. 'But I kind of like this shit show.'

Carlton stood up, his fists clenched by his sides.

'It's not the Hilton,' Coop continued, 'But still-'

Before he knew what he was doing, Carlton was across the floor and pulling Coop to his feet by the collar of his battered leather jacket.

'You need to leave,' he spat, his anger unchecked.

Coop merely laughed and shook his hands away, straightening his collar and rubbing down his jacket as he chuckled.

'Take it easy, bro. There's something in this for you too, of course. At least if I'm here, you can bring the prescriptions home. I don't need to show up at your precious little office and cause a scene, do I?'

Carlton almost flipped, almost let a fist fly straight into his brother's smug face... almost, but then he stopped himself. His shaking fist drawn back.

There could be an advantage here, couldn't there? A sparkle of diamond amongst the coal?

If Coop was here, then Carlton knew exactly where his brother was and what he was up to.

If Coop was here, then there was absolutely no way he was near Willow, and that was all that mattered, wasn't it?

Coop was always better in sight than out of it, their mother had always said.

Carlton lowered his fist, as Coop nodded.

'There,' he said, 'I knew you'd see sense. Don't worry about blankets. I'll pick a duvet up from town.'

'I have a spare,' Carlton said stiffly, 'and you have two weeks. Maximum.'

Nineteen

W ILLOW WALKED THE MILE back to Ivy Cottage alone, the way lit by orange puddles which glistened on the damp tarmac of the road. It was quiet; always quiet here. Only a single car had passed this evening, but rather than finding it eerie, Willow was comforted by the close darkness, the whisper of the trees in the light evening breeze. She had never been afraid of the dark. Never been afraid of anything until the attack.

And now, the stuff with Carlton worried her. How much of her life had he taken? And for what reason?

Sophie had left before Tam had finished going over her plan. She had been concerned about Willow being alone on the walk home, but Willow had waved her on. She enjoyed the peace of her own company, and after the talk with Tam, she was feeling comfortable about what she could do and where to go next. There was a way forward, and she was passing it now.

McGracken House.

The lights from the front of the large house lit the small pavement, and even in the darkness, the house seemed soft and gentle.

Much like its owners.

Willow smiled and pulled her coat up around her ears. From the back came the sound of a strumming guitar, reminding Willow of the weekend's campfire gatherings at the end of each day. Her heart pulled toward something she hadn't wanted for too many years.

People.

The closeness, warmth, and laughter of bodies. Gentle people, wise souls, caring people, people who could be the friends that Willow had lost so many of after the tragedy of the last four years. People like those she had met so recently here, at this house.

She paused by the fence, listening as the music stopped and soft laughter and talk emanated from the garden before the next song began.

With a smile and a last tug of longing, she shook herself and walked onward, turning over the rushing river and up the dark lane.

The cottage wasn't right. The glass door was open, and the hallway, usually lit by moonlight from the corridor and the living room, was now edged with darkness and shadows. Willow shivered in the cold air, and saw her breath cloud before her.

You left the door open, there's no other explanation, just get inside.

There was something heavy though, something off, and the more she stood at the door trying to enter, the more she felt she wanted to get out.

Is there someone here?

Just put on a light.

The second voice inside her head was calm, rational, but Willow felt stuck, like she had grown deep roots which held her firm. The moon slipped behind a cloud and the hallway darkened. Willow's breath quickened.

'Put on a light,' she said into the darkness, raising the hairs at the back of her neck. It was quiet.

Too quiet.

Willow blinked at her own stupidity.

'How can it be too quiet when you're the only one who lives here?'

She paused, trying to calm her racing thoughts, but the feeling persisted. Cold and snake-like.

What if you're not the only one who lives here?

Willow blinked and sweat gathered above her lip as she thought of what Maud had said earlier.

You don't see her, but she sees you...

Icy hands crept down her spine and she closed her eyes. Under her coat, her heart was thumping hard.

The feeling that something was close, pressed around her. A soft sigh of breath on her cheek. Her eyes snapped open.

'No! There's no one here. You made a mistake, just get inside.'

Willow lunged forward, hitting the light switch which was ludicrously only a step in front of her. The old-fashioned flick switch bit into her palm and the shadows were dispelled, the corridor normal.

'Nothing here,' she murmured. 'There's nothing here.'

Steadying her heart with some long breaths, she moved into the living area and switched on the light in this room, too.

She should have felt better.

She didn't.

It's just a house, Willow, you're on edge. Your head was bad when you left, you left the door open. It's no biggie.

Willow scooted around the settee and clicked the button on the remote. The television came to life, filling the room with cheery music as a lady talked about her move from the city to a farm in the countryside.

Willow watched the lady feed some cows in the old barn before moving to the kitchen, swirling the kettle to check the water, and flicking its switch. She pulled a cup from the cupboard, added coffee and milk, and stood peering through the doorway at the television as she waited for the kettle to boil.

Behind her, the open mouth of the bathroom doorway gaped. Willow felt its presence as she would a living, breathing, human being. She didn't have to see it, she just knew. The hair on her neck prickled.

HELLO.

Her mind conjured up the face on the mirror, and a shudder ran through her. She crossed her arms and bit her lip.

Come on kettle, boil.

Cold seemed to wrap itself around her, slow, sly, and conniving, its fingers icy and cruel.

Willow glanced behind her. The bathroom door was shut. Not open.

Somehow, that was worse.

The kitchen seemed filled with a presence. Something that pressed around her unseen.

She stared at the door, expecting the handle to turn, expecting the door to swing wide with a creak, its dark maw releasing a malevolent laugh.

Maybe the lady would be behind it. The lady who *saw.*

Willow swallowed hard and shook her head.

'Stop it. Turn every light on if you must, but stop this, you're getting carried away.'

The solid white door mocked her with its normality.

Look at poor scared Willow, it seemed to say, so scared of everything... and I'm just a door.

'Just a door,' she whispered before crossing the kitchen and throwing it open. She grabbed the corded light string and pulled on the light with a ping.

The bathroom was empty. Nothing on the mirror, the shower curtain pulled back to reveal the bathtub as she had left it.

She huffed a laugh, but her heart banged ferociously, and her head felt light and off centre.

'See? You're being silly, letting Maud into your head.'

Even so, she left the light on as she increased the temperature on the thermostat, made her coffee, and went to sit down, taking a blanket with her to ward off the chill.

The woman on the farm was now trying to locate some lost sheep up on the hill, and with the warm blanket and the warm coffee inside her, Willow began to doze.

It couldn't be much past 9pm, but she let her eyes drop, enjoying the comfort and the familiar murmur of the television.

Th-ud.

The sound was so low that Willow barely heard it. In fact, she wondered if she had heard it at all. Freezing air encircled her face, the only part of her outside the blanket, travelling up her nose and into her lungs with each breath.

'Why is it so cold?'

She pulled the blanket closer, almost ready to check the thermostat again.

Th-ud.

She froze. That was a definite noise from the hallway.

The door?

Rising, Willow walked to the bay window ahead, which afforded her a full moonlit view of the doorway and driveway beyond. There was no one outside. No one at the door.

TH-ud.

Willow flinched and swung round, facing the open living room door, which afforded her a tiny glimpse into the lit hallway.

TH-ud.

She stared. There was no movement, no shadow. She swallowed hard, the beat of her heart in her ears, and crept past the settee, heading toward the doorway.

TH-UD.

Willow jumped and stopped in her tracks. That wasn't an outside thud, it was coming from the hallway.

Inside.

There was a low hum that Willow wasn't sure wasn't inside her own head as she edged to the doorway and peered round.

The hallway looked normal. The sideboard sat as it always did, its pot-pourri sitting on top. The only other place the sound could be coming from was the-

TH-UD.

Willow let out a little scream as the door to the storage cupboard wobbled in its frame and then fell still.

Heavy air pressed against her, thick and tangible as she stared. The silence was all-encompassing.

Did it move? Or were you imagining it?

Was this a reaction to the pills? Or was this her normal crazy mindset that the pills were putting right?

Breathing hard, Willow stared at the cupboard door. It sat still and quiet, seeming to stare right back. The thuds fell quiet. Cheery music played as the television announced the end of the program and the commentator announced the next show before the adverts began.

In the hallway, the air was tense and cold.

You should see what's in the cupboard.

Nope, that can wait.

What if it's an animal? A cat? Maybe it got trapped.

A cat that managed to slip between two locked doors without me noticing before locking itself in a shut cupboard?

One locked door, she reminded herself, as if that made a difference. She chewed the side of her mouth.

Well, what else could it be?

The cupboard door was poised, challenging her to open it, to look inside.

I don't want to look inside.

You won't sleep if you don't, and what if it starts banging at 3am? What if the cat is dead in the morning just because you were too much of a wimp to open a door?

With a large swallow, Willow pulled the blanket around her tightly and moved to the door. She stood to the side so that if anything jumped out it wouldn't leap into her. Her vision wavered, and her lungs felt crushed as she tried to drag in ragged breaths, but she put out a shaking hand and reached for the handle.

TH–UD!

The door rattled and Willow jumped back with a screech.

It's an animal. Let it out.

She pulled on the door with a quick twist on the handle and jumped away as it swung open, fully prepared to run if anything lunged at her. Instead, there was nothing. The door stood open, but nothing came out.

Nothing?

Her breath clouded as she made her feet move into the doorway on boneless legs.

Inside was as it should have been. An ironing board sat up the left-hand side, a clothes airer, an iron, and a 'henry hoover' sat on the floor. Empty shelving sat above. Behind the items was the thick bedroom wall. The cupboard was empty.

Empty?

With a frown, Willow held the door open with a foot while she checked further inside, but there was nothing there, no hiding holes, no spaces for an animal. Nothing but whitewashed walls of the cupboard.

How is that possible?

As she shut the cupboard and ran her hands over the flush frame, there was a click from the kitchen. A click that Willow knew well. The kettle.

Swinging round, she strode to the kitchen. Steam poured from the kettle's spout.

Something had switched it on in the first place, which could have been anything from a fault, to her leaving the button half depressed, to a power surge possibly... Maybe.

But what freaked Willow out the most wasn't the unruly kettle; it was what was on the window.

Drawn into the condensation from the steam was another face. This one wasn't smiling. This one had a straight horizontal line for a mouth. Below, in uneven letters, was another message, this one not as cheery as the last. This one simply said LIE.

Willow stared. One face may have been the owner, but two? This was too much of a coincidence alongside the kettle. This one sent Willow running to the bedroom, where she got undressed and hid under the covers, leaving the lights on and the television blaring behind her.

Twenty

WILLOW WOKE TO LIGHT and birdsong... and warmth. The house felt quiet and passive again this morning, almost as though last night had never happened. She slipped out of bed, pulled on her dressing gown, and walked to the kitchen to flick on the kettle, pausing momentarily to glance at the window.

There's no point looking, there's nothing there. You wiped it away last night.

She remembered flicking the tea towel over the message before running to the bedroom, adamant that she never saw it again. Now, in the light of day, she thought she would like to know for certain. Just to make sure it wasn't in her head.

'Well, you'll find out if this thing likes steam writing, because you need a shower. Next time take the sodding towels with you and shower at the centre after yoga because this will not be fun at all.'

A little unnerved, she took her coffee into the living room, and only then did she realise what was wrong. Last night, the television and the lights had been left on, now every single one was off.

She put a hand to her forehead.

Impossible.

Willow checked herself for a reaction, but even that couldn't rouse much on this cheery, sunlit morning.

Maybe it was all in her head, anyway.

No maybe about it, really, is there?

'You like to conserve electricity, huh?' she tittered, and then fell silent. The eerie feeling of last night would be too close on its heels.

Not looking forward to this evening much, either...

She stopped the train of thought as it began.

'I am looking forward to today though,' she said aloud as she checked her watch. 8.30am. She aimed to be at McGracken House by ten. Plenty of time for that shower, and heaven knew she needed it.

The day looked glorious, but the air was chilly this morning. The wind blustered down the lane, scattering alder leaves around Willow's feet as she turned at the bridge and walked past the old house.

Autumn will be in full swing soon.

At the gates of McGracken House, her breath hitched, and she paused. The panic came from nowhere, a fluttering in her stomach that rapidly constricted her chest and throat.

Why now?

She realised she had never entered this place without Sophie, and suddenly felt more like an outsider than ever before.

Except everyone is an outsider here, silly.

She tried to smile, but the panic climbed, and willow gave in, placing a hand on the fence.

Picture a flame, concentrate on nothing but the flame, Tam had said yesterday.

Willow closed her eyes and pictured the flame, concentrating on slowing her breathing.

Her breath was beginning to steady when she felt a light hand on her arm, and a man's voice. Deep. A soft Scottish lilt.

'Breathe, sweetheart.'

Mr McGracken. Willow found herself relaxing in his presence, keeping her focus until the panic passed. Before she opened her eyes, she gave herself a check over. The fluttering and constriction had gone with barely a haggard breath. She smiled and opened her eyes.

'Thank you,' she said, and immediately felt the heat in her cheeks.

She had expected Mick at the immediate understanding of her condition, but here was a man she had never seen before. Square jaw, soft pale green eyes, freckles across his ruddy cheeks. His thick hair a short, deep auburn. One hand was casually in his jeans pocket, the other still on her arm as though this were an everyday occurrence. A wheelbarrow was set beside him, empty of everything but a spade.

'It's not that bad in there, I promise,' he said with a grin that lit his eyes.

Willow felt herself grinning with him. 'I know, it's just they... well...'

'They come out of nowhere.'

'Right,' she said with a puzzled smile.

He chuckled at her expression. 'You can't be at this house as long as I have without learning a thing or two about the human condition. Part of the territory. Are you okay, now?'

Willow nodded. 'I am.'

The gate had swung shut behind him. Now he leaned to pull it open for her to pass through.

'Thank you,' she said, ducking under his arm.

'Pleasure.' He smiled, letting go of the gate and turning back to the wheelbarrow. She had almost passed through before she remembered her manners and turned back, catching the gate before it closed.

'Oh, and thank you for...' She shrugged, 'you know.'

The man turned, his face open and non-judgmental. They really weren't bothered around this house, and it gave her confidence. Confidence that she was welcome here, and confidence that she was normal after all.

'Aye, no worries,' he said, picking up the handles of the barrow and wheeling it to the front of the house. Willow let the gate shut and moved into the world of McGracken House under the glow of the strangers' care.

'Willow!'

Helena was immaculately dishevelled as she strode across the field. Green wellingtons sat under a long brown cotton boho skirt and a long knitted jumper made of multicoloured squares. A tartan scarf finished the look, wound around her neck for warmth. It should have looked a conflicted mess, but somehow, on Helena's tall, thin frame, and with a messy blonde plait that fell down to her waist, she managed to look almost elegant.

She smiled and held out her arms to Willow, who felt almost pulled into a warmth that met her before the embrace. After a warm squeeze, Helena pulled back, holding Willow's shoulders as she scrutinised her.

'How are you, darling?'

'Good,' Willow flushed, wishing that she could be half as warm and charming as this lady, while knowing she fell a great deal short on both counts. 'I'm good, thank you. Um, I'm here be-cause-'

'I know why you're here, Willow. Tam came over yesterday evening. But look, you're welcome here either way. I don't ask questions. If you come here to rest, to help, to gain enlighten-ment, or to get free of an affliction, that is your business, not mine.'

Willow paused with a frown. Tam had wanted to know every-thing yesterday, chapter and verse, but the person she had said would be best to help wanted to know nothing?

'But...'

But she does know, Tam told her.

Helena laughed softly, like the ripple of sheets blowing in the wind. She placed an arm around Willow's shoulders. 'Walk with me,' she said.

They walked back toward the house, Helena pointing out the various parts of the land. The animals, the paddocks, the tents, the orchard, the allotment, the gardens, the river that flowed across the back of the property. The same river she crossed to get to Ivy Cottage.

As Helena spoke, Willow looked up at the wooded hillside, trying to locate the grey building that was home, but it was completely hidden among the trees.

'Would you like a drink, darling?'

'Tea would be lovely, please,' Willow said nervously as they crossed the threshold into a large, beamed kitchen. The walls were crisscrossed brick and beams, and were adorned with an eclectic mix of horseshoes, baskets of dried herbs, and a single tapestry that simply stated, 'Home is where the heart is'. A fire roared in the grate opposite the worktop, and a large wooden table with many chairs filled the centre of the large space.

'Please, sit,' Helena said, motioning to the chairs with a smile as she filled a tin kettle and lit the gas to boil it. Willow pulled out a chair, noting the handmade cushion sitting on top of the wood. A glance at the other chairs showed that these were as mismatched as the owner of the house herself, and yet, they still worked to provide a simple but comfortable space.

Helena was rummaging through tins on the wooden worktop. 'We have green, chamomile, peppermint, oolong, white, or English breakfast left.'

Willow stared. She felt as though she ought to answer, but had no idea what Helena had just said. Helena looked back at her with a smile, confirming that there was something Willow needed to say.

'Um...'

'Which tea?' Helena prompted.

'Oh! Well normal, I mean, you know, tea, milk, sugar...' she trailed off, colour flushing her cheeks for the second time that morning.

Helena laughed politely. 'English Breakfast then.'

'Sounds fine, thank you.'

Helena turned back to the kettle, which was now whistling, and finally brought two mugs over to the table, along with a small jug of milk and sugar cubes in a ceramic bowl. Willow added one to her tea and stirred in milk, aware of Helena's eyes on her.

'I think he's doing something to me, and I don't know why,' she blurted, wondering what in the world possessed her to say anything. 'He put me on pills I don't need. I didn't know, but I know now. I just don't understand why.'

Helena sat quietly, as though this sort of thing was said around the kitchen table on a daily basis. She circled her mug with her hands.

'Have you asked him?'

Willow frowned and shook her head.

'Well, I'm sure that would be the easiest way to find out.'

'I told him not to contact me.'

'Oh.'

'And I don't want to contact him.'

'That's one of the easiest ways to tie yourself in knots, darling. One of the best ways to find something out is to go to the source. There's no use trying to figure out what's going on in someone else's head using your own. It's utterly impossible.'

Willow sighed and stared at the pale liquid in her cup.

'I don't know what to do.'

'It's simple. Either contact him, and find out, or put it to the back of your mind until you wish to find out, if you ever do. Why don't you want to speak to him?'

'I learned a few things the other day, from Tam, and from my mum. He lies. A lot. Not just small ones, but I couldn't see it. I feel like I've been kept in a drug fuelled haze. I don't think I'd get the truth, that's the reality.'

'So, you thought you'd make it up for him?'

Willow looked up at Helena. Her face was soft and warm, her attention fully on Willow despite a commotion going on at the pig barn outside.

'What do you think he'd say?' she asked.

'He was doing it for my own good. He's the doctor. He knows what's best.' She took a sip of tea, trying to force the lump back down her throat.

'And you don't believe he might think that to be the case?'

'No. Well, I suppose on a level, yes, but he's a psychiatrist, and he has spent the last four years telling me I would die from what I now know is a simple panic attack.' She huffed a breath and wiped a tear from her cheek.

'There's nothing simple about a panic attack,' Helena said, reaching to clasp Willow's hand in hers.

'No, but why would he do that? He's stopped me from doing things as small as going to the shop on my own, in case I got 'hypoxia' and died. He's told me that things I think I've seen haven't been there, now I wonder. I wonder whether they were, or whether I'm as mad as he says?'

'He's said you're mad?'

'He implied it.'

'So, he hasn't said it.'

Willow heaved a breath. 'No, he makes me feel it.'

'But darling, he can't *make* you feel anything. You are in full control of what you feel, and when you talk like this? I can understand why you feel edgy and panicked, because you don't know what is real. But you must remember that this is your doing. Yours alone.'

Willow snatched her hand away from Helena and their cups wobbled on the table.

'I didn't ask for this to happen, and I didn't ask to be fed pills I didn't need. I trusted him!'

'Do you love him?'

'I did. I do. I think. I don't know. I don't know if I even know him anymore.'

'So, speak to him.'

Willow shook her head. Outside, there was a bang and a curse, followed by raucous laughter.

'Well then, you need to put this behind you and move forward. If you meet again in the future, you can give him a chance to explain himself. First, you concentrate on getting well, on taking responsibility for that healing, yes?'

Willow frowned.

'But I thought you wanted me to talk about why I'm here, isn't that why you brought me inside?'

'I brought you inside for tea. We don't need to speak about what happened, darling. We move forward here. There is no back.'

'But don't you need to know about-?'

'Your past?' Helena said softly. 'Everybody has a past, darling, even me. I don't deal in pasts, only presents.'

'Presents?'

'As in the present.' She swooped her hands around her in a smooth circular motion. 'Here and now. The past doesn't exist, and neither does the future.'

'Ah, okay. But don't you need to know what happened? I mean, if you are meant to be getting me well here-'

Helena held up a hand.

'I can't make you well, Willow, all healing is self-healing. As I said, you need to take responsibility for yourself, and for your own healing, but I will be here alongside you on your journey if you need me. All of us here will help you along the way in our own ways. We all help each other to a degree, but the main work? That is down to you alone.'

'What does that mean?' Willow said, suddenly unsure whether she wanted to be here at all with this charming lady who obviously had a very loose screw herself. 'I don't understand. Tam said that you could help me. She said that you would be the best person to help!'

There was shouting outside now, but Helena focused solely on Willow.

'We can help you,' she said. 'All of us, but the healing is down to you. That's all I'm saying, darling. You need to master what is going on in here.' She tapped at her head with a smile. 'I know you don't understand now, but you will. We can have so many more chats, whenever you want to, if you decide to hang around. Would you like that?'

This conversation was so far removed from what she had expected, but she liked McGracken House and its eccentric owners. It wasn't like she was going anywhere for another year either way. She could sit up at Ivy House alone with the creeps, or she could help out here. It was a no-brainer now that she knew she was okay without pills, and that panic attacks could be tolerated, and even eased here.

'Yes, of course I want to hang around. I want to help. I want to help you all here, and I want to help myself.'

Helena smiled and moved her cup aside to clasp both of Willow's hands with her own.

'I'm so glad you've decided to join us. You'll get something out of this. People always leave with something. Mostly, it's not what they're expecting.'

The kitchen door banged open and both Helena and Willow swung their gazes to the door as a burly pig ran inside and on into the next room without so much as a sideways glance. Close on its heels was Mr McGracken, dressed in a tweed under a wax jacket and flat cap, followed by two men that she had met while painting the sheds. One of them, dark curls, and no teeth, raised a hand in greeting before running on into the other room.

'That is absolutely not what I was expecting,' Willow laughed.

'I told you so,' Helena smiled, then she clicked her fingers. 'And I have it!'

'Have what?'

'The very place for you. The allotment!' Helena reached to cup Willow's cheek with a smile, narrowing her eyes. 'Yes, I think the vegetable garden will be perfect for getting to the root of this.'

The pig squealed and scraped as the three men tried to wrestle it back out of the door. Willow tried to focus on Helena as horror filled her gut.

'The vegetable garden?'

'There's nothing like growing your own food for putting life into perspective.'

Willow highly doubted that.

The door banged shut behind men and pig, and then reopened as someone else came inside. Willow tried to ignore the commotion. This was obviously just a day in the life of McGracken House.

'Okay,' she said, keeping her eyes on Helena's. 'Well, er, I know nothing about gardening or growing anything, I'm afraid, but I'm willing to try as long as you don't blame me for spoiling the food.'

'Ah,' a deep male voice said, 'No one blames anyone for anything around here... not to their face anyway, but don't worry, no one can spoil food like Betsy used to. I'm sure you won't even come close.'

Willow turned to see the man from the front of the house. My saviour, she thought. She grinned at him with a shrug.

'I don't know. I'm pretty clueless.'

'Then I'll have to teach you all I know before we starve to death,' he said.

Helena clasped her hands before her with a delighted smile, wispy blonde tendrils of hair blowing across her face in the breeze from the open door as she stood.

'Fabulous! That's settled then. I'll leave you in Jack's capable hands. Excuse me while I sort out Mildred and check on Babe.'

Willow looked at Jack, who seemed unruffled by all the activity. 'Who are Mildred and Babe?'

'The pigs,' Helena said, as Jack opened his mouth to speak. He raised his eyebrows, his eyes twinkling with amusement as Helena clomped out of the open door, her long floaty skirt billowing behind her.

'The pigs,' he repeated, 'and I'm Jack, by the way.'

He moved to the table and offered a large hand, which engulfed Willow's with warmth as he shook it firmly.

'Willow,' she said, standing up.

'Like the tree?'

'The very one.'

He grinned and finally let go of her hand. 'Someone had hippy parents,' he said. 'Come this way, I'll show you what's what.'

Twenty-One

C OOP FLICKED OFF THE television and paced the small living room. And that was a fucking hard task here, where the living room was three paces by two, but if he carried on sitting on his butt all day, he'd be in no fit shape to do what he needed to. Mentally or physically.

He stopped in the doorway, grasped the architrave, and tested his weight. It held. He completed fifty pull-ups with the tips of his fingers before lowering himself to the floor and completing fifty press-ups. Next, he did twenty-five one handed press-ups on each side, until his arms were screaming, and he dropped onto the carpet panting. His mind whirled with inactivity.

Being in jail had been no fun when there were things he needed to do out here, but abiding by the rules now that he was out was driving him equally insane.

He flopped back on the settee, his eyes flicking to the clean corners of the ceiling before he picked up his phone.

It was time.

He scrolled to Radar's contact and dialled. He answered immediately.

'Hey buddy, News?'

'Of the best kind.'

'They're home?'

'Not exactly. It's been four years, man.' Coop forced a chuckle and tried to act casual, flopping back on the settee for effect.

Cool and calm. Cool and calm.

'Mr Simpson gave up and bolted?' Radar said.

'Mrs Simpson.'

'Fantastic, so you have a handle on both of them?'

Radar was good. He didn't miss a beat. He knew they couldn't afford to now there were only the two of them left.

'Only Mr Simpson. He's happy to help with business.'

There was a pause, and Coop knew that Radar was choosing his words carefully. He could smell bullshit from five hundred miles, but it was a fight Coop would have when he joined him tomorrow.

'Hmm, well, Mrs Simpson's wellbeing is more important. We'll find her first and deliver the message before starting up. Ask him where she is.'

Coop rolled his eyes and worked his jaw. He wished they could talk normally, but he didn't have a burner phone right now. This one could be traced straight back to him if it went tits up and it would land him back where he didn't need to be. If it landed him there before he'd finished this, he didn't know how he would function.

He was also certain that Carlton had cameras here. He would have been keeping a very close eye on what Willow was up to, and now he could almost certainly monitor what Coop was up to, too. *The devil is in the fucking details.* What would have helped him enormously was now only hindering him.

'I have,' he said, keeping his voice calm as his hand gripped the side of the phone, 'he doesn't know.'

There was silence, and Coop knew that Radar was trying to keep his head as much as he was.

'Okay, Buddy, I'm in town in a few days. Shall we catch a drink?'

Coop clenched his jaw and ran a hand over his face.

A few fucking days?

'Awesome,' he managed. 'Catch you soon.'

Coop ended the call, and mindful of any cameras, picked up his leather jacket, and dropped his phone in the pocket. His hands were shaking with restrained frustration as he slipped on the coat and left the apartment.

He strode down the pavement toward the park and the other side of town. The side that people like Carlton and Willow and their perfect rose-tinted world knew nothing about. If he could have stayed anywhere else, he would, but he had to keep Carlton as close as possible while they located Willow.

He pulled out a cigarette and lit it before pulling out his phone and opening the trace app.

Carlton's little blue dot pulsed. Not at work, though.

Coop frowned. Holding the cigarette between his lips, he pinched his fingers to zoom the map in.

The Wagon and Horses.

With the sexy secretary, no doubt.

Coop had a feeling there was more to Willow moving out than Carlton's pride would let on. But if Carlton wasn't telling the truth, then where did that leave him and Radar?

Nowhere fast.

He flicked the screen off in agitation.

Bugs would have had this down right now. Bugs had been the mastermind, and without him, they were floundering. Never had Coop spent so long stuck in one place waiting for an answer.

But wishing for Bugs was futile.

His best friend was dead, and four years had done nothing to dampen the pain.

Twenty-Two

'D RINK?' SUZIE ASKED AS she locked the filing cabinet and put the key into the key cupboard. She held out a hand for Carlton's office key as he pulled the door shut and locked it.

'I don't know,' he said.

And that was the truth. He didn't know.

Going for a drink with Suzie had become a habit over the last week. A habit he was enjoying a little too much.

'Come on, hotshot. When she's back you'll be back to going home every day. Enjoy yourself while she's gone.'

'I would if I knew she was okay.'

He had messaged her this afternoon, unable to leave it any longer, but so far there had been no reply. If she was going to deaf him out, she could at least tell him where she was so that he could check up on her without her knowing.

'She's fine. She's a big girl.'

'A big girl with colossal problems.'

Carlton felt her hand on his back as she threw the keys to the lockbox into the drawer. 'She wanted to go, hotshot. She can look after herself.'

Carlton thought of Coop, and the shit that he now had to deal with all over again.

'I beg to differ. But you're right, if she isn't going to message me, I'll never know.'

'Unless the police turn up at your door, they haven't done that yet, have they?'

'No.'

'Then she's fine, see?'

Carlton felt a smile pull at his lips as he looked at Suzie. Pencil skirt, heels, pixie face and bright red lipstick. He wondered for a moment how his life would have turned out if he had met her first. If he hadn't fallen in love with Willow.

'So?' she said.

'Fine.'

'Back to the Wagon and Horses?'

'As long as Coop doesn't spoil the party this time.'

'I won't allow it.'

'So, what has Coop been up to?' Suzie said, talking over the murmurs and laughter of relaxed people and the clinking of cutlery on plates.

Carlton felt the noise grate on his nerves. He swirled the half pint of Stella Artois in the glass. It tasted like shit tonight. He wasn't in the mood for drinks, or chats, or small talk. All he needed right now was to find out what his brother was planning and to keep him away from Willow.

It was eating him up that Coop was out of sight. The apartment door had signalled to his phone that his brother had gone through it, and a quick check of the surveillance had proved him right.

'Carlton?'

He looked up at Suzie and shook his head.

'Nothing, really. He just sits about in the house all day.'

Except today. Where did he go today?

'So, what do you think he's here for?'

'Out of jail and nowhere to go until he gets sent back.'

'That's harsh, Carlton. He's your brother. Four years in jail may have changed him.'

Carlton shook his head. 'It's changed the dynamics, that's all.'

Suzie laughed and shook her head.

'Well, lying around on the settee doesn't sound like Coop. Give him a chance, he-'

'Has you wrapped, too? He hasn't changed. My brother will never change.'

Suzie glanced about them, and he knew he had spoken too loud. He scanned the room for Coop. He hadn't announced himself yet, but Carlton hadn't known he was there the first time either.

He lowered his voice. 'I've already had to fulfill a prescription.'

Suzie's smile slipped. 'I had a feeling,' she said. 'I just didn't want it to be true. So, what *do* you think he's here for?'

Carlton knew there was only one answer to that question. He had known in his gut that this day would come. He had hoped to be prepared, but now he was more out of control than ever. He checked his phone, no messages.

Putting the phone on the table, he met Suzie's eyes.

'Oh, I know what he's here for,' he said. 'To finish what he started.'

'Fantastic. News of the night. Then it's good she's not here, and that she isn't taking messages, right?'

Carlton sighed and downed the rest of his beer in a long gulp. He was trying not to think about the fact she hadn't answered his message yet, and whether it would be wise to say anything to her either way. Wherever she was, she was alone, but down here, she would be in trouble.

While Coop was here, he could figure out just how much he knew, and gauge his response from there.

Suzie placed a hand over Carlton's, giving it a squeeze but not letting go. The contact made his skin buzz. He had missed a woman's touch, and waking up with Suzie the other morning had almost set his soul on fire whether he had thought she was Willow or not. Willow had been unresponsive for far too long, although he knew that was mostly his own doing. He had changed her through his need to protect her. It was a catch twenty-two.

'Are you okay?' Suzie said.

Carlton nodded, his heart thumping as he stared at their hands, his underneath Suzie's. She'd been good all these years, even after he had turned her down, and through all the times he had rushed back for Willow after the attack. Suzie had always been there, always been loyal.

She never cut me out, even when I hurt her, and I hurt her a lot over the years, I know that. And what if Willow had never been in my life?

Carlton knew the answer, and his heart thundered as he slowly turned his hand over and linked his fingers with Suzie's. She smiled and reached to link her other hand with his. A strange mixture of intense desire and guilt flooded his veins.

He knew he didn't really want Suzie; he loved Willow with all his heart... but right now Willow wasn't here. She wasn't even answering his goddamn messages. She had cut him off completely and it hurt like hell. After all he had done for her, all he had given up for her, for her own good, not his. It hurt more than he had let on, even to himself.

'Let's get another drink,' he said.

Twenty-Three

B Y THE END OF the afternoon, Willow was dirtier and far more exhausted than she should have been. Digging potatoes and planting winter cabbages and onions had been different, that was for sure. Jack was an excellent teacher; patient when she misunderstood, laughing good-naturedly when she turned soil 'like a lass', and helpful when she was all fingers and thumbs over the tiny seeds. His deep tones were softly spoken. He was funny, chilled, and good company. The afternoon had flown by, and she was almost dejected when the sun began to slip behind the mountain, until he reminded her that she could stay for dinner.

'Does dinner include a shower?' she laughed.

'It'll have to,' he said, leaning on the fork handle as he assessed her. 'You realise you were supposed to leave the dirt on the ground, right?'

'I told you I was clueless.'

'Aye, come back Betsy, all is forgiven.'

Willow threw a screwed up empty seed packet his way with a laugh, and he returned the favour by flicking the dirt from his fingers at her.

'Come on,' he said, with a chuckle, 'let's get this lot put away and get inside. It's dropping cold.'

Willow grabbed the spade, trowel, and seed bodger, as Jack took the fork and tidied the unused seed trays before picking up the sack of pulled potatoes.

The poly tunnel and potting shed where they had been working was cold, but outside was colder, the wind biting at her cheeks as she followed Jack across the field.

Cheeks that ache, she thought, I haven't laughed so much in... years. Literally, years. She felt a tinge of sadness that her life had escalated so far as to be out of her control.

Not anymore. From now on, you're in control, and there will certainly be more laughter.

Today she really had felt in control, and she felt better than she had in a good while, too. Maybe it was the unused pills that sat on the coffee table at Ivy Cottage, maybe it was the laughter, or maybe the company.

Maybe she was actually getting better.

As Jack put the potatoes in the large barn, a man who appeared to be fixing the old tractor called out. Jack signalled for her to wait and met him at the front of the vehicle. They chatted in voices too low and heavy with accent for her to make out, and then Jack picked up a hammer and gave something a few quick taps.

Willow pulled her phone out of her pocket as she waited. There was a message from Sophie asking how she had got on, a missed call from Mum that she could return later, and a message from Carlton.

Her finger hovered over Carlton's as a strange mixture of emotions flooded through her. Pleased that he had remembered her and did care after all. Hope that he was genuine. Sadness that this would drive a wedge of sorts in the relationship, because she couldn't unlearn this information. Anger that he had possibly played a game with her. And what for? What had she ever done wrong?

She pressed to view the message.

Hi, babe. Just want to check you're all right. I'm a little worried that you can cut yourself off so easily. Can we talk? Are you taking your pills, because I think you may need a change of prescription? Please call me, it's quite important. Miss you, love you lots, C.

She read the message through a few times, her heart banging in her chest. A change of prescription? Did he know that she had found out? What was so important?

Nothing, he's trying to get you to call, that's all. Still checking that I'm under control.

She chewed her lip, unsure of his motives, as Helena's talk from this morning filled her mind - the only way to know what he's thinking for sure is to talk to him.

No, stick to the plan. You don't need any medication, never mind a change. Let's give this a go first. If it doesn't work, call Carlton, by all means, but don't you feel better already?

With a sigh, she turned the phone off and placed it back in her pocket. A niggle of doubt sat at the edges of her mind.

What if he's sincere, and it really is important?

'Trouble in paradise?'

She forced a smile at Jack, who was wiping oil off his hands onto an old rag.

'Not really paradise.'

Jack narrowed his eyes and tilted his head.

'Just trouble?'

Willow smiled a little more easily this time.

'Nothing a shower and a good meal won't fix.'

Jack nodded and threw the rag onto a stacking shelf next to the open side of the barn as they turned toward the house.

'There's nothing a hot shower and a good meal doesn't fix. After you,' he said, opening the back door and ushering her through to a room filled with people chatting and laughing over the clink of glasses and earthenware.

Willow's body processed the scene faster than her mind could react. She stopped short, her legs refusing to pass over the threshold, her chest immediately constricted, and her stomach clenched. It was like she had hit a glass wall. Her mind, taking notes from the response of her body, flailed and screamed at her to GET OUT!

She turned, plowing into Jack in her haste to leave.

'Woah,' he said, catching her arm, 'what's the hurry?'

'I just remembered I need to go,' she mumbled, pulling out of his grasp and running for the gate.

'Willow!' he shouted.

As she ran through the gate the last voice she heard was Helena's.

'Let her go, Jack. She has to deal with this her own way.'

Twenty-Four

W ILLOW STOPPED RUNNING AT the bridge. She pressed her hands onto the cold stone, barely noticing the lowering sun's wavering reflection as the river roared downstream.

Breathe. Breathe.

In for four, hold, out for six.

Focus on the candle.

When her breathing settled, she turned to sit on the low wall, and watched the trees wave against the darkening sky.

What the hell were you thinking? Just because you had a good day doesn't mean you're healed. What the hell made you think you could eat with a whole group of people, when people are the problem here?

Just because you've been with a few of them outside the last few days doesn't mean you can crowd into a small room and eat, drink and be merry with them.

Carlton said that you weren't ready. He's right about that.

Willow stared at the toes of her boots and wondered for the first time just what the hell she was actually doing out here all alone.

Getting well, supposedly.

Or getting worse?

Well, she hadn't had any pills for the last few days, had managed without. Didn't that count for something?

Maybe it counted for seeing doors rattle from inside an empty cupboard, or drawings on steamed glass.

She shivered.

Well, whatever it counts for you've mucked it up, that's for sure. Where do you go from here? Certainly not back to McGracken House. They'll think you're nuts by now. Mad as a hatter.

Willow clenched her jaw and banged a hand against the stone as she rose. Tears welled in her eyes as she made her way up the road to the cottage.

Just when you have a chance to do things differently, you fuck it up. You always fuck it up! Just like booking The Green Man for dad's birthday, it's all just fucked up... and you'll never get better because you're fucked up.

How many times has Carlton told you? How many times? How you hear things that aren't said, you see things that aren't there, your stupid body panics at every little thing. Fucked, Willow, you're fucked. And you'll end up going back to him, fucked.

Willow was running now, tears streaming down her face as she tried to outrun the barrage of self abuse.

She reached the door to the cottage and let herself inside with a sob. The door shut behind her as she threw off her boots and coat in the small porch, her tears dropping to the floor as her chest heaved painfully.

She pulled the keys for the glass door from her pocket, and they slipped from her hand onto the floor. Willow sniffed and wiped her blurry eyes.

'Can't even hold a god-damned set of keys now, either. Completely fucked,' she grumbled, as she stooped to find them in the darkness.

Who the hell didn't think to put a light in this part of the house?

Willow pulled her phone from her pocket, using the screen to light the floor to retrieve them. She stood and then paused as movement caught her eye.

Behind the door, the half-light in the hallway darkened as a shadow passed across the corridor from the bedrooms to the living room. Willow froze and sniffed, blinking her sore eyes, scrunching them shut, and then open again. They stung, and her vision blurred.

Did I see that?

Her drumming heart seemed to think so, but last time she thought she had seen something, she had checked around the outside of the house and caught no one. Slamming the key into the lock, she twisted and threw the door open.

'Who's there? I saw you. The police are on their way.'

She hoped that the person inside didn't put two and two together and know that it wasn't possible to call the police in under thirty seconds.

The house was still and silent, which only fuelled her anger.

'Hey! Are you listening? I said the police are coming.'

Forcing down her anxiety, Willow strode up the corridor and spun into the living room.

Empty.

As were the kitchen and the bathroom - shower curtain still pulled back, thank goodness.

After checking the bedrooms, she concluded that there was no one here. Again.

So, what the fuck was that?

The house was silent. So quiet that when the boiler kicked in with a small roar, she almost had a heart attack.

What the heck is going on here?

Maud's voice answered in her thoughts; *have you seen her? She sees you.*

A tingle spread through willow's body and goosebumps ran down her arms. 'Well, I don't want to see you.'

There was a small tap as something fell from the coffee table and Willow began to shake. She was facing the table. There was no one there that she could see, and certainly no breeze, although the house was almost bone cold again.

She felt her chest constrict.

'No. No. Please, not again. I don't want to do this again tonight. I don't need this bullshit.'

Willow tried to calm herself, tried to breathe, but she was too wound up.

This is ridiculous. What fell from the table? There's probably a logical explanation.

Inching round the settee, willow saw the small box on the floor and picked it up. Prozac. Her pills.

Coincidence?

She paused, holding the packet in her hand, feeling the cold encircling her arms. The feeling of being watched was intense, the atmosphere dense and tangible. She turned to look back across the room, but she was the only one here.

Wasn't she?

Willow was no longer certain. She threw the pills back onto the table and pulled both the door to the hallway and the kitchen shut, locking herself in the living area. It should have made her feel better, but the full-length glass meant the doors were giving her the creeps shut as much as they had when open.

There's nowhere safe, nowhere not to see!

Willow wiped her sweaty palms down her jeans, and held onto her knees, bending forward as her breaths came in quick gasps.

Enough. Get a grip, Willow, you sound as mad as Maud. There probably wasn't even a shadow. It could have been the sunlight blocked by the trees for a second in the wind.

Her mind stalled and ground to a halt.

Yes. It could have been. It had been a quick pass of darkness, for sure, and it could have been the previous time, too. The more she thought about it, the more it made sense and the calmer she felt. A shadow from the trees. Of course it was.

Just a bloody shadow!

Willow huffed a laugh, the tension loosening in her chest, making her woozy with relief as her breathing finally slowed.

Okay. That's better. Turn the heating up. Put the kettle on, settle down with the TV, and call Mum. This whole tension has to stop, or you'll never get any better.

The last of the unease held on stubbornly, but she moved to the kitchen, anyway.

'How are you, love?' Mum said, and warmth swirled around Willow at the sound of her voice. As soon as this year was done, the first person she would see was her mum. Not Carlton. Maybe not him at all. He had kept her from Mum too much, but if he was onto what Mum knew, he would, wouldn't he?

The thought left a cold lump in her stomach.

'I'm okay,' Willow said, and then she cracked and broke down into sobs again. 'I guess I'm not okay, Mum, I'm struggling. I just don't know why I keep panicking. Maybe... I don't know, maybe Carlton was right, maybe I need the pills after all, maybe I'm not ready to-?'

'Hey, hey, hold up,' Mum said. 'You said that things were going well a couple of days ago. A doctor confirmed that you didn't need the Prozac?'

'A nurse. Yes, that's what she said, but she doesn't know the full story.'

There was a pause.

'So, who are you talking to? I thought you said that you were talking to someone.'

'Only about the Prozac, really. She said last night I was doing well, and that I was ten steps ahead of her treatment plan, but I just don't feel it.'

'Why would you? You've taken those pills for four years, Willow. Everything you've relied on as a crutch is gone. Carlton, and now the Prozac. It will take some time for the medication to leave your system, and meanwhile you have to learn to trust yourself to handle things again.'

Willow took a shuddering breath.

'It's the only way, honey. I know, I've been there too.'

'How did you do it?'

'I kept good people around me who were happy to talk. Happy to help me when I was low. You have to build yourself back up. Remember though, that I was on Prozac for five months, you've had a dependency for a lot longer.'

'I'm not addicted.'

'No, I didn't say that. I said that you depend on them. Deep down you believe they take the panic away, and now they're gone, you're panicking more, see?'

Willow nodded at the television screen. Yes, that made sense.

'You need to talk to people and let them help. Find a therapist. If you need the money to go private, I can send it to you.'

Willow's thoughts went to Helena. She should have been the perfect person with her calm warm energy, but she seemed not to want to know anything about it. She had also told Jack to leave her when she had run from the house earlier.

'Willow?'

'There's a person I've been put in contact with. I saw her today, but she didn't seem interested. She said that if I wanted to talk, she was happy to listen, but that she didn't need to know.'

Mum was quiet for a beat.

'I don't know what to say, in what context?'

Willow swiped at her tears and started at the beginning. She told her mum exactly the type of place that McGracken House was, about Helena, and the other people that were there.

'Okay, well, I mean, is that the best place for you? They're just putting you to work for their own gain? Is that it?'

'No, I don't think so. People are free to come and go. No one has to stay, but my yoga teacher Tam says that so many people have got what they need from a stay there.'

'But you need to talk, not to work. Can you talk to this Helena?'

'Yes, she just says that she doesn't *need* to know, but that I can chat anytime. There's a man that's been helping me today, too.

I think I could talk to him. He helped me through a panic attack this morning without prior warning. They do seem to know what to do there.'

Mum gave a sigh, and Willow could almost feel the relief flooding through the phone.

'Okay. Well, do that then, love, if you're comfortable. But listen, if it's not working after a few weeks, we'll reassess you going private. You have time, and I trust your judgment.'

'I'm not sure it will be that easy now. I don't know if I can go back, Mum.'

Willow's lip trembled and more tears let go as she thought of how she had run from the house.

'Oh, honey, why not? What on earth happened? You said you'd had a good day there.'

'I did. I laughed so much, Mum. I like everyone there, and I enjoy the work, but I ended up doing something stupid. We had to... I was going to stay for dinner... but the room. Mum, the kitchen is large, and there were so many people.' She stifled a loud sob. 'Too many people. The music and the talking, and the cups clinking... I just...'

'You couldn't stay, and that's understandable,' Mum said, her voice low and soothing. 'It took me an awful long time to get back into a close public setting, and I'm still not completely happy in a pub, love. These things take time. You've been nowhere for four years.'

'I know, and I thought I could handle it, but I made a fool of myself, and I'm not sure if I can go back tomorrow.'

'Yes, you can. They sound like the kind of people who would understand, didn't you say you had a panic attack this morning?'

'I did.'

'And someone helped you?'

'Jack, yes, but having a panic attack and acting like a lunatic are two different things.'

'Fear, and the way it unfolds, are the same, no matter how we act. I'm sure if this man knew you were having a panic attack, he will understand. And this Helena?'

Willow bit her lip.

'She will get it, yes.'

'So, the thing stopping you from going back is embarrassment, that's all.'

Willow sniffed and went to the bathroom to get toilet paper for her nose.

'I guess so.'

'Well then, you push it down. Go back tomorrow, apologise, and move forward. If these people laugh or judge you, you're in the wrong place, love. Then you can find somewhere else, but at least you'll know either way, yes?'

Willow scrunched her face. Going back tomorrow was going to be above embarrassing, but she knew her mum was right. She needed the help and McGracken House was the one place here where she seemed to have fallen lucky.

'Okay, Mum. I'll go back.'

'Promise me, Willow.'

'I promise.'

'Good, and call me tomorrow to let me know how you get on. Okay? Keep talking. I know it's hard, but keep going.'

'I will.'

'For the record, I agree with this... Tam, was it? You are doing exceptionally well. You're only a few days clear, honey. Give yourself a break.'

Willow nodded, and then a thought occurred to her.

'Okay, I'll try. Mum, can I ask you a question? When you came off the Prozac, did you feel funny? Like, I don't know, more anxious, a little sick, some hallucinations?'

'No, love, but I remember the doctor saying I may. Don't worry, this is all normal, I'm sure.'

'The doctor said you may?'

'I can't remember now, but he did say the medication would take a good few weeks to clear from my system. You're possibly still feeling half effects that are making you feel off. Take it easy, take care of yourself, and tell the people around you so that they can take care of you too.'

'Okay, thanks Mum.'

'Anytime, love.'

Willow ended the call, caught sight of Carlton's unanswered message on her phone, and stared at the Prozac packet on the table.

'I don't need you. And I don't need Carlton to tell me what I can and can't do from all the way down there. I'm going to do this my way.'

TH-UD.

Willow had been dozing to the reassuring babble of the television, but the noise startled her awake. She pushed herself up and stared back over the settee to the glass of the shut hallway door. It was the same noise as last night.

And it's worse, she thought, worse with the door shut.

TH-UD.

She swallowed and ran her hands over her face.

Maybe the animal is still alive, maybe yesterday it was too scared to come out?

It was a thought that pulled her to her feet and moved her to the door, where she peered through the glass. The distorted hallway came into view, and the hairs stood up on Willow's neck.

There was something in there.

She couldn't see it, but she could feel it. It was still and intense. Watching. Waiting.

TH-UD.

She jumped, her heart thundering as she stepped back.

Fuck.

Just go and let it out.

It doesn't feel right.

She licked lips that felt as dry as paper and moved back to the doorway. With a shaking hand, she pulled the door open.

The cupboard was still. The air static, the pressure immense.

Willow forced herself toward it.

Nothing happened yesterday, just pull it open. Let's get this over with.

With a single stride, she grabbed the small handle and pulled the door open.

Something large charged toward her and she screamed, jumping out of the way as there was a crash. Willow dropped to the floor and lay there screaming for what felt like an eternity until she realised that there was nothing except her own screams.

Where is it? What was it?

Shaking uncontrollably, she pushed herself up onto her forearms and forced her gaze back to the cupboard.

On the floor, poking out from the doorway, was the ironing board. Willow almost laughed.

The ironing board fell on me. Shit on a stick, I almost dropped into hell, and it was the bloody ironing board!

With a small titter, she got up and picked up the ironing board. She placed it back into the cupboard, but as she was leaning it against the wall, she saw something else. With a frown, she moved the board to the side and stepped into the cupboard, keeping one foot over the threshold - just in case.

At the top of the wall, just below the shelf, was a small hole. Willow wasn't tall enough, or stupid enough, to look what was on the other side, but she did place her fingers by it.

Air.

Air from an internal wall?

Either way, that must be what was making the hallway cold, and possibly what was causing the banging of the door. It was only a small hole. She could patch it herself, then maybe the door would stay still. For now, she placed the ironing board back over it, hoping to dispel some of the draft, and shut the door.

I don't know if this is you or the pills, but for God's sake, you need to sort yourself out, Willow. I don't know about hypoxia, but I do know you'll have a bloody heart attack up here.

In the living room, she thought she might just do that. The pills were back on the floor and another face had been drawn into the low line of condensation on the bottom of the window. This one was an angry frown. Its message was simply LOOK.

'I don't want to see,' Willow whispered, and for the second night running, she went to bed early.

As she lay shaking under the covers, she hoped that nothing was in the room with her. And if it was? That it left her alone.

Twenty-Five

B Y THE TIME COOP had finished business in town, it was late. He had earned three hundred pounds, spent two on an hour with a woman, and stolen a bottle of Budweiser from the local off-licence. Not because he didn't have the money, but because he could. Because he knew one bottle of Bud wouldn't get him thrown back in jail if he was caught. Because he couldn't stand not to feel the thrill of the steal, the buzz of knowing he may get caught, and the high when he got away with it.

It almost made him want to *get* high, but other than the weed he had just smoked after sex, he hadn't touched the stuff for four years, and the clarity in his mind now was unmistakable. The hard stuff messed with his head; he wasn't quite as sharp, not quite as agile, as he had found out on the night that put him in jail.

The night that fucked up his life.

The night that he wouldn't be able to put right for a further week.

Earlier, Radar had messaged to say his job would take a little longer than he had thought. Coop decided a week was enough. If Radar put it on hold again, then he would go ahead alone. He wasn't out of the pounder now just to sit in his brother's apartment scratching his ass all day, waiting around for other people.

But he *was* out, though. That was the main thing, and as he walked back to the apartment with the swagger of satisfaction and release, an idea popped into his head.

He staggered to a halt, wondering why he hadn't thought of it earlier, and wondering at his own genius.

'What a fucking idiot,' he said aloud.

A woman in stilettos pulled her coat around her and eyed him warily before she tottered quickly past with her head down.

'Child's play, Coop, this is fucking child's play. You need to get your game on, or you'll fuck this up.'

The thought took shape in his mind. He rolled it around, filling it out. He would need to bide his time, play it right, but he had days before Radar was back now. There was time, and plenty of it. A wide smile spread across his face. It had been a good night, and now things were looking up.

Hey, maybe he would smoke more weed, after all. It seemed to make his thinking clearer.

Twenty-Six

T HE NEXT MORNING LOOKED as miserable as Willow felt. Rain battered the windows and wind pushed at the little cottage. It was warm in bed, and it was all Willow could do not to pull the duvet back over her and go back to sleep.

She looked at her watch and saw that it was after nine-thirty.

Nine-thirty! When was the last time I ever slept in that late?

She lay her head back against the pillow and stared at the uneven white ceiling, her stomach tense with nerves. Today she had to go back to McGracken House and see if they were going to make anything of what happened yesterday afternoon. She had no idea what to say if they asked, although she realised that the truth was probably the best thing to tell them. She wasn't ready to go into that whole scenario with a bunch of strangers, though, however nice they appeared.

Maybe I should leave it today and go tomorrow instead?

She felt her eyes shutting at the thought and quickly snapped them open. Before she could argue with herself, she threw back the covers and slipped out of the bed.

The house was warm again this morning. That was something. In fact, it wasn't just warm. It was hot. No wonder she had been so comfy in bed.

Throwing on fresh Jeans and a t-shirt, she carried her jumper to the living area and went to check on the boiler thermostat. Thirty-two degrees.

What? I don't remember turning it that high last night.

But she had turned it up, she remembered, just before the ironing board had almost crushed her to death.

Lowering it to twenty, she popped a couple of slices of toast in the toaster and got her coat and boots ready.

She had planned to be at the house at 10am each morning, and in line with the person she was now becoming, she wouldn't allow herself any excuses, even death by ironing board.

She pulled on her boots and jumper, then added her hat and scarf as she waited. The coat was just one layer too many. That could wait until she was outside.

She ate half a slice of toast on the way down the road, the other she fed to the forest animals as she walked by. Her stomach felt inclined to feed the animals with its own contents if she put another crumb to her mouth. The fact that it was soggy from the steady rain didn't help.

She knew it was nerves, and she also knew that she would suffer later in the day, but there was no bypassing this sickness. She gagged just thinking about it.

She paused on the bridge, trying to pull her nerves into check, the mist and rain stretching out before her, blocking the view of the village as the lane disappeared into the grey. Underneath the bridge, the water rushed ahead, white heads foaming in its swollen volume.

It never stops, never pauses, Willow thought, it just forces it's way downstream.

I need to be more like a river, not a Willow. A Willow is stuck. It can't move forward or back; it simply stands and watches. At the moment, I don't know if I can even watch this next episode.

She heaved a long sigh, and forced her legs to move, her stomach swirling as she passed the corner of McGracken House and moved to the side gate.

From inside came a shout and laughter, and she nearly turned tail, but her mother was right. She had to find out if this was the right place for her, the right people.

She pushed the gate and waited for the familiar feeling of a panic attack. When it didn't come, she walked inside and was immediately greeted by a cheery wave from the man with no teeth. His dark curls folded out from under a beanie hat, and his shirt was wet as he stood under the roof of the open barn.

'Hey there, lassie,' he called. 'Bright and early this morning.'

Willow nodded and wondered if she should mention yesterday afternoon. She tried to remember if he had been at the table, but couldn't remember seeing his face.

'I try,' she said. 'You're earlier though.'

'I live here,' the man said with a chuckle. 'How far are ye?'

'Just up the road, in the village.'

'Ah, I see. Planned?'

Willow frowned. 'How do you mean?'

'You didn't want to stay here? The rooms and facilities are very nice. Very cozy. I can recommend it.'

'Oh,' Willow said with a smile, 'No. I moved to rented accommodation in the village. I didn't know this place was here, and I kind of fell upon it, really.'

'I think that's the story for most of us. A few people head here after falling upon it from someone else. You had a lucky stumble, lass.'

Willow nodded, water running off her hood. 'I did. How far have you come?'

'Ah, I come from all over. Don't stop travelling. This is my longest stay anywhere and I'm loath to leave, but I am getting itchy soles now, ye ken?'

'I do,' Willow said with a smile. 'We all have to move on to somewhere, I suppose.'

'Aye, it's true. I'll spread word of here though, as others have before me. I'll be away a different man when I leave. You make sure you stay as long as you need. It heals, this place, it'll see you right.'

Willow felt her lip twitch. He had been there then. At least he was being nice about it.

'I intend to. I'd better get on before I'm soaked through.' She held her hands up to the sky with a shrug.

'Aye, weather's on the turn for sure. I'll see you around.'

Willow raised a hand and wondered if she should announce her presence at the house or check the poly tunnels and shed first. She was spared the decision as she turned to the house and saw Jack waiting on the stoop with a smile.

Her stomach somersaulted with nerves as she smiled back, hoping it didn't look too strained. After all, Jack could hardly say he hadn't noticed what went on yesterday. She had elegantly face-planted his chest while leaving.

'Morning, princess,' he called. 'Come on inside, get dry a bit first. We'll start after a brew.'

Willow felt herself break into a genuine grin as she pulled her hood further over her hat and jogged toward the house. At the doorway, she could see that the kitchen was empty and let out a small sigh of relief. A roaring log fire crackled in the hearth, and a swathe of heat hit her as jack shut the door behind them.

'Ah, that's better,' she said, shrugging out of her coat as jack took it and hung it on the back of the door. Her hat was only wet at the front, but he took that and her scarf and placed them on a small stool next to the fire.

'There. They'll be dry in no time. This rain is supposed to ease in an hour or so. We'll make an easy morning of it, eh? What do you want to drink?'

'Tea, please.'

'Fancy or bog standard?'

Willow suppressed a laugh as she thought of Helena asking her what tea she fancied yesterday. The difference was night and day, but Jack's question was so much easier to understand.

'Bog standard, milk and a sugar, please.'

'Coming right up. Sit down, get warm, make yourself at home.'

Jack made the tea and brought it over to the table. No sugar lumps today. Maybe that was Helena's thing, too.

'Didn't know whether you'd turn up today,' he said, putting the cup in front of her. Her stomach flipped over, but he hadn't finished. 'What with the rain and all. You're not a fair-weather worker then?'

He pulled out a chair opposite as Willow shook her head, wondering whether to say anything, and then deciding to get the elephant out of the room sooner rather than later.

'I thought you were going to say after yesterday's little performance,' she said.

Jack looked genuinely confused. 'What performance?'

Willow almost wanted to hit him for making her say it, for not giving her an easy way out. She felt heat rush up her neck to her cheeks.

'At dinner, when I ran out like an idiot.'

'Ah, no one thought anything of it. You said you had something to do. People rush off all the time.'

'Some of them will have thought something.'

Jack clasped his hands on the table with a smile. His fingernails were clean, his tanned hands smooth. One point to him after all the dirt they had been covered in yesterday. She pulled her hands into fists to conceal her own nails.

'So what?' he said. 'Willow, it's none of their business. None of anyone's business.'

'No.'

Willow cast her thoughts back to Helena.

I don't need to know anything. Your past is your business.

Was that so true here that someone could act like a nutcase and get away with no one even noticing? Was that a good thing? She had almost been traumatised, and yet no one had batted an eyelid.

Jack reached across the large table and placed a warm hand on her arm like he had read her mind.

'That's not to say no one cared, sweetheart. I didn't mean it like that. We all care, we just respect people's privacy as their own.'

Willow thought back to how he had called her name, how Helena had told him to leave her, and she wondered if he would have come left to his own devices. The way he was talking, most probably not.

She felt a bit disjointed. This caring place with its caring people and healing atmosphere was full of people who minded their own business? How did that compute?

'Well, aren't you interested in what made me run headlong into you on the way out of the door?' Willow asked.

Jack's pale eyes held a little humour. 'If you want to talk about it.'

Willow almost rolled her eyes.

'Not especially,' she found herself saying.

He may have been part of this place, and he may know a little about the human condition, but he was a man, after all, and he wasn't a therapist. Besides, how could he brighten her day if she brought him down with her crap first?

She sighed, and he studied her.

'Are you sure?' All traces of humour were gone, and she may be wrong, but he almost seemed a little dejected. Had he wanted to talk?

For a healing house, this place sure confused the heck out of her.

'I'm sure,' she said. The moment was over. No one had been interested in her leaving and it looked as though no one would ask her why, either. She felt herself relax as she finished the last of her tea. 'Looks like the rain is clearing up a little,' she said with a smile. 'Shall we get out there?'

She looked at Jack and found him gazing seriously back at her. His cheeks held a hint of colour, and this close she noticed the amber flecks in his eyes. An unusual, but striking, contrast to his tanned face and auburn hair.

He sighed and dropped his gaze to his cup.

'I'm not supposed to ask, Willow, if that's what you're thinking,' he said softly. He paused, pursing his lips before continuing. 'It's the way we do things here, but for the record, I do care, and I am curious. I want to know. If you want to say, that is.'

Warmth swirled in Willow's stomach, and she smiled at Jack's obvious frustration with a 'system' that she hadn't known existed. Maybe she had someone to talk to here after all, and maybe her gut wasn't lying when it told her that this was the right place to be.

'Thank you, Jack. That means more than you know, but right now the rain has stopped. We should just get outside while the going is good. I can talk anytime. We have work to do.'

'Leave it for a rainy day, eh, lass?' he said, humour back in his eyes as his forehead creased above his eyebrows.

She grinned. 'Looks like there'll be plenty of them.'

He huffed a laugh and dipped his head. 'Aye, that's the truth. Come on then, let's get outside.'

They worked over the beds in the poly tunnel for the rest of the morning until Jack gave in and brought lunch out to her as she was loath to stop. She was enjoying the physical exertion and was also a little on edge about going back into the house. Surely this morning was a one off because she was late. People would be in there for lunch for certain.

Out here she felt content, refreshed from the manual work, and Jack was good company. They had spent much of the morning laughing and chatting, bouncing off each other, her mum would have said. No awkward silences, in fact no awkwardness at all, and the thought of anything breaking the perfect mood, especially on such a drab day, was not welcome.

By two that afternoon, they finished in the tunnels. The rain was getting steadily worse, and the air was dropping colder. They put the tools back in the corner of the small potting shed and Willow watched the sheeting rain from the doorway as Jack eyed the seeds.

'How about we get these seeds potted, and then we can go inside, get warm, and go over the plan for the year? What do you say?'

Willow felt her stomach constrict at the mention of going inside. A rainy afternoon would surely bring some of them in. Would her body go into flight mode again?

'I'm not quite here for a year now,' she said, turning to him.

Jack laughed and shook his head. 'Aye, it's a shame, but fortunately, the vegetables stay long after you've gone.'

Willow rolled her eyes with a grin. 'Of course, that was stupid.'

'Not stupid. People come and people go, but food needs planning either way.' He rolled up his sleeves to show arms as tanned as his face from the late summer sun, as he set out some pots on the rack. 'Who knows whether you'll even stay the year, you could be gone next week.'

Willow frowned.

'Absolutely not,' she said, pushing up the sleeves of her own coat and jumper, which promptly slid back down. 'I love it here.'

He glanced her way with a grin that lit his face. 'Well, that's good to hear, but are you going to work while you're around, princess, or are you going to watch me do it all?'

Willow slapped his arm playfully, catching the warmth of his skin over the tautness of muscle that only daily manual work built.

'Are you saying I haven't done anything this morning?'

'Not at all, you turn over a half-forkful of soil beautifully for a city lass.'

She raised an eyebrow. 'I'm not sure that's a compliment.'

He nudged her shoulder with his.

'You're doing better than Betsy,' he said, grinning as he pulled the seed trays from the racking.

'Maybe her instructor sucked,' Willow murmured, trying to keep the grin off her face.

Jack eyed her, and then they were both laughing.

'He's a sarcastic bastard, isn't he?' Jack said.

'Very much so.'

'I'm only playing, princess. You're doing great.'

'Too late to take it back now. Let's get these seeds planted, I'm freezing.'

'So bossy,' he said under his breath.

She laughed as she squashed next to him at the tiny bench. He filled the trays with compost, while she planted, covered, and watered. She enjoyed the work, but mostly she enjoyed being this close to Jack. His presence was warm and calming, despite the playful jibes that were thrown her way, and she loved that they never seemed to run out of things to talk about.

They worked methodically, and it was a quick and efficient method. All too soon, the last tray was filled.

'All done,' Jack said, looking at his compost encrusted fingers. 'Let's go in, get washed up, and get warm.'

Willow nodded, but at that moment she felt rooted to the spot, the cold, damp air seeming to crawl under her clothes and right down into her bones. She shivered as she turned to the small door ahead of Jack, and that's when it began.

It was the house, she knew. It was going back into the house knowing there may be people in there. And this one slammed down on her fast.

Her throat closed, cutting the air from the rest of her body. She tried to gasp a breath, but it wouldn't come.

Not again, please, and not now. I don't want to do this again here.

Breathe, stupid lungs.

Not here!

Just breathe!

Her panicked thoughts sent her spiralling downward at an alarming rate, and she grabbed the rack beside her for balance as the shed seemed to tilt. The rack tipped with her; she didn't know if that was in her head too, and then Jack grabbed her hands from behind, lack of room not enabling him to move past her in the tiny space.

'Willow? Hold on to me, sweetheart, the rack isn't safe. You're okay, breathe through it.'

She grasped at his hands, trying to imagine the flame. To concentrate on the flame. But the flame wouldn't come, embarrassment and fear climbing together to make her symptoms worse, not better.

Her thoughts raced and her mind flitted with worse case scenarios. Blackness closed in at the edges of her vision and sweat trickled down her neck.

Not again, please. I don't want to faint here. I don't want to do this. Breathe, just fucking breathe!

Why can't I BREATHE?

Panic escalated along with the pain in her chest, which seemed worse than she'd ever experienced. Her vision wavered, and she fought down a fresh wave of fear. The website had said that a blackout was safe, but now she wondered.

Am I dying? Carlton was right. I should have taken the pills. I should have called him. I don't want to die!

I don't want to die!

'I... I don... Jack,' she croaked, as terror engulfed her, and pain circled her chest. She gasped for air as tears filled her eyes.

'It's a bad one, I know, I've got you. I won't let you go,' Jack said as he moved closer behind her and pulled her back against his chest. His deep voice rumbled through her back, soothing and gentle. 'It'll pass. You're okay, sweetheart, you're going to be fine. Don't think. Empty your mind and just breathe. There's nothing else to do right now but breathe, nice and slow. You'll be all right, I promise.'

He took soothing breaths behind her as he murmured at her to breathe in and out, and she felt herself following his lead, breathing in and out along with him.

As the clutches of the attack eased, she felt her legs go to jelly. Her body felt depleted of energy, and her hands hurt from the pressure of holding on to Jack

for what literally felt like her life.

Willow closed her eyes and leaned her head back against him as her chest finally loosened and her throat began to open again. He stood behind her quietly now, and she knew she should move away, but she couldn't quite find the will to let go of his hands or step out of his arms.

When was the last time she had felt safe and protected through an attack like this?

Never, Willow, because the person who should have done it was busy telling you that you would die instead. What does that tell you?

She shunned the thought as relaxed into the warmth of Jack's body, her shaking hands still clutching his. He circled his arms around her, pulling her closer from behind, holding her up. She felt the warmth of his hands intertwined with hers, the warmth of his breath as his chin rested lightly at the side of her bobble hat, and the fresh smell of aftershave intertwined with the earthy smell of the potting shed.

'Are you all right?' Jack murmured, and Willow was almost sad that the moment had to be broken.

'I think so,' she whispered. 'I'm so sorry, Jack. I don't know what happened.'

'I think I do,' he said, letting go of her hands gently and turning her to face him. 'The house, or something to do with enclosed spaces, isn't it?'

She searched his eyes but found only kindness and question.

'Yes. Enclosed spaces where there are lots of people. They scare me. I was okay yesterday, just me and Helena, and the pig, obviously, but when I walked back in to all that noise and those people? I just couldn't do it.' She tapped his arm with a shaky smile. 'I thought you weren't supposed to ask?'

Jack shrugged and sighed. 'Well, that's the way Helena works, and it does work, to a degree. I agree people need to work on themselves, but personally, I think it leaves out a little caring, as you implied this morning. I also think some people need to be opened up a little. They need to talk.'

'And I'm one of them?'

Jack finally smiled and brought a hand to her arm.

'I don't know, maybe. I just know that last night you seemed too vulnerable to be left to deal with this alone. If I'd had my way, I'd have followed you out, but Helena talked me out of it. She said you need to work it out alone. Helena is an angel, not a bad bone in her, but I would do things a little differently. I mean, what if that had happened just now, and you'd been alone?'

'I'd have been okay,' she said, although she wasn't entirely sure she would have been.

So, open up. Talk to him.

Tears sprang into her eyes as she thought about the evening before, and how right he was in his judgement - although she wouldn't have picked the word vulnerable, of course.

'Well, no, I probably wouldn't. I needed help, Jack. I needed it yesterday, too. I was a mess. I almost didn't come back today.'

Something passed over his face. Worry? Concern? She couldn't make it out properly.

'In that case, I'm glad you're here, and I'm really sorry I wasn't there for you.'

'It's fine. It's not your fault.'

He nodded, glanced out of the shed door, and then met her eyes again.

'I need your number,' he said, and Willow's heart stalled.

He wants my number?

Her mind flailed. She loved being with Jack, but she barely knew him, although she had enjoyed being in his arms, and he seemed to know how to handle her attacks, which was nice. But Carlton was her boyfriend, and there was far too much to deal with at home before she handed her number to any other man.

Willow opened her mouth to object, but then her cheeks flushed as Jack continued and she realised she had taken his meaning out of context.

'If anything like that happens again, at least we can message or talk. If it's really bad, I can get to you without upsetting Helena, and you can call me if you need me. Any time, understood? That was a bad attack, Willow. Please don't think you have to deal with this alone. I'm always here whenever you need help.'

Willow nodded, utterly grateful. She felt a couple of tears let go as she pulled out her phone and passed it to him to enter his number.

What is your problem? Why are you crying just because he cares?

You haven't had actual human contact for so long, that's all. How long has it been since Carlton wrapped his arms around you like that? You forgot how nice people can be.

She watched as Jack gave his own phone a call, saved her number, and handed it back to her.

'Thank you, Jack,' she said. 'For everything.'

He smiled, reached forward, and wiped the tears from her cheeks with both thumbs, then he frowned.

'There aren't many people inside the house during the day unless it's the depths of winter. I should have told you that before, it may have helped. It may also help when you look like you've been to war.'

Willow added her own frown. Did she really look that bad? It had been a harsh attack, but Jack was grinning, and then he laughed and held his dirty hands up, now with clean thumbs.

'Sorry about that,' he said.

Willow put up her own hands to wipe the dirt off her cheeks and saw they were just as bad. She wanted to be mortified and embarrassed, but somehow the laughter took over, anyway. It didn't seem to matter around Jack.

'Ready?' he said as their laughter subsided.

'I think so.'

'If you feel anything begin, stop. I'm right here with you. These things are better nipped in the bud before they completely take over.'

Willow nodded and thought of yesterday morning at the gate. He was right. When she caught them coming, they were a great deal easier to stop. Today's knocked her off her feet, but that wasn't normal. She was just glad that both the attack and the physical part of the day were over.

'I'll be fine. I've got added battle stripes to prove it.'

Jack raised an eyebrow.

'I suppose I deserved that. You can be a real bugger, princess,' he said as she flashed him a grin. 'let's go get a hot drink.'

Twenty-Seven

TWO WEEKS LATER, CARLTON found himself working late. Again. Mrs West always scheduled the last appointment of the day because she knew that he would have no one else waiting and she could take the time she needed. A fact she never failed to take advantage of.

The fact that she was prompt with fees and paid extra cash in hand for his time was something that Carlton was usually happy with, but tonight - on a Friday, of all days - the lady's whining had almost got on his last nerve. His composure almost slipped several times until he had decided, extra money or not, he couldn't take anymore. If she didn't offer it, he couldn't care less.

'I'm sorry Mrs West, I'm afraid I have to cut you short. I really have to go.'

Mrs West instantly stopped talking, her mouth in a small red 'O'. Her eyelids fluttered as though processing what he had said.

'I am terribly sorry, but this can't wait.'

'But it's barely six. I've only been here two hours, Dr Mathers.'

'I understand, and I'll make it up to you next week, but I have something to do tonight. It's very important, obviously, or I wouldn't stop you here.'

'Well, I'm a little bemused as to why you've scheduled something on an evening when you know I'm coming in, but there we go.'

She rose and picked up her coat. 'Well, I suppose next week will have to suffice. Thank you for your limited time this evening, Dr Mathers. I appreciate it all the same.'

Carlton led her out of the office and through the small reception to the door. 'Thank you, Mrs West, and I am truly sorry. How about we schedule you for three next week? I'll have Suzanne move the diary around to get you in earlier, then you'll have even more time.'

Mrs West beamed. 'You'd do that for me?' She placed a hand on her chest and fluttered a kiss to his cheek. 'Thank you, Dr Mathers, you're one of the best. I recommend you to everyone I come across. Did I ever tell you that?'

Carlton stretched his mouth into a smile.

'You did, and I appreciate it. Thank you.'

Mrs West left in a flash of camel Cashmere and Chanel perfume, closing the door behind her with a wave.

'You realise she'll demand that extra hour at every appointment now, don't you?'

Carlton whirled and saw Suzie still at her desk.

'It crossed my mind, but I couldn't listen any longer. The woman was driving me to distraction.'

As Suzie was also doing in front of him with that white shirt, collar open to her chest, one shirt button barely holding her breasts inside the cotton. He looked away as his face flushed. 'What are you still doing here?' he said.

'Catching up. I knew you'd be here late. I took advantage. Sorry. I don't expect overtime.'

'Right,' he said, and cleared his throat. 'Um... your shirt is a little past the point of decency for a first point of contact.'

She looked down and gasped, but Carlton knew her well enough to know that it wasn't a genuine reaction. For starters, her hands didn't automatically move to cover herself. 'Oh God,' she said. 'I'm sorry, this shirt is a little unruly. I hope to God Mrs West didn't get an eyeful. On the other hand, maybe she won't come back. She'll have you down as a seedy psychiatrist.'

Carlton felt a flutter of desire. His eyes fell to her breasts, and the neon pink bra that barely held them in under the shirt. Then he forced himself to look back at her face with a flick of his hand.

'A seedy psychiatrist? She'll be back for more than just talking if she believes that. Keep covered, Suzie, we're a reputable firm.'

Suzie grinned, adjusted and buttoned the shirt, and picked up her coat, along with his.

'I am truly sorry. I'll throw the shirt away,' she said, handing him his coat. 'I honestly didn't realise. I wasn't trying to sway your decision about us. I wouldn't. Drink?'

'Suzie...' Carlton said. He swallowed hard, hating himself for the weight of the restraint he had to pull. 'I can't do this. You know how I feel, this can't go on.'

'I do,' Suzie said, 'and do you know what I think? Because I think it's high time you heard me out for once.'

His tongue flicked nervously between his lips. 'Okay, what do you think?'

'That I'm a single girl with a crush I've had to sit on for far too long. I've respected your wishes, and your relationship, for years, Carlton. I've never interfered, I've never put myself in front of you, even though I *know* there's a spark between us. I know we could be great together, and I know you're holding back.'

'I'm not holding back, Suzie. I love Willow.'

'Sure, you love Willow. The same girl that you've put your life on hold for. The same girl you've dropped everything for numerous times, the same girl you've nursed and looked after for the last four years. FOUR!'

'Suzie?' Carlton said softly, but she was still venting, and going into therapist mode, he stood quiet, letting her.

'The same girl that up and left a few weeks ago with barely a word about her plans. The same girl who won't tell you where she is, or what she's doing. The very SAME GIRL who won't answer your goddamn messages when you're heartbroken! Not only that, but with barely a word about when she will return. She's probably having a fucking ball, and you're still on hold!'

Suzie stepped to him, her face contorted with anger, so close to his. Something about her words was striking home, the truth behind them something he wouldn't have admitted to himself.

'You're on hold. Paused. For how fucking long? Because what if she doesn't come back? What if you've been paused for a year when you could have been having fun, living a normal life? A YEAR of your fucking life, Carlton, and she may never come back!'

Carlton felt something close to tears rise into his chest, not only at what she was saying, but the passion and caring that went into her speech.

'You work so hard, Carlton. You don't deserve this. I hate it! I hate how much you love her, and I hate how much she hurts you! Most of all, I hate that I have to pretend. Every. Damn. Day. That I'm happy for you. When I'm not.'

Carlton stood silent as her anger trailed off and she stood panting before him, her eyes full of hurt and injustice, but not for herself. For him.

Of course there was a spark, there always had been, but he'd had no idea how deep her feelings had run. As he stood before her under the fluorescent light of the office, he thought she had never looked so beautiful.

'Suzie...' he murmured, about to contest, but his heart had other ideas. His lips met hers with a hunger he hadn't felt in years as suppressed desire and heat exploded through him.

Twenty-Eight

A TEXT MESSAGE WOKE Willow the next morning. She yawned but didn't reach for her phone straight away.

After the last few weeks of silence, she had given up thinking that it may be Carlton, and even the hurt of that thought was diminishing. She was moving on, moving forward, and life was good. Friends messaged her instead these days, and after four years of nobody but Carlton, it felt great.

She clasped her hands behind her head with a grin.

The days at McGracken House were almost idyllic, and as they got colder and wetter, Willow was glad to have something to do other than sit in a house with an unruly cupboard, and something that liked to draw faces on the windows. It was almost like living with a small child, this one unseen, and quite frankly, it was beyond freaking her out.

The previous evening, she had placed a spare sheet over the glass of the living room door and sat with the television up loud to cover any noises in the hallway. This had worked well until she wanted to go to bed, and had spent ten minutes staring at the sheet, terrified to pull it aside and open the door in case something was peering in at her.

The feeling had been so intense that she had almost slept on the settee. Then she had chastised herself for allowing this 'thing' to cut her off into one part of the house. It made her wonder about the presence, and it almost made her want to speak to Maud about it.

Not today, though.

Willow rolled over to grab her phone and checked the message. It was from Sophie.

Hey stranger! I have the mutt and a free morning. Fancy a walk in the woods?

Today was Saturday, and although Helena had told her she was free to have a day off whenever she wanted, she hadn't. After two weeks constantly in Jack's company, she was almost addicted to his laid-back attitude and humour. Horizontal, Helena called him. Unflappable. And Willow could only agree, especially when her attacks came on. He made her laugh - all day - and he made her feel safe, both of which gave her confidence she wouldn't have found up here alone.

I'm certainly due a break, though, and I can pop into the house this afternoon.

Willow bit her lip and grinned, excitement circling her abdomen as she fired off a quick reply.

It would be good to see Sophie. She had been absent from yoga over the last week and Willow had missed her, although she had been glad of the opportunity to speak to Tam alone. They had discussed the scarier attacks - the ones that slammed down on her with no warning - and what she could do further. Then she had shown Tam Carlton's last message, now over two weeks old. Tam had immediately called 'Bullshit', as her mum had only days before.

Willow still hadn't called Carlton and wasn't sure she wanted to. Whenever she thought of her life back in Bristol now, it seemed too small, almost claustrophobic in its limitations.

If he could see you now, eh?

An uneasy swirl landed in Willow's stomach. Did she even want to see him? Things would never be the same, especially now that she knew what her mum and dad had thought too. Going home seemed a step backward, but she knew she owed him an explanation, and owed it to Carlton to explain himself too.

But do you want to go back there? Honestly?

Willow swung her legs out of bed and sat on the edge with a sigh.

No... I don't know.

The last few weeks, she seemed to have become a completely different person than the one who had arrived at the door in early September. She wasn't even sure she was the same girl who loved the minimalistic greys of the sleek apartment with its soft closers, controllers, apps, and beeps for every automated appliance.

There's a long way to go yet. You don't have to decide now.

But she already knew the answer as she opened the curtains to see the forest and the front drive. Although it was murky with rain, there was a pull of comfort that she never got thinking about the Bristol apartment.

Here was simple. A switch was a switch, a door lock, a door lock. There was no beep in or out - just hair-raising thuds from the hallway now and then.

This was the type of place that she had craved, though she hadn't ever known it. Or maybe she had just changed. It should have made sense, though, growing up in a rambling old country house, the only child of wealthy parents.

The trouble with living on the edge of the city was that from the moment she was allowed out alone, she was in it, and that was where she had loved to be, with the modern buildings and sleek lines, and glossy surfaces. No beams or uneven walls with dusty nooks and open fires.

From the moment she could work, she was out in the city, earning a wage. She was focused and opinionated, but she had an eye for detail and a head that could twist the hardest negotiations to her advantage. Her drive had taken her to marketing manager in a retail company at just twenty-three, and when the attack had happened, she had been just within reach of regional manager at twenty-eight.

The attack had changed everything, devastated her world, and turned it on its head, but Mum had been right; before that she had been fiercely independent.

The Bristol apartment had been hers when she met Carlton, but after the attack and subsequent loss of her job a year later, Carlton had handed her a piece of paper that she had signed without real thought. The paper had signed the apartment and all of its debt over to him. The mortgage was his, he said, and the apartment safe. She would keep her home.

Now she not only wondered, but she also felt betrayed. Legally, her apartment was Carlton's and if they split and sold now, what would happen? He had paid four years mortgage, and they were common-law partners, she supposed, but the place had been hers. She had fronted the twenty-thousand-pounds deposit. She had furnished it, and she had paid the mortgage alone.

It had been around that time that he had set up surveillance on the house and the phone too, also to keep her safe, he said. He could track her at any point in the day and watch her at home from his phone at work if he wanted to.

Willow shuddered and wondered why she had let it get so far, but again, that hadn't all been Carlton either. She had agreed to the surveillance and tracking, too. It made her feel safe.

Safe.

She thought about life up here and how Jack made her feel safe and gave her confidence in handling the attacks. A completely different context. At home she felt watched, anxious, and caged. Up here she felt supported, confident, and free.

At least you removed the tracker when you left.

When she thought about it, there had been no point in her life until four years ago that she had been dependent on anybody. Since *that* day, she hadn't depended on herself once.

Even now, she was depending on her mum for income that covered her expenses. Mum was more than happy to pay, but now that Willow was getting back to herself, *she* wasn't happy. She had thought of picking up a part-time job, but Mum had been dead set against it.

'This year is about getting well. Focus on that. You don't need the money. I can pay what you need. Promise me, Willow. Just one year.'

Willow had promised, and it was a promise she would keep - for now anyway.

There was a ping, and Willow blinked back into the present. She stepped away from the window and picked up her phone as she left the room and entered the kitchen. She looked at the message as the kettle boiled.

Brilliant! I'll be there just after ten.

Willow looked at her watch - half an hour to go.

Sitting with toast and coffee at the dining table, she messaged Jack. Not that he would be waiting for her. There were always a million jobs to be done at McGracken House, he had told her. Willow had a feeling that showing her what to do was keeping him from his own by a good margin, although no one seemed to mind. Things got done when they got done.

Jack answered the message quickly.

No worries, have fun, you don't need to check in. I'm not even supposed to have your number, remember! Don't panic if you can't get here later, just enjoy your day off.

Willow smiled and then a figure appeared outside, coming up the road in the drizzle, a big black dog straining at the lead in front of her.

Sophie.

A grin spread across Willow's face. She gulped the last of the coffee, pulled on her hat, coat and boots, and went out to meet her.

'Hi-ii!' Sophie screeched, almost hopping from one foot to the other as Willow pulled her into a hug. Frodo was so bouncy it was more of a three-way hug. He licked at the side of Willow's face with a whine, dirty paws landing on her jeans and jacket.

'Down, Frodo,' Sophie scolded, squeezing her hard. 'It's so good to see you, Wills. I've missed you.'

'Me too,' Willow said into her friend's padded jacket, before pulling back and giving her the once over. 'Where the hell have you been? How are you?'

'Oh, just working, you know. Deadlines. The usual crap. Fuck!' Sophie jolted out of Willow's grasp as Frodo lunged and barked at a squirrel. 'Frodo! Bad boy. Leave the squirrel alone.'

Frodo turned Sophie in a full circle, lost interest as the squirrel scampered away, and bounced back up Willow, who scrubbed his head, secretly delighted that he was stationary, even if it meant paw marks on her coat.

'Crazy dog,' Sophie said with a laugh. 'Honestly, my brother needs to sort his life out, any bigger, and Frodo will be walking me.'

Willow grinned. 'Looks like he already is, aren't you, boy?' She scrubbed Frodo's ears with both hands, bending a little too close and ending up with a face full of lick. 'Urg. Okay, I like you Frodo, but that was waaaay too much.'

Sophie tugged the dog down.

'Christ, he's annoying. I've had to bring him out, though. He's driving me flipping bananas and I've only had him since half seven this morning.'

Willow looked at her watch with a grin. 'Three hours and counting.'

'Only another seven to go.' Frodo lurched again, almost pulling Sophie down the road after an invisible smell. 'Let's get into the woods, where I can take his lead off. Is it going to rain all bloody day?'

'Pretty much.'

'Great, I'll have to bath him when I get back, too.' Sophie made a face as she turned the dog back around and forced his backside to the floor with a knee. 'Sit, Frodo. For the love of God, just sit still.'

Frodo was still for a second, and Sophie looked at Willow.

'I can't believe how different you look, Wills.'

Willow looked down at her wet, and now dirty, clothes.

'The dirty drowned rat look will do that,' she laughed.

'No, I mean you look fresher, less tired, more colour in your cheeks.'

'Christ, Soph, you sound like my mum. Come on, let's walk, I'm getting soaked.'

'It's certainly wet rain today,' she said.

'Another mum quote. How old did you say you were again?'

Sophie laughed and tugged Frodo so that he faced up to the woods. Willow grasped her arm to stop her from being pulled over as he got the gist and shot forward.

'Fuck,' Sophie yelled as the lead ran out and her arm was yanked forward.

'I totally see why you had him off the lead that first day we met.'

'He's a nutter, right? He'll calm down, but seriously, he needs to run off that energy.' She leaned down, unhooked his lead, and he was gone. Racing past the cottage and onto the path.

'Fro...' Sophie began, then she rolled her eyes and flapped a hand after him. 'Never mind, he'll come back eventually.'

Willow and Sophie set off up the path into the woods after him. It was good to get moving in the cold air, even with the drips from the trees above them.

'So, how are you getting on at McGracken House, then? By the looks of it, you feel at home there. It's been good for you, hasn't it? I can tell.'

'Oh God, Soph, I actually love it. It's like coming home, and I've learned so much, I can't even begin to tell you.'

'Aye, you've been getting on well. I spoke to Jack in the store a couple of days ago.'

'Oh?' Willow stumbled at Jack's name. She knew he wasn't confined to the house any more than she was, but to have been speaking to someone in the store seemed almost alien.

'Yeah, he said you're a hard worker. Good job because Jack hates a slacker. He clashed with Betsy something rotten. Oh my God, the fights that they had. Not in front of Helena, of course, but yeah, clash central.'

Willow frowned. 'Fights? I can't imagine Jack shouting at anyone. He's always so calm.'

Sophie laughed. 'He is around you, yes, he likes you. Buttons pushed, he can lose his temper as much as the next man, and wow, did Betsy push his buttons, like constantly.'

'I remember he said I couldn't make as much of a hash of the growing as she did, or something like that, when I first met him. That's all I know about her, really. He never mentions her.'

'No, he wouldn't. She was a spiteful little thing. Treated the house like a hotel. The thing is Helena allows people to use it as they want. It's part of their healing, she says. Betsy had no time for work, ploughed through the food like one of the pigs, and was often found trawling through other people's things. Jack flipped when he found her in his shower.'

Willow's mouth dropped open, and Sophie nodded.

'In his *room*,' she said pointedly. 'He lost it and told Helena to 'remove the girl from his room or he would do it himself', but Helena said that she would learn the lessons she needed in time, and to let her be.'

Willow winced. It was a very Helena-like thing to say. She could even imagine the look on her face as she said it. 'Oops, what happened?'

'Jack didn't want to leave it. He was mad as hell. He went up there and dragged her out. She told him it was her house too, and he had no right. He told her to put her clothes on or he would drag her out of the place naked and lock the gate.'

Willow's cheeks flushed. 'Jack said that?'

'Oh, aye. He was absolutely bloody furious. In the end, Helena had to interject, and he said that it was him or Betsy. She went, or he did. He could take no more of her lazy, bone idle, waste of space, idiot face. I think it was that order he said it in. Anyway, next day she was gone, haven't seen or heard from her since.'

'Helena must have known that he was right then. I couldn't imagine her put into a situation like that and having to throw someone out. In fact, I'm sure she said to me that everyone is welcome, whatever their reason. I can't imagine she would tell anyone to go.'

'Exactly, but Jack made her choose. She hated that. She got angry, Wills, really angry. I haven't seen her like that before or since, but aye, ultimately, you're always going to side with your family over a stranger now, aren't you? No one expected Jack to go, and to be honest, a few would have walked if he had. Betsy had only been at the house a few months, and already she was a known troublemaker. Jack is a solid part of the foundation there, especially now he's been back a while.'

Willow nodded, and then she almost stopped as Sophie's words sank in. She flung a hand to her friend's arm.

'Wait. You said family, is that right?'

Sophie nodded, surprise on her features. 'Yes, Helena is Jack's mum. He grew up at the house.'

Now Willow had surprise on her face.

'What? No, I mean, that can't be right.'

'I assure you it is,' Sophie said with a laugh. 'I went to school with his sister. Helena and Mick have two children. Beth is my age, and Jack is five years older. Both of them left the House, but Jack came back around three years ago now to help out. Beth works abroad somewhere. She hasn't been home for a good while now.'

'Wow, okay, but Jack calls her Helena, never mum, or mother or anything else. I just thought, well presumed, that he wasn't related. That no one there was. I assumed that Helena and Mick didn't have children, to be honest. I don't know why. Judging a book by its cover, I suppose. She almost seems too frail and ethereal to have had a baby.'

Sophie laughed. 'I know what you mean. She really does. Jack has always called them by their first names, as far as I know. Tam knows more. She used to look after them as bairns. I guess Helena likes to be known as the leader. To have someone shouting mum at her across the field would probably cramp her style.'

They both laughed at the thought.

'No, Helena probably wouldn't appreciate that, but Jack is a grown man. Why is he so under the thumb there still? What's with the rules?'

'What rules?' Sophie said with a laugh.

'Jack isn't allowed to ask anyone why they're there or what's happened. He's not even allowed phone numbers, or to show concern, as far as I can tell.'

Sophie stopped, a drip of rain running down her nose as she wrinkled it at Willow.

'What on earth are you talking about? Things are as they are. Everyone minds their business to a degree, but that's just be-cause the peace allows you to work things out for yourself, that's all. I can't imagine anyone wouldn't ask how you are, or how your day has been.'

Willow felt the rain patter on her hood as she tried to make sense of what Jack had said all those days ago after she had ran out of the kitchen.

'No, that's just it. They don't. No one asks anything. It's weird.'

Willow stopped herself from saying more instinctively. It wasn't that she didn't trust Sophie, but... she did talk an awful lot. It would only take one Freudian slip.

'Well, that's Helena's thing, yes. Always being present, and mov-ing forward, if that's what you mean. She never asks about the past. You can talk about it if you want to, though. She's always there.'

Willow felt something click in her brain. Sophie had almost re-peated what Helena had said word for word. There was nothing she could put her finger on, but something about Helena and McGracken House suddenly felt off.

Weird.

'...Jack would be the same,' Sophie was saying. 'I'm sure you just misheard him or misinterpreted what he said. That's the whole point of McGracken House. There are no rules.'

Willow nodded, keeping her thoughts to herself. 'You're prob-ably right. I must have misheard.'

'There would be no reason for Jack to get so mad about Betsy if there were rules, and no reason for Helena to get so mad at Jack for not allowing someone to be themselves and do their own thing, would there?'

Willow laughed, hoping it sounded genuine. 'No, you're right. I must have got it wrong. Never mind.'

As they walked further up the hill and out into the clearing, Frodo dashing in and out of the bushes beside them, talk turned to Sophie and her work, Tam, yoga and finally what had brought Willow up here.

Holding nothing back, she told Sophie about Carlton, and what she thought he had been doing to her for the last four years, accumulating in the message asking her to call.

Sophie was wide eyed. 'Have you called yet?'

'No.'

'Well, why the heck not? I mean, we all know you're doing perfectly well without medication, but seriously, have you not asked his sorry ass what the hell he was playing at?'

'No.'

Sophie shook her head. 'Don't you want to know? I'd grill him to within an inch of his life.'

'No, you see, I can't. I want to know his thoughts, but I... well, I suppose I don't trust him-'

'Too bloody right, you shouldn't!'

'I had to cut off all ties to get out here alone. I don't want him up here, especially not while I'm working all of this out.'

'Oh, so you broke up?'

'No, not at all. I came up here with a man I fully trusted and loved. It's only now I've stepped away from him that all this has come to light.'

'Fuck. That's a lucky coincidence, don't you think?'

'Not really. This is all thanks to Mum. There's no doubt that I wouldn't be here if not for her. I'd still be down there with him. Locked up, tracked, watched, fed pills like some lunatic from the asylum.'

'Wow, what a freak.'

Willow grinned. 'Well, thanks, Soph, I love you too.'

Sophie reddened and put a hand over her mouth. 'Not you! Idiot. I meant him, Charlie, or whatever his name is.'

'Carlton.'

'Right, what a freak. He tracked you? how?'

'A location app. I had to link his phone with mine. He knew where I was at all times.'

'I hope-'

'I took it off before I came here, yes, and removed all permissions. I had to leave no trace because he would have followed me. He used to have cameras in the apartment that could see in every room, even the bathroom, in case I tried to, I don't know, kill myself, I suppose. I wasn't even allowed to go to the shop by myself. If I left the apartment, the door chime went on his phone. He would call within seconds and ask what I was up to.'

'He told you to go back?'

'Sometimes. Sometimes he came out of work to escort me back if I was being particularly 'difficult'. Usually, I would get an extra dose of pills and end up sleeping the day away after that.'

'What a controlling fuck.'

Willow blanched at Sophie's reaction. She had never thought of Carlton as controlling. He'd only been like this since the attack.

'You think?' she said with a small flicker of worry.

'You don't? Wills he was literally controlling every single second of your life, wasn't he? For fuck's sake, he could even see you on the toilet?'

'I suppose.'

'That is wrong on so many levels. So wrong.'

Willow frowned across the wet bracken and heather as the hill fell away at the side of them. Within the mist that hung in the low cloud, Willow could just make out the loch and the small willow tree she had sat under back when she'd had time for walking.

'If you linked phones and gave him permission, then you allowed him to track you?' Sophie said as Frodo bolted from the trees, jumped the path in two strides and ploughed into the bracken at the other side.

'That dog is going to be the death of me, you know. I'll be the only ever thirty-three-year-old woman to die by dog.'

Willow smiled. Funny how Sophie was a year older, and yet Willow felt a decade older than the bright, chatty girl next to her. 'Hopefully he'll tire soon, and yes, to answer your question, I allowed him to track me.'

Sophie stopped and pulled Willow to a halt next to her.

'Why? I mean, that means you knew, right? You knew he was doing it?'

'I did. But you don't understand, Soph, the way he sold it - it was like he was keeping me safe. It was for my protection, he said, and yes, I believed him. I did feel safe. I felt like he was always there, looking out for me. That he would drop everything in a second to get home and help me if I needed it. I was scared, Soph, I've been scared for far too long. Mum could see it, I suppose.' She shrugged and stopped. There was nothing she could say that would make what she had said to Sophie any better. It was wrong. It was all wrong now that she could see.

Sophie's eyes widened, and then she tugged Willow back to a walk, linking her arm with hers.

'That's some scary shit, Wills. I mean, like mind blowing shit. Does Tam know about this?'

'Not really. She just thinks he's my crazy therapist boyfriend who was keeping me drugged.'

'Ex-boyfriend, right?'

Willow glanced at Sophie, and then over to the black shape that was bounding back up the hill.

'Wills!' Sophie said, shaking her arm.

'I said I left with a boyfriend I loved and trusted. I haven't spoken to him since, so I guess he still thinks things are the same.'

'Christ! But seriously, you're not going back to him after the year is up, right?'

Willow swallowed hard.

'Right? You can't, not after all this.'

'No, I mean, I doubt it. I haven't thought that far ahead, really. Carlton and this controlling person don't seem the same. He was good to me, kind, considerate. I'm still not sure why he did all of this. Maybe it was to actually keep me safe. I've been through a lot. Maybe he thought he was doing the best thing... I don't know.'

Sophie stopped Willow and turned to face her, hands clasping her biceps.

'You can't be serious. That shit is not right, Wills, and I won't let you go back. He's a fucking therapist! He knows! He knows exactly what he was doing. Taking advantage of your state, keeping you in, while... what? He was swanning around living his alternate life?'

Willow was shaking her head. 'No, it wasn't like that. This affect-ed both of our lives. I was a complete and utter mess, scared of my own shadow for years. It was a daily struggle. He said-'

'I don't care what he says. Or what you say, for that matter, I won't let you go back!'

Sophie squeezed her arms so hard that Willow thought there may be bruises later. She let the intensity of Sophie's reaction flood through her, setting every fiber of her being on edge.

Was it that bad? It didn't feel that bad.

But said aloud it sounds that bad, Willow, so it must have been.

'I guess I'll need to get a job and renew the rent next year then.' She smiled, and then Sophie was smiling too.

'Well, that won't be a problem. I'll message Mel and tell her you're in love with the place and want to stay on. She'll possibly let you buy it if you have the money. She has no intention of coming back now.'

Willow saw an opportunity not only to get away from talk of Carlton, but to get onto the house.

'Did Maud's ghost chase her out?'

Sophie rolled her eyes. 'Maud is a stupid old lady with nothing better to do with her time. The house is fine. You've had no problems, have you?'

Sophie frowned as Willow chewed at her lip.

'I may have had a couple,' she said, and Sophie's eyebrows shot up. Willow put her hands out at her friend. 'Nothing major, I'm certainly not ready to run screaming from the building or anything.'

Well, not yet anyway.

Sophie was looking at her like she belonged in that asylum the Carlton had her locked in, and Willow was regretting saying anything at all.

'It's probably nothing,' she said quickly as they turned and walked back under the cover of the dripping trees. 'The ironing board has a habit of falling out of the cupboard on its own. It's probably the way I'm putting it back in.'

Sophie relaxed and huffed, 'Yeah, I can understand that. Mel always said that cupboard was a pest too. Maybe it needs new catches? At least then the ironing board won't open the door when it falls.'

Willow's stomach caught.

Mel had trouble, after all?

'Great, then it can murder me as I open the door and it's waiting to fall on me.'

'Frodo!' Sophie called as they took another path. 'Well, it's better than death by dog.'

'Marginally,' Willow said, as they paused and waited for Frodo.

There was silence for a beat, and then the black bolt was back, running down the path with what looked like more of a lollop than a run. 'Well, look at that, I think he's getting tired at last. How big a walk do you fancy?'

Willow was glad that the subject of the cottage was dropped. She had an email address for Mel, the previous owner, maybe now was the time to use it.

'I can go for a while yet,' she said. 'What are you thinking?'

'I'm thinking of tiring this fucker out,' she said, scrubbing Frodo's wet, slobbery head. 'If we head this way, we come to the back of the hill above McGracken House. The problem is there's pretty much only one way back to the village there. It's downhill, but it's a long path right round their land and across the back of the houses in the village. We come out on the other more well-used path I told you about?'

Willow nodded. 'Okay, well, we can't get any wetter. I'm game if you are.'

Sophie nodded, 'I'm game, if only to keep my sanity for the next few hours.'

It was a few hours, too. They finally reached the village road just before three, tired, hungry, and gasping for a drink. Sophie apologised and bought Willow a bottle of water and a KitKat from the shop. Willow took the opportunity to stock up on a few things she needed, regretting it when she realized she had to carry four bags back through the village and up the hill to the cottage. Sophie offered to help, but Willow didn't mind. She was tired, but refreshed and clearheaded. The walk had done her good, and Sophie had Frodo to wash now that she was almost home.

They said goodbye at the shop and Willow began the mile walk back to the cottage.

What normally took around twenty minutes managed to take forty-five before she was at the door and putting the key in the lock.

Willow paused before opening the second door, her heart skipping a beat, but inside, all was normal. The house was warm, and the boiler hummed as the central heating did its job.

Willow stripped her soaked clothes and threw them into the washing machine before getting dry. She put the food away as the kettle boiled and the ready to eat lasagna whirled in the microwave. She chopped some salad, and ten minutes later was sitting at the table feeling as though she must be in heaven. Her body tingled with exertion, and her stomach growled with satisfaction at the warm tea and food.

And you've been fine all day. No attacks. Not one.

Well, I've not really been near civilisation, either.

When was the last time you had a day free of a panic attack, Wills?

She frowned as beefy pasta slid down her throat, hot and tasty, and she couldn't remember. Even on her own in the flat, under surveillance twenty-four/seven, she'd had a few attacks a day.

You were sitting listening for sounds, waiting for the men to come back, waiting for the next attack. Today you haven't thought about it once... until now.

She pulled her small laptop out to divert her thoughts, powering it up and connecting to the Wi-Fi before logging onto her email. She found Mel Harding's address on the last communication they had had before the handover, and quickly typed her an email. Nothing ominous, just asking if she had had any trouble with the cupboard and the condensation on the glass. If she had, Willow thought, then Mel would know what she meant.

She pressed send and sat back. Short of speaking to Maud, there was nothing more she could do.

Twenty-Nine

I T WAS LATE. MUCH later than Coop wanted it to be. The street-lights offered the only glint of light in the heavy darkness of the night. He hurried down the side street, head down, pulling the hood of his black hoodie up and over his head against the driving rain.

'Shitty weather,' he mumbled, as he glanced both ways and crossed the street, heading for the park. At least the transaction had gone through easily, if a lot later than planned.

A glance at his phone told him it was 10.45pm.

He glanced at the Golden Jockey as he passed, half wondering whether to grab a pint before last orders, but decided against it. His jacket was thin, the hoodie not much better, and he was frozen from the hour hanging around in the rain. He could have a beer at the apartment when he was warm and dry, though the atmosphere certainly lacked there, and at this time Carlton would probably be in bed.

The park was quiet except for the squeak of his trainers on the tarmac path, and when his phone rang, he almost jumped out of his skin. Darkness was his friend in more ways than one, but it really wasn't his forte.

He fumbled with the phone, his wet fingers not working on the screen. It took five swipes to answer Radar.

'Yeah?' he said.

'Any news your end?'

Coop almost laughed out loud.

'Nope. I'm still waiting for you to get into town. Then the party starts.'

'Mr Simpson didn't cough?'

'Nothing. I have a plan, though. He'll be amicable.'

'Great. Get on it. Thing is, the job here is wired, man. I know I'm late, but I'm up to my neck in work. It may take longer. In fact, a chat with the boss says it could be up to a month.'

Coop came to a halt and closed his eyes, feeling his anger flare.

'A fucking month? It's already been almost three weeks! Are you having a laugh, bro?'

'Afraid not. I have no choice.' Radar had the pity voice on that said he was sorry, but he would not be swayed.

'It's only fucking deals man, what the hell is wrong?'

Radar gave a small cough. 'There's more to it than that.'

'Bullshit. Are you going chicken on me?'

'Careful, bro. I'm not. I was just thinking, you know, this whole shit put us on standby. I'm not sure I need another dose of medicine if anything goes wrong.'

'So, you're going fucking chicken? Nothing will go wrong. I'm not asking you to rob a fucking bank! What about Bugs? What about Floss? They gone for no reason?'

'Course not. They were brothers, man, it's not like that. I'm tied up, that's all. Give it some time.'

Coop worked his jaw.

'I haven't got time. Don't worry, I'm going in alone.'

It was a sentiment that always pulled them back on side when one slipped. They were a band, a pack. They worked together and looked out for each other. Coop knew that Radar couldn't refuse. Whatever chickenshit nerves were keeping him wherever he was, he would come now; Coop had made clear their position.

Except that Radar did refuse.

'Be careful, bro. See you around.'

The connection cut off and Coop stared at the screen before hurling the phone into the nearest bush with a roar.

'Not if I see you first, fucker,' he shouted at the empty park. 'You'd better be waiting for me. I'm coming for you.'

He pressed his hands against his face and sank to his heels.

What the fuck just happened? What the fuck?

Looks like you're on your own, Coop, buddy.

He dragged his hands down his face, and then he froze. Then he began a chuckle, which turned into a moan.

Your phone is in the middle of the fucking bushes, moron... and it's dark.

He spent the next ten minutes shouting swearwords as though he had Tourette's as he fished it out of the bushes... which had spikes. Of course, they did.

When he got back to the apartment, Carlton's light was still on. After 11pm it was a fucking miracle, but Coop was in no mood to jibe him about it. In fact, he wanted to be left alone to work through his plan. He had been holding off with his idea until Radar got here, when they could put it into action and split. Now he just wanted to work out the quickest way to get out of here with the information he needed.

Locking the door behind him, he went through to the dark living room, switching on the light as he kicked the door shut and pulled off his wet clothes. He stood in his underwear as he searched through his new clothes, both stolen and purchased over the last week, and pulled on a pair of jeans and a T-shirt. He wrung the water out of his hair onto the floor before selecting a new hoodie and going into the kitchen to grab a beer.

He opened it, took a swig, and placed the bottle down on the worktop, his palms sitting flat on either side of it.

Fucking Radar. I knew he was a no-good tosser, he thought. Then he stopped himself.

Forget him. You have a plan. All you need is a way to execute it. You can go for Radar afterward.

'Right,' he murmured, taking another slug of beer. 'What would Bugs do in my position?'

He moved back into the living room and opened his phone, pulling up a photo of his best friend. Both of them with long hair and leather jackets, arms firmly around each other's shoulders as they smiled wide for the camera. Coop's chest constricted, and he rubbed a hand over his nose.

Brothers, Radar had said. He had no fucking idea. None.

Coop shut the phone off and finished the beer in three large gulps.

As he sat with his mind going a hundred miles an hour, he suddenly had a flash of just how idiotic he was being. He didn't need to take Carlton's phone to carry out his plan, he could manage without if he just had a location. All he needed was to borrow it.

He glanced at the shut living room door, then rose to open it. Light filtered down the stairs.

Carlton is still up. All I need is his phone for a few minutes. I'll just tell him I lost mine in a bush and I need to make a private phone call. There's no house phone, and he's a pussy. How hard can it be?

'You have to toughen up Coop, think quicker, be smarter, you're taking the load now. For Bugs.'

Then I'll take Radar for Bugs too. If he loves him so much, they can burn together in the hell he is surely in right now, because there is no fucking way Bugs is in heaven, that's for sure.

With a grin, Coop pocketed his phone and took the stairs two at a time.

Thirty

I T WAS DARK WHEN Willow opened her eyes to something clang-ing at the back of her brain. She let her eyes adjust and glanced around the dark room.

It was cold. Again. So cold that she was dithering underneath the duvet.

That's what woke you, go turn the heating up.

She pulled the duvet from the bed and wrapped it around her with a yawn as she moved to the bedroom door. Her hand was reaching for the doorknob when she heard it.

Th-ud.

Quiet. Ominous, but sounding like thunder to her brain.

She closed her eyes. She could feel the cold air coursing round her - through her - chilling her lungs, making her shudder. Or maybe that was just the oppressive energy.

She swallowed hard, the hair at the back of her neck prickling.

Someone is behind me.

Willow's eyes flew open, and her breath caught. She swung round, but the room was empty. She felt a light touch on her head. A small tap.

Shit!

She thrust the door open.

TH-UD.

The sound was louder out here, and Willow froze in the doorway.

Oh shit. Stay out here with... it, or shut myself in the bedroom with... it?

The force behind her seemed to press against her back. She dashed across the threshold and shut the door, putting a barrier between herself and one of the 'its'.

Unfortunately, the other was now between her and the rest of the house. She stepped back until she pressed against the wall at the end of the corridor. Cold immediately seeped through the duvet, which she clutched with both hands. She shivered as her heart thumped and her chest heaved.

TH-UD.

Shit, shit, shit! What do I do?

A calm, logical voice answered, one that surprised her.

The bedroom is out of bounds. The living area is the only place you've not seen anything untoward, and you can get out of the back door if you need to. Get to the living room. Get the sheet over the door. Stay until light.

Willow thought it was the only good idea, unfortunately the living area was past the cupboard, and both seemed to stretch away before her in the darkness.

TH-UD.

'Stop it,' she whispered. 'I'm just going to go past, then you can thud all you like, but please. I'm scared.'

She licked her dry lips, her teeth chattering.

Just got to go for it.

She eyed the doorway to the living area. Not far. Around ten steps at most.

If you run, even less. You can be in there in seconds.

TH-UD.

Willow jumped and whimpered.

'Stop,' she said, raising the hair on her arms.

Next to her the door of her bedroom rattled in its frame and cold circled her ankles.

TH-UD.

'No,' she said, fear spiking, catching her breath as her eyes bulged. 'This is a dream. It's not happening.'

The door beside her clicked and began to creak open, and Willow felt her fear crack.

She ran down the corridor as though in slow motion, each step shuddering through her as the duvet trailed behind her like a cape. As she passed the small corridor that led to the front door, the cupboard door exploded open with such force that Willow actually leaped into the air, crashing into the living room just as the ironing board crashed to the floor. She turned to push the door shut, almost pulling down the makeshift curtain in her frenzy to cover the glass.

'It was there. It was there. It was there. It was there,' she chanted, unable to calm her own terror.

A door slammed shut in the corridor and Willow screamed.

'Stop it! Please, stop it!' she screeched, trying to erase the memory of the darkness that had been silhouetted behind the glass as she pulled the curtain across.

Black. Figure like.

She ran for the settee, jumping onto it, and pulling the duvet around herself. She watched the curtained door, shivering and waiting, her heart thudding against her ribs.

The watch on her arm lit, and she caught sight of the time.

11.15pm? Shit.

It was going to be a very long night, but she vowed not to close her eyes for the rest of it.

Thirty-One

C OOP STARED AT HIS brother and the secretary with his arms folded across his chest. It was a... what did they say? A mass of tangled limbs?

He cocked his head. It appropriately described the shambles that was in his brother's normally tidy room right now. He stooped in the doorway and hooked up a pair of neon pink panties with his pinkie finger as he surveyed the room.

Clothes were strewn around the floor, along with a lamp and the bedclothes. Coop whistled through his teeth and grinned.

This had been one frenzied fuck session.

So frenzied that both parties were now out for the count, and looked like they were participating in a naked version of Twister.

Coop raised an eyebrow. Then he dropped the panties, retrieved the phone from his pocket and snapped off a couple of shots.

This could be interesting leverage when the time came, especially as his brother was denying all knowledge of both Willow's whereabouts and a relationship with this woman.

Even fucking was a relationship, wasn't it?

Coop moved forward, slowly now, snapping photos from different angles. Being sure to get in faces and just how very naked the bodies that were attached to those faces were.

He grinned.

Every cloud has its silver lining.

He snapped a few photos of the room for luck, and then counted his blessings again as he scanned the room. On the floor next to Carlton's jacket was his phone. Coop bent to pick it up and pressed the screen.

Password or fingerprint?

Coop looked at the bodies on the bed. Carlton's right hand was thrown over the top of his hot secretary. The fingerprint should be easy as long as he didn't wake. He would access the phone within seconds that way instead of faffing around trying passwords.

The way his luck was going tonight, he thought he'd chance it. God was obviously making up for the fact that his ex-partner in crime - no pun intended - was a dick.

Thank you, oh heavenly Father, for showing up at least one moment in my life.

Coop sniggered at his own wit and crept around the bed. Small snores were coming from the secretary, whose mouth hung open almost as wide as her legs.

Classy lady.

He pressed Carlton's phone to light the screen and bent to his hand level, hoping his brother used his thumb as it would be the easiest to access from down here. Carefully, he pressed the thumb to the screen, turning the phone to straighten it. The screen lit, and for a second, he thought he'd managed it first time, but the phone remained locked.

Twisting carefully underneath the limp hand, Coop bent backward and pressed the first finger.

Nothing.

For fuck's sake, come on. Give me a break.

The middle finger was raised slightly. He would have to press down from the top too, meaning he was stooped, bent backward and not able to use his hands for balance.

Hilarious, Father, now fuck off.

His hands shook with effort and his core protested as it fought to keep him upright. He twisted his arm, placing the phone under Carlton's finger and then gently pressed the top, pressing it down onto the screen.

The phone flickered and lit, and Coop almost screamed with frustration at the ridiculous position he was holding himself in. He brought his hands down to the floor and stood, stretching out his back. Carlton hadn't moved yet, and he could do without waking him, but he would just have to pick his hand up and hope.

He raised the phone again and looked at it.

Unlocked.

He swiped a finger across the screen, accessing the apps and messages.

Unlocked, it's fucking unlocked!

He almost whooped with joy as he took the phone back downstairs. If God wanted to hang around, Coop may also be able to get it back upstairs before Carlton woke and realised it was missing.

Downstairs, he grabbed another beer and sat down with the phone. He flicked through the apps coming across the house security, which accessed the cameras. He flicked through the different screens, waiting for the feed to load. There was even one in the fucking john. Why the hell Carlton needed to watch her pee was beyond him.

On the bedroom feed, he saw that Carlton and the secretary were still in the same position.

This could be useful to check on you while I'm searching. Thanks, bro.

He left the app open and flicked back to the list, flicking through until he found the tracking app.

His grin widened.

Here it was, the gold he had been waiting for, and the reason he knew damn well Carlton had lied when he said he didn't know where Willow was.

He pressed the app and waited for it to load. A map came on the screen and a small blue dot sat like a beacon. Coop pinched the screen.

Bristol. His heart flipped with excitement. This would be easier than he thought. She was in fucking Bristol. He almost wet himself as he pinched in further and saw that she was close. Really close.

So close she's in the apartment?

He frowned.

That isn't fucking right.

Coop zoomed back out. One dot.

It has to be her, right? Who the hell else can it be?

He found a small menu and opened it.

One phone following, only one. Carlton Mathers. Coop wrinkled his nose.

Carlton is following himself?

He flicked back onto the 'about' page.

-A blue dot will show your location at all times. In an emergency-

Coop scrolled down.

-Connected devices will show as orange on the map. You can name these devices to show on the map with a tag. To add children as a -

Coop shook his head and flicked back onto the map.

There was only one blue dot. No orange.

He zoomed out, out, out, until the whole of the UK showed on the screen.

No dot.

Fuck.

He took a swig of beer and scrolled out further. The world.

No dot.

He checked back through the menu. Was there a bin? Had she been deleted when he arrived here?

Coop felt his heart thump as his search turned up nothing. The only person on here was Carlton himself.

Had Carlton known that Coop was due for release? Had they warned him? And in that case, had he warned Willow, sent her away, and removed all traces of her? What did the secretary have to do with this? Was she in on it, too? Was this all an elaborate plan?

Coop felt his blood boil as he tapped the screen, shutting down the tracker and checking the surveillance. They were still asleep. Only Carlton had moved a little. Coop stared at the bodies and wondered if he could slit their fucking throats as they slept and get away with it.

He flicked through the other apps on the phone, but there was nothing that would serve him here. He curbed his temper and tried to think, injustice banging through his brain.

Surely I didn't have had the luck to get the phone open, just to reveal nothing, because that's shitty, Father, just a fucking finger in my fucking face.

No. There had to be something. Anything.

He couldn't call Willow, but messages?

She would tell Carlton where she was, surely, even if he said he didn't know. In fact, Carlton didn't have to be telling the truth, did he? Maybe she'd already told him.

A flash of inspiration came to him. Even if Carlton didn't know, she would tell him, surely. All he had to do was text from Carlton's phone and ask her.

Coop swiped the phone to messages and almost danced around the room when he saw Willow's name at the top of the list. He still had her number, and there was contact.

We're in business, he thought with a grin.

I'll just check she hasn't told him already. Cut out the middle-man.

He scrolled through the messages to Willow, which were all the usual lovey-dovey stuff, until about three weeks ago, when Willow had told him not to contact her. Carlton had sent a message a few days ago, but she hadn't responded.

Interesting. Did that mean she knew about the secretary, after all?

He finished the beer and re-read the last message.

It appeared Carlton was trying to get her attention, and to get her to call about her medication. Coop felt an uneasy jolt land in his stomach. He wasn't so sure. It felt a bit too intense a message to be just about medication.

He accessed the call list, but Willow hadn't been in contact.

So, she wasn't speaking to Carlton at all. Interesting. But a flick through the messages also told him she hadn't revealed her location via text previously, either.

Fuck. What now?

He stared at the wall opposite and thought.

I could call from my phone, but she doesn't know me. She wouldn't speak to me, and certainly wouldn't tell me anything, even if she answered.

Maybe I could call and say something has happened to Carlton. Get her to come to me?

It was risky. It could work, but Willow was sassy and sharp, if he remembered rightly. It would depend on why she wasn't speaking to Carlton in the first place, and Coop only had one chance at this.

He tapped the phone, keeping the screen alive, and then a name came to him.

Text Track.

It came into his mind so fast that it took him a second to remember what it was. An illegal service Bugs used to use to track the location that a message was sent from.

A message. He didn't have to call at all, and best of all, he didn't have to use Carlton's phone. In fact, it would be better if he didn't, then he wouldn't have to change the password as he had intended, which would alert Carlton if he ever used the passcode instead of his finger.

He scrolled back to contacts and added Willow's number to his own phone. If she had a message from this phone, she wouldn't know who it was. That was risky. She could delete it and never answer. He had to find something to say that he was sure she would respond to.

Upstairs there was a series of thumps and Coop felt his heart accelerate. He swiped to check the surveillance and caught Carlton going into the bathroom.

Shit.

The secretary was still asleep. If he was quick enough, he could throw the phone back onto the floor and no one need know any different. It would buy him more time if Carlton didn't know that he was physically doing anything to track Willow. At the moment, he was certain that Carlton thought he had plans to hang around until she came home. He wasn't stupid enough to think Coop would leave it. They were brothers, after all.

He climbed the stairs as quickly as he could, cursing every creak. At the open door, the toilet flushed, and out of adrenaline fuelled anticipation, Coop slid the phone across the floor as the door from the bathroom opened.

Coop slid back into the shadow of the small nook opposite the stairs. It was barely big enough to conceal him from the doorway, but he couldn't chance going downstairs. He listened to the sound of the bathroom door shutting, the creak of the bed. Coop was letting out a small breath of relief when the bed creaked again and there were more footsteps. There was a pause and Coop held his breath.

Just go back to sleep. What the fuck is going on in there?

Coop shrank back further as Carlton stepped through the doorway and stopped at the top of the stairs, right next to him.

Coop held his breath, wondering what was going on, and then Carlton's hand dropped to reveal his lighted phone.

Fuck. Fuck. Fuck. You idiot. The screen was on.

Carlton looked at the phone again, glanced to the stairs and disappeared back into the bedroom, shutting the door behind him.

Coop closed his eyes and cursed. He would have to work fast now, he could deny it, but who the hell else would have had his phone? Carlton would know.

Well done, Coop, he heard Bugs say in his head, that was amateur. Really fucking amateur.

Thirty-Two

W ILLOW WOKE ON THE floor tangled in the duvet. Sunlight was peaking through the bottom of the living room curtains and carving a rectangle down the wall.

Sunshine?

Willow sat up and looked at her watch. 9.50am.

Not again. This is becoming one massive habit.

Not my fault I can't sleep at night, she pouted to herself. She sat up and scrubbed her hair, which felt like a wild mess after yesterday's walk in the rain and last night's floor sleep.

I need a shower.

She swallowed as she turned to the little kitchen and then looked at the makeshift curtain across the door to the hallway. Gooseflesh crawled across her skin, and she shuddered.

You want a shower? You need to go out there first to grab some clothes.

Willow stood, her heart thumping in her ears. She pulled the duvet around her, opened the curtains, and walked to the living room door.

She remembered being here in the darkness last night trying to pull the curtain across as something came down the hallway.

Crappy glass doors.

She toyed with not going out there at all, a strong feeling that this was her side of the house, and the other side belonged to something else.

Except it wrote on the mirror in the bathroom and the window in the kitchen, and you really need fresh clothes.

Oh, and by the way, you need to get a wriggle on if you're making it for 10am this morning.

She swallowed, heaved in a breath, and pulled the curtain across. The hallway was dark, and willow remembered that her bedroom door was shut. It looked like the others were, too.

She pulled the door in toward her and reached a hand for the light switch on the wall to her right. Her heart was banging, and her hands shaking as the cool air circled her.

Light flooded the corridor and Willow had to keep a little scream from escaping her lips at the sight of the ironing board lying across the floor. A small chunk of wooden sideboard lay on the floor next to it. The cupboard door stood open. A gaping maw in the wall. It seemed to grin, mocking her.

Better get that over with first.

With every nerve on edge, she stepped into the corridor and around the ironing board. Dragging her eyes away from the dark hole of the cupboard, she picked it up and pushed it back inside. She didn't want to look. Didn't want to check out any part of the damn cupboard, but the leg of the board got caught on something on the floor.

Willow huffed.

Can this not just be easy? Really?

She leaned the board up the wall at the side of the cupboard and tentatively looked inside.

On the floor, something white caught her eye. She frowned and bent to pick it up. It was solid, but bore a small hole in the middle, almost like a polo mint. She turned it over. It looked like part of a board of some sort but was no bigger than a fifty pence piece in her palm. Paint one side, and wood the other - chipboard by the looks of it.

The hair on the back of her neck rose as she realised that this could only be from one place. Still kneeling, she looked up at the wall.

The hole that she had discovered a few days ago was still there, but now it was bigger.

She stood, and with her heart thumping wildly, Willow placed the piece in her hand over the hole.

Not perfect, but too close a fit to be a coincidence.

The feeling that something was watching her from the other side of the wall was overwhelming. Something with its eye to the small hole that she now had her fingers inside.

Then willow had another thought. One that almost sent her running from the house in terror.

The wood was on the floor of the cupboard, Wills. You know what that means, don't you? It was knocked out from the other side. Whatever is in here? It's in the walls.

Cold air blew across her fingers, and she stepped back with a strangled screech.

It's in the walls, Wills. There's something in the fucking WALLS. Oh shit. WHAT THE FUCK IS IN THE WALLS?

Then the calm voice, the same one from her head last night, was back. It was a voice she recognised as her own, but one that she hadn't heard in a very long time. A self-assured voice. One that had been suppressed for too long.

Put the ironing board back in the cupboard. Get a shower, go to McGracken House. While you're there, get some wood and some nails and block the fucker up. Nail it inside. Any thumps ignore until it breaks its way out of the cupboard door. At that point, get more wood and block it up again.

You've done so well here, Willow, you're just getting your life together. Do not let this fucker mess with your mind, since when did a thud and some smiley faces hurt anyone, anyway?

'Depends what's living in the walls, I guess,' she whispered. A nervous titter left her lips, unease following it up through her chest. She clamped a hand over her mouth before it turned into a full-blown scream she knew wouldn't stop for a long time.

Instead, she put the ironing board back over the hole, threw the wood piece into the cupboard, and shut the door. Then she grabbed new clothes and took a shower, pulling the curtain around her and closing her eyes against the mirrored glass.

She made McGracken House at 10.15am, but to be honest, if she had let her fear take over, she could have easily made it by 10am.

'Willow?'

Willow blinked and swung to Jack, who was staring at her, his eyebrows raised.

'What?' she said, pulling her fork from the soil. They were working in the second poly tunnel today, digging up parsnips and swedes.

Jack huffed a laugh and shook his head, both hands on the handle of his embedded fork. 'Three times I've asked you to dig the first row. You're too far forward. See the rope?'

Jack had been quiet this morning, more solemn and serious than usual. Willow had followed his lead, wondering if she was learning too slowly and he'd enjoyed his day alone yesterday. Her stomach rolled as she remembered Sophie telling her about the fights with Betsy. Had she been slow, too?

You're thinking too much, you're just tired and on edge.

'Oh, right,' she said, flushing as she stepped back. 'I'm so sorry, I don't know what... I was miles away. I'm sorry, it won't happen again. I'm sorry.'

Jack's smile slipped and a frown replaced the usual kindness on his face. He left his fork in the ground and stepped over the rows. Willow took a step back as he took the fork from her.

'Something's eating you today. What's the matter?' he said, stabbing the fork into the ground behind them. 'Did you have a good day yesterday?'

Willow looked down at her hands, struggling to find words that formed a coherent sentence.

'Yes. No. I mean, yes, I had a good day. I'm fine. I'm just tired, I didn't sleep well. I'm sorry. Don't be mad. I'll concentrate. I can do better, I promise.'

Jack's pale eyes narrowed, but now that he was closer, she saw they were kind as he assessed her. 'You don't need to do better. Where did that come from? Why on earth would I be mad at you?'

Willow gestured to the rows. 'I stood over everything and ruined it. I'm such an idiot. I'm sorry. I didn't mean it, I'm just tired. Maybe I shouldn't have come.'

The overwhelming events of the night before and findings of this morning crashed into her mind and her bottom lip wobbled.

Not now, Wills, Christ.

The tears spilled over regardless.

Jack stood for a moment, quite probably wondering why she was crying over a few stepped-on parsnip beds, and then he stepped forward and wrapped her in his arms. One hand stroked her back as she sobbed - actually sobbed - against the front of his coat. The more she sobbed, the more came, until she was sobbing for every sorry thing in her life.

'Okay. It's okay, princess. What's this all about?'

'Everything,' she mumbled into his coat. He hugged her tighter before pulling away and assessing her tear-stricken face.

He nodded and then grabbed her hand and pulled her toward the house. 'There's no one in there,' he said over his shoulder, 'don't worry. Helena and Mick are at the farmer's market twenty miles away, with some of the others. There's only me, you, and Warren here. Okay?'

He kept her hand firmly locked in his, and Willow jogged to keep up with his stride.

'Jack?' She sniffed. 'I'm okay, really. It's nothing. We should get the beds dug. I'm here to work.' She tugged on his hand. 'I'll be okay, really.'

Jack threw her a look of pure disdain, and Willow kept her mouth shut until they were inside the house.

He slammed the door shut behind them, rattling the framed embroidery on the wall, and making the baskets of dried herbs swing. Then he turned and pressed his back against the door, Willow's hand still firmly in his as she stood before him, trying to catch her breath.

He stared at her, his face stony, cheeks red, and a tremor ran through her. She didn't understand his anger, which had flared out of nowhere, but she knew it wasn't directed at her. She wanted to make him feel better, to step into his arms and remove the funny mood of the morning.

His face didn't indicate he was in a hugging mood, however, so she stood watching him instead. Uncertain. At least her tears seemed to have dried up for the moment.

Jack heaved a sigh, and she watched his Adam's apple bob as the fluttering in her stomach increased.

'Okay, first, you are absolutely not here just to work. You are neither bound here, nor do you have a contract. If you feel bad, or lost, or tired, or fed up, or even just want a rest. You say so and take it. No one is watching over you. Ever. Understood?'

Willow dropped her eyes and nodded.

Jack used his free hand to lift her chin gently.

'Got it?' he said.

'Yes,' she said, looking up into his eyes, which were glinting angrily. He took his hand away and her skin tingled where he had held it. Willow felt her heart banging against her ribs.

'Second,' he continued, 'I'm not mad at you for stepping on a bloody parsnip. Why in the hell would you think that? I'm not mad at you at all. I don't want or need to be. I enjoy being out there with you. Where in the hell would you get an idea like that?'

Willow chewed on her lip, because right now he did look pretty mad. She wondered whether to point that out, but decided against it as he continued his rant.

'Third? Yes, I am angry right now. I'm angry with the pussy-footing around in this house. It drives me batshit. Why is it that you can feel so bad, and look so...' he threw his free hand up at her, 'So miserable, and I can't ask why, and what I can do about it? How is it that you can turn up here for help, and yet you feel you can't talk to me, because I don't ask, because

I know there'll be a ton of crap with Helena if I so much as ask you if you took a shit this morning?'

Willow felt her lip wobble again, but this time it was different. She looked down as a grin began to spread across her face. She pulled her bottom lip into her mouth, trying her hardest not to laugh, and feeling the giggles rise, anyway.

'Don't laugh at me. I'm trying to be annoyed,' he said with an exasperated look. Willow looked up at him, giggles shaking her shoulders as she tried to hold them in.

'I'm sorry,' she spluttered as the laughter forced its way out with a snort. More followed uncontrollably, and she put her free hand on Jack's coat as she gasped for breath.

'It's not that funny,' he grumbled, but a smile was twitching the sides of his mouth as she laughed harder.

'Kind of is,' she gasped, and Jack shook his head with a grin.

'You certainly know how to ruin a moment, princess.' He pulled her into a brief hug and kissed the top of her head. 'Shall we have a brew? I think maybe we could both do with the break today.'

Willow looked up at him with a grin and nodded, glad she had washed her hair that morning. If this had been yesterday, it would have been a different story.

'Maybe we could both do with a chat, too,' she said, the scent of him lingering, bringing a sense of security, and a flush of warmth that told her she could never go home.

This was real caring, and this was safety. This was what it felt like when someone cared enough to have her back, and make sure that she was truly okay. Whether it was a good day or a bad, and whether they were allowed to, or not.

Despite what Carlton had already done, in that moment everything pivoted. She saw, really *saw*, what he had done, and how she had let herself be treated and she knew she could never go back to that again.

Thirty-Three

I T TOOK THREE OF Jack's 'brews' for Willow to get everything that happened with Carlton out, everything he had done, her mum, and why she was here. Now that she was listing it out to people, it shocked her just how much she hadn't been in control of her own life. She told him everything she had told Sophie about the surveillance, the watching over her, the limitations on what she could do and where she could go. Right down to the pills and his insistence that she would die if she so much as had a panic attack.

'I didn't know what they were, I didn't know what was happening, and I really thought I was dying each time I couldn't breathe.'

'Which only made things worse.'

'It did. It was all I ever thought about, which often brought on another, and made Carlton reassess the Prozac. I was in a constant terror cycle. I just didn't know it.'

'This Carlton, he's what, your husband? How was he getting his hands on the medication?'

Willow's stomach flipped. 'He's a psychiatrist, and no, we're not married. He's my boyfriend - partner - I suppose. Or was.'

'You broke up?'

'Not as such. I just can't go back after this. I don't know how things could ever be the same.'

Jack nodded slowly. 'Okay, I can understand that. Does he know?'

Willow shook her head and felt the tears well up again. How did everyone manage to make her feel like the bad guy for not talking to him?

'I can't talk to him. I don't want to yet, I can't take his lies at the moment, I'm not strong enough. I know I should-'

Jack reached across the table and squeezed her hand.

'Hey, hey, calm down. I'm not suggesting you should have done anything different; I'm just asking if he knows about all this. It's a question, that's all.'

'He doesn't even know where I am.'

'Okay. That was your mum's idea, you said?'

Willow nodded. 'She said that I should get away. Just take a break to work things out alone. She said she knew I'd under-stand from a distance. To be fair, I'm not sure she meant not to talk to him at all. That was my idea. He could talk me into believing I needed more, or that I couldn't cope with things. I had already questioned that myself. I had already tried to go out to the shops alone, but he would always ring and make me go home. I knew that would happen here, and I'd end up back there. Mum made me promise to try, and I felt like it was the one thing I had control of while my body and mind were letting me down.'

'It was a big ask, especially with what you were going through.'

'Mum knows me well, she also...' Willow took a breath. 'She also went through the same thing. It put us both there, but she was off the medication after five months. It concerned her I was still on it after four years and she questioned why I didn't seem to get any better. She knows people are different, but I'm her daughter, right? There were also things she had seen and heard that she didn't trust about Carlton. Things I didn't pick up on. That's why she pushed. She knew it was the only way I would understand, I think.'

Jack took his hand from hers, grabbed the cups, and rose to put them on the side. He stood, looking out of the window for a beat, and Willow wondered if she had said too much, but then he turned back to her.

'Where are you at now?' he said. 'You know what he was doing, but don't understand why? Where are you at with the Prozac?'

'That's exactly where I am, questioning my future. Carlton put the Prozac up again just before I got here. He said to message him for more when I ran out. He would send it, or bring it-'

Jack pursed his lips and heaved an agitated sigh, and Willow paused. She didn't understand why he was getting annoyed.

'Have you seen a doctor here?'

'No, I spoke to Tam. We ended up at the pub after yoga.'

Jack sighed and sat back down opposite her, clasping his fingers in front of him on the table. 'I bet that ended well,' he said with a wry smile.

'Well, I suppose it did. I had an attack and ran out. Tam told me exactly what they were, that I wouldn't die, and how to control them. I researched myself too. I'm getting better at dealing with them.'

Jack's hand found hers again and Willow felt warmth surge through her. 'You're doing really well with them. Admirably so, and I've never met anyone who wasn't scared and upset by them. That's a given.'

'I've spent too long being scared, Jack, I don't want to be that person anymore. I ditched the pills a couple of weeks ago. Not touched one since. Tam told me off, and then told me to come here when I refused to take a lower dose and come off it slowly.'

Jack's eyebrows pulled together.

'You've been okay?'

'Fine. A little sick, I suppose once or twice. I feel much better now, and the attacks are beginning to calm. I used to have to stand and breathe a few times a day. Yesterday, I didn't have a single attack.'

Jack nodded. 'Good. So, the anxiety hasn't worsened? No hallucinations, no dizziness, no sweats, no shortness of breath?'

Willow thought of the 'presence' up at the cottage, and a trickle of relief slid down her spine. She could have hallucinations? That explained a lot about her state of mind since being at Ivy Cottage.

'Not really. Sometimes shortness of breath, but that's usually when I get panicked,' she said, meeting his eyes.

'That's a panic attack, sweetheart. You must have a high toler-ance level. The Prozac couldn't have been doing much for you. Four years?'

He frowned as she nodded.

'Jack, if you want me to see a doctor, I will. I didn't know I needed to. I'm clueless, completely clueless.'

Jack smiled and squeezed her hand. 'I was thinking more about your boyfriend being a professional, and what he would make of that. But no, if you're doing well off them, we can try to deal with the rest here, and you have my number, you can call anytime, sweetheart. I'll help you as much as I can whenever you need me.'

He held her gaze as gently as her hand, and Willow felt her heart thumping as she nodded.

Did Carlton ever look out for you like this?

Not really. He was more smothering.

Suddenly Willow was eternally grateful that she had landed on this doorstep, here in this village.

'I will. Thank you, Jack.'

Jack stared at her. There were questions behind his eyes, but Willow was almost out of talking. She felt better, already, know-ing that people here had her back and were willing to help. Back in Bristol, all of her friends had eventually disappeared. She had thought that no one was bothered, but she knew now that Carlton could have been the one to push them away. Most likely he had.

But why? Why would he do this? I don't get it. I thought he loved me. He said he would do anything for me, anything to get me better. His life has been affected too. He couldn't have wanted to restrict himself so much, surely?

'What happened to you?' Jack said, breaking her from her thoughts.

She looked up at him with a frown. She had told him all she knew. 'How do you mean?'

Jack swallowed hard. 'What happened to you four years ago to put you on Prozac and give you an intense fear of enclosed spaces and people?'

Willow felt her chest constrict and a flush of panic rose into her cheeks. 'It was a long time ago,' she said, trying to veer him off.

'You don't have to say, but I'd really like to know,' he said quietly. 'I want to understand.'

The air became thick, so thick that she felt she couldn't breathe.

Except that you know it's just a panic attack and it can't hurt you.

She pulled in a few long breaths, calming her body's instant reaction as that self-assured voice came back into her head.

You need to talk about this. You won't die. It's just words, Willow, and it was a long time ago. It's ridiculous that in four years you've never spoken to anyone but your mum. Jack wants to know, speak to him. It's the only way to get this out and get over it. Talk about it.

Her chest stayed tight, and her stomach clenched, but the attack wasn't worsening yet. Jack took her other hand, and Willow clutched them both tightly for support.

'Steady, princess, take it easy. Don't feel pressured. You don't have to talk about it if you don't want to.'

Willow wondered how he read the signals so easily, and she nodded lightly.

'It was... It was my dad's birthday,' she said.

A flashback of her father's laughing face came to her as she carried the cake to him, a rendition of 'happy birthday' in her ears. The cake was complete with sixty-two candles - no cheating, Mum had said - and Willow had cursed her mother as she nearly burnt her hands lighting them all. Half of the candles had burned almost right down as she carried the cake to the table, the smiling bar staff clapping along next to her.

The only person missing was Carlton. He had declined to attend, said that he had work to do, and tried to tell Willow she shouldn't go either. She had been furious, telling him he was a selfish prick and that if she meant anything to him, he would be there. By the cake reveal, he still hadn't turned up and her blood had been boiling, but she kept her smile in place. For her dad.

'We were in a small pub, local. Lots of us. Family, friends. We were rammed onto four tables. Almost forty of us. Squashed.'

The heat of the room, and the closeness of the people who had come to celebrate, pressed against her shoulders.

'You couldn't move without bumping into someone. It wasn't supposed to be that busy, but more people came than we thought.'

Something crawled across her scalp, and she shuddered and swallowed. She felt the warmth as Jack cradled her hands gently. There was a small scar across his right knuckle, and it hit her just how little she knew about this man.

What are you doing? Her mind screamed, you have a boyfriend, why are you holding this near strangers' hands, and telling him the deepest parts of your life?

Willow looked back up at Jack. He held her gaze, steady, strong, giving her confidence. She calmed her breathing, pushing away the thoughts.

'Okay?' he asked.

Willow nodded and blew out a breath.

'Do you want to stop?'

'No,' she said.

I need to get this out or I may never speak of it again.

Jack dropped quiet with a nod and held her hands tighter, giving her strength.

'I thought I was going to set someone on fire, and I was worried about the cake.' Her breath caught, words choking in her throat.

Jack squeezed, and she breathed until she felt a little calmer.

'We hadn't finished the song, and dad was laughing, singing with us. Then there was a... a bang. Like a fire... like a firecracker, but loud. So loud.'

In her mind she saw Dad's face go from laughter to shock to terror. She watched it melt and morph before her as she stood with the burning cake in her hands, her mouth still singing happy birthday.

Sweat rolled down Willow's back as she was transported back in time. She could feel it on her lips, could taste the salt as her tongue darted between them.

'I couldn't see what was going on, it was behind me, but dad saw. He grabbed his chair as he stood, knocking grandma... I was... I was going to tell him off, to tell him he had hurt her, but... then the screaming started, and there was another bang.'

Willow closed her eyes and managed to put herself immediately back inside the room. It was hot, close, there was the smell of something burning, and a sharp metallic tang. Smoke rose from something next to her and she turned to look.

Willow snapped her eyes open. Everything seemed raw, and painful, and unstable. Her hands were almost thudding on the table as they shook, although Jack was holding them above the wood.

'Okay, princess, I think that may be enough. We can do this some other time. You need to calm down.'

But Willow shook her head. The anger, not only from that night, but from the years after, was sitting like something sour and bitter in her lower belly.

'No. I want to get this out.'

Jack looked concerned as sweat stung her eyes, and she blinked. He let go of her hands, which immediately went cool, and fetched a couple of tissues from the side. She dabbed at her eyes, and wiped her face, sitting with her head in her hands for a moment.

'I don't know-' Jack began above her, and Willow felt the anger spike. She brought her hands back to the table with a thump.

'Do you want to hear this or not? I don't know if there will be a next time, and I'm sick to death of trying to push this down, to keep it in, to pretend everything is fine, and I'm sick to death of people telling me what I'm capable of handling, are you getting that?'

'Loud and clear,' he said, his cheeks flushing as he sat back down. 'I'm listening, of course I am.'

Jack took her hands back in his and looked at her. 'I'm just worried-'

She cut him off. 'Don't be. I'm okay, and I'll stop when I'm not, but I need to get this out.'

'Still worried,' he said, his mouth lifting in a half smile, his eyes uncertain.

Willow nodded and held his hands tighter. 'I need to talk about this, Jack. I need you to trust me.'

'And that's why I'm listening, sweetheart. I do trust you. Just take your time.'

Willow nodded and pulled in a breath.

Focus, let's get this out. Pretend it's a story. Detach.

Willow pushed the images in her mind away and began to talk.

'There was a funny smell after the bangs, and then the man next to me disappeared. I mean, like I thought he had literally gone.' She flicked her fingers in the air. 'Poof. Like he was a magician, but then he knocked my legs and I saw he was on the floor. There was a hole in his back, and blood,' she swallowed, 'so much blood. It was steaming. The hole. I thought how strange that was. I don't know why.'

Her hands were shaking again, and Jack tightened his grip.

'There were so many people, they stepped on him, on the floor. I don't even know... I don't even know if he was dead, but they stamped on him, anyway. Fear, I suppose.'

She looked down at the table, as her eyes filled again, the emotion raw in her chest.

'Then I saw Dad. He was somehow on the other side of the room. There were two more bangs, screams so loud I thought my ears would burst, and then... air.' She frowned down at the table as a couple of tears let go. 'It was like people were literally sucked from the building. They just left. Saved themselves. I saw Mum in the corner under the table, hands over her ears, screaming – but I couldn't hear her. It was as though the sound muted for a moment. I looked for Dad. Two men were helping him wrestle someone to the ground, but there were more of them.'

Willow felt her entire being shake as her mind played the scene out with high-definition clarity.

The intruders came from three sides, all wielding guns, all wearing masks. The one that her dad had wrestled to the ground was still, with two men on top of him. There was another local man who threw himself at one of the remaining intruders and was shot. Willow saw him fall and finally lunged for a table herself. The cake flew, candles put out by the wind, she pre-sumed. She sat under the table as the three men advanced on her dad and the two that were holding the final intruder down.

There were the sounds of sirens in the distance, the smell of blood and faeces in the air.

'There were four men. Masked,' she stopped, shuddering as she breathed. Jack said nothing. He waited, staring at her hands, which he stroked gently with his thumbs. 'Dad and some men had one of them down. One of the others - blonde. He was blonde, I saw the hair sticking out of the bottom of his mask at the back - he shot someone, and then he aimed at Dad.'

Willow closed her eyes, and her tongue darted to moisten her dry lips. She saw herself run from under the table. All three intruders now had their backs to her, and to her right, one of dad's friends, Alan, was also running toward them. They locked eyes. She saw the terror in his, just as he must have seen it in hers, but they lunged together united in putting an end to this. Willow leapt onto the blonde intruder's back, sending him toppling forward and down.

'I... I ran. Knocked him down and he fired. I heard the ping of the bullet off the brass light. Alan had one of the other intruders. I saw dad grab the gun and shoot. I was glad. I remember feeling...' Willow cut off, trying to think of a word to explain. She frowned. 'Jubilant.'

She nodded, and Jack met her eyes. The sadness there almost knocked her guard, but she was on a roll.

Keep focused. Keep going.

'I was glad he was dead. So glad, but then there was another shot.'

Willow saw the gun fly from her dad's hands and land on the floor. The force of the shot propelling him back through four tables.

'Your dad?' Jack barely whispered.

Willow nodded, and a tear tracked down her cheek.

'He was knocked so far... he had broken ribs and a broken arm, but that didn't matter. He had a hole in his abdomen that seemed like it was the size of my fist, although... I... I'm sure that can't be right. I remember it vividly. The look of shock on his face, the blood that ran from his mouth, the way...'

'Willow, please,' Jack said, his voice catching. He squeezed her hands. 'I hear you, sweetheart.'

Willow felt more tears roll down her face.

'I was so mad, Jack. I was mad at Carlton for not coming to the party. I was mad that the place had been so full that we were like sitting ducks. I was mad at my dad for trying to be a hero and getting himself shot. I was mad at myself for not stopping the blonde man, although I could never have known. Two of the intruders were now down, Alan was tackling the blonde one with another member of the party, and... and then I saw the gun. I saw it there and I couldn't help it. I meant to kill him, Jack, I meant to kill them all for what they'd done. I did.'

Her voice shook and tears streamed down her face as she saw herself crawl toward the body of her father. She grabbed the gun, which she found out later was a machine gun, aimed it at the one intruder still standing and pulled the trigger. Even with all the spray, the kick of the gun ensured she missed, but the sirens were getting louder now. The blonde man punched Alan, knocking him down, and together the two attackers left standing fled, straight out of the front door onto the street.

'Did you kill him?' Jack said, hesitancy clouded his features.

Willow shook her head.

'I fired but missed. The two attackers left standing ran out of the front door and were caught by the police a few minutes later. Of the two inside the pub, one was dead by then, pummeled to death by another pub goer. Alan, who had helped me to help my dad, took the gun from my hands and shot the other man on the floor as he tried to get up. I still remember what he said, Jack, I'll never forget it.'

'What did he say?'

'He said, that's one less fucked-up fucker for us to have to deal with in the world. But I didn't want to have to deal with any fucked-up fuckers, Jack. I just wanted to go back ten minutes and be singing happy birthday to my dad, who was smiling and laughing and happy, until they walked in and changed it.'

Willow's chest hitched. The tears were coming fast now, and Jack handed her more tissue.

'I know, princess,' he said, 'I get it. Do you know why it happened? what they were there for?'

Willow sniffed.

'The police said it was an attempted armed robbery. They'd done a few around the area, apparently. One robs the till while the other three keep everyone in check on the floor. They take the money, thank everyone and go. The police said they just picked the wrong pub at the wrong time. They didn't realise there'd be so many people they couldn't get to the till. The report said that it was coincidental. They hadn't been planning on killing anyone, just taking the money. They just didn't expect the birthday party at midday on a Tuesday afternoon. The police said it caught them by surprise.'

Willow sniffed again and shook her head.

Jack heaved a sigh and sat back in his chair, finally letting go of her hands to rub his face.

'Was your mum okay?'

'No. She wasn't okay, none of us were okay, but she was unharmed, yes, and so was I. There were five people in that pub who walked in for a lunchtime pint, or the party, and never went home, Jack, that's how life can turn in an instant. They never made it home, and one of them was my dad - on his birthday.'

'Right,' Jack mumbled, and Willow snapped.

'That's it? That's all you have to say?'

'No, I don't *know* what to say. I'm sorry, I really am. That is one of the worst things I've heard someone go through and you obviously remember it all so vividly. There are just no words, that's all, sweetheart. I have no words that would make it any better. How could anything make that better?'

Willow looked down at the table, the fight gone out of her because he was right. No words would ever make it better.

'I think... I think you may be the bravest, and strongest person I've ever met,' he said. Willow looked up, expecting a joke that would break the tension, but his eyes were serious, his expression awed. 'Tomorrow there'll be no digging. Fuck McGracken House, tomorrow I want to show you something, if you're game?'

Willow wiped her eyes and nodded.

'Okay,' she said. 'I'd like that.'

Thirty-Four

C ARLTON WALKED BACK IN from the office on Sunday with a headache that wouldn't go away. He knew it wasn't only what he had allowed himself to do last night. It was the fighting Suzie and her insistence that they go out again later, that she came over, that he go over to hers, that they do *that* again. That they make the most of the year together.

It was the most amazing night of her life, she said. Carlton remembered it differently. A less spectacular, drunken fumble that had been great - don't get him wrong - but amazing wasn't quite the word he was looking for.

In fact, he had no idea what he was looking for, or why he had allowed it to happen.

She got to your emotions, she knows how to twist you, and she goes in until she gets what she wants.

'That you, bro?' a voice called from the living area.

Carlton put the files down on the small side table and then took off his coat and hung it in the tiny hallway, just the same as he always did, as though nothing had changed.

But everything had changed.

He had slept with Suzie. He had done the worst possible thing he could have to Willow, who was still out there struggling while he was getting his satisfaction, and now he couldn't take it back. He had paid for the ride with his conscience, and he would pay for a lot longer yet.

When Willow comes back, we'll move. I can sell the practice, sell this place, start up from home somewhere else. I don't need a secretary. In fact, Willow could do it with her hands tied behind her back. We'll work together, it will be perfect.

Carlton felt a flood of warmth as he took off his shoes and lined them up under his coat.

Yes, that's exactly what we'll do. Get away from here, away from Coop, away from Suzie, and we'll tell no one where we are. Willow can come off the pills. She'll get better, she'll be safe, and we'll live-

'Bro? I asked you a fucking question. It wasn't rocket science. I was checking you weren't an intruder, man, protecting the apartment?'

Coop was standing in the living room doorway, two beers in his hands. He offered one to Carlton, who frowned.

'Intruders don't usually possess keys,' Carlton said. 'That for me?'

Coop nodded with a grin. 'You're back earlier than I thought. I have a pizza in, we could maybe chill together, for old times' sake, if you're not going out, that is?'

Carlton sensed that something was off. Coop was being too friendly, too smiley, too... unusual. He took the beer anyway and moved to the living room.

Coop went into the kitchen, where the smell of cooking food emanated. There was a clang as the oven door was opened and then Coop was back in the doorway.

'Not out tonight, then?' he said.

'Why do you want me out?' Carlton said, sipping the beer.

'I don't. Man, you need to loosen up. I just thought we're living here together, and we haven't really chatted. A little catch up, you know? How's life going? How's things?' Coop grinned, his hands spread in front of him.

Carlton felt his stomach sink. He'd been seen then. Coop knew. Not that it could make him feel any worse than he already did.

'It was a mistake,' he said. 'It won't be happening again.'

Coop took a swig of beer with a grin.

'Shame, it looked fun. You should have some fun, bro, you work too hard. Office on a Sunday? Come on, man!'

Carlton felt his defences lower a little as Coop checked the oven again and Carlton sat on the chair and massaged his head with his fingers.

Coop brought in the pizza and gave half to Carlton on a plate. Literally. It was burnt, but he thought he could make out pepperoni. He took a bite anyway; it was like eating tough cardboard.

'Headache?' Coop said.

'Yeah, had it all day.'

'Heavy night last night, then?'

Carlton ran his hand over his face.

'Come on bro, tell me what's going on. It's good to talk, you should know.'

'Nothing. I drank too much and slept with my secretary. Now I feel pretty shit.'

Coop took a bite of pizza with a loud crunch.

'Bit overdone,' he said. 'Why do you feel like shit?'

Carlton stared at Coop.

'Because I slept with my secretary,' he said, his words pointed. He rolled his eyes and pushed the plate aside. The pain in his head was getting worse.

'So what? She's a stunner. She's quite possibly one of the only birds you've done that I'd do, too. I can't see-'

'You wouldn't,' Carlton said, slamming his hand on the arm of the chair. 'You wouldn't see because women are toys to you. You've never been in a long-term relationship!'

'Molly Kendrick. Three years.'

'School doesn't count. You were seventeen when you broke up.'

Coop laughed. 'Yeah, three years and she wouldn't put out. No point hanging on any longer.'

'She was a child. So were you.'

'Seventeen! can you believe I was dating for so long, and yet one of the last in my year to actually get laid?'

Coop laughed. Carlton sipped more of his beer. Why was Coop so jolly, and why was he being so nice?

'To reiterate, and to state a fact, you've never been in love,' he said.

'Never. Love is for pussies. Emotional blackmail a lot of it. I mean, look at you?'

'What do you mean, look at me?'

'All fucked up and miserable because you had a shag with a beautiful woman. Fuck me. We're meant to shag. It's what we're made for. We're not meant to stick to one person and never get our end over again. It's biologically and mentally insane. You did what humans are made to do, people are doing it every second, you're not going to die.'

Carlton felt his anger flare.

'I cheated! I cheated on Willow, not once, but four times, and not only that, but I didn't use protection, either.'

Coop waggled his fingers in front of his face. 'Ooooh. Bad boy. Willow isn't even here, bro. Get over it. Four times in a night, eh, you lucky bastard.'

Carlton stood, and Coop's smile fell away as he also stood in imitation.

'Willow will be back. You know that as well as I do, or you wouldn't even be here! I love her. She's ill, and I was weak.'

'She's not here!' Coop said opposite, his arms spread wide.

'It doesn't matter whether she's here or not-'

'Of course it does, you crank. Does Suzie have her number?'

'No, of course not,' Carlton said.

'So, who's going to tell her? Is she psychic? There's only us three know, bro, and I couldn't give a flying fuck. You know what I'd do?'

Carlton felt his anger diminish with a little relief. Coop was right. No one had access to Willow. If he made sure he never did it again, then maybe he could forget about it when the year was up. There was time to work this out. Maybe by the time she came back, Coop would have given up and Suzie would have forgotten.

'I have a feeling I already know,' he said.

'I'd have some fun while you can. Go fuck her. Willow will be back all too soon, then you can go back to boring-ville.'

Carlton sighed. Good job he had his own plan. Coop's was as failsafe as a speeding car with no brakes.

'I'm going to my room,' he said, 'but thanks for the pizza, and thanks for the chat. I think.'

'Anytime, bro,' Coop's smile was a little too wide. It put Carlton on edge.

As he walked up the stairs, he remembered something from last night. A small memory of walking in the dark to the toilet, and his phone lighting his way back to bed. He turned and went back downstairs.

Coop was sitting on the settee on his phone, a smile that said he was probably fixing his own shag date with a girl. He looked up, hiding the screen as Carlton came in through the doorway.

'What?' he said, a little too quickly.

'My phone was on last night,' Carlton said.

Coop shrugged. 'I had to piss. I saw you were in the bathroom and went outside. I stood on your phone, which was on the floor. Sorry about that.'

Carlton nodded. He had been in the bathroom, that was true.

'Okay,' he said and went back upstairs.

The bed smelled of Suzie. He stripped and remade it, leaving the pile of laundry in the corner, then he sat on the bed and checked his phone.

The locks were all in place, and everything looked normal. Even if Coop had got into the phone, Willow had taken herself off the tracking app before she left. He hadn't liked that bit of the deal, but now he thought it was the best thing she had ever done.

'Well done, babe.'

He flicked to a photo of her, fresh faced and beautiful, the summer before the attack, and his stomach lurched.

Freckles scattered her small nose, her sun lightened hair was tied back in a loose bun, strands had blown across her face, her deep brown eyes were bright and alive, and as wide as her smile.

'I'm so sorry, babe,' he whispered. 'I'll make it up to you, I promise.'

His chest ached. He turned face down on the bed and then he sobbed.

Thirty-Five

C OOP LISTENED TO HIS wimpy brother cry upstairs. Fuck knew he was an idiot. Willow wasn't a patch on the secretary, and what Carlton didn't know was that Willow wasn't coming home. By the time Coop had finished with her, she wouldn't be able to.

Oh well, I tried to tell him to have some fun, up to him if he wants to cry over nothing for a year. How are we even from the same fucking family?

He opened up the phone screen again and selected the photos he needed. Five, from different angles, just to make sure she got the gist.

He opened the message box.

You don't know me, but I think you should know who your boyfriend is fucking while you're away.

Coop stared at the message and rethought. If he could make it sound like a female, that may be better. He readjusted the text.

Hi, you don't know me, but I think you should know what your boyfriend is up to while you're away. If I were you, I wouldn't come home.

He stared at it again, scrubbed out the last line, because, hey, that wouldn't be an issue anyway, and readjusted again.

Hi, you don't know me, but I think you should know what your boyfriend is up to while you're away. I was cheated on. It sucks, us girls have to stick together. Message me if you need to talk.

Coop stared at it. Fuck, no, if she actually messaged with a sob story, he didn't think he'd be able to keep his shit together. He took the last line off.

Hopefully, the message itself would prompt a response.

Hi, you don't know me, but I think you should know what your boyfriend is up to while you're away. I was cheated on. It sucks, us girls have to stick together. Sorry to have to do this to you, but I would want to know.

The sentiment was good. It almost begged a response without asking directly. Much better. He added a heart emoji, because that's what girls did, didn't they? Then he added the photographs to the message.

He read it through once again, closed his eyes, and prayed that she would be thankful enough to answer this kind person with at least a simple thank you. Then he pressed send.

Thirty-Six

W ILLOW LEFT MCGRACKEN HOUSE just after four. It was dark, and the quiet seemed to echo around her as the cottage came into view up the little lane. She watched it watching her come home, and almost swore it grinned.

Then she remembered the cupboard.

'I forgot the boards and nails,' she said, slapping a hand to her head.

She half turned on the road, but she was more than halfway up the hill now, it would have to wait until tomorrow. She would sleep in the living area again tonight. There would be no more looking in that cupboard in the dead of night. Not a chance.

She assessed the dark windows as she neared. They looked back at her, impassive, but still somehow menacing.

She blew out her breath.

Look what you did today, Wills. If you can speak about the attack, then you can deal with a poxy cupboard rattling... thing! Just don't look.

She took a few more steps and then stopped. Something about the cottage looked wrong somehow.

She pulled her coat closer and stared.

Nothing moved, and nothing seemed out of place.

'You're not even getting to the cottage before you're seeing shadows now, Wills,' she whispered. 'How much more before you're classed as clinically insane?'

She smiled as she began to walk, keeping her eyes on the cottage.

Then her heart staggered to a halt. There was movement. Movement on the roof.

The thing looked flat as it crawled up the slope of the tiles to the ridge, made its way across the top, and disappeared down the back slope.

Willow blinked.

What in the name of holy God was that?

She kept walking slowly, wanting to find out what it was, whilst simultaneously wanting to run as far from the place as she possibly could.

It had looked like a cross between a huge spider and an ape. Four legged, definitely more ape. Were there monkeys in the forest? Because that was the only thing she could put it down to right now.

She reached the foot of the driveway and paused.

There was no movement, and no sounds from the foliage. Whatever it was, it had probably gone by now.

At least the house is locked up. It's outside. Definitely a curtains closed job tonight, I don't want that staring in the windows.

Willow entered the house quickly, locking the door behind her, and feeling a flood of relief.

Safe from the thing outside.

There was nothing in the hallway waiting for her, either. A good sign. She focused on the living room door, keeping her eyes off the cupboard as she passed and went into the kitchen to make something to eat. She ate and drank with the television on, but she wasn't really watching. She was thinking about Jack, and where he would take her tomorrow. He hadn't told her much more, just that she was to meet him at the corner of the bridge at 10am tomorrow, and to wear good shoes and wrap up warm.

She presumed that meant walking, and there was certainly plenty of it around here. It would be nice to get out into the hills again. She had been enjoying the walks since she got here and had loved the exertion of the walk with Sophie yesterday. She was also looking forward to spending the day with Jack outside of McGracken House.

Jack had been an angel over the rest of the day at the house, and they had chatted long after Willow had told her story. He had told her some stories about the house and the things that had happened there. He made her laugh, made her feel comfortable, brought her mood back up with his ability to tell a good story, and took care of lunch for them.

That afternoon, they had gone back to digging the first row of parsnips. He had jibed her for getting off track that morning, more gently than usual, but she had enjoyed the giggles either way. Finally, he walked her back to the bridge when the day was over.

Willow smiled as she chewed the last of the 'one pot' casserole, it's spicy flavour and chunks of beef warming her to the pit of her stomach - or maybe that was the thought of Jack.

The way he'd hung around a little too long until Willow had laughed and shooed him back to the house. The way he'd asked if she would be okay for the hundredth time and told her to ring if she needed him.

She shook her head with a grin, before taking her plate out, disposing of the carton in the rubbish, and flicking on the kettle. On the table, her phone pinged, and she walked back through to get it. She swiped it open where she stood, the light of the corridor mocking her peripheral vision as she looked at the screen.

It was from an unknown number.

Hi, you don't know me...

Willow frowned.

Then why message?

She felt her blood run cold.

Has something happened to Carlton?

Her stomach lurched, and she quickly opened the message.

Hi, you don't know me, but I think you should know what your boyfriend is up to while you're away. I was cheated on. It sucks, us girls have to stick together. Sorry to have to do this to you, but I would want to know.

Willow blinked and read the message through again, the words not really sinking in. Boyfriend, cheated, sorry, want to know.

What?

The message didn't seem to make any sense, and then she realized that photographs followed it.

Her heart in her mouth, she opened the pictures and felt the room spin in disbelief.

The first photo only showed close up limbs and genitalia. The woman's could have belonged to anyone, but the penis was most certainly Carlton. The mole that sat above the nest of hair gave that away instantly.

Willow immediately began to rationalise.

Well, he may be naked next to a naked woman, but they're not actually doing anything. He's not even hard.

She flicked to the next photo, which had zoomed out a little. A slightly different angle showed their intertwined legs, the woman's large breasts, and Carlton's arm slung around her naked waist.

Bile rose in her throat as her heart pounded her ears.

What the hell is this? A set up?

She flicked to the third photograph, which showed a room in dishevelment. Clothes spread over the floor, neon pink underwear. It showed two people in a rush to get undressed, which was disturbing enough, but then Willow saw the lamp on the floor.

Her lamp.

She looked closer at the photograph, and a strange whimper left her throat. This was their apartment - her apartment - her room, her *bed.*

My fucking bed? Why is there a woman in my fucking bed?

Blood roared past her ears as she felt her cheeks get hot and her breath get ragged.

The fourth photograph showed what she already knew. Carlton, asleep. Naked. Next to this woman with a voluptuous body and short, dark hair.

I'm none of those things, she thought erratically. I'm blonde, not as curvy, smaller boobs, longer hair.

She flicked to the fifth photo and stared.

Suzanne.

It was Suzanne from the office.

In her bed.

With her boyfriend.

Who was obviously missing her terribly.

Willow slammed the phone onto the table as she began to heave, getting to the toilet just before she threw up.

Sophie made two cups of coffee and took them back to the settee, where Willow was staring at the photographs through a blur of tears.

'Come on, now,' Sophie said, placing the cups on the coffee table, sitting next to her, and taking the phone from her hands.

'I can't believe he'd do this, Soph. I feel like it's a setup. It has to be a setup, right?'

'Well,' Sophie scrunched her face, 'I don't see how. I mean, what did they do? Drug them both, undress them, place them in your bed and take some photos?'

'It's possible, isn't it?'

Sophie shook her head slowly. 'I don't think so, Wills. I'm sorry, I just don't. The photos speak for themselves, don't they? And if Carlton woke up like this, you don't think he'd be straight on the phone to tell you this may be coming, and that it was all a joke?'

'He did contact. I didn't call him back, remember?'

'About the pills, aye. He didn't mention anything about this.'

'He asked me to call,' Willow said. Her bottom lip was wobbling so hard she could barely talk.

'He did, but you didn't call back. In this situation, if he really cared, there'd have been more, Wills. More calls, more messages, wouldn't there? He'd have been desperate.'

'Maybe he doesn't know?'

Sophie heaved a sigh. 'Then we're back to square one. The phone call wasn't about that, and if it were a joke, I'm sure they'd let him in on it, right? It's no joke if the participants don't know.'

'It was her,' Willow said. 'She's done this on purpose, that's why he doesn't know. She's trying to break us up. She's always had a thing for him. I used to think it was funny.'

Willow huffed a wry laugh and swiped at the tears that were rolling down her cheeks and dripping from her chin.

So much crying. All the time.

Sophie took a sip of coffee and sat quietly, which was wholly unlike her new friend. Willow looked at her.

'Soph?'

'Wills, I know this is hard, but you have to take this for what it is. He cheated, and someone was good enough to let you know. I'd be thanking them and getting on with my life. In all honesty, this Carlton sounds like a prick, and now you have the evidence that he's acting like one, too.'

Willow felt a stab of hurt run through her.

'He's not so bad, Soph, he's a nice guy-'

'Aye, he seems it,' she said, sarcasm unchecked. 'What sort of boyfriend does all he has done to you, and then sleeps with his secretary the moment you're out of the room? For fuck's sake, Wills, you've barely been gone a month.'

Willow reached for her phone, and Sophie pulled her arm away.

'No amount of torturing yourself with photos and trying to make sense of them is going to make it better. He shagged the secretary, end of. He's a prick.'

'I just think, maybe that-'

'What? She accidentally fell into your bed naked and he landed naked next to her? Happens all the time, I know.'

'No.' Willow's chest ached and her stomach hurt. 'There has to be another explanation. He loves me.'

Sophie shook her head and handed Willow her coffee. Willow sipped, but the liquid seemed to sit on top of the bile that was waiting there. Her stomach churned, and she felt a wave of nausea.

'I think I'm going to be sick,' she said.

Sophie followed her to the bathroom, holding her hair back and rubbing a hand on her back, as she vomited violently.

When she had finished, the tremors that ran through her body were so strong that Sophie almost had to carry her back into the living area. She lay her head on the arm of the settee and asked Sophie to put the television on. Anything for a distraction.

Sophie fetched a couple of blankets, flicked the remote, and grabbed some biscuits from the kitchen as Willow lapsed into silence. Then she stretched an arm to hold on to Willow's hand as she sat by her feet.

Willow barely felt it as her thoughts whirled.

How could he do this?

She thought back through the years that they had been together. She didn't know Suzanne, had only seen her a handful of times over the eight years since he had started his practice. Each time, though, there had been something between them. She had sensed it, but had thought it was one-sided.

He did humour her a lot, though, and when she was around, he touched her a lot. On her arms, the small of her back, the head, the hands. Willow had thought it was Carlton being nice, but now she thought about it, had he done that with anyone else?

Not that she could remember.

And what about the Christmas party, where Suzanne had got so drunk Carlton had physically escorted her home? Willow had been left at the roadside to go home alone while they got into a taxi for the five hundred yards back to Suzanne's house. Willow had waited up for him for two hours, although Suzanne's house was only a fifteen-minute walk from their apartment. He had said that Suzanne was very sick, but now she wondered. Two hours?

There were also all the evenings that he had to work late over the last few years. He had blamed Willow, saying that his patients had to be rescheduled late each time he had to attend to her during the day. Of course he wanted to be there for her, she was ill, and it wasn't her fault, but sacrifices had to be made. He had a business with clients to see.

Or was it Suzanne he wanted to see? How long had this been going on?

Tears of anger and disbelief rolled down her face.

He had drugged her, kept her inside, controlled her movements, watched her, tracked her... and didn't that just make it easier for him? Easier for him to have his cake and eat it? Was the attack just a perfect excuse?

Willow closed her eyes.

Why not just let me go? Why cheat?

The attack.

Maybe he was going to, but the attack happened, and he couldn't do that to you?

So, he drugged me instead?

Whichever way Willow turned it, it seemed ridiculous to go to those lengths. It didn't make sense, but there was one thing that she couldn't deny.

She saw them laughing together at the bar at the party, his hand on the small of her back, waving his hand at her as he paid for her drinks.

She saw them at the office when she popped in. Suzanne leaning over his desk, her hand brushing his.

Pain crossed Willow's chest.

'He's been sleeping with her behind my back, hasn't he Soph?' she said.

Sophie looked at her from the documentary on the television. She nodded. No kid gloves with Sophie, just exactly what she thought, no sugar-coating the bitterness. Willow appreciated her directness.

'Aye, I'd say so, Wills.'

Sophie gave her a sad smile, and Willow closed her eyes.

'Probably for years,' she said.

'Almost certainly once. There's no denying that,' Sophie agreed.

Willow nodded. She didn't need to look at the phone to see the pictures run through her mind.

The casual, relaxed faces of sleep, their limbs locked together, her hand up by his face, his arm over her naked waist.

Comfortable.

They looked comfortable.

Certainly, more than once.

Willow closed her eyes as more tears fell.

When she opened her eyes it was almost light, that kind of dull dawn light that makes everything seem surreal and dreamlike.

Her head ached and her throat was sore. She half wondered if she was ill, and then the images came back.

No. It was a dream, wasn't it? Carlton would never cheat. That's ridiculous, he loves me. Must have been a dream, it had to be, stupid head.

Willow felt relief surge through her. There had been no noises from the cupboard either, she thought.

Maybe I'm running a fever.

She sat up, and caught sight of Sophie, asleep next to her, her mouth open as her head leaned back against the settee.

Her stomach plummeted, and the world looked a little greyer.

Willow glanced at her phone.

It was real, wasn't it?

She clenched her jaw and dragged her eyes away, decided against torturing herself again, and moved slowly off the chair, trying not to wake her friend. Her body felt heavy and tired, her limbs ached, and her chest and throat were sore. She went to the kitchen.

Coffee. Strong coffee was what she needed. She flicked the kettle as she moved stiffly into the bathroom.

Why do I feel like I've gone ten rounds in a boxing ring?

She checked her puffy face and bloodshot eyes in the mirror, splashed her face with water, and dried herself with the towel.

In the kitchen, the kettle clicked off and Willow got two cups from the cupboard. She placed them on the side and reached to get the coffee. Her eyes landed on the window. The condensation. The face.

Her heart stuttered and stalled.

The face was sad, and this one's message was clear. One word.

HELP.

Willow felt her stomach flip, and then she smiled. The faces had never been anything more than that. A picture and a word. It wasn't like the terror of the cupboard, or the figure in the corridor. The face she could deal with.

'I can't even help myself,' she said. 'I'm sorry.'

'Who are you talking to, Wills?' Sophie said through a yawn. Willow turned and saw her get up from the settee. She grabbed the tea towel and wiped the message from the window as her friend joined her in the kitchen.

'Myself,' she said.

'First sign of madness,' they finished together, and then Sophie grinned as willow gave a humourless laugh and handed her the coffee.

'How are you feeling?' Sophie said, taking a sip.

Willow shrugged. 'Fabulous.'

Sophie pursed her lips, and Willow was suddenly glad she was here, suddenly glad that she had stayed when she hadn't been asked to, glad that she had been over just minutes after Willow had called yesterday.

'Thank you, Soph, just for being here,' she said.

'It's not a problem. You're going through shit, and I'm here for you.' She looked at her watch. 'I have *got* to work in about an hour, though. Deadline to hit. Are you going to be okay?'

Willow shrugged. 'Yeah, what can I do about it, anyway?'

'Are you at McGracken House today?'

Willow nodded, and then she remembered. 'Oh, no. I'm meeting Jack. He's taking me somewhere. He didn't say where, just that I needed good shoes and warm clothes.'

To be honest, she didn't feel like meeting anybody, even Jack. She didn't feel like facing the world at all.

'Jack's taking you out?' Sophie frowned.

'No, not out, just somewhere he wanted to show me. I don't think I'm going to go, anyway. I need some time to work this out.'

'Good,' Sophie said, a little too quickly, 'Do you want me to tell him for you?'

'No, it's fine. I'll tell him myself later, we weren't meeting until ten.'

Sophie smiled.

'Don't be silly, I'm as good as passing. I'll let him know, then you don't have to go out at all if you don't want to.'

'I can message him, Soph. I don't want to put you out.'

'Okay,' she said lightly, and then she paused. 'You have his number?' she said carefully.

Willow nodded, and her stomach dropped as Sophie stared at her.

Oh shit, I'm not supposed to have his number. No ties, no questions. Leave well alone.

She felt a flush run into her cheeks.

'It's just because of the panic attacks, Soph, they've been quite bad since I stopped the pills. Jack has been helping me through them. He said if I ever needed help outside of McGracken House to message him. That's all it is.'

Sophie held up her hands.

'You don't have to explain. I'm not saying anything,' she said, averting her eyes. 'Nothing to do with me.'

Willow felt a little off balance from the conversation - not that she had been balanced before it.

Sophie finished her coffee at the counter and smiled. 'Well, I'll be away, got to shower and change yet, but I'll be back after dinner, okay, just to check in.'

Willow smiled. 'Thank you, I owe you one.'

'Don't be daft,' she said, heading for the doors.

Willow unlocked the glass door and then stood by the front door, watching as Sophie stepped out and pulled her coat around her.

'Take it easy today.'

Willow shivered, watching as Sophie walked away.

'Thanks so much, Soph.'

Sophie waved without turning. 'Aye, see you later.' Then she stopped and did turn. Willow frowned.

'By the way,' Sophie said, 'you were right about that cupboard. It was banging away last night, but there was nothing inside. You need to fix the wall, though. There's a pretty large hole, it's letting in a lot of air. I think that's why the place is so cold.'

Willow felt her smile slip.

Tell me something I don't know.

'Okay, I'll take a look later.'

Sophie nodded and left, leaving Willow alone with Ivy Cottage and its noisy, condensation writing, inhabitant.

Thirty-Seven

W ILLOW MESSAGED JACK AS soon as she got back inside. At 8am it seemed late enough that he would be up, but early enough to stop him from making more plans. It was a simple message saying that she had woken up feeling ill, which wasn't so far from the truth, but he answered immediately.

Okay, princess, no problem. Do you need anything? I can stop by the shop for you if you like?

Willow felt both warmed that he had offered, and guilty that she had lied and had mucked his day about. She felt her cheeks colour as she messaged back.

I have everything I need, but thank you for the offer. Hopefully, I'll see you tomorrow.

A good few minutes passed, and she wasn't sure he was actually going to answer. It wasn't like she had asked a question either way, but then a reply came through.

I hope so. You'd tell me if you were feeling bad about yesterday, wouldn't you? If you're anxious, let me help you. You've been through so much. If you don't want to come out with me today, don't be afraid to say so, I'm a big boy. You don't have to come; it was just an idea.

Willow smiled.

If only you knew the real reason I was feeling bad, and it has absolutely nothing to do with you, Jack, that's for sure.

She sighed, thinking how she could word the message to make him feel better.

I'm just under the weather, I promise. I'm not anxious. Talking to you really helped yesterday, and I've been feeling a lot better in that sense.

Of course I want to go with you, I'm excited to see where we're going! I'll make you a deal - promise me we'll go when I'm better, and I promise I will call if I feel I need help.

She grinned as a message came straight back.

It's a deal! I'll message later and see how you are. Helena is back today, and I have to be a little careful so I won't give you a time, but I will be in touch. I promise. If you need anything, just yell.

There was a noise from the corridor - a new sound, like a squeak, as she messaged back.

I will. Thank you for looking after me.

She peered around the kitchen door into the corridor as the phone pinged again.

Anytime, princess. Always here for you.

Willow smiled and warmth flooded her cheeks. She wondered where she would be now if Carlton had just treated her more like Jack instead of feeding her pills...

...and sleeping with the secretary.

Her smile faltered at the thought, and then fell altogether as she saw that the door to the cupboard in the hallway was open. No thuds this time, just the squeak of the door.

Shit, I could do with some wood to block the door off. Why didn't I remember yesterday?

What's done is done. I'll just go out. I can't stay here.

She managed half a bowl of cereal before her stomach turned, so she grabbed a couple of breakfast bars and a bottle of water and put them into a backpack.

She pulled on her coat and boots in the porch, hitched the bag on her back, and left through the front door.

'Bang as much as you want. I'm not bothered,' she shouted as she walked down the drive and turned up the track to the woods.

As she settled into the walk, she thought of how well yesterday had gone - she had spoken about everything to someone other than Carlton, or her mum, and she had managed. She hadn't cracked, or died, or burst into flames. She had been upset, of course, but it had been liberating.

It was amazing just how liberating living here was, allowing her to do all the things that she had thought she couldn't in Bristol. Talking about the attack was one of the major things - but she had done it. Alone.

And then she thought of how the day had turned so dramatically that it couldn't have been written. She had so much to process with Carlton and this latest revelation, and she still wasn't sure that she even believed it.

He had been so supportive... and yet the evidence was clear for all to see.

Wasn't it?

Willow took a breath, pushing the thoughts away. The air was crisp and the day clear. She kept a brisk pace, watching her breath pump before her in the cold. She saw no one, and expected to see no one, but she knew where she was heading.

Her namesake. The Willow.

She had to think, and the solitude of the tree was more accommodating than Ivy Cottage and its restless tenant.

She pulled out her phone and flicked open her messages. The photographs were still there, just as she remembered them, although this time they weren't such a shock. She flicked through them, landing on the last one.

Suzanne, content, asleep.

After sex with my boyfriend.

Willow flicked back to Carlton's face.

She looked at the fall of his shoulders, the slope of his hips, his hairline, eyebrows, and nose. All so familiar, and yet now so unfamiliar.

Had he really kissed Suzanne with that mouth?

Willow felt the anger rise from the depths of her soul.

How dare he. How fucking dare he.

Another voice, the calmer Willow, her rational self, protested.

How easy does this make it for you to confront him and listen to his lies properly now? Call him, see if he denies it. He will, and then you can dump him on his ass and move on.

But how dare he? How dare he put me through all of this, and then he gets to cheat and call the shots? I don't even get to work this out and kick him where it hurts?

Leave it Wills, just message him, tell him it's over and move on.

My fucking stuff is there! My stuff that he has knocked all around the room and goodness knows where else. It's my apartment!

Rational Willow laughed.

Try telling that to a court of law when the place is in his name.

Willow gave a grunt of frustration, kicking at a stone on the path as she stomped past.

It's mine! He's taken my life for the last four years, and now he gets to take my stuff too? My whole life is there – just as I wanted to live it. He joined me! I didn't ask him to move in.

Willow pulled her lips between her teeth as she thought of the way he had maneuvered himself into her life. He had stayed over once a week, and then all weekend, and then half a week until finally she had laughed and told him to bring his stuff.

He had done so that very afternoon, nearly ten years ago to the month.

You wanted it too.

She nodded as she focused on the path ahead. She had, but then, she wasn't the one cheating now, was she?

Spineless prick.

Willow was back to the rolling anger.

How dare he. How dare he do this and not let me break him first.

It doesn't matter, it will be easier now. You wouldn't have enjoyed breaking him.

It does matter. I wasn't going back anyway, but I was sparing his feelings.

Sparing his fucking feelings by not contacting him and asking him to explain himself. By giving him the benefit of the doubt, by thinking the best of him, not the worst. By not wanting to hurt him, although it would have been inevitable, eventually.

She gave a harsh laugh as she stomped out into the clearing. The trees flanked her right as the open hills dropped away to her left, and the vastness of space poured into her, fuelling her anger.

He won't get hurt now, will he? I will just give him an excuse to live the free life he always wanted to with Suzanne. Even if I didn't mention the photographs and just called it off, he would be silently punching the air with glee, wouldn't he?

I'm going to give him an escape, and he will get away guilt free.

Willow found the tiny path in the bracken that led to the loch and the tree sitting very much alone.

She felt the tears well up. She'd never felt more alone, either.

Weeping Willow. Always.

Tears blurred her vision as she reached the valley, and by the time she got to the tree, she was sobbing. She placed a hand on the bark and let out a scream of pain and frustration. And then she did it again, and again. Louder, and louder, and louder, until she had screamed herself hoarse.

Three hours later, weary with grief and cold, Willow sat watching the wind scoot across the water of the loch, knowing she should get back before she caught a chill. She was shivering hard, her hands and feet frozen, and her legs numb, but couldn't find the will to move. The Willow and it's comfort had sapped all of her tears, and all of her strength, there was nothing left in her to give.

Carlton was no more. She could never go back now. It was over. She didn't know whether she should text him, or call him, or just leave him hanging indefinitely. Preferably whichever hurt him the most, and she had to think about which one that was.

Maybe she would even turn up in person and cut his balls off.

She was so lost in thought that she barely heard the ping of her phone. She frowned and pulled it from her pocket.

If this is Carlton, I'll–

How are you feeling, princess?

Willow felt an unprecedented barrage of tears hit her again. How was it that someone she had just met could be so kind, and yet the man she had loved for ten years could turn his back with no thought?

Shit.

She pressed send and immediately regretted it.

Stupid. You're being stupid. This is not Jack's fault, or Sophie's. You need to be careful with your anger. What do you want to achieve by sending that?

Shit as in you need help? Or shit as in sick?

Shit as in my boyfriend is a dick?

She was still thinking what to type when the phone rang. She frowned.

Jack.

She toyed with not answering; she didn't know how normal she could be, but she knew she would just worry him if she didn't pick up.

'Hi,' she said. 'Sorry, that was uncalled for, I didn't mean to worry you. I was trying to think how else to put it... but, here you are.'

'How else would you put it? Because you're worrying the hell out of me today, princess.'

'I'm fine. I'm sorry,' she whispered. Her lips quivered, and she sat on the verge of losing control again. She took a breath and rolled her eyes at her own selfishness.

Can you stop taking things out on other people? Jack has enough to do, as does Sophie.

'Where are you? At home?'

'No.'

'Where?'

'I took a walk in the woods. I needed to think. I found a willow tree - out here - can you believe that? I'm okay. Really, Jack. Don't worry about me.'

'So, what was the shit about?' he said. 'Why are you feeling shit? talk to me.'

Willow hesitated. 'I wouldn't know where to start.'

There was rustling on the other end of the phone, and then echoing.

'Start,' he said. 'You're on speaker so I can keep going, there's no one around me, I promise.'

Willow felt a pain cross her chest, and she shivered in the cold air.

'I just had a bad night last night. I didn't sleep well.'

'Because of what we spoke about?' There was a clang. Jack was obviously working as she spoke. She felt guilt crawl up her spine.

'No, I promise that made me feel better. I've never spoken to anyone about that before. I didn't think I could.'

She stared out across the loch, the wind-scurried current reflected the sunlight in a myriad of broken reflections.

'So, what is it then?'

Willow stared, the ripples catching her tired eyes and mind in a hypnotic daze. She felt she could sleep for a million years.

'Willow? Princess, talk to me.' There was snapping and another clang and the guilt intensified. Jack was working, he didn't need this.

'I can't,' she said. 'You're busy Jack, and it doesn't matter. I'll be fine. I'm sorry I worried you.'

'Willow, if this matters to you, then it matters to me. Anything here can wait, you're more important. There's obviously something very wrong. Speak to me.'

Willow took a shuddering breath and let out a sob that she couldn't hold back.

'I had some photos sent to my phone yesterday evening.'

'Okay.'

'They were bad, Jack,' she whispered.

'I can't hear you, princess.'

There was a rustling, and Willow rolled her eyes.

Well just stop working and listen.

She got up with a sigh, stamping some life into her feet before walking from under the tree's branches to catch the warmth of the sun. Any warmth she could get. She was shuddering, but she had no idea if it was the photos or the cold.

'I said they were bad. They were... oh God, I don't want to say it.'

'Just say it. Get it out.'

'Carlton. It was my boyfriend and a woman. He... he's sleeping with his secretary.'

'Ah.'

'It's not even like I care. I wasn't going back either way, but I wanted to be the one to hurt him, Jack. He wasn't supposed to get to hurt me first after all he's done.'

'That's shitty sweetheart, and I understand how you feel, but you can't make it about who hurts who, it'll drive you insane. So, the photos were of...'

'The two of them... in bed.'

She was shaking and crying now. She looked up at the sun. Her chest hurt, her back hurt, her legs hurt. Everything hurt.

Jack huffed.

'Who the hell would send you shit like that? Carlton?'

'No, it was a number I... I didn't recognise. Some girl... I don't...' she couldn't finish, and it didn't matter anyway. Her chest lurched and the landscape seemed to tilt before coming right again.

'All right. Willow, it's all right, we can sort this out, don't worry.'

The sunlight on the loch was too bright, the ground too hard, the wind too loud in the trees, the rustle of the foliage like gunfire. She shuddered as a trickle of fear ran down her spine and she suddenly wished she was back at the cottage, in the warmth.

'Willow? You've gone quiet, keep talking to me. Are you okay? Can you hear me?'

'Yes. I'm so cold, Jack, I should get back.' She closed her eyes, her chest heavy. 'I need to go.'

'No. Princess, stay with me, and keep talking. Can you do that?'

The world tilted and Willow snapped her eyes open, fear jolting through her.

I need to get back.

Everything was so bright, so loud, and so cold. She wanted to get home, but her feet didn't want to move, and her numb brain couldn't seem to make them.

'Willow?'

'I'm so tired, Jack. So tired of fighting everything. I don't even know how I'm going to get home, I don't even know where home is any more. Everything is fucked up, and I don't know what to do.'

She shuddered, and the phone slipped from her frozen fingers. She stared at it, wondering if she could find the will to pick it up.

Somehow, Jack was still speaking to her, anyway, his breath huffing.

'All right. It's okay, princess, we'll work it out. We need to get you home.'

Willow frowned, wondering if she was imagining the entire conversation, and then she felt a hand on her shoulder and turned.

She just had time to notice how his cheeks were ruddy from the biting wind, and how his green padded jacket brought out the green of his eyes, and then he pulled her into him. Willow clung to him as he held her tightly, encompassing her in warmth, and her only thought was how she never wanted him to let her go.

'Jack, how are you here? How did you find me?' she whimpered against his coat.

'I'll always find you, Willow. Whenever you need me. I told you that,' he murmured into her hair, holding her tight as she found more tears to cry.

Thirty-Eight

C ARLTON TOOK THE DAY off on Monday, and he intended to on Tuesday as well... and maybe the rest of the week. He felt like a family member had died. Knocked sideways and off kilter.

He didn't bother to shave, didn't bother to dress, and didn't bother to answer Suzie's barrage of messages asking if he was okay. He didn't even bother getting out of bed until one in the afternoon. There was just one person he needed to hear from, and she still hadn't responded to his message.

Now he had only one mission, and he didn't intend to go to work until he had completed it in any way he could. Get rid of Coop, find Willow, and keep her safe somewhere they would never be found. Somewhere away from all of this shit, somewhere he could live happily ever after, appreciating how much he loved her with no more stupid mistakes. He would never look at another woman again.

He had underestimated just how serious it was that Coop was out of jail. Not only had he been writing prescriptions for his brother, but he had put them in his own name, Willow's name, Suzie's name, and a false name, too. And still his brother asked for more.

Carlton never saw Coop high, even with all the pills, which meant that he was dealing. In turn, that meant that Carlton was supplying with intent.

If he was caught, he would be in a whole heap of shit that would land him in jail and ensure that he never worked again.

To top it off, Coop had been moody and snappy all day yesterday, and with all the banging around downstairs, he had clearly woken up in the same mood today.

Carlton rolled his eyes.

He had known it would slip. Living side by side like best buddy brothers would never work. They were chalk and cheese, and now Carlton wanted his brother out, before he broke everything that was his and Willow's.

Carlton was halfway down the stairs when he heard the low, urgent talking. He stopped on the bottom step, hidden from view, and put his ear to the wall.

'...Radar, I'm asking for one fucking favour. One. I don't need to see you, and if you like, I won't speak to you ever again. Please.'

There was silence while Coop listened, and Carlton registered the name. Radar had been a part of Coop's gang.

Absolutely no chance of going straight then. Carlton almost laughed.

Of course there wasn't. They were probably discussing their drug ring.

And, even funnier, you're their supplier.

Carlton closed his eyes and ran a hand over his face.

I need to get rid of him. He hasn't mentioned...

His thoughts stopped in their tracks, his hand still on his cheek as he listened.

'No, she hasn't,' Coop said from the living room, 'But I'm close.'

There was another pause, then his voice rose.

'Carlton doesn't know shit. I'm not that stupid. He'd be in contact and fucking scare her off.'

More silence, the smell of toast, and then a plate banged so hard Carlton thought it was a miracle it didn't break.

'So that's it?'

Another bang, and the slamming of a drawer.

'Never. I will never fucking leave it.' He lowered his voice. 'Just because you're too fucking straight to follow through now. The bitch killed Bugs. When I get him justice, maybe I'll retire. Or maybe I'll just continue as I am and live in a fucking tax-free mansion somewhere while you sit in your shitty council house. I can't believe they meant nothing to you.'

There was the scraping of a knife on toast as it was buttered. Carlton's heart was thudding in his chest. He had been lapse thinking that Coop was waiting for Willow. Of course he wasn't waiting, he would never wait, he would pursue until he got what he wanted.

Revenge.

And revenge was not something you wanted to be on the other end of with Coop.

A cold sweat broke out over Carlton's body. This was the moment he had been dreading since the attack, and it couldn't have come at a worse time. Not knowing where Willow was, he was powerless. He had to speak to her, get to her before Coop. It was a shame that she was so drugged, she would need her wits about her and there was no protection where she was.

I have to tell her to come off them. Fuck. She's going to suffer.

Alone.

This was a bad idea. I should have played it all differently. I shouldn't have upper her dose, I shouldn't have kept her fearful, and I shouldn't have played God.

I'm such a fucking idiot.

He was about to go back upstairs to try calling Willow when the bottom dropped out of his stomach as Coop spoke again.

'I've nearly got her. Right to the doorstep. Last chance to play.'

Carlton's shaking legs sent him sinking down to his backside on the stairs.

He's almost got her? To the doorstep? How?

His heart banged as he listened to his brother. This was more serious than he thought. He had forgotten just how ruthless Coop could be.

'Yeah, well, I don't need your fucking help, anyway. One message and she'll be in the palm of my hand. It should come through today, and then the fun begins, Radar. Don't ask to join in, though. No fucking pussies allowed.'

There was a bang from the living area, and Carlton ran upstairs.

Thirty-Nine

B Y THE TIME THEY arrived at Ivy Cottage Willow was feeling a lot calmer than she had for the last twenty-four hours. Jack twisted things into a context that she would never have thought about on her own.

She was lucky.

Lucky that she knew - most women whose boyfriends or husbands had affairs weren't lucky enough to find out. Lucky she wasn't there and had the time and space to process her actions properly, an immediate reaction almost always did more harm than good. Lucky someone cared enough to show her. She was lucky she had found this out when she was on the mend and didn't need him. She was lucky that she had already questioned the relationship and had already decided she would probably leave. She was lucky to have already left, and that she wasn't searching for somewhere to live now or dealing with kicking him out... and a million and one other reasons that, although this wasn't necessarily a nice thing, it was a good thing long term.

'You need any more?' Jack said as they had walked back along the forest path. Willow had smiled and told him no, she got it, she was lucky.

Only Jack could turn this into such a completely positive experience.

Willow paused at the end of the driveway to the cottage.

'This is me,' she said.

'Ah, the old Otis cottage. I suppose you're renting if you leave next year. How are you finding the place?'

Willow glanced at the house. It looked quaint, squat, and cozy.

Looks could be deceptive.

'It's okay. A little cold.'

'It's an old place, been here a good hundred years or so, I believe.'

Willow nodded. She could believe it, plenty of time to accumulate extra visitors.

'It was recently renovated though,' Jack continued.

'Yeah, so I was told. It's still cold. Want a coffee?' she asked.

Jack hesitated, checked his watch, and then glanced down the road.

'It'll be dropping dark soon, I should probably get back before I'm missed too much. An hour can be passed away in the work shed or the poly tunnels, two? I think they'll send a search party.'

Willow smiled. 'Okay, well thank you for finding me and helping me work through this. I was a mess, I'm sorry, I should never have sent you that message.'

'It's no problem,' he said, holding her gaze as he shrugged down into his jacket to stave off the chill of the wind. 'You think you'll be back tomorrow?'

'Yeah, definitely. All I've done today is drive myself insane. I'll drop by at ten.'

He nodded. 'Good. I missed you this morning. It was like losing an arm after the last few weeks.'

Willow grinned. 'A gangrenous one, I know,' she said, beating him to a quip that didn't come.

He chuckled, his eyes lighting up. 'well, that wasn't quite what I was going to say, but now that you mention it...'

Willow huffed a laugh and slapped gently at his padded arm.

'Nice to know I can count on you to kick me when I'm down.'

'I'd never kick you when you're down, princess, only when you're standing.' His grin softened into a smile that made her stomach tumble involuntarily as he held her gaze, and she flushed as he brought a hand to her cheek. 'I'm only joking when I say these things. You know that, right? I know you've had a tough day.'

Willow nodded as he took his hand away. Her skin buzzed where his fingers had left it and she suddenly wished he would put them back, or pull her into another hug, or at least stay for coffee...

'All right, I'll see you tomorrow then. Call me if you need anything.'

'I will do.'

Jack smiled. 'Take care, princess.'

Willow raised a hand with a smile, and as he turned and walked down the road, she felt a glow that she hadn't felt for a long time.

She watched him a while longer, feeling a little like a teenager with a crush, and then she turned back to the house, which now looked as though it had taken off its disguise as the sun lowered. It glowered at her as she walked past her car to the front door.

Willow had seen the shadow through the privacy glass of the second door one too many times now to use the boot and coat rack in the porch area. It was getting cold anyway, and everything left there just ended up freezing when she wanted to pull on a warm coat to go out into the cold. Pointless.

She pulled them both into the hallway and sat them next to the glass door before pulling off her boots and coat. She shivered as she felt a cool breeze move around her face, pulling her gaze to the cupboard. She placed a hand on the edges of the door.

Cold.

She thought about Sophie and how she had said that the cupboard had a hole that needed patching. Was it as small as it had been when she placed the piece over it, or had it got bigger?

Do you want to know?

She tilted her head. The cupboard remained quiet, but the air felt tense.

Just do it if you're going to.

She put out a hand and tentatively reached for the doorknob.

Her fingers touched the handle.

BANG, BANG, BANG, BANG!

Willow jumped and screeched, pulling her hand away and almost running from the corridor, until she realised the bangs were coming from the front door, not the cupboard door.

'Oh my God,' she breathed, pressing a hand to her chest. 'Shit.'

Jack? Maybe he changed his mind about the coffee.

She moved to the doorway, opening the glass door wide and then opening the front door.

The driveway was empty, long shadows thrown by the wane of the day crisscrossed the driveway.

'Hello?' she called, sending a shiver up her own spine. When there was no reply, she shut the door and turned back to the hallway.

The cupboard door was open.

Willow froze.

'Shit.'

She eyed the cupboard and edged into the hallway, swallowing hard. The feeling that she was being watched sending more shivers through her.

Just hit the door and get it shut.

She edged further forward. The door sat still, impassive, as though someone had left it open minutes before and forgotten to shut it.

Well, it wasn't a human hand, that's for sure.

Okay, Wills, just go.

She wobbled a little, took a breath, and then lurched forward and slammed the door shut, turned, and leaned against it.

BANG, BANG, BANG, BANG!

Willow flinched and closed her eyes.

'I'm not playing. Stop the crap, please.'

BANG, BANG, BANG!

'Absolutely not going to the door, so you may as well stop.'

BANG, BANG, BANG!

Not going to the door, not going to the door, not going to the door...

That was when she heard the voice.

'Wills? Are you in there?'

Willow opened her eyes and swung her head to the door.

Sophie?

Relief flooded her veins. She lurched away from the cupboard door and swung the front door wide. Sophie was just heading back down the driveway.

'Soph!' she called.

Sophie turned with a smile. 'Ah, there you are. I thought you were hiding. You're sitting in the dark.'

Willow waved a hand. 'I've only just got back. I was getting my boots off when you knocked.'

'I knocked a fair few times,' she said with a look that said Willow may have been a little crazy.

I know, nearly sent me over the edge, thanks for that.

'I answered, there was no one there, or so I thought, anyway.'

'Must have been when I was spying through the window. I saw you go into the kitchen, that's why I knocked again.'

Willow felt her composure slip.

'I didn't go into the kitchen. I've been in the hallway,' she said.

Sophie laughed as she strode past Willow and pulled off her boots. 'Aye, if you say so.'

Willow looked back to see Sophie pushing the cupboard door shut again.

'You coming in?'

Willow nodded. 'Yeah.'

She pulled the door shut, shut the glass door, and strode up the corridor, eyeing the cupboard door as she passed into the kitchen where Sophie was feeling the kettle.

'You didn't even put it on.' She said with a laugh. 'First thing I do when I get in.'

Willow smiled.

Well, if it'd have been me that walked in here, maybe.

'So where have you been?' Sophie continued. 'Out getting some fresh air?'

'Something like that,' she answered, pulling some cups from the cupboard as Sophie frowned.

'Didn't do you any good? I usually think better outdoors.'

'Oh, I thought all right. I thought myself into a right mess. When I'd finished I was so tired I thought I would never get back, and so cold I thought I was getting hypothermia.'

Sophie sat back against the worktop.

'How far did you go?'

'Only the willow tree, out in the clearing, but honestly, it could have been the other side of the world.' She sighed. 'By the time Jack found me, I was busy spiralling into another panic attack.'

A confused frown crossed Sophie's face.

'Jack? What was he doing out walking? He usually helps at the house in the week. Weekends too, to be honest, he rarely leaves.'

Willow felt her guard go up as she remembered the conversation with Sophie this morning. She hadn't seemed so happy about her having Jack's number.

Too late now.

'Well, I messaged him this morning, telling him I wasn't meeting him. I told him I was ill, instead of going into the whole Carlton mess. Then he messaged this afternoon to see how I was. By that time, I had worked myself up into a mess by the willow tree.'

I guess he realised because he asked where I was and came out to get me. He walked me back. You only just missed him.'

Willow knew that she had skirted the truth, but for someone who was friends with Jack, Sophie didn't seem too pleased that he was watching out for her.

Sophie nodded and poured the water into the cups.

'That's all?'

Willow frowned. 'What do you mean?'

'He's never normally so protective of those that stay or work at the house, that's all. He keeps a distance, they all do, it's part of the culture there. Except that he isn't keeping distance with you, is he? Far from it.'

'Oh,' Willow said, her stomach swirling. She liked Jack a lot. She didn't know if it was that he was older, but he seemed so much more capable, and more caring than Carlton ever had. Plus, he was a whole lot funnier, more laid back, and those hugs...

'Willow?'

Willow blinked and came back into the kitchen with Sophie.

'Yes?'

'I said he's not supposed to get involved with anyone there.'

'Well, we're not involved, so that's okay, isn't it?'

'You're not?' Sophie gave her a pressing look.

'No, Soph. I told you he gave me his number because of the panic attacks, that's all. And that came about because I told him what had happened to me in the past... you know, to put me on the pills in the first place. This goes way further than my problems with Carlton, Soph. We had a good chat about things, and he said he wanted to help me, that's all. That's what McGracken House is all about, isn't it?'

'I guess so, I know Helena wouldn't like it though. Her way is to-'

'Leave everyone alone to heal themselves, yes, but I spoke to Jack. I needed someone to talk to. Not everyone can turn feel-ings on and off like Helena.'

'Aye,' Sophie said softly, 'I know that. I'm just saying, just be careful with him, Wills. Don't get any ideas.'

'Why? Because he's Helena's son?'

'Because you don't know him.'

Willow felt a niggle of anger at Sophie. What was she being so cagey about?

She remembered Sophie had told her about the clashes with Betsy, and she remembered his flare of anger yesterday after they had been digging the beds.

'You told me he clashed with Betsy. Is it that he has anger issues?' Then Willow almost slapped her head as something occurred to her. 'Is he supposed to be healing from something, too?'

'No, no, nothing like that. Jack is a good guy, and he's fine.'

'So, tell me. What is it? Is he a secret woman, a serial womaniser, a serial killer maybe?'

Sophie's throat bobbed, and she gave Willow a look that said she didn't really want to answer.

'Nothing like that, Wills, he's great with the people that turn up there. I'm just concerned that he's looking after you more than most, and I don't know why that is. I know you said he was taking you walking somewhere today. All I'm saying is it's not his normal behaviour, and I don't know what he's planning, but I don't want you to get carried away thinking you can lean on him... or more.'

'I'm not, Soph, trust me. I have a whole cheating boyfriend mess to sort out in case you hadn't noticed. Jack is not on my radar. He's just being nice, and we get on really well. That's it.' Willow hoped her cheeks weren't too red as she folded her arms across her chest, wondering just what her friend was trying to say.

'Good, because this thing with Carlton has upset you, hasn't it?'

'I'm not getting back with Carlton after all he's done, and I'm not the one cheating here.'

Sophie blew out her cheeks.

'I know that. What I'm saying is that it's upsetting you, no? Even though you were already having doubts?'

'Of course. We were together for ten years. What the hell does this have to do with Carlton? If you're worried about a re-bound-'

'I'm worried about another Carlton situation,' Sophie said, cutting her off and looking pointedly at her.

Willow shook her head in confusion.

'I have absolutely no idea what you're talking about, Soph, but there's nothing going on between me and Jack.'

'Good,' Sophie said, 'Keep it that way, because I don't know what he's playing at with you, but he's married. He has a wife.'

Willow felt the world shift on it's axis for the second time in two days, and then her phone rang.

Carlton.

She declined the call.

Forty

C OOP TOOK THE MONEY, kept his head down, and walked away from the scrap yard gates. The entrance was perfect for hidden deals, at the end of a long road through a disused trading estate - and no wonder it was disused. Crime was high in these concealed corners at the back of the council estate. Even now, when he had thought that a Tuesday evening would be quiet, there was a group of teenagers in the locked yard. A few were sitting smoking in the stacked cars. A few more were watching as another kid tried to jump an old motorbike over a car from a makeshift plank, which looked like it could all go wrong at any moment.

As he walked in the darkness of the evening, his stomach rumbled. He had taken himself out most days since Carlton had taken over the apartment with his wimpy-ness. His face hadn't cracked. He wouldn't talk, didn't dress, and the rough shadow on his face was turning into a fully fledged beard that almost hid his tiny features.

Coop was pissed off, too. Almost a week had passed since he had sent the photos with no reply to his efforts. If Willow didn't answer, he hit another wall, and short of skirting the area and searching for her himself, he didn't know how else he could track her.

She didn't work, and therefore didn't get paid, so he knew tracking payments would be useless.

He could try Carlton's bank, he was surely paying for her care, but the bank app was fingerprint entry, and Coop hadn't had a chance to get hold of the phone and Carlton's finger together without him knowing again yet.

He cursed himself for not getting more involved in the hacking and negotiations side of the business when they had been an organised gang. There must be hundreds of other ways to track people, and yet he had left all of that stuff to Bugs. He had just expected him to sort it out, and he had done.

Since Coop had been inside, things had changed out here, too. The places he had known, with people who may have been able to help, had disappeared without a trace. It was a known thing in the criminal world - any sniff of police, or trouble, and they would disappear and start up elsewhere under a different guise. While you were in those circles, you knew what was going on. When you were out of them, there was no finding out what had happened.

Leave no trace.

It seemed every fucker wanted to leave no trace. Not only people who could help, including his partner in crime, but the victims too.

Should have taken more interest. Crime doesn't pay when you don't know what the fuck you're doing and you're on your own.

His stomach rumbled again as he turned back toward the park.

The thought of going back to the apartment and sitting with Carlton on top of his own problems was so unappealing he thought he may actually kill his brother.

Which would solve the fingerprint problem, he thought, but end the obtaining of illegal pills and his only lucrative source of income.

'Fuck Carlton,' he muttered.

He crossed the road, and the smell of food wafted toward him. Hot food. Chips, pizza, steak maybe? He looked up to see the pub and fingered the money in his pocket.

He had been saving as much as he could for when he needed to get the hell out of here, but this deal had been extra. He was supposed to be gone by now.

Supposed to have her by now.

'Stupid bitch,' he said as he pushed open the door of the pub, ordered two pints at the bar, and sat at a corner table with the menu.

Forty-One

C OOP WAS OUT AGAIN.

He was out a lot these days and every time it worried Carlton that he had found her and just left without a trace, leaving Carlton none the wiser, and Willow in grave danger.

Carlton picked up some of Coop's clothes and threw them in the washing machine. He had no idea if they were dirty or not, but the mess was beginning to drive him insane, especially when he was sitting in with it all day.

He collected a few beer bottles and placed them in the recycling, cleared the dirty plates, and popped some bread into the toaster.

He probably wouldn't eat it. He hadn't eaten until late for the last few days, too worried until Coop had finally returned late each evening. Then he snacked on chocolate and protein bars before bed. A healthy diet, but it was the only time he could eat. The only time his stomach didn't turn over with constant worry.

The toast popped, and Carlton buttered the slices and took them into the living room on a plate. He switched on the television for company and distraction and pulled out his phone.

He had made over sixty calls to Willow over the last week, and she hadn't answered or returned one of them, even after his messages saying that it was urgent. It added to his worry.

Was she okay up there? Would anyone know to call him if anything happened? Had she told anyone they were together and that she was returning home?

Or had Suzie been right? Maybe she had left to start over, and she wouldn't be back at all. It was looking more and more likely.

Well, maybe she can leave and just stop caring, but I can't leave her alone knowing that Coop is coming for her. If she wants out, I can only respect her wishes, especially after my actions, but I can't not call.

He dialled her number again. The phone rang out and the voice-mail cut in.

'Fuck, come on, babe, seriously? What the hell is going on?'

He stared at the phone as an idea came to his sluggish mind.

Irene may know. She wouldn't block contact from her mum, would she? Maybe he could convince her mum to ask her to call him.

It was worth a try.

He dialled Irene's number and listened as the phone rang out.

Forty-Two

W ILLOW WAS STANDING IN the garden of McGracken House, leaning on a fork, listening to Duncan as she now knew the man with the curls and no teeth was called. He was nice, genuine, and genuinely interested in everything around him. Unfortunately, he liked to tell everyone around him what he liked too, all the time.

'So, I took it up high when it was well enough to fly, and let it go from the hills. I swear to God, it circled me before it went, making its little caw sound.'

Willow smiled. 'That's so lovely. It's a shame you'll never know where it is again now.'

'I do,' Duncan said. 'I'm sure the little beauty visits me every day. I see it on the fence over there most days.'

Willow followed his finger as he pointed, and caught sight of Jack, working on the tractor, which had broken down for the hundredth time.

Her heart fluttered a little, and then she focused back on Duncan.

It was polite conversation, a far cry from the jibes and laughter she had shared with Jack, but she wouldn't allow that to continue now. She had to stop leaning on Jack as much as she could, because no matter what she had said to Sophie she was feeling things she shouldn't, and to go on as they had been wouldn't be right. At the moment no harm had been done.

Better to distance myself and let it fizzle out.

It hurt like hell, but she had no choice.

He hadn't been honest, and if Sophie had noticed he was being different then maybe others would, and she didn't want people talking about her in this small village that she was coming to like a lot.

You just have to learn to depend on yourself, Wills, as Mum said.

'...it swoops down and circles round, see? So, what I do is-'

Willow's phone rang. She rolled her eyes, expecting Carlton again, but it was Mum. She relaxed and held a hand up to Duncan with a smile.

'I should take this,' she said, moving away down the field as Duncan went back to the wooden deck he was making at the top of the allotment. Eventually, the potting sheds would go on top, and the deck would wind through the beds like a raised floor. It would be nice, Willow thought, better than traipsing the dirt back into the house as they did now.

'Mum, hi, how are you?' she said.

'I'm fine, love. How are you doing?'

'Good, just working at McGracken House. It's doing me good, Mum, you wouldn't recognise me.'

She laughed and her mum made an 'aw' noise down the phone.

'That's great to hear, honey, and are you still speaking to those lovely people there?'

'Yes, it's really helping. I've told them about dad too. They had some lovely words and advice. They look after me really well.'

Well, one of them did, but he wasn't allowed anymore. Willow had spoken to Helena a few times over the last week, but she was far more nonchalant and dismissive than Jack had been and was far less into giving her advice and taking her under her wing.

Well, she would be. It was the past Willow was talking about, not the present.

She was still very kind, still very giving, just a little more vacant and less warm than Willow had first thought when she had first come here.

'...getting easier a few months after I ditched Prozac,' Mum was saying, 'I remember getting on the bus...'

Mum's voice faded out as Willow looked back at Jack, who was standing by the tractor's cab, calling something to Warren, who was sitting inside. His short hair blew a sideways parting on his head as he wound a hand round in the air at Warren. Then they were both laughing, and Willow felt a pull of sadness.

Why, oh why, did you have to be just like the rest of them, Jack? I trusted you. I loved how you took care of me, and that you were always on the other end of the phone.

'...so, it's easier that way, see? You should try it.'

'Uh huh, I will,' she answered, without a clue what she was agreeing to.

Mum carried on and Willow continued to watch Jack. She was getting better at telling him she could do the garden alone now, but still not good at actually communicating with him without a flood of guilt and sadness. She could leave McGracken House and never go back, but she knew she was getting better by having things to do. Besides, the only other option would be to stay at Ivy Cottage all day. The air there was getting so tense it was like it would snap at any moment, set free like a chaotic, broken guitar string, and probably with the same twang, too.

Willow turned away.

'Anyway, love, I'll let you get on. I'm going shopping now. My chariot has just arrived.'

Willow focused on her mum's voice, her face flushing.

She had missed the entire conversation, watching someone she could no longer be herself around. She blew out a long breath and walked down the field, putting more distance between herself and Jack.

'Okay Mum, thanks for-'

'Hang on,' she said. 'I haven't got around to what I called for yet. I'm going to leave this one up to you, love, but I thought I'd let you know Carlton called me earlier.'

Willow stopped walking, her heart banging in her chest.

'Carlton?'

'Yes, he says he's called you too many times to count, but you're not answering.'

'So, he thought he'd go in the back door?' Willow snapped.

'I'm not saying a word, love. All I'll tell you is that he did sound kind of... well, frantic, I suppose, which is the only reason I'm telling you. I would have told him to stick his call where the sun doesn't shine otherwise.'

'You wouldn't,' Willow said with a grin.

Mum sighed. 'No, I wouldn't. Either way-'

'I know he's called Mum; I've got the messages and missed calls to prove it.'

'I know. I told him I couldn't make you call if you didn't want to, but he made me promise to give it a go. He said he was desperate, and that it was urgent.'

Willow pursed her lips and raised her eyebrows.

'I should think he is desperate, Mum, desperate to tell me more lies. He's been sleeping with his secretary. Someone sent the photographs through to me. He probably found out.'

'Oh!' Mum exclaimed, 'What? Are you sure?'

'I have the proof in full technicolour, unfortunately. Whoever it was sent closeups of their faces so that I can tell exactly who they are. No guesswork. It's him and Suzanne.'

'Suzanne? Well,' she said. 'I just can't believe it. Or maybe I can. Someone who can lie so adeptly about ordinary everyday things is probably expert at lying about things that need to be kept covered. I have to say though, love, he didn't seem the cheating type. That's shocked me!'

'It shocked me too, but the more I've turned it over, the more I think it's been going on for a while. They sent the photos a week ago now, and it's been a good few days that Carlton has been calling. It has to be that, and I suppose it is urgent to him, but I don't want to hear the lies.'

'I don't blame you. Are you all right, love? I can drive up to see you if you like?'

'No Mum, it's a good few hours away for you, and I'm fine. I'm a lot calmer than I was, but I still don't want to speak to him.'

'I should think not,' Mum sighed. 'Well, I'm glad that I didn't make small talk. I thought about it, what with him nearly being family and all.'

'Not anymore. We're done, Mum. Maybe there would have been a chance if he'd had a good explanation about the pills, but absolutely not now. Mum, you didn't tell him where I was, did you?'

'How can I love? I don't even know myself.'

'I know, but I've given you clues, and you know I'm a good few hours north. You haven't said anything?'

'Of course not, no. I wouldn't. Ever. It was my idea you did this, wasn't it? Why would I give the game away? Even if I knew?'

Willow felt herself relax.

'Thanks Mum.'

'I have to go, honey, but keep me updated. If you call him, or answer his calls, let me know how it goes.'

'I will, but I won't be doing either. I don't want to know. If he calls you again, tell him to sling his hook. Enjoy your shopping trip.'

'I will, Bye, love.'

Willow looked down at the phone as the call cut off, paused, and then flicked to the photographs.

She pursed her lips as her stomach pulled, but nothing like it had last week. They were getting easier to look at as she processed what had happened.

She was breaking free, and it felt good. Really good. She should be thanking the person who sent these, not blasting Carlton. He made his own decisions, and he would have to live with them. If he was suffering, that was his own problem.

'Hey, sweetheart,' Jack said behind her, making her stomach flip. She pulled the phone in closer, hoping he hadn't seen what she was looking at as she turned.

'I know,' she said, a flush heating her cheeks. 'I'm getting back to it now. It was just my mum.'

He smiled, but it wasn't full, and she knew he didn't understand what was going on, and why she was suddenly pulling away.

Not that she owed him an explanation.

'I'm not bothered about that, Willow,' he said. 'You can talk as much as you like. I was just going to ask if you'd remembered about yoga. It was an earlier session today, wasn't it?'

Willow was impressed that he had remembered the flippant comment at all.

'Three,' she said.

'Aye, that's what I thought. It's half-two now, you'd better get going.'

Willow stared at him, and then she nodded and checked her watch.

'That went fast, er, well, okay.'

He seemed so lacklustre that she placed a hand on his arm, trying to ignore the pull the connection made her feel.

'Thank you, Jack. I'd have missed it if it wasn't for you.'

Jack nodded and took the fork from her.

'I'll put this away and tidy up. You go.'

A wave of emotion swelled inside her, and she suddenly wanted to tell him everything. She wanted to wrap her arms around him and feel the comfort of one of his hugs, but there was a wife stepping into that place rightfully at home, and the thought that he wouldn't stop her didn't make her feel any better.

'Are you sure?' she said.

He nodded, and her heart thumped as she looked at him.

'Okay, thanks.' She stepped past him before she did something stupid. 'I'll see you tomorrow.'

As she passed the open-sided barn by the gates, she picked up three planks of wood, a hammer, and some nails that Jack had put aside for her earlier.

She swallowed hard, and her stomach rolled.

Don't look back, she thought. Just don't look back.

Forty-Three

T HE CUPBOARD WAS OPEN again when she got back, and the
house was freezing. If it hadn't been late, she would have
hammered the boards over there and then. As it was, she just
had time to get into her leggings and sports top, pull her own
clothes over the top, grab a bag and water, and run the mile
back to the community centre.

The air nipped at her face, and her breath came in clouds as
she ran. Biting air, cold, it made forty-degree yoga seem very
appealing, especially when she could shower there afterwards,
as she had done the last few sessions.

Sophie joined her for yoga but had to leave straight after. Willow
sent her friend off with a hug and then headed back to the
toilets and a warm shower.

It was cold inside the community centre - aside from the Yoga
studio, which was heated via infrared system - but inside the
shower area it was warm, damp, and steamy. An aerobics class
had run in the main room an hour before. They had either
sweated a lot, or it was just a nod to the colder weather.

Someone was in the middle of the three stalls already, so Willow
took the left.

She placed her things on the hooks provided and her shoes on
the bench. Public showers never went the way you thought they
would, and she had been left with wet shoes more than once.

The water was hot tonight, and Willow closed her eyes as she
let the spray massage her face and run down her body.

*I can't remember the last time I was this warm, or even comfort-
ably warm. This is divine.*

She washed and shampooed her hair quickly, but the reluctance to leave the warm water when she had finished was phenomenal.

Just another five minutes.

She closed her eyes and let her thoughts drift to the cottage.

First thing to do when you get home is block up the cupboard, and then maybe you should put a blanket over it to seal the edges.

The cold that was entering the house from one cupboard was ridiculous. Once the cupboard was sealed, she would look at the heating and make sure it was working right. It had been cold when she got back earlier, yet the thermostat had been set at thirty. She wondered if the boiler kicked in and out on a timer, overriding the thermostat, although she knew that wasn't how they usually worked.

She'd had no email back from Mel in the last week, so there had been no help there, and the village was so small that rental houses came up once in a blue moon.

She loved Clover Nook and the people she was meeting here, and she didn't want to move away, so she would just have to get on with things herself as best she could.

Of course, as Helena said, there was always a bed at McGracken House...

No, absolutely not. Not even as a last resort. I'll sleep in the car.

'...low.' A quiet and singsong voice came from the room, so quiet that Willow almost thought that she hadn't heard it. She wiped the water from her eyes, pulled her head out of the spray, and listened.

'Willow...'

Her heart stuttered as the hair at the back of her neck rose.

'Hello?' she called. 'Did someone want me?'

There was silence, and then a faint hum.

'Hello?' she said. 'Who's in here?'

There was no reply, although the shower next to her was still running, as it had been when she first arrived.

She slapped on the tiled wall between her own stall and the next one.

'Hey, hello. Is there anybody in there?'

The low hum continued, a quiet tune. Willow turned off the shower and heard the flow of water in the next stall.

'Hello? Who is that?'

There was no reply, and Willow felt something icy crawl over her scalp.

She stepped out of the shower and grabbed her towel, wrapping it around her. Her instinct was to throw open the door, but she knew that if she did, two things would happen.

The first was that she would want to run - in only a towel. The second was the rush of cool air that always joined a shower when you opened the door. She didn't fancy either.

Get dressed first.

Getting dressed seemed to take forever. Moisture made everything sticky and impossible to put on. She was trying to pull her jeans up over her thighs when the shower next door squeaked off and the humming stopped.

The silence was even eerier than the hum. No doors opened, there was no rustle of bags, and no one announced themselves.

Shit. What the hell is this?

She pulled on her jeans, fastening the button as there was another sound. A slow squeak that set Willow's teeth on edge, like chalk screeching on a blackboard.

Willow pulled her t-shirt and jumper over her pounding heart, pulled on her shoes, and reached for the shower door. The squeak stopped as she pulled it open, leaving silence.

The washroom was empty.

Like you expected anything else.

Swallowing hard, she looked around, her heart thudding in her ears.

'Hello?'

The silence was all-encompassing and eerie. Surely whoever was in the middle stall would hear her now with the shower off. They hadn't had time to leave yet and surely she would have heard the snap of the catch, the rustle of bags, footsteps. Any sign of human life.

Forcing herself to face the closed door of the next cubicle, she raised a hand and rapped on the door. The noise was almost enough to send her skidding for the exit herself.

'Hello, is anyone in there? Are you okay?'

'What are you doing?'

Willow yelped and spun round. In the doorway stood Maud, which was almost scarier than whatever was in this room, humming and squeaking. Her grey hair was slicked back with sweat from the session, her eyes unnerving as the fluorescent beam cast her deep features into awkward shadows.

'Um, there was someone in here, in the next cubicle, but they're not answering.'

Maud chuckled. 'There's no one in here, child. Everyone has gone. Even Tam had to run.'

Willow clenched her jaw and forced a smile.

'No, there's someone in here. They've just stopped the shower. I wanted to check if they were okay, but they're not answering.'

Maud walked towards her, and Willow inadvertently took a step back. Maud stopped and tilted her head to one side.

'Are you afraid of me, child?'

'No,' Willow said quickly, 'I'm not. This whole thing has me on edge. I want to know who's in there. What if they're hurt?'

'Then open the door,' Maud said, stepping past her and giving it a push.

'It'll be...'

Willow trailed off as the door swung wide. The small cubicle was empty.

'...locked,' she whispered.

'Aye, but it's empty. There's no one here.'

'But the shower was running.'

'Faulty most probably.'

'The handle squeaked off.'

Maud shrugged. 'Nothing and no one here but me and you.'

'I heard it!' Willow said, losing her temper with the older woman.

'There's no one here. What's the matter, child? Is she getting to you? Slipping into your nightmares?'

Willow stared at the old woman.

'She is around you, isn't she? She's trapped, poor soul. Come by my house tomorrow at noon. I have information that may help.'

Willow shook her head. There was no way that she was going to this crazy old lady's house.

'Save your judgment, child. When noon comes tomorrow, I will see you. If I don't, well, there'll be a next time. Keep the card close.'

She handed a card to Willow, turned, and left the room.

In the quiet, Willow heard the door bang, and then the outer door of the community centre.

It wasn't late, and there was an art class tonight, which was why yoga was early, and why no one had to lock up.

Which meant that she was alone.

There was a small squeak from the other end of the room where the basins and toilets were, and then a low hum.

Willow turned.

There is some bugger in here, trying to scare me, I swear it.

She grabbed her bag from the cubicle as the hum continued.

Was this Maud? Did she have an accomplice to help to scare her? It was funny how she was so sure that there would be no one in the shower next door.

Well, rather than get freaked out for the evening, and never have a shower in here again, why don't you scout the room? They probably won't be expecting that, and you can knock this scary shit on its head.

Willow thought she had never had such a bad idea, all she wanted to do was run.

Did she really need to know?

Yes, or you won't have a shower ever again, here or at the cottage. Not showering is not a great look, and this is obviously a person.

Leaving the door to the cubicle open, she walked past the middle one, and then the end. All the showers were now open, all empty.

Of course, because this person is down the toilet end of the room.

She could see the basin area was empty, but two of the four toilet doors were closed.

Willow trembled, her heart banging. She had already gone into panic mode, not realising the constriction of her chest was barely there compared to last month.

Breathe.

In for four, hold, out for six.

In for four, hold, out for six.

She focused on the toilet doors. They didn't quite reach the floor.

Maybe she wouldn't have to open them all after all.

As Willow began to walk toward them, the hum stopped. It was as though the person she was listening for was also listening for her. Her shoes squeaked on the blue nonslip tiles.

One squeak for another. Tit for tat.

Willow almost felt her mind click over to insane as giggles fluttered up from her belly.

She saw herself kneel, water soaking into the knees of her jeans, and then she saw herself lower her head to the floor.

She expected nothing, but in the end toilet there were feet.

Bare feet, dirty, the size of a small adult, or an older child. Long grey material hung around them, almost like one of Helena's long skirts, but more ragged.

Willow took more breaths.

Okay. There's someone in there. Now call them out.

She thought she would do better than that.

There was a soft rustle as she got back to her feet.

I'll give you something to squirm at, she thought.

She strode to the toilet door and pushed it open hard. It swung back, hitting the tiled wall before swinging closed again with a bang.

It had shown Willow enough.

The cubicle was empty.

Impossible.

And the room was getting impossibly small as Willow tried to control her breathing.

She pushed at the other shut door to reveal its empty space, and then stood before the final cubicle again.

There's no one in there. Get out of here!

Her mind screamed as her head tried to rationalise.

How can there be no one where you saw feet? Who the hell walks around in bare feet, anyway? Are you making this up again?

Willow pushed at the last door again. It opened slowly this time, but still revealed empty space.

You imagined the feet, imagined them in the panic. Jack said that you could hallucinate. It's okay, there's no one here.

She scoured the ceiling - just in case - and then she turned.

On the mirrors, which hung over each basin, were lots of condensation faces. Some sad, some happy, some angry, all surrounded by one word, written hundreds of times with a finger.

HELP.

Willow's chest constricted hard now, and she felt the familiar pull and squeeze of her lungs trying to drag in air. The fear gripped her chest, squeezing painfully, and she gasped.

There was another squeak, and she turned toward the exit, past the showers.

'No more,' she tried to whisper, but the words stuck in her throat as she gasped.

The woman with bare feet stood by the shower cubicles, blocking her exit. Dirty dark blonde hair covered her face. As Willow watched, the woman's head twitched, like a stutter in the reel of a horror movie.

Willow felt her breath close off. There was no air. She would be in here forever with this woman... this thing.

The woman moved towards her, and the fluorescent lights stuttered and went out.

The room fell into darkness.

Willow tried to scream with no air. The pain was intense in her chest, and she remembered reaching for a basin as the floor fell away under her feet, and then the world went cold and black.

Willow came round on the floor with a blanket over her. Tam was stooped next to her like an angel. She smiled as she pushed Willow's hair from her face with a hand.

'Ah, here she is. How are you, pet? Maud, could you get a bottle of water from the machine, please?'

Willow tried to rise, but Tam held her down with a smile.

'Not yet, pet, I just want to ask you some questions first.'

Willow's mouth was dry, and her head felt fuzzy, but she nodded as Maud came back with the water, her eyes on Willow as she stood back.

Tam looked into Willow's eyes and took her pulse with her fingers.

'What happened, pet? Does anywhere hurt?'

Willow shook her head and found a spot that ached on the right side.

She put a hand to a small lump and winced.

'Here,' she croaked.

Tam felt around the bump.

'Okay, well, a head injury isn't the best, but is to be expected when you fall from a height. It's swelling nicely though and doesn't feel like anything untoward.'

Willow raised up onto an elbow and motioned for the water in Maud's hand. Maud brought it forward, her eyes concerned.

Tam helped Willow into a sitting position, and she took the water, drinking thirstily.

'Thank you,' she said, folding the cap back over the bottle.

'What happened, pet?' Tam said, still running her eyes over Willow's face, head, and arms.

'I'm not sure,' she said. 'I was having a shower.'

She shook her head.

If you tell the complete and unabridged version, you'll more than likely end up in the nearest lunatic asylum.

She looked at Maud, who was looking down at her worn trainers, still in her yoga leggings and woollen jumper.

'I thought there was someone in the next shower. The water was running. It stopped, and I thought someone was in trouble when I heard nothing more. I called, but no one answered.'

Maud looked up, nodding in agreement.

'I walked in as she was calling out. I pushed the door, but there was no one there. I said the shower must be faulty, that's all. Then I left the building but forgot my towel. When I came back, I heard a noise from the bathroom and went in to find her out cold. That's when I came to find you, Tam.'

'Aye, okay, thank you Maud. What happened after Maud left, pet?'

Willow frowned.

The toilets, the bare feet, and the small lady all flashed into her mind. She didn't want to tell Tam about any of those things. Luckily, Carlton had given her an escape.

'I had a panic attack. I think I worked myself up about the shower running itself, and that I was here alone. I remember struggling to breathe, and then I was here.'

'Oh, pet, I'm so sorry. I didn't think. I should have stayed while you were around. You just seem to be doing so well now that I forget you're still healing. I make you stronger than you are in my mind. I won't do it again.'

'I am strong. I don't need a babysitter, Tam, and I don't expect you to do it. I am doing well, and I've been okay for a few days. The attacks seem a little more intense now, but a lot less frequent if that makes sense?'

Tam nodded. 'It's natural. It's taking far bigger things in your mind to trigger you now, I think that's why. Are you keeping in mind the flame and staying focused?'

'I am, and it's working well. I just couldn't get this one under control in time.'

'I'm sorry, child, part of that is my fault. I would never have left you in those circumstances if I had known, I would have waited.'

Willow smiled at Maud, and the older lady smiled back. Willow wondered why Maud had ever seemed scary.

'It's okay, you couldn't have known.'

Tam sighed and helped Willow to her feet.

'Give yourself a brush down, pet. Any dizziness, just sit back down.'

'I'm fine,' Willow said, although she was still a little shaky.

'Does it hurt anywhere else?'

'No, just my head. Lucky, I guess.'

'Very. Do you want me to walk you home?'

Willow paused. She wasn't really into walking home alone in the dark after what had happened, but she didn't want to worry Tam, and it wasn't late.

'No, I'll be fine,' she picked up her bag and slung it over her shoulder. Her head throbbed with the pressure, and she winced.

'Any vomiting, vision problems, headaches et cetera, please call me. I'll take you to the hospital, okay?'

Willow nodded. 'Okay, thanks Tam.' She looked at Maud, who appeared a lot older than she had just half an hour ago. 'Thanks to you too Maud, I really appreciate you all looking out for me.'

'I'd have looked harder if I'd have known. I'm walking past the bridge on my way home. I'll walk with you there if you like.'

Willow felt genuine relief flood through her.

'That would be great, thank you.'

Maud nodded. 'Come on then, child, let's get you home.'

At the word home, Willow's stomach tumbled over. She thought she would rather stay the night here than go back to that cottage.

On the walk home, Maud mentioned nothing about what she had seen in the showers. It was as though she had known anyway, as though she hadn't needed it confirming. As they got to the bridge, she had simply said, 'Please don't think that this will go away. Come and see me. Noon tomorrow.'

Willow agreed that she might.

Inside Ivy Cottage, Willow shut the cupboard door without looking inside and immediately nailed the wood across it. She made sure to hit the wooden door surround, not the weaker plasterboard of the wall.

Three pieces of wood, like bars across a jail cell.

Willow was sweating, shaking, and her head throbbed, but it was done. The main source of distress was disbanded. The shadow and the faces could be dealt with by not looking.

'Now, please, leave me alone,' she said aloud.

The house was quiet, and warmer than normal, she noticed. Maybe that was a good sign. Maybe the presence agreed that she had been through enough tonight. Willow hung her damp towel over the radiator, pressed the switch on the kettle, and put the television on.

She was sipping at her drink when she noticed her phone ringing. It had been on silent for the yoga session, and she hadn't yet turned the volume back up. She picked it up as the call rang off and Willow saw it was Carlton. Again.

She checked back through the missed calls, and saw he had rung twenty-five times since yoga had begun, not quite two hours ago.

Desperate is an understatement, Wills.

Well, he would be, wouldn't he?

She flinched as the phone began to buzz in her hand again, and anger punctuated her gut.

Fuck off, Carlton.

She pressed the button to turn off the phone.

Forty-Four

C ARLTON LISTENED TO THE answer machine cut in and slammed down the phone on the kitchen side.

His head ached, his eyes ached, even his arms ached from holding the phone too hard. Hadn't Irene told her yet? She had promised to call Willow straight away yesterday. He had pressed how urgent the situation was and she had seemed to take him seriously. So why hadn't Willow called? And why wasn't she answering his calls?

The days at home were beginning to feel like Groundhog Day.

He cried himself to sleep. Got up puffy eyed, called Willow, over and over and over, with a small break for food and to use the toilet. Suzie often messaged in the afternoon to see how he was and to let him know anything urgent or important that was going on at work. Not that he could care less.

Once or twice, she had phoned him when he hadn't answered her message for well over an hour, but he hadn't picked up.

He had thought it funny how he was looking at the screen and neglecting to answer, probably much like Willow was doing with his own name, wherever she was.

It sucked. Quite probably sucked for Suzie, too.

Oh well. The sooner she realised what they had done was a mistake, and not the start of something, the better for both of them. He had bigger fish to fry.

He picked up the phone and punched in Willow's number again. And again.

And again.

Forty-Five

I T WAS RAINING WHEN Willow woke the next morning, her limbs tangled in the duvet on the settee.

She yawned and sat up, blinking in the dull morning light. Something felt off. Weird. She felt like she had slept for a week, her eyes felt puffy and blurry, although she couldn't say that she felt well rested.

She picked up the Prozac packet that had appeared on the floor at some point last night and rose to put the kettle on.

The curtain was shut across the living area door usually, but not this morning. It was drawn back.

Willow peered through the glass. She could see that the cupboard door was still sealed shut, and the corridor looked normal, but she shuddered as she remembered something.

Last night, when she had peered through the door to check the cupboard was secure through inevitable thuds, she had seen her.

The lady. The one with the twitch. The one from the shower.

'No. Not going there today,' she murmured.

But I am going to see Maud. Crazy or not, she may know something that will help. It can't do any harm.

Complete with coffee in hand, she went back to the settee and sat down. She yawned as she picked up her phone to...

'Eight messages? Bloody hell, news travels fast around here.'

She put her coffee cup down and answered the first couple, Sophie and Tam. She deleted the four from Carlton until all she had left was Jack's.

She didn't know how to respond to Jack, although she knew she ought to tell him she wasn't going to McGracken House today now, anyway.

She took a sip of coffee and sighed. Whether Jack was married or not, he had still been more than good to her.

Has he really ever done anything but look after you? Maybe this is your problem, Wills. Maybe you're reading too much into his actions because you like him.

She read Jack's message again.

Hi, sweetheart, I heard what happened and I hope you're okay. I'm worried about you, but don't want to call and disturb you. I'm not sure a call would be welcome, anyway? Well, message if you want to, but hopefully I'll see you tomorrow. Take care of yourself, and I'm always here if you need me. Anytime. That doesn't change.

She stared at his words.

Damn you for being so kind, Jack, she thought, as she heaved a sigh.

It made her own message seem so much worse as she typed in her reply.

Hi Jack, I'm good now thanks. Just letting you know I won't be there today. I have something I need to do. Maybe tomorrow.

As a last-minute thought, she added a bit to the end.

Thank you for caring, though. I appreciate it.

It still sounded sterile and wasn't at all how she wanted to communicate with a man that had helped set her on her feet, but she would have to live with it. She pressed send.

😊 😌 😐 😟 😣 😵

Willow pulled her hood close as she walked down the street to Maud's house, rain driving into her face. She wasn't sure which house it was, but she did know that Maud had carried on past the bridge. There was also a small picture of a house on her card, offering her psychic medium abilities - for a fee.

Willow didn't know whether she was supposed to pay for this sitting or not. She had no money on her either way, but could sort it out if she needed to later on. It wasn't like she or Maud were going anywhere for the foreseeable future.

Jack messaged as she was scouring the little cottages just after the bridge. It had taken him over an hour to reply. A bad sign by all accounts, and Willow bit back the guilt that tried to crawl up from her stomach as she read it.

Okay, sweetheart, see you tomorrow... maybe. Take care.

She pushed the button to lock her phone as she came across a house that looked a little like the one on the card. Grey stone, right off the pavement, green door and window frames. A ginger cat sat behind one window, staring at her as she stared at the house.

The door opened as she was reaching into her pocket for the card to check the house number, and Maud stepped into the rain.

'Come in, child, quickly now.'

Willow crossed the lane and stepped into the house.

Inside was old and dark, and smelled like cats, which seemed to run in every direction as she entered.

'Follow me,' Maud said, taking her through to a tiny room at the back of the house. Two dining chairs and a small round table sat in the centre, and the surrounding walls were hung with Indian style silks and bells. A small bookcase sat along the wall opposite the door, its shelves almost bowing under the weight of the crammed books. Next to it was a large wooden Buddha, a small round red cushion balanced on top of his bald head.

If she was being completely honest, the room wouldn't have looked out of place with a Madam Rosa sign and curtains at the entrance.

'Sit,' Maud said behind her. 'I'll get some refreshments. What would you like to drink?'

'Just a tea if you have it, please.'

Willow turned and smiled at the lady. Her head was beginning to ache, or maybe it was her eyes that were aching in the darkness of the room. A curtain was pulled across the small window and Willow wanted to reach across and pull it open.

Instead, she looked at Maud's back in the kitchen, and wandered to the bookcase, glancing at the titles.

Mediation for the twenty-first century

Crystal healing and therapy

An advanced guide to tarot

Tapping intuition.

The Buddhist Way

Mediumship

Channeling your inner energy

Aligning your chakras

Maud was a serious student for all the village seemed to think she was a meddling old lady.

'Here you are, child. Sit down.'

Willow turned from the books and moved back to the chair, a feeling rather like that of being caught with her pants down bringing a flush to her cheeks.

Good job it's dark.

On top of an old cupboard she hadn't noticed by the doorway was the only thing that had been missing from this room. A large crystal ball, alongside a box of tarot cards, and something called angel cards.

She sat as Maud put the small wooden tray on the table and sat in the chair opposite.

There were two hot drinks, one of which Maud passed over, and a packet of hobnobs which elicited a loud grumble from Willow's stomach. It was past lunchtime, and she hadn't even eaten breakfast yet.

'Go ahead. You need to eat, child. This situation doesn't get any better for not eating.'

Willow reached for them, but as her hand touched the packet, Maud's hand grasped hers. She tried to pull away, but Maud held firm, and when willow looked at the lady's face, her eyes were closed, and a frown was crossing her features.

'Maud?' she said.

Maud mumbled something and shook her head and Willow thought it best just to sit and wait, the hobnobs taunting her under her fingers.

After a few minutes that seemed like hours, and two very loud grumbles of protest from Willow's stomach, Maud finally let go. Her eyes opened, and she smiled as though she knew everything that had passed through willow's tragic life for the last few years.

'I see,' she said with a nod, her gaze holding Willow's. Willow still sat with her fingers on the packet, wondering if she should move.

'Go ahead, child,' Maud said. 'I'll let some light in. The room is a little dark, what with the rain outside.'

Willow finally opened the packet and then a gloriously nutty hobnob was in her mouth. She took another from the pack as Maud sat back down.

She regarded Willow, her head tilted, like she may have once regarded the fine silks on the walls.

'You didn't sleep much, last night.'

Willow stopped chewing and wondered whether she should answer. One look at her face would tell anybody that. She hadn't slept for a good many nights now, and she felt the effects. Although last night...

'But you did sleep heavily,' Maud continued. 'Hmmm.'

She stared at Willow, the two very different colours of her eyes more pronounced now that the light was upon them, and Willow half wished the curtains had been left closed.

She chewed again and swallowed.

'Do I answer?' she asked quietly.

Maud smiled. 'You may stay quiet until I have sorted the information.'

Maud closed her eyes, and Willow raised her eyebrows as she took a sip of tea. Then she turned her gaze to the window, watching the rain streak down the glass under the grey sky.

'Ahhhhhh,' Maud suddenly exhaled a long breath, her eyes still closed, and Willow froze, cup halfway to her mouth.

'Yeeeeeesssssss,' she whispered, a frown crossing her features.

Gooseflesh lined Willow's arms. She tried to calculate how many strides it would take to get to the door, and whether Maud would even notice that she had gone.

Under the table, something bumped against her legs. She flinched and looked down to see the ginger cat winding itself between her ankles with a purr that sounded like a small motor.

Willow wasn't a cat person. She neither had time for cats nor a liking for sharp claws. At least the smell seemed to have gone now, though.

Not gone, you're nose blind. You're just used to it.

She let out a small yell as the cat jumped into her lap and began to pummel her thigh.

'Sorry,' she whispered, but Maud was still, her brow creased. If she had heard any of the commotion, she didn't show it.

To Willow's dismay, the cat curled up on her lap. She couldn't very well tell it to scat with its owner before her, so she was stuck with it. Hopefully, this whole thing wouldn't take long... if Maud wanted to share any of this information with her, anyway.

Willow's hand reluctantly fell to the soft fur of the cat, which sent vibrations through her legs as its engine started up again.

She sighed and took another sip of tea, and then movement in the kitchen caught her eye. She leaned back in the chair, scanning the room, but saw nothing.

The cat carried on purring and Willow sipped at her nearly empty cup, and then she saw it again.

A flicker in the kitchen, like the light had dimmed, as though something had stood in front of the window. Willow stiffened as the dark moved out of her peripheral vision, and the room lightened again.

Shit.

Every nerve in her body suddenly felt fraught, her heart was pounding, and she almost felt... watched.

Maud was still sitting with her eyes closed, swaying slightly in her seat with a small sound that could have been a hum or a moan.

Willow stared straight ahead at Maud, willing the lady to open her eyes. Willing her to be in the room with her, and then the cat meowled and fled from her lap. The shock swung Willow's gaze to the kitchen where the cat was flying past the doorway, and the small lady stood.

Willow jumped, and her throat closed over as the woman's head twitched.

The scream left her lips as she stood, knocking the table, and Maud's hot drink all over it. The hobnobs rolled onto the floor, and then she was rushing for the door, and Maud was shouting.

Willow had her hand on the front door catch, about to throw it open, when Maud yelled.

'She will be there, too. You can't outrun her, child, she will follow. Let me help you to help her. It's the only way.'

Willow gasped for air as she paused, and Maud lowered her voice.

'Come, child, there is much to be explained.'

'I can't go back in there. I don't want to see her, I'm scared.'

'Then tell her. Running is useless, child, she is trying desperately to communicate.'

'What do you mean?'

Maud looked round at the kitchen.

'Martha, the child is afraid,' she boomed. 'The more you show yourself, the less she is able to help, but help we will. Do not come to this house while she is here again.'

Something fell in the back room and Willow felt like crying. Was nowhere free of this. Could she do nothing?

'Could you ask her not to appear at the cottage, too?' she said weakly, fearing that she knew the answer.

'She is tied to the cottage for a reason. It's her home, there the energy is stronger. She won't appear here now, though. She is quite amicable, she doesn't want to hurt you, and she doesn't want to frighten you. She wants help.'

'Great. Why me?'

'You moved into the cottage.' Maud smiled. 'But I'm not sure that was a mistake. She has linked to you for other reasons. That is why she is restless now. Fate in action.'

Maud held out a wisened hand and Willow looked at it.

'How do you know all this?' she said.

'I hear her too, child. I knew her in the past, but I can no longer help, for I am no longer at the cottage.'

'Could we swap houses until it's over?' Willow was only half joking. She would even look after the cats.

Maud smiled again. The fingers on her hand flicked back and Willow placed her hand in Maud's.

A jolt of warmth ran through her and Willow felt herself relax.

'It's not possible. Let's sit.'

'Can we shut the door to the room?'

'If you wish.'

Willow let Maud lead her back into the tiny room.

Forty-Six

'**I**'M CONCERNED THAT THIS isn't the only thing I see,' Maud said. Her eyes were closed again, but this time she was expecting responses.

Willow gave a loud swallow as Maud's eyes flicked open.

'There's more. That's why she's so attached. Your energy is matched strongly with hers. There's something...'

Maud closed her eyes again and Willow sat with her heart pounding.

Why do I have to match energy with some crazy spirit lady?

She wasn't even sure she believed in ghosts, hadn't had any kind of experience before this one. She tapped her fingers nervously on the table and chewed at her lower lip.

'I see something dark around you,' Maud muttered.

Willow stopped tapping and looked at her.

Fantastic.

'Something small at the moment. It's growing though... what is that?' Maud frowned. Her eyes were closed, but she looked over Willow's shoulder, tilting her chin upward. 'It's male, or masculine in presence. Are you having trouble with a man at the moment, child?'

'You could say that. I just broke up with my long-term boyfriend. He had an affair.'

Amongst other things.

'Hmm, maybe,' Maud said. 'It feels threatening. This situation will get worse before it gets better.'

Willow sighed. 'Nothing I didn't expect.'

'Be on your guard, child. I can't see this properly, and I will continue to seek, but at the moment, it's not coming through. I feel a strong attachment to Martha through this darkness. She sees.'

'Could the darkness be Martha?'

Willow almost didn't want to know the answer. If this presence - Martha apparently - was going to get any worse, she wouldn't be hanging around to find out, and thanks for the heads up.

Except that she follows you now.

Bugger.

'No. Martha is there, but she's in the background. It's difficult to explain, but she's a different light. This darkness is very obviously masculine, but she... hmmm.'

Maud creased her brow into a frown and dipped her chin to her chest.

'She, what's the word? She identifies with this darkness. It's that which pulls her to you, which seeks her to communicate.'

'So, if I get rid of this darkness, will she back off?'

Maud opened her eyes and looked at Willow steadily.

'There is no stepping away from this darkness. Nothing you can do, child. This is something in your future that will happen. You may be able to delay it, but it *will* come, and you *will* have to deal with it.'

Willow swallowed hard, the sound washing past her ears.

'Right,' she said.

'I wish I could tell you more, but nothing will come forward. It's like there's a block of sorts.'

'It's okay, if it's Carlton, my ex, it's been pretty rough so far, and yes, it's likely to get worse, I suppose. So, this Martha identifies with this? Man trouble?'

Maud chuckled. It transformed her entire face in a second. Her lines looked softer, her jowls jolly, her eyes twinkled. 'I think, as women, we can all identify with man trouble. I am lucky. I have no man to trouble me, and that's just the way I like it. It's just me and my cats.'

Willow laughed, breaking the seriousness of the moment, and helping her to gain her focus.

So she couldn't do anything about Carlton, that would happen anyway, and that much she knew, but did that mean that she couldn't do anything about Martha, her unwanted houseguest?

'Okay, well, if I can do nothing to avoid this... thing that's going to happen and that links me to Martha, then what can I do about her? Is she going to stay until the darkness is over?'

Maud took a breath.

'Good question,' she said, pushing her fingers together in front of her on the table. 'There's a strong intention around this event. It's almost like her energy is insistent that you listen, but no, something else troubles Martha's spirit. She has been bound to Ivy Cottage for many years, a nasty business. This won't pass easily.'

Willow opened her mouth and shut it again.

'A nasty business? At the cottage?'

Wow, I picked the wrong secluded cottage for sure.

'Oh yes, dreadful affair.'

'So, I'm stuck with her?'

Maud fixed her with one dark eye and one milky eye.

'Or she's stuck with you. You're in her property, remember?'

Willow sighed and sat back in the chair.

'Right. So, I suppose I'd better find out who this Martha was who lived there? You said that you knew her?'

Maud sat back in her own chair with a sigh.

'Oh, Martha Otis. That's a story, child. Are you sure you want to know?'

Willow nodded. What choice did she have?

'She was born in Ivy Cottage,' Maud continued. 'Inherited it after her mother passed. Her mother was an older parent, and Martha was fairly young at that time, around sixteen if my memory serves, although it's been so long now. She married a local man at just eighteen. He moved into the cottage, and there they lived for many happy years. Or so it looked to the outside world. My mother was good friends with Martha's mother, and she looked after her for a while as she grew up. Martha also looked after me a few times too when my mother and father had places to go that didn't involve children.'

Maud looked up at Willow sadly. 'After her marriage, she lost touch relatively quickly, and we only saw her in passing a handful of times - even in this small village. I was a child. I hardly noticed anything, but my mother was worried about her. She said there were problems. When the pair split some twenty years later, it came out that he'd had affairs much of their married life.' Maud looked up at her with a pointed stare. 'Even in this small village.'

Willow nodded.

'I can certainly identify with that.'

'Her death was untimely and unfortunate. Quite brutal.'

Hopefully not in my living room or bedroom? Not in the cottage would be nice.

'What happened?'

'Her husband happened. She finally plucked up the courage to leave him when she met someone else. Turns out he was a very jealous ex, or so the story goes. Murdered both of them not long after she moved him in. So, you see, man trouble. Not only that, but the darkness around you is masculine, too. It possibly triggered her energy.'

Two people murdered at the cottage?

This was getting better and better.

Willow nodded.

'So, what do I do about her?'

'There is nothing you can 'do' child, except to remember that you're on her territory. She is trying to get your attention, that is certain. I rented that cottage for a good many years after the murders, before Melanie brought it and overhauled the place.' Maud shook her head and flicked her eyes to the ceiling. 'Is it any wonder Martha walks with heavier footfalls now? Anyway, for the first few years, there was nothing. The cottage was quiet and cozy, and then she came to me in my dreams. I'd have terrible nightmares, and then the rapping and cold spots appeared.'

'They're still there, although the rapping is more of a thud now, usually from the corridor. She also leaves messages on mirrors and windows. She's knocked things over in the bedroom, rattled the door, and I've seen her too.'

Maud's mouth was a startled small 'o'.

'Oh! You've *seen* her? I thought you were feeling her presence like I do. In truth, child, I thought you were like me, maybe a little mediumistic?'

Willow was shaking her head.

'Not that I know of, and honestly, I wouldn't want to be if this is what you have to deal with. I'm not that interested in the dead.'

'Unless they're hounding you,' Maud said with a smile.

'Indeed.'

'I don't see them, child. I merely feel. I work with energy, and I've learned to channel the energy to open up visions and feelings that are often correct. I've learned that intuition can be harnessed, and often isn't too far out when practiced. I've made a healthy career from it for the last forty years.'

Willow nodded, thinking of the witch comment that Sophie had made way back when they first met.

'I bet that has been fun in a small village, too.'

'Well, there's people's reactions are never normalised. I've had everything from tell me my future, to speak to my dead aunt, to you're a fraud. I've even been called a witch and told what I do is witchcraft.' She shrugged. 'Most don't understand, whatever side of the coin they land.'

She stopped and waved a hand. 'Anyway, this isn't about me. You say you've seen her?'

Willow nodded, and goosebumps tailed up her arms as she thought of the shadow in the house.

'I've seen a shadow a few times now, usually in the corridor. But the shower after yoga was the first time I saw an apparition. A lady with long fair hair.'

Jeez, was she really saying this out loud?

'Ah.'

'She walked with bare feet, had dirty clothes, and twitched her head a lot. Does that sound like Martha Otis?'

Willow shuddered, and Maud placed a hand over hers. She seemed a little pale and shaken, which wasn't making Willow feel any better.

'No, but she may be presenting in an altered state. An apparition, although frightening to witness, will not harm you in most cases, and I have already felt that she means you no harm. But she does want to get your attention, obviously more than I picked up on.'

'She scares me. I don't want to see her.'

'She's harmless. Try making a deal with her.'

Willow balked. 'A what?'

'Sometimes, when acknowledged, a spirit can be spoken to.'

'So I could tell her to go away?'

Maud shook her head.

'No, she wants your attention for a reason, but to a certain extent you could tell her that, for instance, you don't mind the messages, and you understand she wants...'

'Help,' Willow said. 'She said she wanted help in one of the messages. I think. Maybe she meant I needed help? I don't know now. I'm confused.'

'Well, okay, I suppose she wants help with whatever she is suffering with, although avenging her killer will be difficult. He died in prison six years ago.' She shook her head. 'Anyway, you could tell her you don't mind the messages, but you don't wish to see her again.'

'Will that work?'

Willow thought that she wouldn't feel quite so bad if she didn't have to see her again. Banging was banging, and messages were messages, but the figure? She couldn't take much more of that.

'It can. It doesn't always. The main thing is to remember that she can't, and won't, hurt you.'

'She can scare me to death.'

Maud smiled.

'She doesn't want that either, child, I promise you. Her energy is stirred, and it is uncomfortable and restless, but it seems to be directed more around this darkness than at you. There's a change afoot, I can feel it. I wish I could tell you more, but this is what I was compelled to share with you. I can say no more without exaggerating what I know, and I could be wrong.'

'It's okay. Thank you, Maud, and thank you for your time. At least I don't feel so afraid of her now.'

'You shouldn't. You have an ally in her. She feels protective, but she is troubled herself. There is a reason she doesn't rest, possibly the violent way she died. Tit for tat.'

Willow nodded and thanked Maud again as she left the little house.

She felt better, although the fact she had been discussing a dead person who had come back to roam her house and knock at cupboards, like it was the most normal thing in the world, was a little disconcerting.

Tit for tat.

Forty-Seven

T HE SUN WAS TRYING to shine as Willow crossed the lane and walked back down to the bridge. It was still deathly cold for an autumn day, but cold and sunny, she could deal with.

What she couldn't deal with was the man who was working in the front garden of McGracken House.

She slowed. It had been a long time since she had spoken to Jack properly, and she felt a little guilt climb up into her chest as she watched him cut back and pull out the flowers which had now given up believing there was any shred of summer left. Willow was starting to believe that, too.

He should feel guilty, too, she thought defensively, but wiser, calmer Willow seemed to cut the voice off.

Why do you have a problem speaking to people about what is bothering you and giving them a chance to explain? It's very judgmental.

She frowned.

I don't... do I?

You absolutely do, and that is why you walked away from Carlton and told him not to get in touch.

That was–

That is why you didn't contact him straight after the photographs and confront him.

That is why you haven't asked Jack about his wife, even though he's been nothing but nice to you.

That's why you keep running from your uninvited house guest.

'Confrontation,' she whispered, and she knew she had hit a chord within herself. She didn't like confrontation. Even the thought of it aroused a horrible sense of fear and dread in her soul.

Which is strange because you never had a problem standing up for yourself and confronting people before.

It was like a light bulb had clicked on her head.

The attack, it's been since the attack. You confronted the attackers, and they ruined your world. You don't want to give that opportunity to anybody else.

But it's happened either way.

I didn't confront Carlton, but we still had the argument. I didn't know about the affair, but it still came out. The truth has a way of forcing its way to you, whether you want to hear it or not. Whether it changes you or not.

'Hi,' Jack said, and seemed to falter, 'I didn't think you'd be here today, after your message.'

Willow looked up to find that she had overshot the bridge in thought and was now outside the front of the large house.

Good job the road isn't busy.

She looked at the man beside her with new eyes. He had been kind, he had looked after her, and he hadn't said he was married.

So what? Is it any of your business? Jack is doing a job. It's a shame you got carried away, but this is your problem, not his. Can you blame his wife for marrying him? Look at him.

Willow was staring, she knew that, and Jack was smiling, but he looked unsure, quite possibly because her behaviour was more than a little strange. He'd have jibed her by now if they'd have been on normal territory, snapped her out of it, made her laugh, teased her a little.

You did this, Willow.

She shook her head, half at herself, and half at him as he waited.

'No, I'm not. I...' She pointed back at the bridge, 'I was going home. I just overshot the road because I was too busy thinking. Lame, huh?'

Jack's smile softened. Possibly because she hadn't said this much to him in days.

'You've a lot to think about,' he said. 'How are you after yesterday?'

'I'm Fine, thanks, and yes, even more to think about now,'

'Oh? Where have you been?' he said, leaning on the fork.

She felt a pang of nostalgia. This is what she had missed. The fact that whatever it was, wherever she had been, and whatever he was doing, she always felt that she had his full attention. He was good at that.

You can't get that close again Willow, the hugs were way beyond the mark, especially with the way they made you feel. It's too close.

Her heart fell flat. She left it there.

He was married, she would get over it. She couldn't keep punishing him forever.

'To see Maud,' she said.

He cocked an eyebrow, and a small grin began to play around his lips. A glimpse of the old Jack that made her want to cry.

Willow forced a smile. 'She's okay, Jack. She told me a lot of stuff about the history of Ivy Cottage and what went on there.'

Jack's smile faltered. 'Ah, that was a nasty business with Martha Otis and her fella. It hit the village pretty hard. If you wanted to know some history about your house, you could just ask. I was raised here. I was only a wee bairn when the murders happened, but I still remember the repercussions and the fear that took over the village well.'

Willow shook her head.

'I've found out what I wanted to know, but thank you.'

Jack nodded, but he almost seemed to wilt.

He wants things to get back to normal between you.

It can't happen. Not like it was.

She turned back to the bridge.

'I have to go, Jack, things to do. I'll be here tomorrow, though.'

He nodded and smiled.

'It'll be good to see you. Thanks for the chat, sweetheart. I've missed them.'

Willow smiled back and raised her hand as she walked away.

She'd missed them too, and the laughs, more than he'd know.

She turned at the bridge, waved at Jack, who was still standing watching her, and then she lost sight of him in the trees.

She let out the breath she had been holding.

That wasn't so bad, was it?

When her old self began to argue, she shut the voice down.

Ivy Cottage loomed above her as she climbed up the track, but now it looked different, not so ominous. And now she had a name for the presence – Martha – she had almost given it an identity. A real house guest.

A protective ally Maud had called her. That couldn't be a bad thing, could it? That's a good house guest to have.

She also said that she was a troubled spirit herself.

A house guest with problems.

Willow narrowed her eyes. So if she could help with whatever the problem was, then maybe her spirit would leave? Had Maud said that?

She tried to think back on the information Maud had given her about spirits and hauntings and what she did before she left. The boring bit, Maud had said. Like the fire drill advice.

Willow hadn't found it boring. She had been more than skeptical at what sounded like lunacy, but she had tried to listen hard. She was having to live with this thing, after all.

She couldn't remember exactly what Maud had said, but she could always ask at the yoga session on Thursday.

Sophie will hang onto every word of that conversation.

She grinned.

Yeah, well, Sophie doesn't have to live with this incessant fear.

She reached the front door and pulled it open, trying not to hesitate as she had been doing lately - it just seemed to build the apprehension.

She looked straight through the glass into the bright hallway. No shadows.

That was good, but there was something big and white hanging across the carpet about halfway up the corridor.

Willow felt her heart jump.

'Oh, for crap's sake, no.'

She pushed open the glass door and stepped into the hallway.

The cupboard door was open, the three planks of wood on the floor, nails strewn beside them.

Willow wanted to cry. She knew she could nail them over the door again, but she also now knew that it wasn't a failsafe.

She swallowed as she stopped to pick up the planks, feeling watched in her own hallway. She could feel the prickle of hair raising on her arms and the back of her neck.

She thought of what Maud had said as she shut the door and took the hammer from the drawer in the sideboard.

You could try making a deal with her.

That's all well and good in theory, Willow thought, as she hammered nails back into the boards, but it's scary as shit up here, and I'm not sure talking to an empty house is good for anybody's mental health. Plus, if she answers, I'm gone. I can't stay here with a talking ghost.

You won't know unless you try.

Willow went into the living room, because that was the room she felt safest in, as if anywhere was safe from something that could walk through walls.

She pulled in a breath.

'Okay, Martha, I think we need a chat.'

Forty-Eight

W ILLOW SPENT THE REST of the day pottering around the cottage, tidying up, and venturing into the back rooms. Now that she felt better about what was in here with her, it was giving her courage.

Knowledge is power, she thought.

She was straightening the bedspread when the phone rang for the fiftieth time that day. She almost switched it off, but Carlton was really starting to piss her off. Maybe it was about time she confronted the problem instead of expecting it to go away. If she could deal with Carlton, she could certainly deal with Jack, and both problems needed a solution.

She used her sleeve to wipe the sad face, and its word BEWARE from the window, with a flicker of unease as Maud's darkness came into her mind.

She pushed it out and answered the call.

Focus, Willow. The darkness is on the other end of the phone. Let's see if we can get rid of it.

'What?' she said.

'Willow? Babe? Oh my God, Willow, is that really you? You don't know how long I've been trying to get hold of you.'

Carlton's words gushed over the line, and she could almost smell the relief pouring from him. It made her curl her lip in disgust.

'I have a good idea,' she said.

'Why didn't you answer? I've been going out of my mind down here.'

'I told you not to contact, Carlton, that I need the time alone, remember?'

'But this is important, babe. I even called your mum. I need to warn you about something-'

'I know, she phoned.'

Carlton fell silent.

'You still didn't call me back?'

Willow felt a flutter of pity at the sadness in his tone. She wiped her hand over her face.

No pity. You know what he's done. You know why he's calling.

'Why would I?'

'I told your mum it was urgent?'

'She said.'

'Then why...?' he trailed off, and it was like something clicked in his brain.

'I know, Carlton, I know what you did.'

Carlton fell silent, and for a moment his heart stopped.

She knew?

Of course she doesn't know. How would she know?

No, Coop is right, you're the only one with contact, and you haven't told her.

'I... I don't know what you're talking about?' he stammered, his hand shaking on the handset.

'Yes, you do.' She was giving nothing away. 'How long Carlton? How long have I been kept in the dark? How long have you been doing this behind my back? Just since the attack?'

Carlton blinked rapidly. The attack? And then he almost sank back with relief. The attack, the pills. She knew? Okay, that he could deal with. That was neutral ground. He had been calling to tell her about the pills anyway, maybe she had stopped taking them already, and that would be a good thing in this situation.

'Right, that's what I wanted to talk to you about,' he said, regaining some of his lost footing. 'Have you taken your pills, babe?'

There was a harsh laugh on the other end of the line and Carlton frowned.

'It's always about that, isn't it? Always about whether little Willow is seeing or doing more than she should. No, Carlton. I have not taken my fucking pills, and I won't be taking them ever again.'

Carlton felt himself relax a little, although his hand still shook, and a sheen of sweat hung around in the hair that sat on his top lip. She was pissed about the pills, the little white lies, and the surveillance, and that was okay. He knew that he would have had to tell her some of it anyway to get her off the pills. If she had some of it figured out, it would make his life a little easier.

If she had been off the pills for a while, she would be coherent and that would be better, even if she was angry.

'Okay, that's good. That's good.'

'Is it? Because, while we're on the subject, I've been doing very well off them, and the panic attacks are subsiding with the help of good people who don't tell me that I'm going to die each time I can't breathe.'

Carlton closed his eyes and rubbed a hand across his mouth.

'Okay, babe. I know what you must be thinking, but it really isn't like it seems.'

'So how is it?'

Carlton blew out a breath.

Where to start?

'I'm waiting for an explanation,' she said. Carlton thought he hadn't heard her so angry for years, but then she had been doped up for most of the last four.

'Okay, just let me think.'

'Why, so you can work out your story? I don't even care about that crap, Carlton, I don't trust you, I'm not sure I even like you right now, we are so completely done, I can't even tell you-'

Her breath hitched and Carlton felt his own chest well with pain.

'No, babe. No, please, Willow, please hear me out. I love you.'

'There is no love in a relationship with no trust, and you broke every level of trust. You disgust me, Carlton.'

Carlton reeled. He supposed he should expect such a reaction, but it still came at him with the force of a sledgehammer.

'Willow, babe, hear me out, please.'

There was silence on the other end. A sniff. He thought that she may have been calming down, but when she spoke, her voice was still edged with granite.

'You have five minutes, and I'm warning you right now that nothing you say could ever put this right. Ever. We're done.'

Carlton was nodding, sat in his dressing gown, unwashed, on his own settee.

'Okay,' he said. 'Okay.'

He took a few seconds to compose himself or he thought he may lose the plot himself.

'I was protecting you, that's all.'

Willow spat a harsh laugh.

'Protecting yourself.'

'No. No, I know something that, to be honest, won't make you think any more of me, but I need to explain, right from the beginning. Will you listen? Please.'

'I'm listening.'

'Okay, so the day of your dad's birthday, the day of the attack. I didn't come to the pub with you-'

'I know, that didn't go unnoticed.'

Carlton swallowed.

'I didn't go because I was trying to get you all not to go. I hoped that if I dug my heels in, and you bowed out too, that your mum and dad would change the party time, or venue, or something, anything, until a little later on.'

'As if, Carlton. There were forty odd guests in that pub for dad's party alone. There's no way we could have changed anything within the last few hours. You knew that.'

'I did. But I wanted to change it, anyway. I desperately wanted to change it.'

'It wasn't going to change Carlton! And because it didn't, you didn't come, that's not fair!'

She was shouting now, and Carlton's heart gave a pull. She didn't understand, but she would. He had no choice but to tell her.

'I know it's not. It wasn't very courageous either. I should have tried harder.'

'To what? It wasn't going to change.'

'I tried to change it from the other side, too, I just want you to know that. I really tried to change what happened. I tried with everything I have. I guess I'm not a very good negotiator.'

He thought of what had happened with Suzie.

'I don't really have a backbone either. I should be tougher.'

The armpits of his dressing gown were damp, and he knew the future hung in the balance here, whether it had been for his mistake with Suzie or not.

Willow huffed.

'What the hell are you talking about? This is nothing to do with you Carlton, this is about me! What you've done to me, to my life, to our life.'

'Yes, it is, but it started with the robbery, Willow.' He swallowed hard. 'Because I know the gang who committed it, and I knew it was going to happen.'

Willow felt the world grow small and claustrophobic around her. She heaved in short breaths as Carlton's words sank in.

'You knew what?' she said.

The revelation had caught her completely off guard. She had been prepared to go all out at him for cheating, prepared to listen to his reasons for keeping her drugged, but this was one thing she hadn't been prepared for.

The evening of the party came rushing back. The argument, Carlton slamming the door as he left to 'work', although he was probably going to Suzanne, her fury at him for declining to come to something so important to her.

'I know the people who committed the robbery.' His voice cracked. 'I knew where they were going to hit and when. I knew there was a strong possibility you'd be caught up in it, and I was so, so fucking scared. I tried to speak to one of the gang members, tried to push them off course, but he didn't listen. To be honest, he never has. I didn't want this, I really didn't, and I know I should have tried harder.'

'You know them?' Willow's blood was beginning to run cold. 'You were involved in my father's murder?'

'No, no, no! No. I wasn't involved. My brother, Coop, is a bit of a bragger. He'd been stopping by the clinic for prescriptions for drugs for years. He often told me what they were up to.'

'So, what? You thought you'd help him along by fuelling his habit and playing along with murder? What about all the other people in there that day? What about all of the others killed? It wasn't just dad! It was *me*! I could have been killed, too.'

Carlton made a strangled sound and began to cry.

'I know, I know. But, babe, it wasn't supposed to end in murder. They had done a few other pubs over in the area, and they wanted cash, that's all. It was supposed to be about the cash. Coop had never taken a life before that day. He isn't a killer.'

'He *is* a killer, Carlton!'

Willow could feel the horror of the day rising, her stomach swirling with emotion.

He knew. He *knew*.

'I know, I know that. Oh, babe, I tried to stop you, that's why I tried to cancel the party. That was the reason for the whole crappy argument that day. I was terrified. I knew it was going to happen, and I couldn't stop it.'

Willow needed air. In the living room it was too thick, too stale. She moved to the front door, opening it, and gasping the fresh, chilly October air outside.

'Willow? Babe, please say something. I did call the police and tip them off. That's why they were there so fast, and that's why my brother got sent down.'

'What do you want me to say, Carlton? How very chivalrous of you? How very self-depreciating? They didn't come fast enough, did they? Five people died that day, one of them my dad! The carnage was–'

She hitched a breath, feeling the attack coming as her chest constricted.

'It was horrendous,' she finished, knowing it was lame, but also knowing she had to control herself.

'I know–'

'You *don't* know,' she shouted. 'You don't know anything about that day.'

'I know what you told me.'

'You can't even begin to comprehend,' she said, tears spilling over, as Carlton sobbed miles away in her apartment. The cozy apartment with no presence that liked to knock on cupboard doors and let in the cold. The apartment he had shagged his secretary in.

'I'm sorry,' he said. 'If I could take it all back, I would. I'd do anything, babe, please.'

Willow swallowed hard, wiping the tears from her face.

'And the rest?' she said.

Carlton gave a sob and then blew his nose noisily.

'There were four guys that went into the pub, but only my brother and one other got out.'

Willow found herself wishing he had been one of the two killed, but that was sod's law.

'So? Shame they weren't all killed.'

'Yes, I know you feel that way, and I don't blame you, but there's something you need to know. Willow, he knows you shot one of them.'

'I didn't shoot anybody.'

'You did. He says you had the gun, and you were spraying bullets - I've never told you I knew because it meant... well...'

'Admitting that you had contact with criminals, that you helped them to ruin lives?'

'No, because it meant admitting that *you* had killed someone, and you didn't seem to remember that bit. I didn't want to bring it back up in case it sent you further down.'

'I don't remember because I didn't shoot anybody. Someone else took the gun from me. He killed the other man after they'd ran out.'

One less fucked up fucker in the world.

Willow ran a hand over her brow. She was shivering hard.

'Willow, are you sure? Because Coop says-'

'So, you'll listen to his side over mine? He's a fucking criminal who nearly killed your girlfriend. I did not kill anybody. The two of them ran out, then someone took the gun from me and finished the second man off. The first man had been killed before that, and I was nowhere near him.'

'Okay, well, I suppose it doesn't make much difference-'

Willow almost threw the phone to the ground and stamped on it.

'Doesn't make a fucking difference? It most certainly does. I am not a killer–'

Carlton cut her off with a yell.

'No! no, I didn't mean that the way it came out. I mean, it won't make a difference to Coop. He won't listen to me. He's convinced you're the one.'

'Well, ring Borstal and tell him it's not fucking me. I killed no one. Have you spent all of this time drugging me because you think I'm dangerous?'

'Absolutely not. Of course not. I, I prefer the term protected, not drugged–'

'I couldn't give a fuck what you call it. You drugged me.'

Carlton stuttered.

'Well, I suppose, in a way.'

'In every way. How do you explain drugging your fucking girl-friend for four years?'

'Coop called me from prison. He told me he knew you had shot his friend. He told me that you'd pay, and that he would send people after you.'

'He was in jail.'

'Yes, but he said he was in contact with others outside. He promised when he was out, if they hadn't got you, that he would... follow up, I suppose.'

'Four years ago, Carlton, the attack was four years ago.'

'Yes, but I didn't know when these people would pounce, and I wasn't certain he wouldn't be released early and not say. He knows where the apartment is. He would have known exactly where to find you. You're stubborn Willow, even with the pain and the panic attacks, I knew you wouldn't be chased away by a threat. I knew that you wouldn't sell up and move, and I knew that you wouldn't let me track you and keep you safe if you were well. I knew you would carry on as normal even knowing that, but I couldn't have you out there when he could be scouting you out. I gave you the pills to keep you inside, to keep you protected.'

'You told me I'd die if I had trouble breathing, that I'd black out and die, Carlton.'

'Same reason, babe. I couldn't have you out there walking the streets. It was too risky. I set up the tracker and the surveillance so that I would be ready, without putting you through more than you already had been. You could stay safe and carry on living fear free.'

'You call that living? It was like living in an asylum. You can't keep someone locked up, Carlton. You can't. It's kidnap, it's holding someone against their will.'

'I could keep you safe-'

'So, this was all about you, and making you feel better? What about my mental health? What about the trauma I had just been through? What about the effects the pills had on me? What about the effects of being told I was going to die? What about the effects of being locked away and monitored? What do you think that did to me? Why the fuck do you think I'm here?'

Carlton released another sob.

'Coop is unruly, he was angry, babe, so very angry. He still is.'

'He's been locked up for four years now. He's probably forgotten and is planning his next poor victim.'

'No, no, he's not. He's still angry, and he's still out to get you. He thinks you killed his best friend. He's focused on you.'

'And you know that how?'

'Because he's out, babe,' Carlton said, his sobs growing heavier. He sniffed. 'He's out and the first place he's come is here. He's already trying to locate you. I've heard him speaking to people...'

Willow felt her heart roll right over. She stared round at the darkness as his voice faded into the background. It was pitch black out here, the trees thick, the cottage isolated. If someone wanted to stake her out, they could. Easily.

But somehow this didn't ring true. The attackers were out of the pub when the second man had been killed, probably being arrested. What reason would there be to think she had done it? How much of this was true? Was he even really out? And if he was, why was Carlton letting his maniac brother stay in the apartment with him anyway, after all he had done? Still covering for his brother? Or was this a lie to cover up the affair, which sounded much more probable? Hell, in that sense, she even had the pictures to boot.

He lies, Mum had said, *and he does it so convincingly, without missing a beat.*

Willow felt another stab of anger that he would make up something so ridiculously elaborate, and deeply personal, and expect her to believe it.

'Why did you message about the medication, Carlton?'

He stopped, cut off mid-sentence. 'What?'

Ah, see. Caught you out, didn't I?

'You messaged me about the medication a while ago now.'

'Oh, yes. I did. I wanted you to call so that I could discuss this with you. It wasn't about the medication; I was just trying to get you to speak to me. I needed to tell you to come off the tablets. You'll need your wits about you if he finds you, unless, well, you want to tell me where you are, and I can come up. I know him best, but I can't help you down here-'

'No, thank you.'

'What?'

'I smell bullshit, Carlton.'

'It's not, babe, I promise you, please, listen to me. He's *here*. He's out, and he's looking for you. I can't do much from where I am, can I? If you'll just let me know where you are-'

'Well, it's bloody simple from where I'm standing. You failed miserably last time, nearly ruined my life, took the next four years away from me, and now you're telling me this? If this is true, and I highly doubt that it is, then for fuck's sake, grow some balls and stop him this time.'

Willow ended the call with her heart pounding.

He had asked for her address too many times. Lies, all lies. She was glad that she hadn't only got that to go on, that there had been more.

It was time to put Carlton behind her and forge a new future, free of pills and panic attacks and visions of that day in the pub. She felt stronger now, more alive, more in control, and she knew that one person, the only one who had her back down there apparently, had helped her out hugely with making the break.

She opened the message from the person who had sent the photographs. Here was a girl who could smell bullshit, too - not only that, but she would call it. Willow hit reply and messaged two words back.

'Thank you.'

Forty-Nine

C OOP WAS GLARING AT the old man at the bar when the message came through. He was so drunk that for a second, he thought he had a bee inside his jeans. After a few minutes slapping his leg, he finally pulled out his phone, and ignoring the looks from the down-and-outs who drank here.

He threw up a middle finger at anyone willing to look at him, probably as drunk as he was anyway, and plopped back down onto his chair.

Except the chair wasn't where he had left it. His right buttock hit something hard and then he bumped down onto the floor as something came round to hit the back of his head.

'What the fuck?' he yelled, swinging around on his ass to square up the person who had hit him and finding the wooden back of the fallen chair.

There was raucous laughter and Coop threw up a few more middle fingers as more faces watched him stand and try to right himself.

'Yeah, yeah, show's fucking over, boys and girls.'

The patrons went back to their own drinks and Coop pulled the chair right, kept a hand on the centre of the seat, and then sat on it.

When he was stable, he pulled his pint toward him, took a long swig, finishing the glass, and pulled the next one over to him. He took another long drink as he watched a tattooed couple in the corner, heads together, in deep discussion. The guy's knuckles were tattooed with 'Fuck' on his right hand, 'off' on his left.

Coop wondered if he ever showed them to people who pissed him off like he was going to do a double fist bump, but not following through. Maybe he wasn't much of a talker, although he was doing some talking now.

Coop swung his gaze back to his pint and saw his phone on the table.

He blinked.

What was that doing there?

He picked up the device and stood, scraping his chair across the old wooden floor.

'Okay, which of you dickheads has taken my phone?'

The room was small, and it hushed as people looked his way.

'Looks like it's in your fucking hand to me,' said an older man with a shock of chin length gray hair. Badges covered his denim jacket, and there was more gold around his neck than B.A. Baracus from the Eighties series, The A Team.

There was more laughter. A cheer.

Coop moved to the front of the table, holding onto it as the room tilted and swayed.

'I'm not fucking around here. Who touched it?'

'Dude, pipe down,' a skinny black lad at the bar said, his jeans belted halfway around his buttocks, green pants on show. 'You've obviously had a skinful. No one touched your phone.'

'Yeah? Was it you?' Coop said, wobbling to the bar and waving the phone so close it tapped the lad's nose.

'Get the phone out of my face.' The lad was squaring up now and Coop saw that he was tall. He had at least a good foot on him.

Skinny though, I could take his ass.

'Touch my fucking stuff again, and I'll put the phone down your fucking throat.'

The lad frowned and grabbed Coop's wrist. It hurt. His grip was strong.

'Get your fucking hands off me,' Coop slurred, trying to pull away. The lad held firm.

'The phone was in your pocket. It went off. You ran around like a pussy and then you slapped your drunk ass on the floor. You want to know what I think happened here?'

The lad was so close now that Coop could see the whites of his eyes were tinged with red.

'Not really,' Coop said.

'You had a call or a fucking message. Probably from your trashy wife. Check your phone and go home. You've had enough.'

Coop raised his eyebrows.

'*You're* telling *me* to go home?' He looked around the pub and pointed a finger. 'This wimpy little scrot is telling *me* to go home?' he shouted.

'I'm telling you to go home,' the man behind the bar said. 'Get out, and if you make a scene like this again, you're barred.'

Coop smiled at the man's lined face. He could probably take both of them at once, but now someone else was shouting at him to leave.

'I can't go anywhere while this young man has my hand now, can I?'

He smiled at the lad, whose full lips smiled back as he released his grip and held his hands up.

'Go,' he said.

Coop turned around with a swagger that felt a little too big. He staggered, and then he turned back, swinging his fist. The lad had moved back, and was sipping his pint, coolly watching as Coop's fist hit the bar with a bang.

Pain exploded through his hand, and stars exploded through his vision.

There was laughter as the lad smiled, raised his pint, and took another drink. Coop staggered toward him, and then hands grabbed him by the arms, and he felt himself dragged to the door.

'Let me go,' he grunted, as he fell down the pub's three steps and onto the pavement. He lay on his side, his hand agony, and now his leg throbbing too. There was a thump on his jacket, and he winced, thinking someone had followed him down onto the street, but as he looked, he saw his phone lying in the crook of his arm.

The lad had said something about the phone. What was it?

Coop pulled the device off his arm as the pub door swung open and then he flinched and sat up as cold water hit his chest and face.

'What the fuck?' he said, looking at the man in the doorway. The older man. The B.A. lookalike.

'Forgot your pint,' the man said, then he saluted, two fingers from his brow. 'Have a great night,' he said, and went back into the pub.

Coop thought about following him, but if there was one thing he knew, it was when he was beaten. He was too drunk, too cold, and too unsteady.

'I'll be back for you,' he mumbled, getting to his feet, and pointing to the pub door with his good hand.

Then he turned, stepped into the road, and stumbled back at the blare of the horn.

'Fuck you,' he said. He tried to raise his middle finger and grunted as pain flew down his arm. 'Fuck, that hurts,' he yelled, and stumbled across the road to the park.

Fifty

C ARLTON'S EYES AND NOSE were sore when he woke. He had cried all evening, and eventually cried himself to sleep.

He crawled out of bed. His limbs hurt, and his chest ached.

This is what you get, Carlton. This is your karma, your dose of reality, after trying to have your cake and eat it.

He shuffled to the bathroom and checked his face. His nose was bright red, his eyes weren't far behind, although they sat in dark puffy circles.

She left you. She left you and is it any wonder? Look what you did?

He averted his own gaze as he felt the tears threaten behind his eyes again. He wanted to go back to bed, to pull the covers over himself and wake up to reveal it had all been a nightmare.

He had no such luxury though, because he couldn't just leave this alone.

Willow was in trouble, and whether she wanted his help or not, he knew Coop best, and he would have to make his way to her aid, anyway.

Somehow.

Two days ago, turning off the tracking had seemed the best idea she'd had, now he thought it was the dumbest. He could have been with her today, talking her round, helping her get well, and moving her on to somewhere Coop wouldn't find either of them.

Now that wasn't possible. He had no way of knowing where she was.

Turning on the tap, he splashed water over his face before brushing his teeth and returning to the bedroom to get dressed.

He would just have to keep a close eye on Coop, and if needs be, he would trail him to her location when he had located her in whatever illegal way he was using.

He shuffled downstairs, pushed open the living room door, and his heart stopped.

The living area was empty. The duvet wasn't out. This room hadn't been slept in last night.

'No,' he whispered. 'No! He has not gone already. He can't have.'

Carlton banged his hand against the architrave as his heart seemed to somersault in his chest. He knew all too well that Coop could have, and wouldn't even bother to tell him, because despite his bragging, he wouldn't let Willow's boyfriend in on his plans. Before last week, he'd had no idea that Coop was tracking her at all. That was a lucky overheard conversation. Without that, he would still be clueless.

He was clueless, and now he was completely stuck short of calling Willow, and he didn't hold out much hope of getting an answer.

Carlton staggered into the living room, fell down onto the sofa and put his head in his hands, tears threateningly close to spilling over again.

Why couldn't he get a break? Just one goddamn break.

Fifty-One

E ACH TIME WILLOW THOUGHT she was doing well, she slipped. It was bad enough that Carlton had been cheating, but to make up the lies he had about his reasons for drugging her and keeping her inside had infuriated her. To bring up the past, and that day, and say that he knew all along? Surely that was bullshit, a way of deterring her from speaking about his affair, maybe? He was running scared, but she couldn't fathom what was truth and what wasn't... and she still hadn't heard his explanation for shagging Suzanne. Was that for her protection, too?

She had trawled over the infuriating conversation all night, ranting her house guest into silence, until she decided he wasn't worth her time and energy any longer. She had confronted him, she had told him they were done, she was off the pills and doing better, she was getting a life up here. That was it. Enough. Time to move forward.

With Carlton forced to the back of her mind, she had gone to McGracken House early, eager to lose herself in physical work. In the vein of sorting things out instead of sitting on problems, she vowed to stop punishing Jack for her own emotions, too. She had to get over herself and stop wallowing. Jack had been kind, and he didn't deserve the way she had been treating him.

And so, this morning, after a chat at the gate, they agreed to work together to dig the last bed in the third poly tunnel, before getting manure from the muck heap over at the back of the pigsty and stables, which was a badly thought out distance from the vegetable patch where most of the manure was used.

Willow was enjoying the pace. Jack was one of those rare people who could talk and work at the same time. He didn't stand around like some of the others here who seemed to only work their body or their mouth in turn, which was frustrating when she simply wanted to get on and lose herself in the work.

She was doing well, enjoying his company, but keeping her feelings in check, although she knew he was picking up on it. It was a tentative affair, but it was keeping her the right side of the line, and she had to admit, after the last week working alone, working closely with Jack again felt good.

When the third bed was dug, they took the wheelbarrow to the muck heap.

'You barrow this time. I'll shovel, then we'll swap if you like. It's much easier on the arms that way,' he said.

'Sounds good to me,' she said, watching him roll up his shirt sleeves before shovelling, and trying not to notice his tanned muscles.

When the barrow was full, she followed him across the yard to the beds they had dug just over a week ago, her arms straining satisfyingly with the weight and effort.

'Just wheel it to where it's easier, don't worry about walking on the soil. It'll be dug again after, okay?' Jack called over his shoulder.

'Got it,' she called back.

Just as they reached the bed, Warren called for Jack from the barn.

'Bugger,' Jack muttered as he raised a hand, turned back to Willow, and took the wheelbarrow from her.

'Okay, just tip it where you need it,' he said, moving easily onto the soil and flipping the barrow over. 'Then scatter it loosely around with a fork and give it a dig into the soil for now. Not too much, just a light covering is enough. When you've scattered this lot, give me a shout. I'm just going to give Warren a hand.'

'Okay,' she said.

'That okay?'

'I just said so,' she said with a smile.

'You can wait for me if you want, this isn't urgent.'

'No, I'll be fine. Thanks.'

'Right,' he said. 'Well, er...'

She knew he was stalling for time, and although she would have loved him to stay with her, she had to push him away for her own good.

'Just go, Jack. I'm fine. Any problems, I'll call you over.'

'Right,' he said, hooking a thumb back over his shoulder. 'I'll be in the barn.'

She nodded, took the fork from him, and almost died as their fingers touched, sending a jolt of electric around her body.

This was going to be harder than she thought.

She was digging manure into the second bed, lost in her own thoughts as she hummed Madonna's Vogue, and struck little poses with the fork, when she noticed Jack stood at the side of the vegetable bed, hands in his pockets, watching her. His eyebrows were raised, and a small smile played around his lips.

Her eyes widened as she felt the heat flush right up from her chest in a tidal wave of embarrassment.

'Oh, God, Jack, what are you doing?'

'Watching someone enjoy their work, I think,' he said with a small laugh. 'I threw some lunch together for you up at the house. I'd have brought it down, but I presume you want to wash your hands after digging this.' His eyes scanned the two large beds. 'You've done a lot, Willow. A hell of a lot. You didn't call me back to help you with the manure.'

'I didn't need it,' she said. 'I managed fine. I like the physical bit of the work a lot. It's almost therapeutic.'

'So, they say,' he said with a smile that didn't quite touch his eyes. 'You coming up?'

He nodded toward the house.

'In a sec, I won't be long. Just want to finish this section.'

Jack nodded. 'Okay, see you up there.' He began to walk away, then turned back. 'Oh, and there's only me and Duncan in there at the moment. Mick is out fixing a fence with warren two fields down, Tilly isn't here, and Helena has gone for a nap. Doesn't feel too good, apparently. You won't walk in to a crowd, I promise. You want a brew?'

Willow felt her stomach go to butter.

'That would be nice and thanks for the info.'

'Aye, see you in a bit.'

He turned and walked away, and Willow closed her eyes. Why was he so thoughtful and considerate?

Willow blew out her cheeks as she looked over the land, past the tents and down to where she knew the river ran, although you couldn't see it from here.

The hill rose steeply from the river up through the trees to the path that she and Sophie had walked down with Frodo. Just over a week ago, Jack had fought his way over there after realizing where her willow tree was, and getting to her exactly when she needed him.

He couldn't even do that wrong.

It would have been annoying if it didn't make her want to cry.

Fifty-Two

W HEN COOP WALKED INTO the house late that afternoon, he was pissed. Not literally. All the alcohol was now well and truly out of his system after a night and most of today spent lying on the park bench, with a throbbing hand, throwing his guts up into the grass.

He was tired, wet, and cold, and if he didn't have hypothermia, he'd be amazed.

At least his stomach had stopped complaining now.

He saw Carlton lying on the settee, staring at the television, his face red and puffy, and unwashed from the smell that radiated around the apartment. Coop felt his stomach roll over.

'You ever going back to work?' he said.

Carlton glanced at him, looked back at the television, and then flipped his head back up.

'You're back,' he said, swinging his legs off the settee with a relieved smile.

Coop raised his eyebrows.

'You're not going to tell me all of this-' He swung his hand from Carlton's head to his feet. '-was for my benefit, are you? You look like absolute shite.'

Carlton smiled, not biting.

'I can't say that you look any better,' he said. 'But no, this isn't for you, although I was slightly worried that you'd disappeared.'

'Scared I'd found her?'

'Not really.'

Coop smiled. His face hurt. Why did his face hurt?

'You won't know when I find her, bro. I can't have you interfering in business.'

'She dumped me. I couldn't care less anymore, Coop. Do what the fuck you have to.'

Coop paused in the doorway and narrowed his eyes.

'You been taking something, bro?'

'No. I told you she dumped me.'

Coop wrinkled his nose.

'That's what that look is? Looks like you care to me.'

'No.'

'Thought you were having no contact?'

'She called me. Told me I was a wanker. That's it.'

Coop raised his eyebrows, and a small flutter of anticipation filled his chest.

'So, you know where she is?'

'No, she didn't offer that information as she was balling me out.'

'What about? Found out about you and sexy Suze?'

Carlton flicked a look of disdain at his brother. 'No, it was other things. Do you know she basically accused me of drugging her?'

Coop walked through the room to the kitchen and opened the fridge. He located two bottles of Speckled Hen, took them out, held them in his arm as he popped the tops off, then he glanced at his phone.

One message.

His heart nearly jumped out of his chest as he opened it up.

It was from Willow. It simply said thank you.

You're mighty welcome little lady, he thought with a wide grin, physically restraining himself from fist pumping the air. It had worked. She had answered, and from here it would be easy. He had already spoken to the guy who would trace the number for him. He wanted a fee the size of his egotistical head, of course, but that was no longer an issue now that he had had extra time to hang about here getting deals. Now, the real fun would begin. He was going to little red riding hood's house, and she'd better be home.

The bottles clanged between the fingers of his left hand as he picked them up. His right didn't feel it could pick up a teaspoon right now, and it throbbed like a bugger. He walked back into the living room and handed Carlton a bottle.

'Have you seen the time?' Carlton said, indicating the clock on the wall which said 3.30pm.

'Beer-o'clock,' Coop said. 'You having one or not? Tell me about this riveting dumping, then.'

Carlton took a bottle, and Coop took a long swig of his own, feeling better than he had in hours.

Hair of the Dog, he thought, and the result of a great text message.

On to phase two. Get the fuck out of this dump.

Fifty-Three

C ARLTON'S STOMACH ROLLED AS he sipped at the beer, but the inclination to keep Coop on side until he had discovered just what he knew was strong. He had slipped from his sight last night, and he couldn't let it happen again.

'So that's it. She accused me of drugging her, trapping her, and trailing her,' he said, trying to keep his voice free of the guilt and fear he felt.

Coop frowned.

'But you just said that you did,' he said.

'I know that, but I did it for her protection, from you or your... people,' he said for want of a better word.

Coop patted a hand on Carlton's arm.

'It was a nice try, too, but you'd never have seen me coming, bro, just like she won't see me coming now.'

Carlton quelled the ember of anger that sat boiling in his stomach.

'Yeah, well, I know that now, don't I? The point is everything I did, I did for her, and she just threw it back in my face.'

'Bitches will twist and turn things all day long, they love it. She's a fucking waste of space, bro, always was. Be grateful you've had a lucky escape. How's Suzie these days?'

'I don't know, I haven't seen her. Left her messages to cancel patients, that's it. If my practice survives this, it will be a miracle.'

Coop whistled through his teeth.

'You have landed yourself at the top of the self-pity pile, haven't you? You know what you need?'

'What?'

Coop winced and took another swig of beer. Carlton noticed sweat forming on his forehead.

'A bath, a shave, and a change of clothes. You stink, bro, I'm not even joking. I almost hurled when I came through the door.'

'It's my apartment...'

Carlton almost added 'you can leave,' but he remembered he was supposed to be buttering Coop up, and if he left, Carlton would be back where he had been an hour ago. Hopeless, and scared for Willow.

'Good that I won't be here much longer then, eh?' He clapped Carlton on the back and then yowled. His face contorted in pain, and Carlton saw actual tears in his brother's eyes.

'What's wrong?' he said.

'Fucking hand,' Coop hissed through his teeth.

Carlton looked at Coop's right hand, which was swollen and beginning to go purple.

'What did you do?'

'Fight with the bar last night,' Coop said. 'There was supposed to have been a guy's face in the middle. He moved. Fucker broke my hand; he'd better hope I don't see him again.'

Carlton was still looking at the hand, but Coop pulled it out of sight.

'It's fine, it'll heal. Could do with some paracetamol though, or something stronger.'

Carlton flicked his eyes to his brother. It did look painful and was probably broken.

'What you need is a hospital,' he said.

'Nope, I need some painkillers and a bandage.'

Carlton sighed. 'Why don't you just get it checked out? I'll come with you. It must hurt like hell.'

'It does, and I don't need a fucking babysitter. I'm not going. Can you get me some painkillers or not?'

Coop raised eyebrows that looked too dark on his sheet white face.

'You know I can,' Carlton said. 'I'll need my prescription pad, though. It's locked up at work.'

'I suggest you get it, then. I'll allow you to take a bath first, you look like the homeless guy at the station. You'll be outside the front door with your sleeping bag soon, begging for scraps.'

Carlton held back the quip on his tongue.

Coop may not be so far off the mark if he didn't get back to work, and yet, he had no choice but to stick as close to his brother as he possibly could right now.

It would be Coop's fault if everything fell through. Coop's fault that the landslide had already begun with Willow.

He hoped if he could get to her, then he could make her see. She would understand and take him back. Her words last night had cut like a knife and gutted him like a fish.

'Can I ask you something first?'

It was a long shot, but it felt like a way forward. He had to try.

'If you fucking hurry up.'

Carlton licked his lips and tried to sound angry.

'When you go - after her - I want to come with you. Teach the bitch a bit of a lesson myself. I was keeping her safe from you, what a fucking joke when she throws it back in my face. I want to teach her she should see just what-'

Coop curled his lip at him. Even Carlton knew he hadn't quite hit the spot.

'Don't try to talk tough Carlton, you sound like a care bear on steroids.'

Carlton shook his head.

'I don't care what you think,' he said, trying for more edge. 'I need to see her. She doesn't get to dump me over the phone, raging about what I've done wrong. I want to show her *she's* done wrong, and I want to tell her we're through. She can't come back. Ever.'

Coop took another swig of his beer, unconvinced.

'Well, you have done something wrong. You slept with your secretary - who is fitter and hotter - so why don't you just let this slide and hook up with her? Sex four times a night without the guilt. Or you could start a pansy relationship if you like, I suppose. Nothing stopping you now is there. Just get her out of your head.'

Carlton felt panic and real anger emerge in his chest.

'I don't want to get her out of my head, and I don't want Suzie. What I want is to teach that bitch a goddamn lesson!'

Coop grinned, showing a line of straight white teeth.

'Okay, brother, now you're talking my language. Didn't think you had it in you, Mr Nice Guy.'

Carlton was breathing heavily.

'So, can I come with you when you find her?'

Coop assessed him with a swig that finished his beer.

'Nope. You'll get in my way, and nothing is getting in my fucking way. If you find her first, go for it, but I finish her. Me, and me alone.'

Carlton felt deflated. Of course it hadn't worked. He had never strayed onto the wrong side of the path any more than Coop had strayed over to the straight and narrow. Why had he thought that he would convince him otherwise?

'Also,' Coop added. 'If you do anything to her first, or back down like a pussy and warn her? Make no mistake, I will kill you. Do you understand?'

Carlton swallowed the lump in his throat and nodded his head.

'Fantastic. Glad we sorted that out. Now can you get changed and get my fucking pills? I'm in agony here.'

Carlton had a headache that was taking over his whole body as he drove to the clinic. Every set of headlights seemed to beam into his brain like lasers, he could almost feel them burning a hole. He was also aware that he had drunk a bottle of beer, and now he was driving. Quite probably not over the limit, but he wasn't a drinker, and his ability to drive had to be reduced. If the chemist hadn't been so far into town, he would have left the car at home, but Coop was steaming for his pills, and his mood was getting worse with each passing minute.

He was almost at the clinic car park when he realized his mistake. Asking to go with Coop and revealing that he may be after Willow too officially put them in a race - in Coop's mind, anyway. Carlton should have stayed quiet and trailed him instead.

Too late now. You're certainly no mastermind, Carlton.

Then his mind threw him a new idea. Maybe there was something he could do after all.

He had heard Coop on the phone with someone last week saying that he was expecting a message that would lead him to Willow, hadn't he?

He was pretty sure that was it.

A message.

And as Coop was still here, was it possible that the message hadn't come through yet?

Maybe he just had to monitor his brother's phone.

Sounded easy enough, but he had no idea what his password was, and if it was fingerprinted like his own, he was no further forward.

Except that he knew someone who had experience with tracking and hacking into phones. She had learned out of necessity too, after her husband had cheated on her for eighteen months and denied it furiously. The phone revealed more than she could have hoped for and gave her all the ammunition she needed.

Suzie.

And it just so happened that he was going to the office right now.

Maybe this was fate in action after all.

Fifty-Four

W ILLOW FELT CALMER THAN she had in a long time as she walked back up to the house in the dark after yoga. The wind pulled and tugged, but the rain was holding off.

Sophie had made her laugh so much after the session, with an account of an embarrassing moment with her agent earlier, that she had almost choked to death, causing Tam to rush to the vending machine for water, and talk her though a panic attack that wasn't happening.

Which only made Willow and Sophie laugh even more.

The smile was still on her face after their last goodbyes, and Willow felt good. She was also confident that the cottage would be better tonight after her little chat yesterday. It had felt at least hospitable when she had tidied it up earlier, despite the small message on the window.

Willow put the key in the lock and felt the hair rise at the back of her neck. She paused.

There was someone behind her.

Watching.

She turned the lock, opening the door and stepping over the threshold, before peering back out into the chilly darkness. The wind rustled the last of the russet aspen leaves left on the trees and swept the rest down the roadside.

There was nothing out there to see.

Still, her hackles wouldn't go down. There was something wrong here tonight.

Willow shut the door, feeling the tension increase. The feeling that she was being watched - or rather observed - was almost crippling.

Guess the bed is out of the question tonight, then?

She had planned on sleeping in it when she had remade it this morning in the daylight. Now she wished the duvet was back in the living room. It was one more step into the dark side of the house that she had to make or freeze to death.

Goosebumps littered her body. She realised she was still facing the solid wood of the outside door and facing the inside privacy glass into the hall seemed like way too much of a task.

Well, you'll be frozen to death if you stand here all night.

She closed her eyes as she turned, and a whimper escaped her lips.

Calm down. You haven't even got in the house yet.

But she knew what she would see before she even opened her eyes. And like the sun rose every single morning, there it was.

There *she* was.

The shadow - Martha - was at the door in front of her, distorted in the swirls of the glass.

Willow saw one twitch before she screamed and turned back to the solid door outside.

'Go away, go away, go away,' She whispered. 'Please go away.'

Her lips trembled and her body began to follow suit. She could feel the figure's eyes on her back. Feel her trying to turn her around.

Then there was a touch on top of her head, light fingers, even though Willow knew the door was still locked between them.

Doesn't matter, she can come through, can't she?

'No!' she yelled, shaking her head and batting her hands at the places the fingers had been. 'L...leave me alone!' she yelled. 'M... M... Martha, you promised you wouldn't sh... show yourself.'

Although that wasn't strictly true, Willow thought. It had been a very one-sided conversation, to be honest.

'Leave me be, p... please. I... I want to help but you sc... scare me.' Willow felt her heart almost pounding out of her chest. 'Oh fuck, I just have to go. I can't stay here.'

She was about to open the front door when an icy breeze ruffled at her neck, taking her breath away in its passage. Willow felt her inside's go to cold mush with it.

Then the breeze disappeared, and Willow knew she had gone. Her shaking hands clenched into fists, she slowly turned.

The glass door was open, which sent her stomach tumbling over, but the form was gone, and the hallway looked normal behind it. Even the cupboard door was shut.

'Thank you, Martha,' she muttered, her relief almost flooring her, despite the door.

She pushed the door before going inside and shutting it behind her. It was only then that she noticed her eyes wet with tears that she didn't know she had cried in the tension.

She wanted to walk into the living room, as though she knew Martha would heed her and stay out of the limelight, but she knew nothing of the sort. The chat with Maud had made things seem so much easier in the daylight.

Willow half ran with her coat and boots still on. In the living room, she shut the door and pulled the curtain across.

She shivered, her heart still pounding.

The ordeal wasn't over. She had to have a shower. She was layered in dried sweat from yoga and the shower here had seemed safer than the community centre after the last time. Now she was questioning her decision.

At least you put fresh clothes in the bathroom ready.

Small mercies.

'Martha?' she said aloud, raising the hair on her arms. 'I'm going in the shower. I'd appreciate you not joining me there.'

It seemed Martha was going to play ball as the rest of the evening fell unusually quiet. Willow relaxed enough to do some dinner and eat at the table. Martha hadn't done any of her artwork on the mirror or the windows, as Willow had asked, and there were no noises from the hallway at all. No thuds, and no creaks.

It was as though the house – or Martha – had settled now that Willow had acknowledged her and offered to help... however the heck she was supposed to do that.

She called her mum, telling her about the argument and what Carlton had said. Then she switched on the television, replied to a funny gif from Sophie with laughing emojis, and answered Tam's apology and enquiry about how she was.

After that she had chanced getting the duvet from the bedroom, not quite willing to sleep in there tonight, after all.

There hadn't been a peep.

Not until Willow was laughing hard at a comedy that was being re-run for what seemed like the hundredth time.

Then there was something. Something she had never heard before. Just faint, but enough for her to turn the television onto mute and listen harder.

But now there was nothing.

Maybe she had imagined it.

It had set the tone, though. She could no longer laugh so openly at the film as she had one ear on the hallway beyond the curtain.

She picked up her phone and looked at the time.

11.25pm.

'Great. Please Martha, don't start now, I'm tired. You've done so well this evening. I promise I will look into you tomorrow and see if I-'

The noise cut her off, and Willow froze.

Scratching. There was *scratching*.

It seemed to come from the hallway. Willow felt her breathing coming faster.

I can't do this for another night.

More scratching, and then a period of silence, and Willow felt herself pulled to the curtained door. She half wondered whether a cat had got in after all and had finally got out of the cupboard itself.

Of course, because a cat can beat off all the nails and planks across the door by itself, can't it? Especially from the inside.

Willow stood behind the curtain, feeling the energy build on the other side of the doorway. Her head ached with pressure, and then there was another series of scratches from just beside the door.

She teased the curtain across a fraction and peered round it.

There was nothing to see, and nothing looked out of place.

Sweat trickled between her shoulder blades as she pulled the curtain more and peered at the foot of the door.

See, there's nothing there. It's fine.

Out in the hallway was a sudden bang, as though a bomb had gone off.

Willow screeched and ducked, throwing an arm over her face as the boards flew off the cupboard, hit the wall and the sideboard before dropping to the floor with a clatter.

Willow crawled back to the door and pulled the curtain back over the glass with a whimper. Her heart thumped an erratic beat in her chest, fast and frantic.

What the fuck?

She stood up slowly in the resounding silence, every limb shaking. As she stared at the curtain, there was a new noise.

A slow creak.

Willow backed away from the doorway, swallowing hard.

'Oh no, Oh no. I can't do this, Martha. I can't.'

Her throat felt like sand had lodged itself down her windpipe. She couldn't breathe.

As she listened to the thin whine in her throat, she staggered back to the settee and flopped down, elbows on her knees, as she tried to control her breathing.

The scratches were coming louder now, joined by an older sound.

TH-UD.

Willow put her fingers in her ears and began to rock.

'Please stop, Martha, please stop, Martha, please stop,' she whisper-chanted, her breath coming in short, ragged bursts.

TH-UD.

There was more scratching and a thump as something dropped - or maybe something had crawled out of the hole in the cup-board.

Willow whimpered as she grabbed her phone. She couldn't be here anymore, but there was nowhere else she could go at half-past eleven at night.

Sophie?

There was a creak, and more scratching by the living room doorway.

WHAT THE HELL IS THAT?

She scooted from the settee and backed up to the living room window on her backside.

What the hell is in the cupboard? Surely this can't be the work of a ghost. Maud said that she couldn't hurt me, but she can tear the cottage apart?

Every hair on her head seemed to stand on end as she unlocked the phone to message the only person she thought would be big enough and strong enough to help her.

Jack? Are you awake?

She typed it three times before her fingers hit the right letters and the autocorrect didn't have a cow. He answered almost instantly, and Willow began to cry with relief.

I am, are you okay?

She quickly messaged back.

Not really. I have some trouble with my hallway cupboard. I don't know what to do. Please help.

There was a pause and willow felt her heart thumping as she waited. The sounds of scuffling and scratching continued from the hallway. She wiped a sheen of sweat from her face as he finally answered.

Well, that wasn't quite what I was expecting, but I'll be right there. Give me five.

Willow put her head into her hands and sobbed with relief. She hadn't the coordination in her shaking fingers to type more, she was just glad that he had responded quickly asked no questions. That was who Jack was proving to be over and again; action first, questions later, and she couldn't be more grateful right now.

Fifty-Five

W ILLOW'S TEARS DRIED AS she saw the car headlights appear
behind the curtains of the living room and tackled the
second hardest task of the night. How to get to the front door
while passing through what sounded like the destruction that
was in her hallway.

She hesitated at the curtained door, frozen with fear at what lay
beyond.

For now, all suddenly seemed quiet, and she wasn't sure
whether that was good or bad.

There was a banging on the door and the only thing that propelled Willow into the hallway was the thought of Jack on the
other side of it.

The corridor was clean, except for the planks of wood that were
now stacked neatly on the floor, the nails atop the woodpile.
The cupboard door was shut, and the rest of the hallway looked
normal.

There was another knock and willow felt fingers crawl through
her hair.

What if it wasn't Jack? Would he really drive two minutes up the
road?

The door was solid, and her phone was in the living room. There
was no way to know except to open it.

She stepped into the quiet, expecting all hell to break loose
around her at any moment. When it didn't come, she unlocked
the privacy door and glanced back into the stillness of the
corridor.

Three bangs echoed around her, and she yelped.

The door, Willow, just the goddamn door.

'Willow? Are you in there?' Jack bellowed.

Relief swept through her as she fumbled with the keys in the lock and swung the door open.

Jack stepped out of the way as fear propelled Willow right outside next to him. She grabbed the arm of his coat.

'Jack, thank god, thank you so much for coming.' Tears slid down her cheeks as her hands grasped his padded jacket, not eager to let go of anything that was real.

Jack staggered back under her momentum, and light from the hallway picked up the frown on his face.

'Woah, Willow, you'll pull us both down,' he said with a laugh that bordered on nervous. 'What's all this about?'

'The... the cupboard. The hall. There's...' Her voice hitched, and she swallowed loudly. 'There's something in there.'

'All right. It's all right, calm down. Have you had a look?' he said.

Willow shivered beside him as the freezing wind raged through her knitted jumper, but the thought of going back inside the house was scaring her to death.

She shook her head hard, windblown hair sticking to her tear-streaked face.

Jack half-turned to face her, her hands on his coat stopping him from turning her all the way.

He swept her hair away from her face gently with both hands, forcing her to let go of his sleeve. She immediately grasped the material around his waist instead as he assessed her.

'Okay, hey it's okay. You've had quite a scare, haven't you? Let's get inside and get it checked out. I've got some tools in the car. I didn't know what you'd need me to bring.'

He eased her back inside the porch, but she pushed him through the glass door into the hallway ahead of her.

The air seemed still and expectant. Willow clutched the back of Jack's coat, moving close behind him, her eyes half closed, ready to run if anything so much as touched her.

'This cupboard?' Jack said, pulling open the cupboard door before Willow could answer and poking his head inside. Willow closed her eyes and pressed her face into the back of his coat.

'Willow!' he said with that same nervous laugh. 'I can't see while you're pulling me back, sweetheart.'

Willow shook as she pushed her face into the padded material harder, grabbing handfuls of it to cover her face.

'Willow!'

He turned, and she let go, not wanting her back to the cupboard where the monster was waiting. She grabbed the front of his coat and pulled him away from the mouth of the cupboard doorway.

'Don't put your back to it, Jack.'

Jack grabbed her hands and prised them from his jacket gently.

'Willow, calm down. I can't look inside the cupboard if you're pulling me back out of it. This is the one, right?'

Willow nodded as she grabbed for him and found one of his hands. 'yes.'

'Okay, well, all I can see in there is an ironing board and a hoover at the moment. If you let me go just for a second, I'll take a better look with the phone light, but I think it's empty apart from cleaning stuff.'

'No, it's not. It can't be,' she said, her voice shaking with fear.

Jack gave her a concerned frown.

'Let me take a look then, sweetheart,' he said gently. 'Whatever it is, I'll find it and we'll chuck it out. It's probably just a cat or something.'

He turned back to the cupboard, pulling his hand out of hers and reaching into his pocket for his phone. She lunged for his other hand and grasped it in both of hers.

If anything was going to drag him inside, she would be going with him. There was no way she would be left out here alone.

'Willow.' He shook his hand to prompt her to release him. When she wouldn't let go, he closed his fingers around hers instead. 'Okay, I guess we just do this together then.'

He opened the phone with his thumb and scrolled down to press the torch. Willow closed her eyes as the light hit the back wall of the cupboard. She could feel the tugging from Jack's warm hand as he shone the light inside and peered in after it.

'Ah,' he said.

There were several tugs on her hand as he knocked against the cupboard wall, and then he was still.

Willow felt her heart begin to accelerate.

'Jack?' she whispered.

'Still here,' he said with a squeeze of his hand. 'This is weird. You have...' There was a tug as he moved, and then he was still again '...your eyes closed,' he finished.

'I don't want to see. What have you found?'

'Just a cupboard. I promise it's empty, but you do have a hole here. Let me just move this.'

He pulled his hand free of hers and she grasped his coat again instead, her eyes still squeezed shut. She could see the hole well enough without opening her eyes. She didn't need to know if it had got any bigger, and whatever he saw in that hole, she didn't want to know what it was.

She heard him move the ironing board to the back wall.

Then there was tapping and a few knocks.

'Jack?'

'Just checking something,' he said.

'There's nothing in there?'

'Nothing, I promise you.'

Willow opened her eyes.

The hole was bigger. Not by much, but the darkness behind it seemed to mock her as she held onto Jack, who was knocking at the back wall of the cupboard.

'What is it?' she said.

'Hollow. It's a stud wall, not brick.'

'What does that mean?'

He turned to her, and she finally felt able to let go of him as the grip of fear loosened. The cupboard was as empty as he said.

'Well, these are brick-built cottages. All the houses around here are, so this wall has been put in at a later date for some reason.'

Willow felt her heart jump. 'What reason?'

Jack chuckled, 'I don't know, Willow, I've never lived here. This hole though... chipboard, you see?' He pulled at the hole and more of the chipboard came away with a snap.

'Don't Jack, I don't like it. There could be something behind it.'

'Exactly. There could be, especially if there's a cavity behind. You could be hearing noises from this cupboard until the poor thing passes.'

Willow thought of the scratching she had heard earlier. Maybe this wasn't supernatural after all. Maybe they could get the animal out and she could return to faces on mirrors and windows, which were a lot less scary.

'What do you want to do?' she said.

Jack rubbed a hand over his chin. 'Well, if you have no objection, we could open this bit of wall up and check behind it?'

The look on her face must have given him all the answer he needed. He took her shaking hands in his.

'It's just an option. I could cut a smaller hole around what's here already and shine a torch inside. It'll need squaring off to repair it anyway, nothing that wouldn't already need doing.'

Willow felt her throat close up as she nodded.

'Okay,' she whispered. 'Just a small hole.'

'I'll repair whatever mess I make, don't worry about that.'

Willow nodded again. She was more worried about whatever was behind there than the mess he made, but if he was going to repair it for her too, at least the hole would be blocked up afterward.

He let go of her hands and squeezed her shoulder. 'I'll get the tools out of the car.'

'Jack!' He turned back to her. 'Do we have to do this now? It's dark and I'm tired and just, well, downright scared, to be honest.'

'Of course not, we can do it tomorrow, but what if there's some poor animal behind there as frightened as you are? How much sleep will you get then, anyway?'

Willow nodded. 'You're right, I'm just being an idiot. Go get the tools.'

Not wanting to watch, Willow made a drink as Jack plugged in the jigsaw and began to cut a square around the small hole that was already there. The teeth of the saw clattering against the chips of wood sent Willow's nerves skittering off into orbit again.

It was 12.05am, she saw, as she checked her phone.

Good, past halfway and on the way to morning. If I could keep Jack here for another couple of hours, I'd be home free.

And his wife would probably wonder where the hell he was.

As the kettle boiled and the jigsaw thrummed, Willow wondered. Tilly was the only other woman at McGracken House at the moment – that Willow had seen, anyway. She was a quiet girl, blonde and slim, and Willow would have thought much too young for Jack.

You never know.

A small spike of jealousy stabbed her stomach.

Are you serious? Have you ever seen them together?

She chewed on her lip, and then she almost laughed with relief.

Hadn't Tilly mentioned a boyfriend when she had spoken to her last week?

Yep, she definitely did. If she was married, she would have said husband. Not Jack then.

So this woman is not at the house often then if I haven't seen her. I thought Jack was staying at the house.

Maybe he goes home somewhere in the village.

He was still here quickly tonight, but maybe that's why he's in the car.

What did his wife make of him shooting out to help a girl in need in the dead of night? Was she okay with it? Was she super nice and super relaxed?

Willow sighed as she thought of Jack's nature and the nature of McGracken House. Probably she was. Maybe she was even a graduate of the house herself.

She was probably like his mother, blonde and leggy and beautiful, with sky-blue eyes and red lips, and...

'Willow?'

Willow shook the thoughts away and poured water that had boiled God knew when into the cups.

'Yeah?' she said.

'Come and look.'

'I'm not entirely sure I want to,' she mumbled, moving into the hallway.

Jack was in the cupboard, chipboard all over the carpet around him. His head had disappeared through a hole big enough to fit his entire body through if he pushed himself up. Willow balked.

'Jack, that's bloody huge!' she heard herself say as she stood in shock.

He pulled his shoulders back from the gap with a grin that made him look almost boyish.

'You have got to see this,' he said, grabbing her hand.

She pulled back, not wanting to see anything that was behind that wall.

'Take a photo,' she said.

He frowned at her. 'What?'

'Please. Take a photo first. I just need a barrier between me and whatever is in there. Is it cute?'

Jack shrugged and leaned back into the hole to snap a few shots. 'Not particularly,' he said.

'Oh, what does it look like?'

'Long and hard.'

Willow felt a stupid grin spread across her face. 'Long and hard?' she repeated.

'Brown,' he said.

A giggle escaped her lips as he pulled himself back out of the hole. He raised his eyebrows. 'I'm glad this is a little less horror movie for you now,' he said as he checked over the photos.

'More a different kind of movie,' she said.

Jack looked up. There was a glint of humour in his eyes and chipboard in his hair. She said no more but saw his mind work, and then they were both laughing.

'Is there a man hanging out in my cupboard, Jack?'

'Well, he's been trying hard to get your attention. Do I board him up or let him out?' he said.

'That depends,' she said as Jack handed her the phone, and she swiped through four angled photographs. 'What the hell is it?' she said.

'Looks very much like a step to me.'

Willow's grin fell away.

'A step? As in a stairway?'

'Could be. Maybe an old attic room. No way of knowing without opening it up fully, but the air that's coming through, I'd say more than likely.'

'How long has it been boarded up like this?'

'Hard to say. I don't remember it ever being two stories, but certainly from the time the cottage was overhauled. The paint is the same age and colour as the walls to look at.'

He picked up a bit of flaked paint and held it to the wall opposite. The colour matched perfectly. Then he stilled, and Willow glanced at him, and then followed his gaze into the hall.

All over the opposite wall above the sideboard, scratched into the paint, were faces. Some large and some smaller. They were angry, sad, happy, worried, and their messages were scrawled everywhere. Help, beware, watch out, hello, peace, Hi.

They were bad enough, but the worst one was bigger than the rest and scrawled over a few of the faces underneath.

MURDER

Willow gasped. Her heart pumped as she took in the sheer volume of faces and their messages. These hadn't been here when she had come in tonight, had they?

'I take it you didn't do this?' Jack murmured, running a finger over the faces.

'No, but I heard scratching in here earlier.'

'You were alone?'

'Of course, or so I thought.'

'And noises from the cupboard too?'

'Yes.'

Jack was quiet as he stared at the wall, and then he came to a decision.

'Okay. Willow, I'm not happy with you staying here tonight. Come and stay at the house, at least until we can get this cupboard sorted and checked out properly tomorrow.'

Willow felt her stomach turn over.

'You think there's someone else here?'

'I don't know, sweetheart, but I've never seen anyone as terrified as you were earlier, and I know you didn't send that message easily. I'm aware things haven't been quite right with us, and I don't pretend to know why, but if you messaged me, then it must have been bad.'

Willow dropped her gaze to the sideboard and nodded.

'So, will you come back? If there is someone else here, I don't want you out here alone.'

There's something here, all right, and I don't want to be alone, and it's only half-past twelve.

It didn't take much persuasion for her to agree.

Fifty-Six

J ACK MADE WILLOW THE tea that they didn't drink at Ivy Cottage, putting a finger to his lips as he took her through to the living room.

'They'll all be in bed asleep by now. Early risers. Just keep your voice low.'

The living room was dark and cozy, the only light coming from the large fireplace, which was still glowing orange. Above it sat a large gilt-framed painting of the house.

Across the room to the right, wooden stairs led up, and ahead, three two-seater settees formed a U shape around a large, tasselled rug, with a low wooden coffee table in the middle.

A guitar was perched on a large beanbag next to the fireplace, and a coat and two bags were slung across one of the settees.

Jack lit a large three-wick candle and set it on the table in its stand.

'No electricity used unnecessarily,' he said. 'Everything from the solar is stored in batteries, but we don't get much at this time of year, as you can imagine.'

'It's nice,' she said. At Ivy Cottage it would have been a horror movie set of shadows and creaks, but McGracken House, although a lot older, seemed a million miles away. Warm and inviting.

She sat down on the settee opposite the fire and stared at the glowing embers. Jack sat next to the coat and bags at a right angle to her. She sipped her tea as she watched the shadows draw angles on his face and light his hair and eyes.

'Thank you for coming up tonight, Jack. And for checking things out, and for coming in every room with me while I grabbed my stuff. I'm sorry you had to come out so late.'

He looked up from his cup, lines creasing his forehead.

'In all honesty, I'm glad you messaged. I'm glad I came out, and I'm glad you're here. Something about that house has always given me the heebies a little, sitting up there alone, knowing what happened in it. I nearly rented it just before you moved in, Mel almost had me sold on it. Changed my mind last minute. I'm glad I did now.'

Willow wondered whether this was supposed to make her feel better. She had to go back there tomorrow alone, she couldn't leave it forever.

Well, people stay here for years, she thought.

She looked at Jack and thought of his wife.

No chance. I'm not staying within an inch of his room knowing he has a woman in there.

She sighed.

'I'd like to say I wish I hadn't bothered either, but the alternative would be worse right now. Still holed up and drugged down in Bristol while my boyfriend shags his secretary.'

She stared at the candle flame, another flame igniting in her belly as Jack reached out to touch her hand. When she didn't pull away, he curled his fingers around to hold it.

'I'm sorry about that too, sweetheart. I am. No woman deserves to be treated like that.'

She should have pulled away but couldn't find the will. She closed her eyes as his fingers grazed her palm.

When explosions sent the butterflies scattering in her stomach, she opened her eyes and turned to tell him she was tired. Anything to take her hand away, but her voice caught in her throat. He was staring at their hands with a small frown. She wondered if he felt half of what she did, and what that meant.

It means he's married Willow. That's all.

She pulled her hand away.

'We should get to bed, Jack. It's late.'

She put her cup on the table, but Jack stopped her as she began to rise, grabbing both of her hands in his.

'Wait. Stay with me a while.'

'I'm tired, Jack.'

'Please,' he said.

She sat back down, her heart thumping more than it had at Ivy Cottage.

'What is it?' she said, pulling her hands away from the tingle of his touch, which slid up her arms and landed in her chest.

The silence was beginning to feel a little awkward, and then he spoke, keeping his gaze down.

'Willow, I have to know... what's the problem here, sweetheart? Because if I've done something wrong, I don't know what it is. I enjoy your company immensely. I love the days with you, the laughs, the chats. I felt like...' he shook his head, trying to find the right words. 'I don't know, like we were on the same wavelength, I suppose. I don't want to overstep your boundaries, and I respect whatever it is that you're feeling, but you haven't been right for days. I felt like we understood each other. I miss you. Can't you talk to me about this instead? I don't care what it is, I'd rather you tell me than have you block me out and chat with the others.'

Jack looked up at her, and Willow could have cried. Candlelight flickered in eyes that were conflicted and pained. His smile was sad, but he was trying to smile. She was hurting him, she knew, and that hurt her.

But he hurt you first.

That's the old Willow talking, the one who liked to push things under the rug. Get it out there and find the truth instead.

She looked away and tried to figure out how to tell him what was on her mind. For someone that she could speak to so easily, she was having trouble finding any words at all, especially words that didn't hurt as she looked at what she couldn't have. Because sitting here, she wanted nothing more than to move into his arms and let him keep her safe.

'Willow?' he said quietly.

He placed his left hand over hers, and electricity jolted through her. She stared at his fingers, and then she realised she had something to say after all.

'You're not wearing your ring,' she whispered.

'What ring should I be wearing, sweetheart?' he said, looking genuinely confused.

She swallowed hard.

'The ring that says you're married.'

Jack looked down at his hand over hers with a small frown, and then he smiled.

'Ah, that ring I took off a while ago. I don't like to wear it.'

Willow bit her lip.

'You didn't say you were married,' she said.

'You didn't ask, and it didn't come up. Is that what's been eating you?'

Willow shrugged. 'I suppose I've just been over sensitive with how Carlton has been, and what I've found out, and how much I've enjoyed you looking after me. I'm sorry. I should have allowed you to tell me your side, I just thought you were hiding it.'

There was a creak from upstairs. Someone moving around.

'I've nothing and no one to hide it from.'

Willow nodded as her stomach dropped. She felt stupid. He wasn't acting in the least bit guilty, which meant that everything he had said and done was out of his care for her, nothing more.

'No, I suppose not.'

'I only know you're not married because of what you're going through, and what you've said, right?' There was a creak from the top of the stairs, and Jack flicked his eyes toward them. 'But, yes, I am married,' he finished. A look passed over his face that she couldn't read. Anger, irritation?

'Right,' she said. 'I'm sorry. This is my fault. I completely misread things, and when Carlton did what he did, I blamed you. Not for his actions, but mine, if you get me?'

She chewed on her lip.

Please don't make me spell it out.

Jack sat quietly, waiting. Willow sighed.

'I leaned on you too much because I didn't know there was anyone else. I shouldn't have. I'm needy, I guess. I didn't mean to take my feelings out on you. I've got a lot of healing to do, I suppose.'

'You're the least needy person here, and aye, of course you do, sweetheart, but you're doing really well. You're a very brave and honest person, and you're teaching me a lot, too, especially right now. I need to be more aware of my actions. I want to help you all I can, but when you push me away...'

He stopped and shook his head.

Willow felt her breath catch. There was something under the words. Something in his energy that misaligned. She couldn't put her finger on it, but she knew he was conflicted.

He's hurting enough, Willow, he wants to be friends. Do you think you can man up and do that?

He had one thing right. He did seem to understand her more than the others, even Tam. Maybe, if he thought she understood him too, then there was something underlying that he needed from her. Maybe to do with the anger that had slipped out so suddenly the other day?

She suddenly felt very young and very stupid next to him. Maybe this was the wisdom that age brought, maybe in six years' time when she was Jack's age, she would laugh that she had ever been in this situation at all.

Maybe in six years' time she would have found a man just like Jack and be married to him too. Maybe... although she didn't think there was another Jack anywhere in the world.

Jack was looking down at his hands when she looked back at him. He seemed tense, that funny air around him still hovering.

Can you put this aside and be friends?

Willow reached out her hand and grasped his. He curled his fingers around hers with a tight squeeze. She pushed down the emotion that swirled within her.

'I don't want to push you away,' she said. 'I didn't mean to take it out on you. This proves why I should talk to people about things, I suppose. If I confused you, I'm sorry.'

There was a constriction in her chest, a burning behind her eyes.

Don't cry, you Klutz.

'Aye, maybe talking is the best cure for most things. Shame that isn't the motto here, because sometimes talking about the past can help with the present and the future. Maybe they shouldn't be dismissed as completely separate things.' He smiled up at her, squeezing her hand before letting it go. 'Just my theory.'

She smiled back. 'It's a better one.'

'Friends?' he said.

'Yeah,' she smiled.

He put a hand out to touch her cheek. She was going to have to get used to this though, he was obviously just a very tactile man.

'We'll check out your cupboard in the morning, okay?'

'I can't wait,' she said, deadpan.

He chuckled and stood. She stood with him, and he pulled her into a hug. He lowered his head to her ear, making every nerve ending in her neck tingle as his lips grazed it.

'You know you can talk to me about anything, right? Nothing is off limits,' he whispered, his breath hot on her skin.

There was an edge to his words, an edge that she couldn't understand.

'I know,' she replied, her heart drumming hard.

What was he saying?

He let her go and smiled, the edge around him gone.

'Let's go and find you-'

'Jack?' a woman's voice said from the stairway. Willow couldn't place the soft twang, although it felt vaguely familiar.

'Yes, I'm coming up now,' he said, not bothering to keep his voice down, or hide his irritation.

'Hurry up,' the voice said, and Jack rolled his eyes.

Trouble in paradise, Willow thought. Maybe she was the trouble, as he had been called out late to help her.

If you meet her in the morning, you can apologise.

Her stomach turned over at the thought. Maybe she would skip breakfast.

'Come on,' he said, herding her toward the stairs as he picked up her bag. 'I'll show you which room you can sleep in, save you walking in on anyone.'

Willow smiled as she followed him up the stairs to a long corridor which stretched to the left and straight ahead.

There was no one on the landing now as he showed her into a large room on the left, complete with a king-sized bed and its own bathroom. A large window overlooked the lane and the hill beyond she saw as he placed her bag on the bed, and then she thanked him as he left.

The bed was comfortable and warm, and she was so tired that she thought she would drop straight off to sleep. Instead, she lay watching the moon through the open curtains, thinking of her dad, Ivy Cottage, Carlton, and then of Jack and his wife a little way down the corridor.

Why had that voice sounded familiar?

A pain ran around her chest and lodged itself into her heart like a lump of cold lead.

I don't want to know her. Please don't let her be nice.

She will be, and this is a small village.

Willow turned her face into the soft pillow and let her tears go as the emotion, disappointment, tension, and fear of the evening came out in one big emotional outpouring.

Fifty-Seven

C ARLTON DIDN'T SEE SUZIE at the office. She had skipped out
early, not that he would reprimand her for it when he
couldn't even be bothered to turn up. If he thought about it,
what he would really like to do is put a match to his whole life
right now and let it burn.

Instead, he rang her from the office phone, and heard the
familiar tone of the answering machine - which he also wished
to put a match to after the last few days.

The second time calling, she had answered, and he had been
right, she did know how to get into a phone, but it was a fairly
illegal and dangerous combination she had used.

Periodically, she had fed her husband tramadol dissolved in
whatever he was drinking, when he became drowsy and slow,
she used his thumbprint to unlock the phone and change the
password. She could then get into the phone when she wanted
until he had to enter the password again.

'He would always get frustrated,' she had said with a laugh.
'Wondering why his damn password didn't work. He would
change it back, and I would get the tramadol out again. It
was pretty simple looking back. He actually thought there was
something wrong with him because he kept having these funny
lapses into complete tiredness out of nowhere. Funny really.

Also extremely dangerous, Carlton thought. He didn't ask
where she had got the tramadol from. The less he knew, the
better, and besides, it gave him an idea of his own.

Coop needed painkillers. Tramadol was a strong opioid that
would work wonders for his hand. Legitimately prescribed,
if anything happened to Coop while taking it, Carlton would
possibly never work as a psychiatrist again, but he might avoid

jail. The only snag was that Coop was a recovering addict. It may not work as well as it had with Suzie's ex.

Carlton considered the odds and decided to run with it. He had to get Coop's phone tonight. There was no time to waste. If it didn't make Coop drowsy, he could slip him a little extra, but he knew Coop would take the pills with a beer. It could be deadly but would hopefully heighten the effects of drowsiness with less.

'Fingers crossed this works,' Carlton whispered as he unlocked the filing cabinet and removed the prescription pad.

He wrote the prescription, accessed the computer, and quickly logged in to pull up Coop's patient notes. All of these pills had to be steadily logged, although some prescriptions had had to be filed under other patients' names as he had demanded so much since leaving jail. Tramadol was a new one on his file, though.

He wrote up a fake patient appointment, changed Coop's med-ication, wrote the prescription, and locked everything back away.

He drove to the chemist on Sharing Street and came out with pills that would not only help Coop, but hopefully help him, too.

As he ran through the rain to his car, he sent up a quick prayer to God. He wasn't religious, but if there was anyone up there, he could use the help right now. This was his only chance.

Willow's only chance.

'Fuck me,' Coop screamed as Carlton tried to apply a square of thin wood under his hand to keep the fingers straight before bandaging around it.

'Do you want the bones to fuse properly or not?' Carlton said.

Coop was white, and Coop did pain well by all accounts. Carlton was no medic, but he thought the hand was definitely broken, another gift that would buy him time.

'I don't give a fuck. Get me the bloody pills,' he said, a bead of sweat rolling down his face.

'Almost there, then you can relax the hand and the pills can take effect after manhandling it.'

'You're a fucking psycho, Carlton.'

Carlton felt his cheeks flush as anger spiked colour into them.

'I'm not a doctor, Coop. You should have gone to the hospital.' He crossed his fingers in his mind, hoping that Coop didn't suddenly decide that he was going, anyway.

'Just hurry up, holy mother of God!'

Carlton bandaged the hand, being careful to leave the fingertips and thumb out of the bandages. Coop was right-handed, and Carlton was sure he had unlocked his phone with a thumbprint when he had seen him previously. It was bound to be on his right hand.

'There,' he said when he had finished, 'that's the best I can do.'

'The pills,' Coop murmured. 'It burns. Holy mother of God, it burns.'

Carlton got up and popped two of the pills out of the packet. True to his form, Coop sat up and grabbed his beer bottle to wash them down.

'What are they?' he said when they were already down the hatch.

'Tramadol,' Carlton said.

'Good. Thought you were going to get me pussy co-codamol. I'd have fucking punched you with the other hand, you know... ah, ow... if you had.'

He readjusted his hand to rest in his lap and sat back in the chair.

'You want another drink or anything to eat?' Carlton said, moving into the kitchen.

'Beer. Got to numb this fucking pain, man.'

'You shouldn't drink with tramadol,' he said for effect. The cameras were watching, after all. It would help his defence if anything happened.

'I said get me a fucking beer,' Coop growled.

Carlton hesitated, again for effect, before opening a bottle from the fridge and taking it in to him.

'Food?'

'Not hungry. Piss off and leave me alone, Carlton. I don't need to make weird chit chat with you just because you bandaged my hand. It fucking hurts and my patience is wearing thin.'

Carlton shrugged, made himself a sandwich and crisps and went up to the bedroom.

He spent an hour scrolling through his phone before moving back downstairs.

Coop was snoring on the settee, not overdosed, but out for the count.

Carlton stared at him, said his name, but there was no response.

On the other chair lay Coop's leather jacket. They had removed it when Carlton had come back with the bandages, and he had noted the weight in the right-hand pocket.

He picked up the coat and took the phone out.

Bingo.

This was almost too easy.

Maybe Coop isn't a very good criminal. Maybe he never was. Intelligence was never his strong point, and he wasn't in a gang now. Two had gone, and the other two had disbanded. Any loss of life was tragic, but Carlton couldn't help but think that this was a good thing.

Carlton lit the phone. His hands shaking as he checked the phone wasn't a simple slide unlock.

It wasn't.

He moved to Coop. His heart pounding harder than he had ever felt in his life.

His hands were shaking more than he would have liked, but he squatted next to Coop.

Coop had fallen onto his right side on the settee, trapping the arm beneath him. The hand, however, was free, sticking out from under him at a right angle, palm face up.

Awkward, but it could have been worse.

He pressed the phone to the unlock screen and turned the screen down toward Coop's hand.

Careful, he thought as the phone shook in his sweaty fingers. If he dropped it, the pain would wake coop for sure - and he would be worse than a bear with a sore head - he would be a lioness whose cub had been murdered.

Carlton gingerly pressed the screen to Coop's thumb.

Coop murmured and winced in his sleep. His eyes remained closed as the pressure of the phone released and Carlton looked at the screen.

Locked.

Come on!

He turned the phone around again and pressed it back onto the thumb, higher this time, hopefully in the right place.

Coop grumbled and pulled his arm closer to him.

Carlton felt sweat trickle down his neck as he waited for his brother to wake.

Coop didn't, but his right hand was now closer to his body.

Bugger.

Carlton turned the screen over to check, anyway.

There was a naked girl on the screen, covered by a handful of apps.

Carlton blinked. It's open.

It's open!

He crawled to the doorway, pressing the screen to keep it alive as he rose and ran upstairs to his bedroom.

Maybe it was a bad idea being up here, maybe he should have stayed down by Coop's coat, ready to replace it, but he was here now, entering the settings, and remembering Suzie's instructions.

Even after all he had put her through, even after the awkward situation, she still treated him normally. Carlton was being anything other than normal with her. He was lucky that she had helped him.

He changed the password, licked his lips, and opened the messages.

Apparently, there would be a message from someone, and he would have her. Carlton had to find out who this someone was.

He scrolled down the recent messages and stopped short.

Willow? He has her in his contacts? How the fuck?

Thank you, was all the message said. The last correspondence was from her. If it was her at all.

It can't be that easy, surely.

He opened the message, reading the thank you first, before scrolling down to read the first message and registering just what he had opened.

There are pictures?

Carlton was more than shaken as he looked through them. His stomach was going over, bile rising up his throat.

She knew. Willow knew.

No wonder she was so angry with him.

She knew, and Coop was the one who had told her.

Carlton took a sip of water from the tap in the bathroom and swilled his mouth, spitting the water back into the basin.

He remembered his phone had been lit on the floor that night, and Coop's pretence that he had stood on it days later.

Coop.

The one destructive force that was not only content with ruining Willow's life, but was intent on stitching him up, too.

Coop.

Whose hand he had just bandaged and pills he had just fetched.

Coop.

Blood. His brother. The one he had offered a home to here, while he plotted and planned against his own girlfriend.

Ex-girlfriend, unless he could claw her back. He had felt a lot more confident about that half an hour ago before he realised just what Coop had done.

Did you expect any less from him? Just a few weeks ago, you sat in the pub and told Suzie that he would never change. Why did you let your guard down so much, not only with Coop, but with Suzie too?

Carlton gritted his teeth, clenching his jaw hard.

For the first time in his life, Carlton thought that he was capable of killing. At the moment, he would do it without hesitation while his brother slept.

In that moment, sitting on his bed, he fantasised about all the ways he could do it, each more gruesome and more painful than the last.

Then he gave a low guttural roar of frustration, and then he simply cried.

Fifty-Eight

T HERE WAS ARGUING DOWNSTAIRS when Willow woke. She lay on the soft pillow, listening to the sounds of the birds outside as the sun tried to stream in through the curtains. Mingled with the tense voices were sounds of the guitar being played somewhere, and a shout and a laugh from the garden below.

Is everybody up? What time is it?

Willow sat up, rubbing her eyes as she checked her watch.

9.45am?

Holy crap. How had she not been woken? It appeared that everyone else was up from the noise downstairs.

She threw off the bedclothes and went into the bathroom to get washed and dressed. The doors here had no locks, except for the bathroom, and as she took a quick shower, her thoughts turned to Jack and Betsy. Why had she taken a shower in his room if they were en-suite? Or maybe they weren't? The house was big but not mansion or hall size.

With no answer, she packed yesterday's clothes into her overnight bag and left it on the bed before stepping out onto the landing.

The argument continued, raised voices in the kitchen. Jack and Helena, by the sounds of it, Jack's voice angrier and more spiked than Helena's softer tone. Willow couldn't hear Helena very well, but Jack was louder.

'What are we here for then?' he was saying. 'What is it exactly that you do here, Helena? If there are no rules, how is it that I can be breaking them?'

Helena's voice was low in the background. Willow held her breath and strained to listen, but she couldn't hear what was said until Jack spoke again.

'I've done everything you say, by the book-'

He was cut off by Helena's voice, a little more raised now.

'We have guests, Jack, they don't need to...' Willow narrowed her eyes, but Helena lowered her voice again, her words fading away.

'I can't do this anymore, it's bullshit.' Jack shouted.

There was a bang from behind Willow, and Duncan shuffled out of the next room.

'Hi,' he said with a smile of surprise. 'You came back to stay?'

Willow shook her head as the argument continued downstairs.

'Just for the night. I was wondering if I should...' she trailed off, hitching a thumb to the stairs.

'Ach, give them five minutes and it'll all be over. Jack can be a wee bit hot-headed, but Helena will calm him soon enough. She has the magic touch.'

He smiled and opened a door opposite into a large bathroom.

Not all the rooms are en-suite after all then, she thought, as she stepped back into her own room and shut the door.

She lay on the bed watching the clouds move over the sunlit hill over the road. No trees on the other side, she noticed, just grass, heather, bracken, and the odd rocky outcrop.

The raised voices finally went quiet downstairs, and she wondered what had started the argument. Duncan was the second person to tell her Jack was hot headed and yet, that wasn't the version of him she saw at all.

Maybe that's because you see him through rose-tinted glasses.

There was a soft knock at the door, and Willow jumped off the bed, her heart thumping wildly. What if it was Helena? What if the argument with Jack had been about her and now she was here to tell her she wasn't welcome?

Stupid, Willow, Helena said you were welcome from the first day.

The knock came again, and she opened the door.

Jack held a mug in one hand.

'Morning, princess,' he said with a smile that didn't quite reach his eyes. Whatever had happened downstairs, he was still annoyed.

'Jack,' she began, 'I've been thinking, maybe I should just go back to the house alone this morning. You have work to do here. I have skill enough to pull down a wall, although I may need help to put it back up later, but if you-'

Jack's gaze hardened as he cut her off.

'Willow? I'm coming to help you with the damned cupboard. You need me there, more than I'm needed here. Helena is obstinate, I don't work for this bloody place, I just happen to be related to the owner, and that means I should be happy to offer my services twenty-four hours a day? I've helped out here every goddamn day for the last three years. I'm pretty sure I'm owed a day off. If you start to tell me what I can and can't do as well today, we'll be falling out very quickly.'

Willow softened. He was angry, but not at her.

'Okay,' she said.

'I'm old enough and ugly enough to make my own damn decisions. Some people forget that around here.'

He swung his gaze to Duncan as the man left the bathroom with a cheery 'morning', and gave him a nod and a smile.

'Yes, you are, you also have a temper,' Willow said, pointing to the mug. 'Shall I take that before it slops all over the floor?'

Jack frowned, but there was a little humour in his eyes. Willow was glad to see it coming back.

'I don't have a temper,' he said, handing her the drink.

'You so do,' she said, taking a small sip. 'That is heaven, thank you.'

'You're welcome. I have a mother who drives me insane. There's a difference.'

'And Betsy?' She almost regretted the words before they left her lips. It was the wrong thing to say.

Darkness passed over his face.

'Willow, there are things you don't have the full story about. If I had to guess, I'd say Sophie has been talking. That's what caused all this agro between us with the marriage, and she's told you about Betsy, too. Am I close?'

Willow couldn't do anything but nod, and Jack huffed a laugh.

'We have a saying around here. Consider well the stream where you fish, its source, and all possible pollutants. I'm not saying Sophie isn't a nice girl, she is, but she often talks about things that she has heard from a second source, or things that she hasn't got the entire story about. Gossip. Betsy is one such story. One day, maybe I'll tell you what really happened that day and you'll have the solid facts instead of half-truths.'

Jack's voice had risen again, and he stopped himself with a shake of his head. 'I'm sorry, princess, I need to calm down. I'm not this person, and I hate that this place forces me to become it.'

'If you hate it so much, why don't you leave?' Willow said gently.

Jack ran a hand over his face with a sigh.

'That's another very long, very complex story, that you shouldn't hear second hand,' he said.

Willow didn't know how to respond, but then Helena's voice floated up the stairwell.

'Jack? Could you do the pigs, please? Warren has to go with Mick to town this morning.'

Jack closed his eyes briefly, his finger tapping rhythmically against the door frame, his mouth a straight line. He was furious, Willow could feel it underlying, and she knew it wouldn't take much of a trigger today to set him off.

'Jack?'

He looked at her, his face stone.

'How long will the pigs take?'

'Half an hour,' he said.

'I'll be ready by half-ten then. If you want to come back up to the cottage with me, I'll certainly be glad of the help, but if you need to be here, then stay. I don't want to cause any trouble for you.'

Helena's voice floated back up the stairs with more edge than Willow had ever heard her use, or even thought she was capable of. 'Jack? You've had more than enough time to deliver a mug of tea. This place won't run itself. There are things to be done.'

Willow was about to retract her statement and tell him to stay. Helena obviously had one on her today too, but Jack was nodding his head at her.

'I'll be ready. We'll take the car. The tools are still inside.' He turned on his heel, disappearing back down the stairs, and Willow pushed the door closed.

She cupped her tea and stared at the grain of the wood running through the large, dark beams. She wondered what sorts of fireworks would go off when he came back after a day with Ivy Cottage's cupboard.

There was something wrong with the atmosphere here today, it seemed that McGracken House wasn't quite the tranquil haven that she had been made to believe that it was.

Fifty-Nine

C ARLTON HAD PUT THE phone back last night, but Coop hadn't noticed. This morning he had been a bear with a sore head, but after his last dose of tramadol at 2pm this afternoon, complete with another beer chaser, he had gone back to sleep.

Whatever he had done to his hand, Carlton couldn't thank God enough. Not much could keep Coop down, so this one must be a doozy.

Carlton took some paracetamol for his headache and grabbed Coop's phone from his jacket.

He entered the password he had made yesterday and clicked back into messages. He stared at the photographs that Coop had sent to Willow. Distasteful close ups that would leave her in no doubt who the pair were, although he hardly recognised himself lying there. It was almost as though he had scrubbed the incident from his mind.

It won't be so easily scrubbed from Willow's now, though.

He read Coop's initial message again.

He had a plan. Carlton didn't know if it would work, but there was no other option. He had called Willow twice late last night, anything to try to persuade her she had got it wrong. This was Coop, and he was not having an affair, but in the end, he was glad she hadn't answered. It gave him a chance to try another tactic. One that may actually work.

He opened the message box and typed.

You're welcome.

He swallowed hard and sat looking at the screen for some time, trying to figure out how to be a girl, trying to figure out how to follow on from Coop's message in the same tone.

If you ever want to chat about it, you're welcome to message me here. I'd want to vent, and I'm an impartial ear if there's no one else where you've moved to. Hope you're okay.

Carlton read it through a few times but couldn't see the woods for the trees. He didn't know if it sounded all right or not, but it would have to do.

He pressed send, deleted the message, turned off notifications, and placed the phone back in the jacket.

Hopefully, he would get to any messages she sent before Coop did. If not, he hoped Coop would think she wanted to talk. That would fluster him right out of his comfort zone.

Carlton grabbed his own beer from the fridge. He flicked on the television and sat thinking how to proceed if she answered. There had to be a way to get her to give up her address to a stranger.

Sixty

W ILLOW FELT HER STOMACH clench as she entered the cottage ahead of Jack. It was cold, but everything seemed exactly as they had left it last night.

'Everything okay?' Jack said, and when Willow smiled and nodded, he went to get the tools from the car.

Goosebumps rose on her arms as she saw the large black opening in the cupboard where Jack had cut the hole. She pushed the cupboard door shut and turned to the masses of faces on the hallway wall. Swallowing hard, she remembered the sounds of scratching and shuffling and creaking that had arisen from the hallway last night. It had almost sounded like the dead were having a party, and now, in the quiet of the morning, it seemed surreal.

How can one dead lady make so much noise?

More to the point, can you spend another night alone here?

She didn't know. She thought it may depend on what they found in the cupboard today, but in all honesty, the bed at McGracken House was looking a lot cosier than her bed here.

But this is home, she thought. At McGracken House, you're just a visitor.

She thought about how she had been scared to go down and face Helena after the argument, although Helena had turned out to be nothing but lovely and seemed genuinely pleased that Willow had chosen to stay the night. There was an air between her and Jack though, and it had been bordering on uncomfortable after Helena requested a word with him when they had been ready to go.

Jack was red faced when they got into the car and had driven a little too fast up the lane to the cottage.

Now, he placed a toolbox in the porch and went to fetch a couple of heftier items out of the car. Willow brought the toolbox in and placed it by the sideboard.

She blew out a long, nervous breath as she stared at the door and thought about what may lie behind the wood.

'That's the last, then,' Jack said, bringing a couple of larger hammers, a dust sheet, and some goggles. 'Get the cupboard open, let's find out the mystery of the boarded-up staircase.'

Jack was smiling, and more relaxed than he had been all morning. Out of McGracken House, he seemed to calm quickly, or maybe it was just out of Helena's way. This was a mother/son relationship that definitely wasn't all roses.

Willow shuddered. 'I'm not sure I want to know what the mystery is.'

'You don't?'

'No. Last night you told me someone else may be here. I don't want to know if I've been living with someone for the last few weeks. It freaks me out.'

'Has this been going on since you got here?' Jack said, opening the cupboard and putting his head back inside the hole. 'Woah! What the-' he flung himself backward out of the hole as Willow screamed.

'What is it?' She yelled with her eyes closed.

Jack didn't respond. Willow sneaked an eye open to see that he was back inside the hole, head and shoulders.

'I'm not sure,' he said. 'Something moved in here before I could switch the torch on. Looks like it's gone now.'

'Gone where?' she yelped, her heart banging in her ears.

Jack pulled his head out. 'Up the stairs if I had to guess.'

'I don't want anything living upstairs, Jack. I don't even want an upstairs in my one-storey cottage! What the hell was it?'

'I don't know, something small, possibly a cat?' He moved out of the cupboard and picked up a sledgehammer. 'Only one way to find out.'

A small whimpering moan erupted from the back of Willow's throat. 'I don't want to.'

Jack looked at her, sledgehammer poised.

'Willow? We can leave this if you don't want to, sweetheart. I can patch the hole up and someone else can find it in the future instead. Just tell me before I make the hole bigger.'

Willow stared at him and licked her dry lips. 'You said last night someone could be here. What do *you* think?'

Jack set the hammer down at the side of the door and stepped over to the sideboard to stand next to her. They both stared into the cupboard.

'The way I see it,' he said after a brief silence, 'Whatever just moved in there is probably the culprit. It didn't look big enough to be an intruder. In all honesty, I'd like to get the poor thing out, but this is your house, not mine. How long did you say you'd heard noises from in there?'

Willow shrugged. Their shoulders bumped and her breath caught. He was standing so close she could feel warmth radiating from him. 'Since I got here, give or take a few days.'

'Whatever it is, it's probably on its last legs, then. It was putting up a real fight to get out last night, that's all.'

But that doesn't explain the creature on my roof that looked like a cross between a spider and an ape, and it doesn't explain the scratched faces on the wall.

The creature was obviously from the forest, and the faces were Martha, you know she draws. If you can get rid of the animal in the cupboard and tone down the scariness, you'll feel much better about being here.

Jack put a hand on her arm. 'Willow?'

She nodded. 'You're right. We need to get whatever it is out.'

'You're sure?'

Willow turned to him and grinned at the look of excitement doing its best to be suppressed on his features.

'You're just dying to use that sledgehammer, aren't you?'

'Don't often get a chance, and it's a great way to offload some tension,' he said. 'And I'm dying to know what's back there – secret stairs? How can you resist?'

'Okay. Go for it. Let see where your bloody stairs lead.'

'Could be you've been hiding the stairway to heaven,' he said.

'More likely, the gateway to hell.'

'It can't be,' he said, picking up the hammer with a grin. 'It goes up.'

Sixty-One

W ILLOW WAS SHAMELESSLY WATCHING Jack, shirt sleeves rolled up to his elbows, goggles on, as he smashed at the board. The hammer crashed through it easily, and it could have taken a gentler tool, but Jack seemed to be in the mood for a good smashing today. Maybe he was venting his frustration, and as long as he put it back together afterward, she wasn't too bothered.

He was tapping at the edges, more gently now as the wood splintered and gave. Then he put the hammer down and took off the goggles, wiping the sweat from his forehead.

'That should do it,' he said, knocking away some of the sharper edges and kicking at the bits with his feet.

'It's done, all the way through?'

She was only three feet from the cupboard but still wouldn't look into the darkness of the hole.

'Yep, all the way through. There are stairs.'

Willow felt her heart accelerate. 'Bugger,' she said, looking at the chipboard covering him and the floor, his hair almost white with board dust and old paint. 'Do you need a drink before we check out hell's gateway?'

He laughed as he wiped his face and brushed down his shirt and jeans. Pale red rings circled his eyes where the goggles had pressed against his skin.

'Just some water would be great, thanks.'

He rubbed the dust and woodchip from his hair as she ran him water into a pint glass which he downed in one.

'Okay, do you want me to check it out first, or shall we do this together?' he said, placing the empty glass on the sideboard.

The thought of Jack disappearing up into the darkness alone, swallowed whole as he disappeared into the belly of the cottage, was too much. He was rummaging in the toolbox on the floor as she stared at the doorway through the wall. Cold air caressed her cheeks. She shivered.

Logic told her it was just an attic and that he would be fine, but fear told her differently.

Why was this stairway boarded up, anyway? What had happened?

Was it to do with Martha Otis and the murders?

Don't go there, she thought.

Jack rose, complete with a small, powerful torch. He clicked it on and shone it into the darkness, highlighting the step that he had seen through the hole. Small and wooden.

'Well?'

'I'll come with you,' she said.

'Right. I'll go first. These steps may not be safe. Could be why it's been boarded over.'

Willow felt a trickle of relief run over her.

Of course, maybe they aren't safe, that's why they've been blocked off. Why didn't I think of that?

Because you have a face drawing crazy woman running around the house, that's why. Can't tell Jack about that one. He'd have you locked up.

'They turn here,' Jack said, two steps up and shining the light around the corner. 'This is why the cupboard has a false wall at the back, too. These must run alongside the front bedroom wall, they'd have been open to the hall at one point, presumably.

Willow lit her phone torch as she stepped onto the first two steps and leaned to see around the corner. The stairs were narrow, and Jack filled most of the available space, but she could see them rising above him.

The cold air that travelled down to meet them disturbed the dust. The dry musty air made her cough.

'Okay?' Jack called back.

'Yeah, fine,' she said, hearing the slight wobble in her voice.

Jack checked his weight on the step above. It moaned and creaked but held. He stepped up and checked the next one. Willow followed close behind, her heart drumming, the cool breeze on her body raising goosebumps. She wished they could go faster, just get these claustrophobic steps out of the way, and get back down, but she knew they had to be careful.

She reached forward, placing a hand on Jack's warm back, wanting to feel him ahead of her, to stay connected. As darkness closed in behind them and the house swallowed them both, Willow began to feel trapped. Hemmed in and watched in the darkness.

She had another feeling too; one she didn't like at all.

If she looked behind her now, back down the few stairs they had climbed, she would be there. Standing at the bottom, head twitching as she watched them rise.

Willow kept her eyes on Jack, as the feeling grew behind.

She could feel Martha, she would rise as they rose, hemming them in.

There was a small tap at the base of Willow's neck. Icy fingers crawled into her hair. She stifled a cry and shook her head, but the fingers remained.

Panicked, she stepped up, sliding her left hand around Jack's waist, pressing herself to him.

Please go away, she thought into the middle of his back.

Jack stilled and reached a hand out to the wall next to him.

'Willow, don't pull us both down, Princess. These steps are steep, and there's a brick wall at the bottom.'

'Sorry,' she said, loosening her grip.

'It's not a problem, just not right here, we've only...' he flashed the torchlight up the stairs ahead. '...six steps left.'

Willow wasn't listening. The hair on her head seemed to rise to stand on end, as her scalp felt the buzz of electricity.

Next to her on the step was something that made her want to scream. There was an outline in the dust. A footprint at the side of the stairs. Not just any footprint.

A bare foot.

Small enough to be an older child — or a small lady with a twitch.

Oh God, she's been here. She's up here. It's her.

The feeling of something menacing behind her persisted and Willow began to shake.

She wasn't up there now, she was behind them. As close as Willow was to Jack, breathing ice down her neck.

Willow felt the panic rise in her chest, the familiar feeling of the air lodging in her throat, the constriction of her lungs. The air was too old, too dusty. She couldn't BREATHE.

She broke out into a sweat.

Fingers were back on her neck behind her, and she was gasping, fighting with the speed that her body was shutting down.

You can't break up here, you can't, you'll fall.

The darkness spun, and Willow felt her legs give way. She man-aged to turn, hitting the wall, her backside landing on a step as her phone clattered down the steps, filling the stairway in strobing patterns of light.

There's no one there, she thought as her chest screamed.

No one there. No one there. Breathe.

Then Jack was in front of her, below her on the stairs, forcing her to keep her attention on him, to breathe slowly. Breathe in, and then breathe out.

It took a while to get herself out of this one, but Jack remained calm, guiding her through it. By the time her airways seemed to open again, she was sweating, her chest hurt, and her nose was streaming. She sniffed.

'Better?' Jack said, his face cast in shadows from the torchlight.

She nodded. 'I think so.'

'Christ, sweetheart, I wish you'd said something. You just scared me half to death.'

'It came on too quick.'

'It's been so long I almost forgot they were a thing,' he said.

'Me too.'

It was true. She had hardly thought about them at all for the last week.

Multiple daily to one a week in just a month.

They were worse now, though, more intense. Maybe that was not taking the Prozac, she didn't know, but she had to get a handle on just how hard they hit and hit them back even harder.

'Shall I take you back down?'

She glanced up the stairs and saw an opening on the left above the top one.

'No,' she said. 'I didn't put myself through all of this to quit halfway up. I want to know what's up there, too.'

Jack nodded and stood. He grabbed the torch and moved downstairs to where Willow's phone light was still shining on the bottom step. He brought it back up, handing it to her as she got shakily to her feet.

'Thanks,' she said.

They went quicker this time, reaching the top doorway in just a few seconds.

Wind howled over the tiles just above their heads, and a cool breeze ran around the large room in front of them. Willow flicked her torchlight around the walls. It must have been the square footage of the entire front and back bedrooms combined, and although the eves ran low at the edges, the floor space was large and the roof high enough for Jack to stand up at the centre. Then Willow noticed the sturdy, long planks spanning the entire surface beneath them.

'Look at the floor, Jack. Surely this wouldn't have been just storage if it was floored properly?' She said into the darkness, her voice echoing around the space.

'Aye, I agree. Maybe a bedroom at some point? It needs insulating, though, it's bloody freezing up here.'

'It's freezing in the cottage most of the time.'

'Hardly surprising with the wind that's coming through here.'

He flashed his torch around the beams of the ceiling. Willow walked a few paces into the room and scanned her own torch around.

'No windows either,' he said, 'strange dark room. Nothing moving up here now, though. Maybe there's a hole somewhere, and it got out.'

Willow's torch found a dark heap in the corner opposite the doorway, and her heart plummeted.

'Jack,' she whispered.

He turned to her, and she motioned the pile with her light. He shone the torch over it, highlighting a pile of dusty old blankets. He walked over and gave them a nudge with his shoe and then pulled the bundle from the wall. Willow shut one eye, ready in case something ran.

Nothing did.

She walked gingerly over to him.

'What are they?' she said.

'Just old blankets,' he replied, pushing the pile back into the corner with his foot. 'There's nothing else up here. Whatever I saw it's long gone, meaning you have a hole up here somewhere that it's getting in and out through.'

'But why does it keep coming down the stairs?'

'Food, maybe. Warmth. Got to be warmer at the bottom of the stairs than the top.'

'Hmm,' she said, eyeing the pile as Jack turned his torch to the other side of the room.

'Ah,' he said, 'It was a room once.'

Willow turned to where he was shining his torch and saw a window recess.

'A roof window? Why is it so dark then?'

'It's been tiled over by the looks of it. From the outside, you'd never know it was here.'

He tugged and pulled on the old latch, but it appeared to be stuck fast.

'Nothing getting in and out of that,' he said, swinging his torch back her way. 'I think that's about your lot, princess, a secret room, but a very bare one. Not a dusty attic chest in sight.'

'No, as secret rooms go, it's pretty uninteresting.'

She shone her light around the edges of the room, looking for footprints like the one on the stairs but finding none. Which in itself was weird.

'Actually, that is interesting,' she murmured.

Jack turned back to her. 'What is?'

'No dust. There's no dust on this floor. We've left no footprints in a room that has been blocked up for God knows how long?'

Jack had a logical answer fast. 'The air running through here could be classed as windy right now, not even a breeze. It'd be swept away before it had a chance to settle.'

Willow nodded but wasn't convinced as she swept her torch back around the edges.

There'd be dust somewhere, wouldn't there? It didn't just get erased by the wind, and this breeze couldn't get to all the corners.

'What do you think, then?' Jack said, watching her from the doorway entrance.

'About what?'

'Moving your stuff up and having a penthouse bedroom.'

'Not a bloody chance, Jack, not even on my radar.'

Jack shrugged. 'It's very spacious, has a convenient dust exclusion system, built in air con, and even comes with spare bedding. I think you're missing a trick.'

'It's also dark. Those blankets look like the old potato sacks in your barn, it comes with an increased chance for extensive nightmares, and the air con can turn you to ice on a cold winter's day.'

'What's not to like?' he said with a chuckle. She jumped slightly as her phone pinged in her pocket. A message. 'Would madam like to answer that in the penthouse suite, or down in the drawing room?'

'The plain old living room will do,' Willow said, moving to join him in the doorway, and then coming to a halt.

It may not be too bad up here, but the stairs belong in a horror movie all by themselves.

'You go first,' she said, turning to Jack.

'You're already there, I'll follow you down.'

Willow grinned in his torch light and swung her right hand toward the stairs.

'I insist, really.'

He laughed, shaking his head. 'A penthouse room would be a bad idea, princess, you're right.'

'Why's that?' she said.

'It'd cost you a fortune to hire someone to escort you up and down the spooky old stairs every night.'

'So funny,' Willow said, a grin on her face as he passed her. 'Tell me you'd like to climb them to bed every night.'

'Wouldn't bother me,' he said jovially.

'After you said the place freaked you out last night? Maybe you should have rented the cottage after all.'

'Maybe I should,' he said. 'It gets more spectacular each time I see it.'

'You've only been here twice since I moved in and both times you've demolished something in it.'

Jack laughed harder as he descended the stairs.

Willow heard the scuffle from behind as she turned to go down the stairs. She turned back to the now dark room and her heart seemed to miss four beats. Somehow, in the corner, was something even darker than the dark. A shape. Tall and still.

Until it twitched.

Sixty-Two

C OOP WAS HAVING TROUBLE focusing. His hand was giving him less trouble now, but his concentration and his ability to stay awake had apparently gone to shit. He looked at the packet of Tramadol. I've taken these in the past, I'm sure, but these are fucking me up.

He shook his head, swallowed a glass of water because his throat felt like a desert, broke out into a sweat as he pulled his jacket tentatively over his hand, and stepped out of the door.

The cold air gave him a jolt of freshness that was almost magical, like an extra boost of energy and awareness. His coat wouldn't keep him too warm today, but maybe that would be a good thing.

He lit a cigarette and started down the street to the park. He had a meeting today with the guy from the text tracking 'service'. It sounded official, he supposed, but really it was a backstreet installation of an app that would allow him to trace Willow's phone via GPS without her knowledge.

Hopefully, she would be on the other end of it.

The message she had sent gave him more hope than not.

Coop kept his head down as he crossed the park and headed across the street for the complex of old units culminating at the scrapyard gate.

Dez would apparently be there at twelve, wearing a black hoodie.

Coop had almost laughed at that. Every teenager that stole through those scrapyard gates had a black hoodie. He hoped this Dez stood out a little more than they did. Maybe a sign around his neck?

It wasn't like he could even message the guy. Part of the deal was to remove any trace of contact straight after a deal had been done. That deal was one of the easiest he had ever made.

'The app installation is £300, take it or leave it.'

'I'll take it.'

Granted, it was a little more than he wanted to pay, but he hoped it would be worth it in the end. The look on the little bitch's face when she discovered who he was would be worth £300 alone, never mind the look when she found out what he was going to do.

He hurried to the scrapyard ahead of him, shrugging his collar up around his ears. Luckily, there was only one black hoodie to-day. Staring through the gates at the scrap metal, not watching the road at all. Coop stood next to him.

'Dez?' he said.

If the guy said 'huh?' He'd simply apologise and move away, but he didn't. He turned. He seemed familiar, but Coop couldn't remember where from.

'Well, well, if it ain't the bloke who likes to fight with bars,' the lad said, skinny, black, deep brown eyes laughing at him.

Coop narrowed his eyes. 'Where do I know you from?' he said.

'The other night, seems the bar won,' The lad wore a broad grin as he gestured to Coop's bandaged hand. 'Good job you didn't hit me, cause I'd have fucking slaughtered you, mate.'

Coop had a memory of the pub, of being thrown out, but not really this lad. He shrugged.

'You win some, you lose some. You Dez?' he said, digging in his pocket for the cash he owed. The lad took it with a nod and grinned again, a mouthful of big white teeth. A charming smile that Coop knew was all false.

'£400 for cocksuckers who like to try it on at the bar, mate.'

Coop wrinkled his nose. 'What?'

'Take it or leave it?' He spread his hands wide, grin still plastered on his face.

Coop shook his head. 'We agreed a fucking price-'

'That's before I knew who you were. £400. Make me ask again the price doubles. Take it or leave it.'

'I'll take it,' Coop growled, anger settling in his stomach. Who the fuck did this little strip of shit think he was?

He rummaged in his coat where he had put the £200 cash, just in case. Bugs had always said deals could be negotiated up or down, sometimes you needed to cover your backside. He hadn't expected to need it, though.

He pulled the notes out and realised he had only one hand to count it with.

'Take your hundred out of there,' he said, handing the wad over.

Dez pocketed the money and held out a hand. 'Phone.'

'Where's my fucking change?' Coop said, the anger beginning to spark. This lad was getting on his last nerve.

'I need the phone,' Dez said, waggling his fingers.

'I need my fucking change, or I'll-'

'You'll do nothing, because I will do this.'

Dez reached out, and before Coop knew what was happening, he had squeezed the bandaged hand, which was only minimally protected by Carlton's small splint.

There was a crunch and Coop roared as fire raged up his arm. He held his hand at the wrist, staring at it as though it couldn't possibly cause so much pain. 'Fuck!' he yelled.

Stars shot before his eyes, and he sank to the floor with a thump.

'Phone,' the lad said.

Coop leaned between his knees and threw up. The pain was fierce and unrelenting. Tramadol, he needed the tramadol he had skipped to make it here with focus.

'Phone. I don't have all day, mate.'

His hand shaking and slippery with sweat Coop unlocked the phone, the pain from the press of the right thumbprint no worse than the pain now growling all the way up to his shoulder. He opened Willow's contact before handing it up to Dez.

'That's the number,' he said.

The lad took the phone and began to tap, then he opened his own phone and tapped that, too. He put the phones close by and then put his own away.

He tapped on Coop's phone again, and then he handed it back down to him.

'Done,' he said, pulling his hoodie closer around his face and looking down the street before stepping off the curb.

'Wait, don't I get instructions?'

'For extra,' the lad said over his shoulder.

'I gave you fucking extra,' Coop said, his jaw clenched against the throb in his hand, which pulsed hot fire.

'Extra means *on top of* what you gave me,' the lad said.

'You're not having any fucking more,' Coop said.

'Good job it's just a GPS tracker and even a moron could use it.' He assessed Coop, his head on one side. 'I'll give you a small tip for free, as you look a little dopey. If you get in trouble, open the app, and follow the orange dot.'

'Don't you even fucking dare patronise me,' Coop raged, getting shakily to his feet as the lad raised his middle finger and hurried down the street. 'Don't you dare!'

Coop watched Dez go, and then he moved away from his vomit and sat back down. No way his legs were taking him back just yet.

I need five minutes.

He stared at his bandaged hand, the arm resting on his right knee.

It's shattered. Your hand's fucked. It crunched. Must be in a million pieces inside there.

Coop felt his stomach roll again but managed to keep the contents down. He wiped sweat from his face and brought up the phone.

Let's see how good this is for my £500.

He opened up the app, which displayed a map. A small orange dot pulsed in the centre of the screen. Only the glow of that dot could dissipate his anger and pain so quickly and replace it with excitement.

'Well, hello there, little lady. That's where you've been hiding. So far from home? Who would have thought?'

He put the phone on the floor and pinched the screen in closer before picking it back up. It was good. The dot went all the way to a particular block that could be a house before the zoom came to a halt.

He pressed a button for a satellite view.

It was getting better. If it was a house, it looked like it was at the end of its own road with a forest around it.

Coop flicked back to map view and swiped the screen with the left side of his hand to take a screenshot.

All the way to Scotland, he thought. There's only one reason she would have gone so far. No matter what Carlton said, he had been in cahoots with the prison service and he had known the release date. He had told willow to run and to have no contact.

Which meant that although she was aware of him, she would think that she was safe all the way up there. Drop a pin on a map a million times and he would still never have found her.

He had her now, though.

'Which was worth £500 all day,' he said with a grin. 'Cheers Dez. Next time you're in the pub, I'll smash your fucking face in as a thank you.'

Sixty-Three

W ILLOW FLICKED THE KETTLE on, pulled her phone from her pocket and unlocked it, ignoring the couple of missed calls from Carlton.

The message was from the same number that had sent the photographs.

She frowned, tapping at the screen, wondering if she wanted to see any more damn photographs, anyway.

Then she pressed the message.

You're welcome. If you ever want to chat about it, you're welcome to message me here. I'd want to vent, and I'm an impartial ear if there's no one else where you've moved to. Hope you're okay.

Willow frowned. The first message she had received with the photographs had said that she didn't know this girl, so why would she think Willow wanted a friendly chat?

I would never follow up a message like this with a want to chat, I'd leave the poor girl to sort out her life. Not that I would ever do this anyway, now that I know how much it hurts.

She hopes I'm okay? Strange.

Something was off. The message didn't feel right. And then something occurred to her. Willow had lost a lot of friends through Carlton and the attack over a progressive number of years. Could it be a friend that she had lost contact with?

Saying I don't know her?

Maybe because you don't know the number, or maybe because it's been so long?

Hell, maybe everyone knew what he had been up to all this time.

She chewed on her lip.

One way to find out, and it wasn't like she had anything to lose.

I'm okay, thanks. Who is this?

She tapped out the message and sat with it on the phone, staring at the words.

'Important?'

Willow looked up at Jack, who was leaning against the kitchen door frame, arms folded across his chest, a smile on his face.

She pressed send, turned the phone off and put it on the work-top.

'Not really,' she said, making the drinks as the kettle flicked off.

'What do you want to do with the hole in your cupboard?' he said when she offered no more.

'Board it up, I guess. I'm not really interested in going up there again. I just wanted the noise in the cupboard to stop. It's been driving me mad.'

'That why you've been sleeping in here?' he said.

She handed him the drink with a frown. 'What do you mean?'

'The duvet, on the settee.'

She could tell him she was just keeping warm; heaven knew it was cold enough in that attic, but why bother lying?

'Pretty much. Only for the last few days, though.'

'Willow. Why didn't you come down to the house? There's always a bed for you there, you know that. Helena told you that you're always welcome, didn't she?'

'She did. I just didn't want to disturb everyone so late at night. The noises always come late, that's all. Sandwich? I have cheese or cheese.'

'I'll take the cheese, thanks,' he said, raising an eyebrow.

'Gourmet or bog-standard?' she said. She hadn't got two packets, but the thing she loved about Jack was his ability to pick up wittily wherever she led. He didn't let her down.

'Is the gourmet as fabulous as the penthouse in this establishment?'

'More fabulous,' she said, grinning into the fridge and picking up the block of mild cheddar.

'I'll take the bog standard then.'

She grinned at him as she held the co-op cheddar aloft.

'As bog standard as it gets,' he said with a chuckle. 'Perfect.'

Willow giggled, enjoying his easy-going humour and his company.

See, you can get the old Jack back, if you just put aside the silly crush and act normal with him.

She did think how nice it would be to have him prop up the doorframe and watch her make tea and sandwiches every day though. Her stomach spun as she glanced up right into his eyes.

Only going to work if you stop stealing glances at the wrong time.

She put the sandwiches on a couple of plates and ushered him through to the dining table, pulling out the chair opposite him.

They chatted as they ate, easily and naturally, about everything except McGracken House, and the real reason there was such a problem here at the cottage, and why Maud thought Martha had upped her game.

Even with Carlton, Willow didn't think she had ever enjoyed eating a sandwich with someone quite so much. She never seemed to stop smiling and laughing around Jack, he was funny and easy-going. Carlton had a much more serious nature. He'd have been more inclined to watch her carefully as she ate... just in case she choked on some cheese.

You used to like that, she thought, his over caring protectiveness.

At the thought of Carlton, her mood sank.

*His over caring protectiveness turned into something much more
sinister, and much more about him that you.*

'What's the matter, sweetheart? You've gone quiet,'

Willow smiled and shook her head.

'Nothing. I'm fine.'

'You sure? You went a little funny after that text earlier, too.'

Had she? Maybe for a second. How did he see every little emotion that crossed her face?

'You're doing it now,' he said with a chuckle.

She sighed.

'The text was from the same person who sent the photographs.
She was asking if I was okay and offering me the chance to chat
if I needed to.'

Jack frowned. 'I thought you said you didn't know who it was
from?'

'I don't. I don't even recognise the number, but it has crossed my
mind that it could be someone I used to know. A lot of friends
drifted away after the attack. Carlton wouldn't let them see me,
said I was too ill.'

Jack had stilled and was staring at her, the last bite of his
sandwich still in his hand. He waited, and she thought maybe
she did want to talk about how weird it was.

'In fact, I remember him coming between me and my best friend
Kelly way *before* the attack. It could be someone like that, if they
have a new phone number and kept my number for whatever
reason. I've not changed my number since my first ever phone.'

'How would they know that?'

Willow looked at him. The sandwich was still in his hand.

'Know what?'

'That you have the same number?'

'Well, I suppose they wouldn't would they? It was potluck.'

'So, if you didn't know that the number was correct, and you were going to send photos like that, you wouldn't check first?'

An alarm was jangling in Willow's head, something that hadn't felt right about the message from the get-go.

'It would be easy enough to send a message asking if it was still your number first, wouldn't it?' he continued.

Willow was nodding. 'I suppose. Maybe they thought I wouldn't answer an unknown number?'

'I'm sure any normal person would at least try before sending a barrage of explicit photographs to an unknown person. And if it was a friend, wouldn't they just have said?'

Willow thought about Kelly, and a good many of her old friends, yes, they would probably have said so first. This person had said that she didn't know them.

'Maybe they're happy with not being friends. Maybe they didn't want to pick up where we left off?'

'So why are they asking how you are now and saying they want to chat?'

Willow felt an uncomfortable turn in her gut. The eaten sandwich sat uncomfortably on top.

'What are you saying, Jack?'

He gave a small shrug.

'Probably just that I'm more analytical and paranoid than you? I don't know, something just doesn't feel right. You know that you can trace someone through a text? Have you ever thought that this may be Carlton trying to track you down?'

Willow shook her head. 'Oh, he would never use those photos as an excuse to get me to answer. I'm absolutely certain that this isn't him. Plus, they were taken by a third party...'

She trailed off as a memory of Maud in the small room came back to her.

There's a darkness coming. You can't stop it.

She swallowed hard. 'What makes you so certain that you can trace through a text message, Jack? I'm pretty sure there are laws against that without consent.'

'Of course there are. I know because I was tracked in a similar situation. Different circumstances, of course, nothing as low as this. But she found me all the same.'

'Who found you?' Willow's lunch was beginning to come back up the way it had gone down, and Jack's sandwich was now back on his plate.

'My wife. The lovely Jennifer who was a miserable manipulating bitch most of the time,' Jack reddened and looked up. 'Sorry, I shouldn't have said that out loud.'

Willow stared. His wife had tracked him. An old wife, or his current wife? Because that didn't sound like very loving behaviour, although he had used past tense when he had called her miserable and manipulating. Maybe she had changed.

'Don't you say that out loud either,' he said seriously. 'I'll be in huge trouble if that one gets out. This is just between us, right? It can't go any further.'

Willow nodded.

'Of course.' She was floored and stumped. She had a million questions, but she didn't know what to say, and Jack was already taking her back to her own situation.

'So, it could be Carlton, or maybe a friend of his, trying to get your location.' He held his hands up in the air, 'But I am paranoid about it now, it may just be that it's forefront in my mind. It's just that with the story as you've been telling it, and the not speaking to him, would he not want to find you? It's bothered me since you first said you'd had the messages.'

Willow felt another conversation pull her stomach over. She ran a hand over her face.

'I spoke to Carlton a couple of weeks ago,' she said. 'We had a massive argument, but he pretty much confessed everything. He asked for my address a few times during that conversation.'

'So, he is after coming up here, then?'

Willow heaved a shaky sigh and looked up at Jack.

'Yes, but to protect me, he says. From the person who is apparently really hunting me down.'

A frown flit across Jack's face. 'Back up. You've lost me,' he said.

Willow took in some breaths and Jack covered her hand with his on the tabletop.

'What is it?' he said.

'It could be nothing. It was something Carlton said, but it sounded so far-fetched that I dismissed it.'

There's a darkness coming.

'The afternoon of the attack, I think I told you that just before two of the attackers ran out and got caught by the police, I picked up a gun.'

'Aye, you did. Someone took it off you and shot one of the other guys in front of you, right?'

'Yes,' Willow whispered. She was shaking, and her chest was beginning to tighten.

Twice in one day.

She brought up the flame and focused hard until the feeling passed. Jack gave her the moment she needed quietly. 'But Carlton said that he knew the group of attackers. Not only that, but one of them was his brother.'

'What?' Jack's face twisted into disbelief.

'That's why he tried to change the party, apparently. That's why he didn't come, because he had inside information. He knew what was going to happen that afternoon, he knew what time they planned it for.'

'He knew what was planned? He was told?'

Willow nodded. 'So, he says.'

'And he let you and your family go?'

'Yes, he says he tried, but ultimately couldn't stop us. So we went, and he didn't.'

'If he knew what his brother had planned, couldn't he have gone with you and tried to change the outcome? What coward sends you to slaughter by yourself?'

'He says there wasn't supposed to be any killing. The guns were for show, but the pub was so crowded they lost control.'

'He still let you walk into a dangerous and volatile situation either way. If he knew, why didn't he stop it? Why would he protect a gang of armed robbers, brother or not? Why? I don't get it. Why didn't he try harder?'

She shrugged. She had asked herself the same question.

'He says he tried everything he could.'

Jack reddened and his jaw clenched. 'There's no everything he could if you were still walking into that pub, and the robbery was still going ahead. That is not all you can fucking do, is it? He should have stopped it from either side, and then he should have got his brother sent down. Saved some lives. That's everything he can fucking do. That's when it fucking ends.'

Willow nodded.

'I agree, Jack, calm down. It doesn't make sense to me either. He did say he called the police to tip them off, and that's why the last two, including his brother, got arrested at the scene.'

'Good for him,' Jack said, the sarcasm unconcealed. 'What a hero.'

'I said the same.'

Jack pushed his hands over his face and into his hair, linking them at the back of his head. Willow felt the cool breeze on the top of her hand where his warm touch had just left it.

'So, he drugged you after sending you to the slaughterhouse, for what reason?'

His words were pointed, Willow couldn't blame him.

'He says to keep me inside. To protect me from harm.'

The words tasted like bile in her mouth.

'Harm from what? Hadn't the damage already been done?'

'Well, yes, but he had been in touch with his brother in prison. The guy believes that because I had the gun when he left, and now his partner is dead, that I killed him. He told Carlton he would come after me.'

'From prison? Why would he say that? And why didn't Carlton tell him otherwise?'

'Carlton doesn't know. He doesn't know any of this because I've never told him. I've never had the chance to just go through it thoroughly with anybody really, not other than Mum, and now you. Carlton said if I had done it, he didn't want to make me any worse by making me relive it.'

'I thought you said he was a therapist?'

'He is. I don't know why he did that. Probably because none of his treatment of me was ethical or professional, anyway? It doesn't matter now; I won't be going back. I told him we were done. Either way, his brother thinks I shot the man. I didn't, but now that's beside the point because he's coming after me anyway.' She ran a hand through her hair. 'To be honest, I didn't believe Carlton when I spoke to him. I thought it was just an excuse that he could gloss over the affair with, but now, I'm not so sure.'

Jack's hand found Willow's again. He squeezed his fingers around hers.

Please help me Jack, tell me it's as ridiculous as it sounds? She wanted to say, but tears were forming behind her eyes, and she wanted to keep her composure. She had cried on Jack enough.

'What are you thinking, Jack?'

He looked at her seriously.

'Is this guy still in prison?'

Willow felt a tear slip out over her cheek and she began to shake again.

'No, he just got out. He's living in my apartment with Carlton. Apparently, he went straight there, which would seem to affirm his story, but if they were speaking when he was in prison, I'm not sure how friendly they are, anyway. Carlton hasn't kicked him out yet, has he?'

'I thought you'd been with this man a long time.'

'Ten years.'

'And he never mentioned his lunatic criminal brother?'

Willow thought about it, but no, she couldn't remember a single time until the phone the other night.

'I knew he had a twin, of course, but he said they didn't get on, so I never saw him. No.' she shook her head. 'It would have made sense if they were estranged, I suppose, but then why would he be chatting to him enough to get his plans out of him beforehand, and in prison afterward?

'Sounds like they're friendly, if not close.'

'I know, it's weird. And I'm not sure what this brother wants with me, but I wasn't there, anyway. He doesn't know where I am, and Carlton doesn't know where I am, so I'm okay, aren't I? Am I okay?'

There's a darkness coming, you can't stop it.

'Did you reply to that message, sweetheart?'

'I did,' she said, the tears slipping faster down her face. 'I've done something stupid, haven't I?'

Jack stared at her, his face crestfallen. Then he got up and rounded the table. His arms circled her shoulders, drawing her toward his stomach. She threw her own arms around him and buried her head in his dusty shirt with a sob.

'It's okay, princess, we'll sort this out. You're going to be fine, I promise. First thing we need to do is get rid of that phone.'

Sixty-Four

C OOP CAME BACK JUST after 2pm and ate a double dose of
tramadol as Carlton watched. At least he took them with a
large glass of water this time, no beer even mentioned.

He was sheet white and grimacing like he was standing on hot
coals. He grumbled about his hand and going to sleep, which
Carlton was more than happy to allow him to do. He wanted to
see if Willow had messaged back.

Half an hour later, when Coop was safely snoring, Carlton
checked his pockets. As luck would have it, Coop was lying on
his right-hand side, his hand hanging over the edge of the chair.
The phone was in the left-hand side of his jacket, which flopped
over his side and hung down toward his trim stomach. Carlton
pulled it out carefully.

He sat on the chair opposite and opened the phone with the
new password.

He opened the messages to see that Willow had replied, and
that by chance Coop hadn't yet read it. He almost stood and
did a happy dance around the room, but he stuck to a grin and
glanced at Coop.

she had answered, and that was fantastic, but Carlton had a
better plan now, one that would almost certainly get her to
reveal where she was, and her own reply led perfectly into what
he needed to do.

He calmed himself and read the message again before forming
his own reply with care, rewriting it over and over until it
sounded like the person he was after. Not that he had known
her all that well, and it had been a good few years ago now. He
knew their nicknames for each other, though; they had come
to him in a flash of inspiration in the night.

When he thought he had it down, he read it through again.

I didn't want to tell you because I know we have history, but I still care about you, and I still think about you. It's Snoop. I know what happened four years ago. I heard. I didn't think that this was something you needed on top of what you've been through. I thought you should know. I'd like to meet up if you're interested? Maybe claw back some of the time we've missed out on. What do you say, Poochie?

Confident that it sounded like he remembered Kelly speaking. He pressed send, deleted his message. Then he downloaded the tracking app to the phone and linked it to his own GPS tracker. He hid the app in another folder on Coop's phone screen and removed alerts and notifications. Just in case this message didn't work, he would have Coop's location either way.

He checked the dot on his own app and then placed Coop's phone back into his pocket.

He stood staring at Coop for a while and then, feeling more at ease, he decided to go to work. Mrs West had been ringing almost daily and was now screaming negligence at Suzanne whether Dr Mather's was sick or not. She had to come in and see him. If he got Mrs West off his back for a while, it would buy him more time. He could explain things better in person too, maybe make up a story as to why he was feeling so bad.

Maybe he would just tell the truth - that Willow had left him. That was something she would understand. It was half the reason she saw him, anyway.

He went upstairs to get showered, shaved and dressed, and then he rang Suzie. She answered on the third ring.

'Mather's Psychiatry. How may I help you?'

Professional as always, he thought, thinking of how loyal she was, and how hurt she must be that he was avoiding her and leaving her with the stress of angry patients.

'Hi, Suzie, it's me.'

'Oh, hi, how are you? Please don't tell me you're calling to tell me you'll be off for another week. Mrs West is already threatening to find another therapist and sue the company for negligence.'

'Empty threats, but actually no. If you could give her a call and offer her between one and three this afternoon, I can see her today. I'm going to pop in for a few hours. Catch up, see a couple of the more urgent cases.'

The relief in Suzie's voice was evident.

'That would be amazing. I'm sure she'll come straight over. There are only two more that are shouting right now. I'll see if they can come in as well.'

'That's fine. I'll see you in five minutes.'

'Great. I'll give these patients a call.' She paused, and then added. 'It'll be nice to have you back, hotshot.'

'It'll be a nice change to be back, but it's only today at the moment. Thanks Suzie.'

'No problem,' she said before ringing off.

He stared at the phone, his stomach giving a small tug of affection.

Whether he liked it or not, there was something about Suzie. There always had been. She was easy, fun, and had a great smile. None of which he had seen in Willow over the last four years.

Can you blame me for wanting some normality, babe?

He doubted Willow would be back after what she had seen, but he would try. If not, he would make sure she was safe, anyway.

After that, if Suzie was still around? Who knew?

Sixty-Five

W ILLOW WOKE TO A horn blasting outside. She threw off the duvet and peered through the curtains. Jack was standing at the open driver's side door of the small Ford, his hand inside, pressing on the steering wheel.

Jack? Oh, shit.

She glanced at her watch and saw it was 9.15am.

A vague memory of a really bad conversation about phone tracking and a vendetta and getting rid of the phone came back to her.

'We'll drive a hundred miles or so west and dump it. I'll get you a new one. Write down all the numbers and info you need because you won't be able to save the sim card either.'

Willow had stared at him through her tears.

'Is that really necessary? I can check if it's a friend first, right? This is all a bit drastic, Jack.'

'Aye, it may be, but this man has already been to prison. He thinks you killed his accomplice. Do you think he wants a chat and an apology?'

'He may not even be coming, I mean, this is all so far-fetched.'

'Aye, but who has access to your apartment at the moment?'

'Well, he does. He's living with Carlton, which means he's not on his way up here.'

'Yet. But come on, Willow, you're not daft. He has access to the apartment, and where were the photographs taken?'

'In the apartment.'

'And Carlton was asleep, so was his secretary. So, who took the photographs?'

Willow began to click.

'His brother must have.'

'Exactly, and who needs a reaction from you to learn where you are?'

'His brother.'

'And you get a message with photographs he took from an unknown number.'

'Shit.'

'Willow, if I am overreacting, and I could be, the worst you get is a new phone. I'll buy you-'

'No, Jack, I won't allow that. I'll get myself one.'

'Willow, it will be my fault if you threw away the phone for no reason. You've had the upheaval of starting over. I'll buy you one tomorrow.'

'No.'

'Yes, if not only because you need to be able to contact me if anything happens, and I need to be in contact with you or you'll worry the shit out of me after this conversation. You absolutely cannot be without a phone. Okay?'

Willow sighed.

'Will you take no for an answer?'

'No. I'll pick you up tomorrow morning at 9am. We'll drive somewhere far away, throw the phone, and pick you up a new one before we get back. At least that way, if he has a location tracker and it goes beyond the phone being turned off, it's tracking him in the wrong direction. If not? No harm done, but do not answer any other messages from unknown numbers on the new phone.'

Willow rubbed her eyes as she padded to the door, shutting the cupboard on the way past, and opened the front door.

'Sorry Jack, two minutes.'

'Did I wake you? I did say 9am, didn't I?'

'You did, I had a rough night. I'll be as quick as I can.'

He nodded, shut the car door, and stepped inside. She left him in the living room while she was dressing and then she headed to the bathroom to wash, and brush her teeth and hair.

Jack was quiet. He seemed tense, which only made Willow feel guilty.

'Okay, I'm done,' she said walking back into a bright living room. Jack had opened the curtains and was folding the duvet. He lay it over the back of the settee. 'Thank you, you didn't have to do that.'

'No problem,' he said with a tense smile, 'let's get going.'

Jack was quiet as they drove - pleasant and polite - but not his usual chatty self. He said that he was taking her somewhere around two hours up north and to the west, so to get some rest if she was still tired. Willow took that as a sign that he didn't want to talk. To be honest, she didn't want too either. She was tired, not only physically but mentally, too. The house, Martha, Jack, Maud, Carlton, and now his brother. She was tired of it all.

She watched the scenery roll by through the rain-streaked windows. Soaring pine-streaked hills and tiny villages, moody mountains, and grey lochs, she wanted to lose herself in its beauty, but her thoughts always seemed to land on last night.

It had been late afternoon when they had finished thrashing out what the messages could have meant and what they did about it. Jack had apologised but said that he really had to get back and could she deal with the cupboard not being boarded for a couple of days?

She had agreed. He had helped her more than enough for one day, and with the trip tomorrow he couldn't be expected to do more – even if the thought of those stairs being open scared the hell out of her, especially after the shadow and the footprint.

They had blocked the cupboard door as best they could to allow the house to retain what little heat it actually held, and Jack had left saying that he would be at the cottage at 9am.

To be fair, Martha had given her a couple of hours' leeway, a few hours of peace before she had begun her antics at just after 9.30pm that evening.

But from then on, it was as though all hell had been let loose in the corridor. There were no more thuds, maybe that was because the wall had gone, but three times the cupboard door had creaked open. All of the things she and Jack had blocked it with had been strewn across the floor. The third and final time she had shut it, she had run back into the living room. As she turned to shut the door, Martha was there. Up by the bedroom at the end of the corridor.

Willow had shut the curtain over and told her she could do whatever she damn well pleased with the cupboard.

There had been creaking, more scratching on the wall, and maybe worst of all, footsteps on wooden stairs. But the bit that had really kept her awake most of the night was when the scratching and steps stopped. It had been like bedlam, and suddenly it was quiet.

She had turned to check the living room door only to find Martha silhouetted in the kitchen doorway, dirt-streaked hair over her face, grey dress, feet dirty and bare.

Willow had wanted to leave at that point, wanted to run, but had nowhere to go. She was still unsure whether she was truly welcome at McGracken House after Jack's argument, and so she had told Martha to leave her alone, over, and over, with her eyes closed and her head under the duvet on the settee.

She had expected more, but Martha had indeed left her alone for the rest of the night. Even so, it had taken Willow until near daylight to fall asleep with exhaustion – just in case.

'You okay, sweetheart?' Jack finally said as she stared out of the window.

'Yeah, are you?'

He shrugged, 'I suppose so. You said you had a rough night. Thinking about the phone and Carlton's brother?'

'Some of it. Some of it was the noises from the stairs and the cupboard again.'

'The animal was back, huh? I'll check for holes in the roof and get it boarded up for you as soon as I can. I need to sort out some time.'

He fell quiet again, and Willow felt like she wanted to cry.

'For what it's worth, Jack, I think you're right about the phone. You're not doing this for no reason, but I could have driven myself up here. You only had to tell me where to go. You didn't have to come with me.'

He swung back to her with a frown.

'I know I didn't have to. I want to. Why do you say I'm right?'

'I got a reply to the message I sent yesterday asking who it was.'

He glanced at her. 'And?'

'An old friend, Kelly, one of my best friends from school. We haven't spoken for around six years or so now. We had a row about something stupid, but we're both stubborn and pigheaded, and so we never spoke again.'

The flicker of a smile crossed jack's face.

'What was the something stupid?'

'She borrowed a dress, and it came back ripped. She swore it was always there, I swore she'd done it. It wasn't even expensive, but the principal ate at me. To be honest, I can't even swear hand on heart now that it wasn't there before.'

'So why didn't you just tell her that?'

'Stubborn.'

Jack looked at her, his face serious but his eyes soft.

'There's a pattern going on here, isn't there?' he said, looking back at the road. 'Of things that you think you know that you'd rather make up scenario's about than ask the people involved?'

The comment hurt a little, but she knew it was true, she had seen it herself.

'I know, I can see that, but I'm getting better. I stopped avoiding Carlton, and I spoke to you, too.'

Jack smiled.

'Aye, I'm glad you did. So, what is stopping you speaking to this Kelly now? What felt wrong?'

'Well, the message reads like her, and I would have been convinced, but she uses the nicknames that we gave each other in school. We always used them instead of our real names, they just kind of stuck. Only in the message she gets them the wrong way round.'

Jack pursed his lips.

'You're sure?'

'Hundred percent. I would never forget that, and she wouldn't either. The other thing that crossed my mind is that she didn't really get on too well with Carlton, which would fit with her sending the photographs, but not with being in the apartment to take them. Now that I know more, and the name is out there? It just doesn't fit. The nicknames are just icing on the cake. This is definitely not Kelly.'

'I don't know whether that's better or worse,' Jack mumbled, running a hand over his face.

Willow shook her head and looked back out of the window.

'At least we're out nice an early and we're already an hour from Clover Nook,' he continued, 'Just have to keep our fingers crossed, that's all.'

'Surely the GPS will move with the phone either way.'

'Aye, but that doesn't rule out anyone doing the investigating yesterday evening, does it? Where was the GPS then?'

'So this isn't fool-proof?'

'Nothing is ever fool-proof, sweetheart, but at least it gives you a chance. You're one step ahead.'

'Where are we taking the phone?'

Jack smiled and glanced at her. 'It's not only about where we're taking the phone, it's about somewhere I wanted to show you. The phone is just a good excuse to get you there. How far have you been into Scotland?'

'I've never been at all before I moved to the cottage, but it's a beautiful country. I'll certainly be back if I don't stay. I love the mountains more than I thought I would, and I love walking through the woods to the clearing. Getting up high, it's beautiful, reminds me how small we really are, and how small our problems are too. I think it's really helped me.'

'Aye, that's exactly it. You'd have liked where I was going to take you before everything went to pot. Do you enjoy hiking?'

'I can't say as I've ever really walked anywhere until I came here. Bristol is a busy place and once you've seen it a few times, well, you know. I wouldn't walk for the sake of it. Out here is a different story. There's so much to explore.'

'Aye, there is. I love hiking for that very reason, but I just don't get out enough, I'd like to do more. It's humbling. Keep in mind just how small you feel at the back of the cottage. The place we're going is mind blowing.'

Willow watched the mountains around her now, and thought that they were just magnificent. Even with the steady patter of rain and the low grey cloud, she didn't see what could be any more impressive.

'The whole of Clover Nook village and its surroundings blows my mind already, and I love that there's a single Willow out there on its own. It makes me feel like I'm in the right place.'

'I used to play under that Willow when I was a bairn, and swim in the loch. It's a strange place for a single variety of tree, makes it pretty special, probably even more so for you.'

'Hmm, weeping willow. My namesake.' She said with a laugh, 'so that's how you found me so quickly the other week.'

'Oh, I knew exactly where you were as soon as you said. Why would weeping Willow be your namesake?'

'Carlton used to call me his weeping Willow. I am always crying, you can't deny that, and I've been stuck, just like a tree, too.'

Jack looked at her with a frown.

'I can deny that. I've seen you laughing much more than you've cried. In fact, you know what? A willow is a really beautiful tree. It's roots are far-reaching and strong, giving it an incredible support system to keep it steady in a storm. It's branches are flexible, allowing them to bend with raging wind, and they provide shelter for lots of animals, not least us. They're a very protective and generous tree. Sturdy, strong, and hardy.'

Willow stared at him. Her stomach filled with lead, and there was the tell-tale burning behind her eyes.

Please don't do this, Jack. Don't show me what I'm missing. I'm not sure I can deal with it today.

He continued unabated, his eyes on the road, one hand on the gear stick.

'Did you know they're also the tree that has the most will to live and ability to survive? If you cut the very end of a willow branch and replant it, it will grow into a whole new tree. I think there's much more to the willow than you think, and you're more like it than you think, but not for the weeping part. Willows don't weep. That's just a name we gave them. If he was going to connect you with the tree, he could at least pick the right bloody qualities.'

Willow blinked, and tears rolled down her cheeks. Her heart ached to tell him to stop the car so that she could feel his arms around her, but she couldn't. He wasn't hers to hold.

'What's the matter?' he said, looking over at her with a surprised laugh.

'That was a really beautiful thing to say,' she whispered, and then she laughed with him as she wiped her face. 'See, you made me cry. Weeping Willow after all.'

Jack smiled, but there was something in his eyes as she wiped her face. Sadness? She couldn't quite tell. He reached to wipe a rogue tear from her cheek. 'No, I still won't have it. Strong, brave Willow, who is merely bending in a storm that will pass.'

'Do you really believe that?'

He nodded. 'You're canny. I'd put money on you still standing when it passes. You'll be fine, princess.'

Willow looked down at her hands in her lap, her tears blurring her vision.

'I have so many things to thank you for, Jack. Hopefully, one day I can repay your kindness and your patience.'

'You've already re-paid me just by being at the house.' He sighed and swallowed, his tongue flicking to wet his lips. 'I was almost at breaking point that day when I found you at the gate. You've made the days so much more bearable, and just having you to focus on has made a real difference to me. Of course, the fact that we get on so well, and you have a great sense of humour, helps too. I should be thanking you.'

Willow chewed her lip as she looked at him. She wondered whether he would go on telling her more about what was eating him, but he was already changing the subject.

'So, did you say that you may stay on at the cottage?'

'Maybe.' She shrugged. 'I'm a free woman now, and the world is my oyster, isn't it? I really like Clover Nook - though I could do without the spooky cottage.'

Jack chuckled. He seemed to be relaxing as the trip wore on, and Willow was grateful. She knew that there was something going on, she just didn't know what it was. The argument with Helena yesterday morning replayed in her mind like a movie on a loop.

'I can't say I blame you. I'm not fond of it either.'

Jack's phone rang. He steered with one hand as he lifted it from the centre console. His face darkened as he looked at the screen and then he turned it off.

'Not answering?'

'I don't want to speak to her.'

Willow raised an eyebrow. 'I hope you're not getting into trouble for me, Jack. You haven't been yourself for a few days now.'

'Things haven't been right for a good while, as I said. The last few days have just got worse, that's all.' He looked at her with a small smile. 'I'll be fine, sweetheart, I promise it's not you.'

Willow looked down into her lap with a frown and then turned her gaze back to the window.

Someway down the A82 they lost the trees, and the landscape opened up around them. Or should that be, rose up around them. The mountains soared, autumn brown, giant and majestic, their tops lost in grey cloud. If these mountains could move, they would be slow and shake the earth with each footfall. They were giants in a landscape of dwarfed trees, rivers, and streams. They rolled and rose so sleekly that they appeared close, protective, but a look at the tiny trees on the hillside showed just how big they really were. They literally took Willow's breath away.

'I've never seen anything so huge in my life,' she said, craning her neck at the window as they passed.

The road rose until it felt they were driving among the mountaintops, and the landscape seemed to flatten as they passed pockets of water dotted with islands. In the distance, more mountains rose, vast and unspoilt.

How was there room for so many mountains? For so many peaks?

The cloud was lying low, but the rain had stopped by the time the road turned and dropped into the valley of Glencoe.

The mountains ahead of them were vast and silent, and the car felt dwarfed by the giant sentinels that guarded the pass. The road turned between sweeping peaks, and Willow gasped. In the valley sat a single white house, so dwarfed by the scale of its surroundings that it almost seemed unreal.

'Jack, this is the most amazing place. I can't even comprehend the size of these things.'

Willow got out her phone and turned it on to take some pictures, but Jack stopped her with his hand.

'Don't bother, they'll end up in the loch. We'll pop up to get you a phone first, dispose of this one, then we'll come back this way, and stop off in a layby.'

'Could we? I'd just like to get out and smell the air, I don't even know why I need to do that.'

She laughed and Jack grinned.

'We'll do it,' he said. 'First we go to Fort William, get you a phone and throw that one as far as we can out into the water.'

'What's Fort William?'

'It's a town about half an hour from here. It boasts having the highest mountain in Britain in it's postcode, but honestly, after this road, it almost pales into insignificance.'

'Ben Nevis?' she said.

'That's the one.'

Willow was looking forward to getting out of the car. She would like to have stopped now, but each moment she had the phone, she was at risk.

The road continued to impress as it carved its way deeper into the valley, passing through the rock itself, peaks rising all around them.

Willow gazed awestruck until the landscape opened up and they found themselves in a small village. To their right was water, the sea, Jack said, coming in from around the Isle of Mull. A good many miles out in front of them, in the murky distance and across the water, were more rugged peaks.

They crossed a bridge and wound through more villages along the coastline until they arrived out of a land that had seemed fit for hobbits and fairies right into a small, bustling town.

They weren't in Fort William long, just long enough for Jack to pay through the nose for a new top-end phone and manage to negotiate a new contract way better than the one she was currently on. Willow negotiated using the shop's electric for half an hour to charge it while they had some lunch and stretched their legs.

As they wandered through the town, it almost felt blissfully like they were on a day out. Even in the cold weather, people bustled along the front, and boats sailed on the loch. Jack was finally relaxed and chatty as they watched the boats and strolled past huts selling seafood and loch tours.

They stopped at a fish and chip shop and ate on a bench in the cold at the side of the loch, watching the boats screened by the mountains behind, and Willow decided that battered Haggis may be the best thing she had ever tasted.

The sun showed its face just after midday, in bright patchwork as it fought for space among the clouds. The fluctuating shadows on the mountains creating the perfect moody scene.

After picking up the newly charged phone, they were back inside the car and heading out of town, and the first chance he got, Jack pulled into a quiet layby. They headed down to the side of the loch, turned the old phone off, and threw it out to sea.

It was an almost liberating feeling as the wind snapped at her hair and bit at her cheeks, and a good throw too, one she didn't think she could replicate if she tried.

'No one getting that but the seals.' Jack had laughed as he helped her back up the bank and to the car.

Sixty-Six

W ORKING THE PHONE WITH only your left hand was a pig, Coop decided, as he threw the device down onto the chair. He heaved a frustrated sigh and clenched his jaw. It wasn't the only problem he had right now.

He had relied on taking Carlton's car up to Willow's isolated little house, but he thought that driving may be just as much fun with a broken hand as trying to work a phone.

He knew it was broken. He had heard the crunch as Dez had grabbed it. Hell, he had *felt* the crunch. It brought him out into a sweat at just the mere thought of it.

His hand throbbed worse now. What had been a dull ache yesterday morning was turning into a major pain fest now. He wondered if it needed re-splinting, and then decided that was just too much fucking pain to bear.

He laid his head against the back of the settee and thought through his plan. He didn't need to hang around Willow's place long, just give her long enough to contemplate what she had done, and then boom. She would be gone, and he could get as far away from there as possible.

The thought of actually killing her gave him a wobble. He had never liked blood, and he had never seen a dead person before the day of the robbery. He wasn't keen on seeing another so soon, and he hadn't particularly enjoyed prison, but she had killed Bugs.

If a girl could kill bugs and walk away, then he could certainly kill her - even if he never touched another gun in his life, and he thought that may be an option.

He would stick to dealing. With his brother having access to a prescription pad and being in close contact, it was actually proving very lucrative. He was getting into his stride alone easily.

Except when Willow is gone, he may not help you at all.

Coop shook his head. Carlton was a wimp. He would talk him round, or force him round, but they *would* be a team. It was his only option, other than working in Sainsbury's stacking shelves for minimum wage, and that had never been on his bucket list.

Carlton had actually gone to work yesterday, and again this morning. He had said that he would be back at lunchtime today, but at least it gave Coop some peace to work things out.

He got off the settee and kneeled before it like he was praying to some deity. He rested his right elbow on the chair, his hand in the air, and pulled the phone back with his left.

Pressing the phone to his right thumb with a grimace, he un-locked it and put it back on the chair in front of him.

If Gods and deities were a thing, there was one working in his favour right then, because the phone opened to his messages. He was about to shut the screen down and open the tracking app, but there was a message from Willow that he hadn't read yet.

He pressed the message with a frown.

Why the fuck was she telling him she was okay out of nowhere? She had already said thank you above. It was the extra thank you that set his intuition on edge. Who is this?

Coop scrolled up the messages. Nothing but what he had sent to her nearly three weeks ago now and her initial thank you days later. Now this?

He scrolled back down and looked at the message. Sent two days ago?

'Why the fuck would she...' his murmur trailed off as a flare of anger rose in his stomach.

Had someone been messing with his phone?

He flicked the phone into darkness and lit it again on the lock screen. He typed in the password five times before it locked him out entirely for sixty seconds.

His hand shook as he waited for the time to count down.

Carlton. It could only be Carlton.

He was marginally impressed. How the fuck did his doo-goody little brother know how to hack into a phone?

Then he almost slapped his head with idiocy.

He had got into Carlton's with his fingerprint when he was asleep, and clearly this had been the same night that he had come back with a broken hand and eaten a handful of tramadol.

He had slept a lot of that first afternoon back after the night on the park bench. Had Carlton really had the skill and audacity to steal his phone and contact Willow through the same messages that he had begun?

There were no sent messages, just a reply. Which meant that he had the forethought to delete his own but missed this one.

Coop's gut dropped.

Or had he?

If Carlton could get into his phone, had he seen the app? Did he know where Willow was?

He pulled up the app and checked on the dot, as though that would tell him anything at all. Willow's dot was still on the map, but now it was moving.

Where was she going now?

A look at the map told him she was far from the location of the last dot.

He grunted and slammed the phone down on the chair. It bounced and fell onto the floor.

There was only one reason she would travel so far, and it wasn't for a day out. Carlton had told her what was going on. She was on the run.

Which meant, broken hand or not, he had to move.

'Fuck!' he screamed. And then something else occurred to him.

Had Carlton actually gone to work this morning? Or had he gone to get her ahead of Coop?

Coop was on his feet so fast it sent a bolt of pain through his hand. Gritting his teeth, he ran to the front door and flung it wide.

Carlton's car was on the small driveway.

Coop let out a small laugh of relief, and then he wondered if Carlton still had the spare car key hanging by the kitchen door. If it was still there, Coop thought, maybe it was better to take the car and go now before she went too far north. The drive was going to kill him either way, but at least he had her location wherever she was going.

It would also give him a few hours head start before Carlton worked out where he was going too.

His hand throbbed and pulsed, and he looked down at it.

'Too bad. Looks like we're driving to Scotland whether the fuck you like it or not.'

First, he had to contact Radar and collect his gun from the lockup.

Just a small detour.

Back inside, he checked the app. She was still moving north.

He grinned.

'You can run, sweet Willow, but you can't hide. I'll always find you.'

Sixty-Seven

O N THE WAY BACK through Glencoe, Jack pulled into a large layby around halfway up. It was just after 2pm, and the afternoon sun was already beginning to dip below the mountain tops, which seemed far higher now that the clouds had cleared.

There were only a handful of other cars, so Jack pulled forward until they had a perfect view down the valley. They were high up here, the land falling away below to a river with a meandering pathway alongside. To their left, the first of what Jack had called the three sisters' rose. The second rose just ahead of the car, and the final sister, which rose in front of them, was just as majestic.

The wind was brusque, but there was no way Willow was sitting in the car.

She got out to take some photographs, walking the perimeter of the large car park, pulling her coat hood up against the chill. Then she returned to Jack, who had got out and was leaning against the bonnet, staring down the valley.

He turned with a smile as she returned to the car. 'All done?'

'Let's go for a walk,' she said, coming to a halt in front of him and grabbing one of his hands.

'A walk?' he said. 'I suppose we could go down along the river for a while.'

'No, not the river. Up there,' she said, pointing to a small track up the side of the mountain just ahead.

Jack raised an eyebrow, laughter in his eyes as he scanned her outfit.

'You want to hike up the mountain in fashion boots?'

'They're flat,' she said, 'and they're boots. I'm not scaling Everest.'

'Aye, good job, too. You'd bloody freeze to death, it's nippy enough here.'

'I'm not that cold, and we'll get warm walking up there. Please.' She pleaded at him with her eyes and tugged on his arm. 'I'd do it bare foot right now. I just need to see the view from a bit higher, not all the way up.'

'We wouldn't get all the way up before dark,' he said, squinting at the path. 'We could make it to that outcrop if we're quick enough.'

He pointed to a spattering of rock a small way up.

'Come on then, let's see how far we can get,' she said, pulling him off the car.

Jack grabbed his coat from the back and locked up before they walked down into the valley and began to rise back up the side of the mountain.

Willow had barely made it a hundred yards up the steep path before she had to stop. Her lungs burned and her thighs screamed.

'This hiking lark isn't as easy as it seems,' she panted to Jack.

His smile was wide, his eyes bright. 'It's as easy as walking up a hill. There's no race, just take your time. We'll turn back in half hour or so wherever we get to. We don't want to get stuck up here in the dark, it'll be treacherous getting back down.'

Willow found that if she paced herself and didn't talk, she could continue to walk without stopping too much. Jack slowed his pace to match hers, helping her around the jutting rock, and up steeper sections as they climbed higher. It didn't take long before they could look back and see the car, no bigger than a toy town model. The people below looked like ants.

'There's the beauty of a mountain,' Jack said as Willow admired the view. 'The climb is a pig, but you get very high, very quickly. You're doing well. We've got about ten minutes, do you want to stop, or keep going?'

Willow looked at the spectacular scenery around them. From here she could get some stunning photographs, and there was rock to sit on just at the side of them. There was no need to be higher.

'I'm good here, if you are,' she said, snapping photographs on her phone, whose settings and scope were a hundred times better than the one now sitting at the bottom of a loch up the road.

'This is fine for me,' Jack said, already sitting, his arms resting on his knees as he took in the view.

Willow snapped off more shots of the pale red sun dropping behind the mountains, giving them an ethereal quality. There could never be enough of a view like this, although what she captured could also never do the scale of it justice.

When she had finished, she turned to see Jack with his phone in his hand, his face stern.

Willow sat beside him.

'Important?' she said, motioning to the phone.

'Nope.'

'Well, for heaven's sake, Jack, put it away. Your mood just dropped six levels by the look on your face.'

'You're right. It did,' he said, putting the phone in his pocket and turning to her with a smile. 'Let me take some of you,' he said, holding his hand out for her phone.

He took a few shots, repositioning her for the best views behind. She laughed at the silly angles he was taking them at, even almost lying on the floor at one point before she had told him to get back up. When he was done, Willow stared at the photographs. Not only was the scenery was stunning, but considering what was going on, she looked fresh faced, happy, and alive. Her eyes bright in the sunset, red glow glistening off her face and hair, cheeks red with the wind. She looked like a different person, out here in the wild, hair mussed, her face makeup free.

It was a person she liked. The new Willow.

What had Jack said? Brave and strong with a zest for life? Something like that.

She'd take that, anyway.

'Look at this one,' Jack said, causing her stomach to roll over as he sat next to her, their knees and shoulders touching as he leaned over her and scrolled through to one that made her look like she was sitting on top of the world.

'That's my favourite,' she said, thinking she would use that to model her future self on. 'Like I really do have the world at my feet.'

'My favourite too, it's bonnie, isn't it? I love how your face glows in the sunset, and the red glints right off your hair,' he said with a smile. 'You look happy.'

'That's because I am,' she said, coming too close to adding that it was being up here with him as much as the being here at all, which was special enough. 'Thank you for bringing me here, Jack, I love it. In fact, I've loved the whole day.'

'Aye, me too,' he said quietly. 'I'm glad we can be friends again, Willow, it means a lot to me. I enjoy being around you. You're showing me there's more to life than McGracken House.'

Willow looked into his pale eyes, which were full of something that was a cross between pain and sadness. She wanted to touch his cold cheek, to rest her forehead against his and tell him it would all be okay.

Except that she hadn't got a clue what was wrong, apart from fighting with his mother and being stalked by his own wife, which was weird enough in itself.

Willow realised she was staring and felt herself flush as he stared right back. She dropped her gaze to her knees.

'What's wrong at the house, Jack? Why do you and Helena fight? What is making you so sad?'

Jack shook his head and frowned toward the car in the distance.

He half stood, but she pulled him back down.

'Please,' she said, 'you've listened to me, you've helped me out, you've been there whenever I've needed you. Talk to me.'

'It's nothing you should worry about, sweetheart. I'll be fine.'

'But I want to know,' she said, still holding a handful of his coat. 'I don't like it when you're like this because you lift my days as much as you say I lift yours. You don't like it when I'm miserable, and I don't like it when you are either. What's wrong?'

He stared at her and sighed.

'Helena doesn't like the time I'm spending with you.'

'So, it *is* me.'

'No, it's *not* you. It's me.'

'It's me. I called you out late the other night. I asked you to help me with the wall, and I've allowed you to drive me here today. I knew you wouldn't say no, I shouldn't have asked and I shouldn't have allowed it. I'll back off, I'll stay away from the house, I feel lots better now anyway-'

'No.' Jack said, grabbing her arm, then he loosened the pressure. 'No, please don't do that. It's not what you think.'

'I don't understand,' she said, her chest heavy.

'I know you don't, sweetheart, and I just don't know how much of it I can or should say. Does it even matter? Like you say, you could be gone in a year, anyway. No difference will have been made other than I've caused ripples that I shouldn't have, and then things will be worse. Maybe I shouldn't be making them worse, I don't know.'

He ran his hands over his face, and stared back out over the mountains where the sun was almost gone, and willow knew that they were almost out of time. They had been here over ten minutes already. She heaved her own sigh and shivered as the freezing wind penetrated beneath her clothes.

'Will it count if I guess?' she said. 'It seems pretty clear to me that Helena - as your mother, and rightfully so - is worried about you spending time with me because it's a small village, people will talk, and you have a wife. She's worried you're doing too much for me, and although we know nothing is happening here, no one else does, do they? She's putting two and two together and getting five. Am I right?'

'Yes and no,' Jack said, wrinkling his nose. 'It's complex, like I said. It's also getting dark, and you're going blue with cold. Let's go back to the car.'

'On one condition,' she said.

'You're going to make me tell you, I know.'

'It'll be a long two hours if you don't, I can make the journey very quiet and uncomfortable.'

In fact, she had no intention of it, and grinned as she said so to make sure Jack knew she had no intention either, but Jack's reply sent her off kilter again.

'If you're quiet with me like you were before, those two hours will seem like weeks.'

'So, you'll talk?'

'Aye, I'll try. Come on, before we catch our deaths.'

Sixty-Eight

C ARLTON SAT IN THE window of the bistro across from the office, the pint sliding soothingly down his throat.

When he put the glass down, it was half empty. He smacked his lips.

'Good?' Suzie said opposite him.

It had been his idea this time. Seeing her at the office had made him feel guilty and reckless all at the same time. He had barely spoken to her since that night they had shared, and really, this was all his fault, wasn't it? It was his weakness that had led them to this point. Suzie was simply a free woman who had spoken her mind. He was the one who had taken her home.

He was the one who had lost control.

'The best I've had since I was last here.'

Suzie smiled. She was being a little coy, and a little quieter than usual, not that he blamed her.

'So, how have you been?' he said.

'Busy. Cancelling a thousand angry and mentally unstable patients day after day.' She flicked her brown eyes up to him. 'You?'

'Not good,' he said. 'I'm sorry I left you with that. I just couldn't process anything that was happening, or what had happened, you know. I didn't really know how to handle it.'

Suzie nodded. 'I know. You're a loyal and sensitive man, Carlton, one of a kind. I shouldn't have led you down that path.'

'I shouldn't have gone down it with you. It's my fault.'

Suzie fingered the stem of her wine glass.

'I'm glad it happened, for what it's worth. At least you're out of my system now. It was a night I'll remember for a long time, but it won't happen again.'

Carlton felt his stomach and heart pull in opposite directions.

Half of him wanted it to happen again, the other half knew it was for the best.

You're out of her system.

That bit he didn't like too much.

'No,' he said, finishing the rest of his pint. 'I have to sort out what is going on with Willow. There've been a few... developments since we last spoke properly.'

Suzie frowned. 'With Coop?'

Carlton sighed. Where did he even begin?

'Yes, I'm afraid he saw us, um, that night,' he said, rubbing a hand over his face.

Suzie raised an eyebrow. 'Can't say that I'm surprised he has voyeuristic tendencies, to be honest.'

'He took photographs.' Carlton licked his dry lips and wished he'd left some of his pint in the glass.

'Of us?'

Carlton nodded. 'And then he sent them to Willow.'

Suzie's face dropped in horror. Her hand covered her mouth. 'Oh, Carlton. I'm so sorry. I didn't mean for anything like this to happen. I'm so sorry. I'm selfish. I'm sorry. Is it worth asking what her reaction was?'

'She called me, balled me out, told me we were done. That's the long and short of it.'

Suzie's hand covered his, and he stared at it, at her long scarlet manicured nails.

'I didn't know, Carlton, I promise you. This wasn't my intention. My thoughts were on you, only you. I even knew that you would go back to her when she re-appeared. I knew this was something we probably wouldn't ever do again, I just wanted to enjoy it for what it was, to dream, that's all.'

'I know,' he said. 'This was Coop. He saw an opportunity to get her to talk, so he stole her number from my phone and messaged her with them.'

'How do you know this?' she said, and then she rolled her eyes. 'You managed to get into his phone? What did you do?'

'As you said. Luckily, he hurt his hand pretty bad in the pub that night. I prescribed him tramadol for the pain which he likes to take with beer.'

Suzie's face went white, and her smile fell. 'No, Carlton, that isn't good. You could get into big trouble for that. Huge!'

'I know. I wrote up his file as though he had seen me, so it's all official. Hopefully, any investigation will come out in my favour. Hell, what am I even saying? I hope to God he doesn't overdose. That's what I really hope.'

'I hope not too, for your sake.'

Carlton nodded, signalled her empty glass, and went to the bar to fetch two more drinks.

'So, you got into his phone?' she said as he sat back down.

'I did what you said. Waited until he dozed off after a dose of tramadol, used his thumb print to unlock it, and changed the password. The irony is, to get Willow's number, he probably had to do the same to me. I feel a bit foolish.'

'There's no need. You're not the one in the wrong here.'

He stared at her, his eyebrows raised.

'Well, okay, a little in the wrong, if you want to see it that way.'

'More than a little. I deserved to have it all backfire. I doubt she'll take me back now, even when I find her and grovel.'

'I'm always here,' Suzie said with a sigh, looking down into her wine.

Carlton smiled sadly.

'Suzie, you're a stunning woman, and you could have anyone you wanted. You don't have to wait around for me. I'm not worth it, really.'

'You are worth it to me. If I need to wait longer, I will.' She met his eyes and his stomach turned over. 'I know that it's only Willow in the way, otherwise you'd be with me, wouldn't you? That night may have been wrong, but it was good, you have to admit that.'

He nodded. 'Yes, and yes, if Willow wasn't around, of course I would have jumped at the chance to be with someone like you. I would. At the moment? I have a lot to sort out. My head is all over the place, that's why I couldn't come in to work.'

'I understand that, and I can deal with it for you. That's what I'm here for. Take all the time you need.'

Carlton smiled and restrained himself from leaning across the table to feel those full red lips on his again. She made it too easy for him to want her. He took a long sip of beer and turned his gaze to the window. Outside, the traffic was heavy and a look at the wall clock told him it was 3.05pm.

Not quite rush hour. Between four and six every day, and around lunchtime on a Friday, the traffic always snarled up. It was one reason he had wanted his office so close to home, but today it was starting early.

In the queue Carlton saw a silver Vauxhall which looked familiar. Funny how the salesman had told him that his Astra's sleek sports pack was a one-of-a-kind job built by the last owner, and yet, here was another with the same kit, even down to the nineteen-inch alloy wheels. He stared, wanting to get a good look at the person who wanted the same car as he had. Maybe this guy had been told it was a one off too.

The person at the wheel had long hair and a dark jacket, and now that he was closer, as the traffic pulled through the lights, Carlton could make out the first part of the number plate.

LJ65

Carlton frowned.

'What is it?' Suzie said, bringing his attention back to her.

'That car,' he said, pointing at the Astra, now waiting patiently as the lights turned amber and then green.

'Looks suspiciously like yours,' she said with a frown of her own.

Carlton caught the last of the number plate as the car sailed through the lights and disappeared down the road.

'It was my car,' he said, feeling the heat in his cheeks as he rose out of his seat. 'Do you have any plans tonight, Suzie?'

'No,' she said, 'other than being here with you.'

'Good, ditch the wine. I need to borrow your car, but I've had too much to drive. Fancy helping me find out what Coop is up to in my car without asking permission?'

'Sound like fun to me,' she said, 'let's go.'

Sixty-Nine

J ACK TURNED THE HEAT up full and faced the heaters toward Willow as the car engine warmed. It was only 3.05pm, but it felt as though it should be much later as darkness set in.

'I can share the driving back if you get tired,' she said. 'Just ask.'

'It's three in the afternoon.' Jack grinned as Willow yawned.

'Well, I could sleep for a week. Must be the mountain air.'

Jack turned the car carefully out of the car park and back onto the road. The car lights illuminated the craggy roadside rock as they pulled back up the valley toward the mountain tops.

'You go to sleep then, sweetheart. I'll be okay driving.'

'You can tell me what's going on first,' she said, putting her fingers to the warm blown air from the heater, her feet thawing nicely under the foot heater below. She shivered and tried to huddle closer.

'What did Sophie say to you about it?' he said.

Willow frowned at him. 'Sophie? Nothing, really. She just said to be careful how much I lean on you because you were married. I said I hadn't known and that I would back off. I *was* leaning on you a lot, and you were helping me out a lot at the time, as was the work at the house. I just presumed that it was okay. You hadn't told me that I was overstepping any boundaries.'

'Because you weren't, and you aren't.'

'But you are married, and in more ways than one, you have dropped everything to look out for me, even I know that's wrong. Your wife may be the most laid-back woman on earth, Jack, but there's no way any husband of mine would be running round after any other girls. Job or not.'

'It's not a job. I enjoy looking out for you, it gives me purpose, and she's absolutely not,' he said, easing the car around a bend, the inky blue sky opening up before them. Stars were glinting above them already.

'Who's not what?'

'She's not the most laid-back woman on earth. In fact, she's the most pig-headed and spiteful woman on earth. If I ever see her again, it'll be too soon.'

Willow's mouth dropped open, and she spread her hands.

'See? This is so confusing, Jack. What the hell is going on?'

'Jennifer and I split up over three years ago. I was sick of the arguments, sick of being under the thumb, sick of trying to make someone happy who had no intention of trying to make me happy, sick of working a job I hated, and sick of living in the city.

We lived in Edinburgh, and I struggled not being around the mountains and the wilderness. I never really got a chance to travel out to the beach or the mountains, even though they're fairly close to the city, you know? She was never interested, so it was never something we would do together. I'm not bothered about doing it alone, but I always had to do something that she organised on my days off. I never felt like I got a chance to be me. It was my fault. I did walk out and decide I couldn't go back, and I did leave her in a mess. I snapped. I'd had enough.

The problem was that I worked for her family firm, her dad is the owner, and he decided that I should have nothing if I chose to leave his daughter. He offered a substantial raise if I went home to her, but I couldn't go, so I didn't take it. He fired me on the spot. I tried a rental just outside Edinburgh, just like you have really, just needing my own space somewhere out of the city, but she tracked me, wasn't quite so keen to let go, apparently.'

'I can't imagine why,' Willow said, rolling her eyes, and then she clamped her lips together and flushed as she looked down at her hands.

Keep yourself in check, Willow.

'Sorry,' she said, 'uncalled for. Carry on.'

Jack smiled as he shook his head. 'She didn't want to let me go because she had appearances to keep up. It destroyed her perfectly made world. She hated that everyone would know I had left her. If it had been the other way round, she wouldn't have cared less - it was all about protecting her perfect identity, and being in control of exactly what people thought of her. Of us.'

'So, what happened?'

'Well, the money ran out fairly quickly. Well-paid jobs are scarce for labourers, and her family were quite well up in the industry. They made sure my name was mud. No one was interested in hiring me for quite a few miles around. Right at the time I was having to choose between a car, a roof over my head, or food, I decided I had no choice but to come home.'

'That's not so bad though, Helena and Mick were happy to take you in, I bet?'

Jack wrinkled his nose and shrugged.

'To take me in, aye, but happy? Not a chance. They still - well, Helena really - still wants a reconciliation. It was an arrangement, you see. A good deal for both families. So no, I'm not flavour of the month at the house, because Helena is not happy that I'm looking after you when I should be chasing after my self-important wife - ex-wife - and begging for forgiveness.'

Willow blinked and shook her head.

'Back up a sec, an arrangement?'

'Well spotted,' he said with a sigh. 'Jennifer and I were childhood sweethearts. It was always assumed that we would get married and have children, and that I would work for her family firm, and take it over in the future. Jennifer only has a much younger sister, and I was the ideal son-in-law material for them, apparently. For Helena and Mick, they got a son who wasn't messing about on the hills after dropping out of university. That son had a future, a good job, and a well-to-do company almost handed on a plate. By the time I had decided that I really didn't want to marry her, the wedding was already being arranged, just after her eighteenth birthday. I was young, Helena and Mick seemed really happy, I didn't really know what to do, so I went along with it to keep the peace.'

Willow stared out at the stars through the windscreen. The sky was clear, the moon bright, but wearing a frosty shawl that would deliver a white blanket over the land by morning.

'Following so far?'

She turned to him and nodded her head.

'How long did you stay together?'

'Too long. I was twenty-two when we married and finally decided there was more to life at thirty-four.'

'Twelve years! But you just said that you didn't want to marry her at all.'

'No, but I didn't know how to let people down. I don't particularly like confrontation. I knew the arguments would come from both families, as well as her. It was easier to go ahead than not. I just wanted an easy life.'

'You don't seem to do too badly with confrontation. Both Sophie and Duncan say you're hot headed.'

Jack huffed a laugh.

'I hate arguments, Willow. Sophie and Duncan are good people, but they don't understand the frustration of the situation. Remember Betsy?'

Willow nodded. 'Yes.'

'Betsy is Jennifer's younger sister. She came purely to make trouble on behalf of Jennifer. Helena and Mick could say nothing because she had them over a barrel. They didn't want anyone to know the truth about the split, and so Betsy followed me round being nasty and generally upending anything I did for a good many months. I told Helena, Helena told me to ignore her, that it was worse that the truth came out, and that karma would get her later, which is a load of shit. They watched as this child made a mockery of them, the house, and me. The morning Sophie told you about when everything kicked off? I found her snooping in my room and told her to get out. She wouldn't, so I asked Helena to remove her, but she told me to leave it. I was furious that Betsy was being allowed in my personal space, so I tried to deal with it myself, and yelled at her to leave. She told me to make her, and then she stripped.'

Willow did a double take.

'She what?'

'Stripped. Said if I as much as made a move to stop her, she'd call rape and say I was attacking her.'

'Are you kidding?'

'I wish I was.'

'So, what happened?'

'I put the shower on and pulled her in. She was screaming, of course, but I turned it on her and told her to get out of my shower and get out of the goddamn house, or I would dump her outside the gate naked. Everyone knew I had been outside two minutes earlier. They all believed she had been in the shower. I made Helena an ultimatum because she had such a need for me to be in the right, to be her angel and not the failure she thought I really was. Keeping up appearances again. I knew she would choose me over Betsy. It was the only way to get rid of her. Luckily, I haven't seen or heard from her since.'

'Would you have done it?'

'Dumped her outside the gate naked? Aye, I'd have loved it, but she got dressed rather hurriedly after that.'

Willow laughed. 'Quick thinking, though.'

'Don't think I've ever thought so quickly in my life, the last thing I needed was to be accused of rape, too. By then, I'd already been through enough with Jennifer. I couldn't take much more.'

Willow nodded.

'Did you love her?'

'When I was fourteen, aye. We used to spend time up in the hills, swimming, climbing, fishing. It was really starting to wane by the time we married. Her family moved to the city when she was sixteen, and she was growing up a different girl. By that time it was makeup, tan, perfect hair, and designer dresses. She was getting a nasty attitude too, looking down on other people a fair bit. I didn't like that side of her. Still don't. That side only got worse as she got older.'

'Do you have any children?'

'No. She was just getting out of the parties and into families as I left. I couldn't let that side go ahead. It would have been unfair on the child. It was part of why I left, the pressure to conform.'

'You don't want a family?'

Jack huffed a laugh.

'The irony is, I really do want a family. It's all I ever wanted. My sister is the career woman, I just want the hills and the kids, I think that's why Helena and Mick despaired. For all they seem chilled, they wanted to raise high flyers. I should have left Jennifer earlier, and that family will possibly be a sacrifice now, but I couldn't have children with her for my sake. It wouldn't have been fair.'

Willow chewed her lip.

'What a mess,' she murmured.

'Aye, and it still is. Helena is adamant that I tell no one that we've split up. I'm to say I've come back because my family needs help at the house, but that I'm going home when I'm done. So that's what everyone thinks. Helena loves that the village thinks I'm a hero, not a failure, and she is determined that her plan should work out, that we make up, and the whole thing will never have happened to the outside world. Disaster averted.'

'In her eyes, anyway.'

'Right.'

'Doesn't she think after three years that it isn't going to hap-pen?'

'No, because I've never said I wasn't talking to Jennifer, it seemed easier to let that slide too and just have a peaceful life for as long as it lasted.'

Willow shook her head. 'Wow, and you say I've got issues facing up to things.'

'Aye, but I never had a reason to fight it before, and the thing is, when you find something worth fighting for, you wonder why you put up with the crap. By not telling them what I want or need, I've been letting them know exactly how to treat me - as a doormat. I don't want to be that person anymore. I don't want her to have that hold over me. I want a divorce. I want to move out of home. I want to move on. I want...' He trailed off with a sigh. 'I just want a life.'

Willow wasn't sure there was anything she could say. She put a hand on his arm.

'You'll get one,' she said.

'I hope so.'

There was a layby on the left and Jack indicated and pulled over. Willow was confused for a second, and then she saw the tears on his face.

'Jack,' she said, unbuttoning her seatbelt.

'I'm sorry,' he said, pinching the tears from his eyes with a finger and thumb. 'I'll be okay, just give me a sec. It gets overwhelming.'

She squeezed his arm, and then she abandoned thought of being polite, and pulled him into a hug instead.

'Take whatever time you need. It's not like I have to get back to my spooky cottage with a secret penthouse and a hole in the cupboard. In fact, I'd prefer it if I didn't anytime soon.'

Jack spluttered a laugh and pulled away with a sniff, wiping his eyes.

'I'd take staying at the spooky cottage over going back to Mc-Gracken House at the moment. I'm in for hell when I get back. Helena has called five times so far today.'

'I've a spare room,' she said, half hoping he was serious. 'Take it if you need it.'

'I'd make things worse.'

'Did you tell her where you were going today?'

'Of course, but she didn't like it.'

'I'm not Jennifer.'

'Not by a country mile,' he said with a small laugh, his tears finally dry. 'Sorry about that, princess, shall we carry on?'

'Whenever you're ready,' she said with a smile.

Now that Jack had opened up about Jennifer, he couldn't seem to stop. He told Willow more about their life together in Edinburgh, her family, his job, and more about Helena's obsessive need for them to be together and for Jack to be successful. In fact, he didn't stop until he drove onto her driveway and cut the engine.

'Home sweet home,' he said. 'Let's get the serious bit out of the way first. The phone is gone, and that's a relief, but remember it may not be over. If this man is serious about getting to you, he will probably know other ways around it.'

Willow felt her stomach sink as she nodded and looked at the house.

'Willow?'

She looked at him. 'I'm listening.'

'Keep everything locked at all times, doors and windows. And don't forget to call or message if you're worried. Don't worry about how late it is, how early it is, don't even think about it, just call.'

'I will.'

'And please always remember you can stay at the house if you want to. Anytime. Helena's issue is with me, not you. You're always welcome if you don't want to be up here alone.'

'Okay,' she replied. 'Thank you for everything today, Jack. You don't know how much I appreciate it. You sure you don't want me to come back down with you and speak to Helena?'

'Not unless you want to stay there tonight,' he said. 'Honestly, it'll be bad enough. You don't need to see that. I'll probably just head up to my room after, anyway. No doubt the others will tell you about the argument tomorrow.'

'I'll stay here tonight, but I'm sorry you have to go back to that now, and I'm sorry for what you've had to go through.'

'That's okay, sweetheart, it's my own doing,' he said, unhooking his seatbelt, curling an arm around her shoulders, and pulling her in to him. She lay her head on his shoulder. 'Guess we both got the rough end of the deal with long-term partners, eh?'

'At least you didn't really choose yours,' she said.

'You have such poor judgment,' he said into her hair. 'I knew from the beginning mine was a bad seed.'

'At least I wasn't led into it.'

'No. Like you say, you chose it.'

'Rub it in.'

He chuckled and squeezed her tight.

'We'll make it through, princess, we both will. Thank you for listening today. It's been nice to share the burden.'

She smiled and closed her eyes, for once not feeling the least bit guilty about being in his arms.

'I don't mind. I feel like I understand things better, and now that you're not married, I guess I feel better about being myself around you.'

'I am married,' he said with a laugh that reverberated through her and sent tingles down her spine. 'And you never need to be anyone but yourself.'

'You know what I mean.' She looked up at him seriously. 'Jack, there aren't any more secrets, are there? Nothing else that's going to break me? I feel like you hold me together. I don't want to feel like I have for the last week. I enjoy being around you.'

Jack looked back at her, his gaze soft in the moonlight. 'No. I didn't know that you had been told or I could have explained. Not that you're to repeat any of it mind, Helena would kill me. But yes, I am married, separated, living at home with my parents. Living the dream. Wanting nothing more than to get the hell out of that house. That's the only secret.'

He grinned as she giggled.

'It's not such a bad place, Jack.'

'No, but how many almost thirty-eight-year-olds are still living in their childhood home, with their parents? I don't even have a job because part of me being able to live there is working the land and helping out, and of course they think I'll go back to my old job when I get my marriage back on track.' He huffed a mirthless laugh. 'Do you know Helena and Mick give me an allowance each month, like a child, and I can't spend any of it because I'm expected to be there seven days a week? And I have absolutely no choice in the matter. Look what happens when I take a day out.' He held up his phone. 'I'm stuck. It's not a good look, is it?'

Willow pursed her lips. It was almost worse than her situation had been. Almost.

'I'm sorry.'

'Don't be.'

He tightened his arm around her shoulders and pulled her close. She turned toward him, twisting in her seat, and tucking her face close to his neck. She placed a hand on his chest, warmth rising from beneath his jumper, his heart beating steadily. He put his hand over hers and placed his chin on her head with a sigh.

'I've nothing to hurt you with, princess, nothing at all,' he whispered. 'I promise.'

Her heart thudding in her chest, she closed her eyes and wanted time to stop and hold her right there, in the warmth of his arms, his heart beating under her hand, surrounding her in a veil of safety.

And that was all she needed.

Seventy

'T HIS IS LUNACY,' SUZIE said as she started the engine of her
Subaru. 'How will we ever find out where he went? He
could have gone to the shop and be home now.'

'He's hasn't,' Carlton said, getting into the passenger seat and
buckling the seatbelt. He looked at the phone screen, drawing
the map in closer. 'Turn left out of the drive, first right, then
keep following the road up. At the 'T' junction, go straight across
until the main road and then turn right.'

Suzie did as he said, driving a little too fast for his liking. 'How
on earth do you know where he is, hotshot? Spill the beans.'

'I've got a tracker on him.'

'GPS? Good thinking.'

She was coming to the "T" junction now and crossing straight
over with barely any hesitation. Carlton closed his eyes.

'He's got the contacts. I know he's been onto Willow for a while
now, but I couldn't understand why he hadn't made a move. He
said he needed a message from her. He had one in reply to the
photos so I knew it wouldn't be long.'

Carlton closed his eyes and put a hand to the roof as the car
bounced over a couple of speed bumps, jerking him out of his
seat against the seatbelt, as Suzie screeched to the end of the
road.

'Right?' she said.

'Yes, right here and keep going straight.'

She eased the car onto the main road with a roar and there was the blast of a horn behind. Carlton watched the old Volvo disappear into the distance as she put her foot down.

'I thought he'd wait a little longer with his hand being so bad, but getting even is obviously worth more to him than the pain.'

'How do you know he's even going after her?'

'Educated guess.'

'He's probably driving your car doped up to the eyeballs.'

'It's crossed my mind,' he said, relaxing back into the seat now that the car was sailing along a clear main road. 'I'm trying not to think about it too much.'

Suzie kept her eyes on the road.

'How far is he?'

Carlton zoomed back out of the map a little so that he could see the dot, which seemed to be heading toward the Bristol Channel.

He clenched his jaw. If Willow had been in Bristol the whole time, he would not only kick himself, but kick her, too.

'Not far. He's heading toward Portishead by the looks of it. Keep going, we're gaining on him.'

Suzie seemed to think that this meant she should put her foot down and her speed rose to 80mph. Carlton put his hand out onto the dashboard.

'Slow down a little. I don't want us to get pulled over.'

Suzie slowed to around 78mph. Carlton swallowed. It would have to do.

In a little over twelve minutes, they reached Portishead, and Carlton guided her round to the marina where Coop's orange dot seemed to have stopped.

'Be careful now,' Carlton said, his head beginning to ache. 'He's parked just around the corner, I think. His dot is on its way down to the boats, but I don't think cars can go down there.'

As they rounded the corner the Astra sat parked haphazardly on the edge of the kerb next to a block of flats. Suzie pulled past it and bumped the Subaru up the kerb opposite the entrance to the marina itself.

'There he is,' she said, and Carlton saw his brother's retreating back heading along the concrete toward the mass of sails and large hulls. He put a hand on the door handle and Suzie stopped him.

'Where are you going?'

'I'm following him. If Willow is down there, I don't want him to get to her first.'

'You have the GPS, and these boats are all private. Does she know anybody down here?'

'I have no idea, but if she's on one of these boats, then he knows about it.'

Suzie nodded and pulled some trainers from the backseat. She slipped off her heels and pulled the trainers on.

'Let's go, but we keep our distance. And if I get a parking ticket, it's the company's problem, not mine.'

'Fair enough,' he said, his eyes on the orange dot as she locked the car, and they crossed the road. 'He's stopped.'

Suzie took the phone from him and navigated down the large concrete walkway.

'He's down there,' she said, pointing to a smaller gangway.

Carlton turned to it, but Suzie pulled him back.

'No, he's not moving. If we walk down there, he will see us. Let's wait here.'

'But what if he has her?'

'He doesn't,' Suzie said, turning him away from the small walkway, putting her arm around him and walking him quickly away.

'What are you doing?' Carlton said.

Suzie stopped them to look at an information board, waited, and then turned him around. Coop was ahead, walking back up the concrete toward the car.

'I don't think Willow is here. Maybe some sort of help, Something illegal probably, but not Willow.'

Carlton felt his headache thump worse as they trailed him back to the car, keeping a good distance behind.

At the car, Coop threw something inside and then got into the driver's seat. He started the engine and drove past the Subaru, out of sight.

Suzie and Carlton jogged up to the car, although Carlton could see the orange dot was crawling at the moment.

'He's moving back toward the main road,' Carlton puffed.

They jumped into the car and Suzie lurched forward, following Carlton's directions.

'I wish we knew how far he was going. I'm low on fuel.'

'Fill it up at the next garage. I'll pay. We can't drop too far behind him now. You know what I wish?'

'What's that?'

'I wish I'd brought a manual car. He'd be having a much harder time with that damaged hand right now.'

'We'd be trailing him either way,' Suzie said as she pulled onto the main road and resumed her unsafe speed after the orange dot that was Coop.

'That's the other thing. I wish I knew what he was up to, because if this is a wild goose chase, I'll kill him. I don't know what he's going to do, what he's planning when he gets there-'

His voice hitched, and Suzie glanced at him.

'Well, we'll be there to stop him either way,' she said, easing her foot down harder on the accelerator.

Seventy-One

W<small>ILLOW HELD UP A</small> hand as Jack turned the car around and drove down the lane, the red of the brake lights the only sign of him as he drove down the hill to McGracken House.

She held onto the outer door as she watched them, almost wishing that she was going with him, but she was home now. She would just have to deal with whatever came her way tonight and at least the following couple, too.

Jack had been honest about not knowing when he would be able to put the cupboard back together, and understanding more about his situation, she had told him she wasn't too bothered, and not to worry.

Maybe I'll have a go. Take some of the pressure off and block the thing myself.

She shivered as she stared down the road, which was now completely dark, the noise of the engine gone.

I wonder if the thudding will be back tonight.

What's worse? The footsteps or the thuds?

Either way, she got no sleep.

She turned to the dark hallway, adrenaline flooding her veins as she looked at the glass ahead.

Is she in there tonight?

Where the hell else would she be?

Willow swallowed. She was shivering uncontrollably now, the icy wind blowing through her as the frosty moon upheld its promise. She held the door and peered into the darkness.

Was that movement?

Was she at the door?

Martha, please go away. I have enough to deal with without this crap. If I don't feel safe here, how can I possibly be safe against an intruder?

Even Martha hadn't been safe here against an intruder, she thought, running a shaky hand through her hair.

SHUT UP AND GET INSIDE.

Willow felt frozen to the spot. She squeezed her eyes shut and reopened them with a breath. Never had she felt such a force at the door that she couldn't enter, but tonight, coming back in the dark, with an unknown threat hanging over her and with a hole in her cupboard that led to spooky stairs?

You're terrified of a cupboard when there may be something much worse coming your way. Just go inside and lock up before you get hypothermia.

She stared, her heart thumping so hard she wondered if it could be heard outside her body, and then she had an idea. A brilliant idea.

Use the back door into the kitchen, you klutz!

Relief making her dizzy for a moment, she laughed as she shut and locked the outside door and walked around the side of the house. In the moonlight the vegetation was silver; stalks of bushes that had lost most of their leaves, and plants that were long dead when the summer warmth had gone, were rattling hollowly in the breeze.

It reminded Willow of a rattlesnake. Or maybe a hundred rattlesnakes.

The cottage seemed just as deadly with its black eyes as she edged to the back door.

She scanned the garden where dark pockets concealed who knew what creatures. Maybe even the primate from the roof.

At the thought of the thing on the roof, Willow's neck prickled.

Was it in the bushes, watching her?

From the edge of the garden, by the woodland, came a low rustle, a snapping branch, and then silence.

Willow swallowed hard. Whether there was a legitimate reason for the feeling or not, she felt watched. Her eyes scanned the garden again, searching inside the darkness for...

What? What are you searching for? Something to tell you that you're right? Get inside.

Willow put the key in the lock and opened the door, walking into a wall of cold no warmer than the wind outside. She flicked on the light and turned to shut the door.

It was there.

On the lawn.

A figure, facing the house, staring at her, just ahead of the blackness around the edge of the garden.

Shit. Shit, shit, SHIT.

She slammed the door shut, the walls of the cottage reverberating with the blow, and turned the lock over before pressing her back to the door.

Her heart thudding, she flicked off the light and peered out of the half curtain, wishing the kitchen had a full blind instead.

More material like you have in the living room doorway. This house will be little more than a hovel if you keep going.

The figure on the grass was gone.

Had it been there anyway, or was this her imagination again?

She squinted, and then there was a squeak beside her.

She could feel her thudding heartbeat in her ears as she looked at the door.

He's found me. It didn't matter about the phone because he found me anyway.

The round handle of the kitchen door was turning slowly.

Is it?

In the darkness, she stared at the handle so hard that her eyes ached.

The squeaking stopped, and there was silence.

Is somebody out there?

Willow pressed herself to the door, listening.

Maybe just throw open the door and confront the intruder now. Get it over with.

Not a chance in hell.

A shadow passed the kitchen window.

Is that the moon?

If it is an intruder, the cottage is secure, but the front curtains are open. They can see inside.

Willow lunged into the living room, around the settee and dragged the front curtains shut, and then the side. Then she moved back to the front and pulled the curtain back to peek outside.

There was nothing there. The driveway was empty of everything but her car. The trees swaying in the wind.

From the hallway came a noise. A scratch.

Willow swung her head to the living room door. The curtain was open here too, darkness pressed against the glass. Willow put a hand to her forehead.

How much fear can one person take before they keel over? How many sleepless nights before they go insane? Am I insane?

The intruder thinks there's no one inside. Put the lights on and turn on the television.

Willow froze with indecision.

No, they saw you come inside, remember? Keep it dark, then you have the advantage.

The scratching persisted.

Maybe there was no one there, you just imagined it?

And the squeak of the door handle?

Scratch. Scratch. Scratch.

It was like the noise was scratching at her brain, right inside her skull.

If there is someone outside, are they any worse than the thing inside?

Scratch. Scratch.

Willow clenched her jaw and placed both hands over her ears with a roar.

'SHUT THE HELL UP! ALL OF YOU, JUST SHUT THE HELL UP!'

When she took her hands from her ears, the cottage was silent. Pensive.

Willow shivered. Every hair on her body stood on end.

'Martha?' she called to the empty room. 'Please. I don't know what you expect me to do about any of this if I'm so damn tired!'

The cottage was still, almost holding its breath. Or maybe it was Willow that was holding her breath.

And then she had a thought. Maybe she knew why the activity was increasing. Maud had said that Martha felt a connection to her, but Willow was avoiding the issue as adeptly as she could.

I do have my own issues, and my own intruder to look out for now, too.

But isn't that the issue that Martha had? In this very cottage? Is it any wonder that the girl is trying so hard when you're just ignoring her?

'Okay. I get it, and I will listen, but please, Martha. I'm begging you. One night where the cottage isn't freezing, and noises don't come from the hallway. I just need one night of sleep. Tomorrow, I promise I will look into what happened here. I will.'

From the hallway there was a small thud and a click. Then there were soft, slow steps. The creak of the stairs. Someone was going up.

Willow knew that she would have to check the front door. Was that person real or Martha?

'Martha? No more! I've had enough for tonight. I hear you, and I see your messages. I will look into it tomorrow, I promise. I will listen, and I will listen to your warnings. What happened here will not repeat itself. I will make sure of it.'

The cottage was quiet again. The only sound was Willow's heart thudding against her ribs. She went into the kitchen and peered out of the back window. There was nothing out there that she could see, and it was the same at the front. Whoever the intruder was, it appeared they had gone for tonight.

If there even was one.

Maybe you're making too much of Martha's 'beware's' and Jack's talk of tracking, and Carlton's talk of revenge. It's putting your mind in overdrive.

When this guy comes up here, I don't think he'll be the type to go sneaking around the house watching. I think he'll blow his way inside and come straight for you.

Willow felt her stomach drop through the floor.

This was real.

Someone was possibly chasing her down. Someone who didn't want to talk about things.

Haven't I been through enough?

It doesn't matter. If he's coming, you'd better be ready for him.

Oh, I will.

Her mind fell silent, and she realised the cottage was also still silent.

With more confidence and an almost certain knowledge that Martha was gone too, Willow looked out into the hallway. There seemed to be nothing untoward, so she opened the door and switched on the light.

The cupboard was closed, the hallway clear. No sign of Martha herself.

Willow went to the bedroom and looked inside.

It felt warm, and the bed looked like heaven.

Why am I sleeping on the sofa? Pushed out of my bed by a ghost?

And Martha had been seen in the kitchen doorway, anyway. Was the bedroom any less safe than the rest of the cottage?

'Martha? I'm sleeping in my bed tonight. My promise still stands. If you'll keep your end of the bargain, that would be great. Thanks.'

She checked the other two bedrooms and then she went back into the living room, turned on the light, and then turned up the heating, which had fallen to a record ten degrees on the thermostat.

No wonder it's so bloody cold.

She made a drink, snuggled in the duvet, and watched television until her eyes were dropping at 10.30pm. Then she went to bed.

In peace.

And fell into a deep, almost instantaneous sleep.

Seventy-Two

C OOP WAS WET WITH sweat when he pulled into Lancaster services. The traffic on the M6 had been particularly slow, especially around Birmingham, which he managed to hit at rush hour. From Bristol, Lancaster was a mere three and a half hours, but tonight it had taken him almost six, and even slipknot and Limp Bizkit had begun to get on his nerves.

It was barely 9pm, but he was exhausted. His hand was throbbing, he was shaking, and his vision was blurry at best. He also needed fuel and a piss.

The services seemed the best option for killing ten birds with one stone.

Earlier that afternoon he had tracked Willow to a place just below Fort William, which was a good deal further up into Scotland than her first location, but he supposed that would be the way it was. If she had been tipped off, then she would move higher. It stood to reason, but he would get to her eventually.

He pulled into a space at the edge of the busy car park and turned off the car.

He got out, took two tramadol dry, and made his way to a squat building that announced Burger king and Costa Coffee waited for him inside.

His stomach rumbled as he swung open the entrance doors, and the smell of food hit him.

He stopped at the toilet first, then the shop for a few snacks, drinks, and beers, and then burger king for tea.

Struggling back to the car with everything in his arms and trying not to use or hit his hand was proving almost impossible.

His hand was a fucking pain in the arse.

Period.

He put everything on the floor before opening the car door and throwing it all inside. He followed and shut the door firmly.

It was freezing out there. He wished he had brought a thicker coat. One of Carlton's padded numbers would have gone down nicely now, but it was too late for regrets. No way he was turning back now. He was closer than he had been earlier, much closer.

He ate his burger and fries, dumped the rubbish in the back seat, and opened a beer.

He wanted to have a look at the GPS, and wanted to have a look at the gun, but he could only hold a beer in his good hand and the car was too close around him. The thought of balancing his beer between his legs was just too cold for comfort.

He drank the beer and discovered another problem.

It was freezing. Not the best way to enjoy a beer, shaking in a cold car in front of a rubbish strewn hedge. It wasn't like he was going to get any sleep here, no matter how tired he was.

He did have his stash of cash, though, and he had seen a sign for a Travel Lodge just around the corner. He could just take the cheapest room.

It didn't take much persuading. The more he shook with cold, the more his hand hurt. A bed for the night seemed like a good way to go. At least he would wake refreshed in the morning.

He started the car and fuelled up as he passed the garage, before driving round to the Travel Lodge car park and checking in.

He fetched a small black holdall from the boot. Took some of his clothes out and placed the gun and beer inside. He zipped it up and made his way up to the room on the first floor.

Warmth hit him first. It was warm in here, and there was a small bathroom, and a television, and more to the point, a bed that looked half cozy.

He threw the bag onto the floor, popped another beer, and took a swig, then he took out the small revolver. Zippy had given him an extra round of ammunition, but Coop didn't really think that he would need it. He hoped to get the job done swiftly and quietly and move on with his life.

The gun was one he had used before, but he was right-handed, and he hoped he could get to grips with it being in his left. He tried it out for size and thought that he had a good chance.

To be honest, he was too tired to care either way.

He threw the gun back into the holdall and grabbed the remote before sitting with his back propped against the headboard.

He flicked through the channels until he came to something at least watchable, an old Top Gear episode, and then he pulled out his phone.

He'd had no messages, which was a little strange as he was missing, and so was Carlton's car. Carlton must be home by now... unless.

'He's having his fucking way with the secretary again. Maybe that's the reason he went back to work.'

He huffed a laugh. At least that gave him more time and more of a run.

He flicked onto the Text Tracker app to see whether Willow had run any further. Last time he had looked she had been stationary.

He scrolled through the map and frowned.

No dot.

No dot? Which means no GPS. Is she somewhere without a signal?

Could be, so far up.

He opened the menu and clicked on her number. A message flicked onto the screen.

Location not available at this time.

Coop tapped the screen.

Had she turned the phone off?

Maybe she turns it off at night because that's when Carlton gets all whiny.

He raised his eyebrows and checked the gallery for the screen-shots he had taken of her last location before he had left.

He had only taken them so that he could route himself without the dot fucking off the end of the map and confusing him.

Now he was glad he had.

He opened Google Maps and typed directions to Fort William.

Motorways all the way up to the M8. From there it was A roads. His biggest problem was time.

Almost six hours from here, and that was with no traffic.

He stared at the television where Jeremy Clarkson was driving a four by four down a huge sand dune followed by Richard Hammond and James May.

Six hours.

And with no GPS, and no idea why, that seemed like an awful long time to take.

He could make it tomorrow, he hoped, but the way his hand had been after six hours driving today, he wasn't sure he would be able to pull off a convincing revenge shooting.

The important thing was not to make a mistake. There was a small square by the dot that had been at Fort William, and a look at Google Maps told him it was a house.

He only hoped to God that the phone was back on, or that she hadn't left the house by the time he got there.

Chill out, Coop, he thought. She doesn't know that she is being tracked, I'd put money on it. Even if Carlton has told her and she is running, she can't run forever.

Coop kicked off his shoes, picked up his beer and settled for a night with the television, beer, and Tramadol.

There was nothing else he could do.

'He's stopped,' Carlton said, his stomach rolling over. 'Just below Lancaster.'

'Let's hope it's a service station because I could really do with the break.'

Carlton zoomed in to the map. He hadn't thought of that, and when he looked closer, he saw that she could be right. Why would Willow be staying in a trading estate and service station?

Chill Carlton, it's probably not her. Coop needs to rest too, probably more than us, and we have the advantage with his hand being hurt.

'Seems to be just around the corner. Let's just get off at the services and see.'

'How far?'

'Around ten miles? Half an hour or so now we're actually moving.'

'I gotta tell you, hotshot, this adventure became somewhat less adventurous when the traffic got involved. I'm pooped.'

Carlton looked over at Suzie. She still looked as fresh to him, like she had just risen out of bed. It struck him as funny, and he grinned.

'I don't know what you're smiling at. I think this is over and above my line of duty. Where was this in my contract?'

Her voice was stern, but the smile pulling at the edge of her lips gave the playfulness away. Carlton couldn't resist.

'Any other duties as deemed necessary,' he said. 'We're a two-man band, got to stick together.

'So, I don't get a raise for going above and beyond?'

'In January,' he said.

'I always get a raise in January.'

'That's right.'

'You're such a difficult and stubborn man,' she said, her laugh deep and throaty.

'Also right,' he said and began to laugh with her. After the stress of the last few weeks and the enhanced stress of the last few hours, it felt good. He felt some of the tension slide off his shoulders at the possibility of food and a decent rest.

'Okay, so off here?' she said, indicating and pulling from the third lane to the first in one fell swoop.

Carlton zoomed back at the map. Coop's dot was still there, and still dormant.

'Yes, I think he may be at the travel lodge.'

Carlton felt his spirits rise and Suzie voiced his thoughts.

'Ah, food, a toilet, crap television, a bed, and rest. I hope he's in this for the long haul.'

'The long haul? Go round this way,' he said as Suzie turned the car into the car park.

'As in all night, and this isn't just a pit stop.'

'I think he would have gone to the services for a pit stop. Either way, we'll get some rest. If it wasn't for the traffic, we'd have been on top of him anyway with your driving.'

'My driving?' she said as she parked and pulled on the hand-brake. 'Nothing wrong with my driving, hotshot.'

'Not if you're Lewis Hamilton.'

'I have a Subaru. It's meant to go fast.'

'Subaru began life as four-wheel-drive farming vehicles,' he said as he got out of the car.

The freezing air circled him, and he wished he'd brought a coat. This suit jacket wouldn't do much to ward off a chill. Suzie had little more than a shirt and a thin jacket over her above the knee pencil skirt.

Even in trainers, she was taller than he was. She probably could have earned more as a model than sitting at his reception desk.

Not that he was complaining. How many secretaries would have gone this far for their boss?

'If you say so,' she was saying now, 'but I'm not sure my Impreza has ever been on a farm. I wonder if they sell knickers here.'

'Knickers?' Carlton wondered if he'd heard wrong.

'I didn't expect to be out all night. I don't have spare clothes, never mind spare underwear.'

She pulled open the front door of the building and Carlton felt his gaze travel to her backside. He remembered the jiggle of it under his hands...

Stop.

'Turn them inside out,' he said, his face growing warm as he shook the thought away.

'Gross,' she said as she led the way to the reception desk. 'One room or two. I'd go for cheaper, but you have to do what you have to. I don't want an atmosphere in the car tomorrow just because we slept in the same room.'

Carlton struggled with the answer. He knew that two rooms were best, but she was right: if he was just a bigger man, it could save them a fortune. Who knew where Coop was headed and how long it would take to get there?

He swallowed hard. Both Suzie and the receptionist were looking at him for an answer.

'One is fine, I'll pay.'

Seventy-Three

W ILLOW SLEPT IN AGAIN, but this time she woke in a fuzzy haze of perfect sleep. She hadn't had such a great night for a good many weeks. She smiled.

'Thanks Martha,' she whispered.

She wondered if it had been this easy all along, but she hadn't been willing to chat.

Seems you're never willing to chat, and it just makes life harder, Wills.

Well, not anymore.

She sat up and swung her legs off the bed. The air was warm this morning, and the sun was already hitting the back of the curtains, making it feel summery outside.

She pushed her feet into slippers and moved to open them.

Outside was white over. But not snow. This was frost. Thick, beautiful, and very, very cold.

The condensation on the inside of the windows rose halfway up the glass. At the bottom of the left-hand pane was a message.

HI, and a smiley face.

Happy this time.

Willow smiled at it.

'I can deal with these, Martha. It's the others that bother me. The 'Murder' in the hallway? That could kind of do with a facelift, and the angry faces too.'

She raised her own finger to the side of the face and wrote her own message.

HELLO.

Then she smiled and left the bedroom for a shower, hoping that the creepiness had left the house for good. It felt pretty awesome here right now. Warm and cozy, as it was when she had first arrived.

She carried her clothes into the bathroom and turned on the shower. She left the bathroom door open as she stepped under the water, not knowing why that felt better, but it did.

The shower was glorious and there were no ominous feelings of anyone being on the other side of the curtain today. However, there was another message on the shower mirror. This face had a mouth that was a straight line.

HELP

Willow wrote her own message next to it.

TODAY.

Funny how the first hello she had found getting out of the shower had terrified her. Now she was answering the messages.

Hey, if I can communicate, and she can leave the freaky stuff out, I'm fine. I can even live with her. I just can't deal with the spooky shit, and I really don't need to see her again, either.

Willow made some toast and sat down with her breakfast and a cup of coffee. She pulled her new phone to her and pressed the screen.

It was a good few models above her old one, and Jack had paid a hefty price to get the monthly payment down lower, but it was stunning and sleek. The photographs were a thousand times better, too.

First, she messaged everyone who needed it her new number, then she pressed the gallery.

Fifty-two photos already. All of the mountains, and the few that Jack had taken of her.

They were the only photos she had ever had of herself that she didn't want to delete, each beautiful in quality and light. They were different somehow, like she was different, and she supposed in a way she was.

This wasn't weeping Willow. This was flexible, well rooted, strong Willow. Willow who wanted to survive, and who would fight for her future.

She flicked the phone screen onto Google and did something she had never done before.

She Googled the attack.

There was a whole page of stories about the robbery and shootings, and each had photographs of the assailants.

One, the Daily Mail, even had the good sense to name them under their pictures.

Willow took a good look. It unsettled her to note that she wouldn't have known any of them if she had passed them in the street. Without the paper's help she couldn't even pick out the two that had died, and Carlton's twin brother she wouldn't be able to pick out of a lineup.

The two that had died were named as Henry Castle and Benjamin Ford. Henry had been just twenty-nine, Benjamin had been thirty-six.

What a waste, she thought.

She glanced at the other two pictures. The men that had been arrested at the scene. An Asian man with short dark hair was Rahib Khan, thirty-four, and the other, a stocky man with greasy shoulder-length blonde hair, was Cooper Mathers, thirty-five.

Mathers. He was Carlton's brother. She stared at the photograph. She had never met him, and the relationship between Carlton and his twin had always seemed strained. Carlton fell on one side of the tracks, Cooper obviously on the other. What made her uneasy was the lengths that Carlton would go to protect his brother, even letting her go to the very place that he would be committing armed robbery. He had never let on that Cooper had fallen this far fowl of the law before. She'd had no idea until now that it had been Cooper who had been involved, never mind the fact that Carlton knew and had said nothing to her either before or after.

She understood they were brothers, twins, but when he said that they weren't close, Willow would have taken that to mean that he would have chosen her safety over his brother's protection, especially in such a scenario.

He did say he called the police, and that got him arrested.

Well done, she thought. It had cut him up apparently, but they're not close.

'Although he was close enough for Cooper to tell him what would happen that day,' she murmured, staring at the photograph. 'Close enough that he now lives with him discussing revenge plans.'

What the hell had gone on under her own nose that she hadn't known about? How much more? Was her whole life a lie? Was Carlton so adept at lying that he didn't know the lies from the truth?

More to the point, would Carlton stop him from taking that revenge? He said that he was protecting her with all he had done, but when the crunch came to the crunch, who would he choose?

Willow didn't know and wasn't sure she wanted to find out.

She stared at the picture of the man who looked nothing like Carlton. She had to commit him to memory. He may have changed, and could even have shorter hair, but at least it was a clear picture. His face was chiseled, his eyes blue.

The more she stared, the more a lump of cold hard lead grew in her stomach.

Had she averted disaster by getting rid of the phone? She swallowed hard and thought about Maud's words.

You can delay it, but it will come.

Shit.

Her hands were shaking now. The cottage wasn't two minutes from McGracken House at a run, but if someone was here? Someone like Cooper, or Martha's husband? It was as isolated as it got.

The phone pinged a message and Willow's stomach flipped, and then she remembered it was a new phone. No more messages from random friend trackers. She let out a breath as she looked at it.

New phone? It's Saturday, got the monster! Fancy a walk?

Willow hesitated over the reply, only because a walk outside in this weather sounded perfect, and exactly what she needed to clear her head, but she had promised Martha that she would check things out here. After such a quiet night, she thought she'd better uphold her end of the bargain - for all the good it would do.

The company would be nice though, she thought, as she messaged Sophie back.

Yep! Have a few things to check out here first, a bit of a mystery. Not sure how long I'll be, but you're welcome up here if you like. Two heads are better than one. Maybe we can get out with him this afternoon?

Willow had barely pressed send when a reply came back.

Sounds mysterious! I'll be there in ten. See you soon!

Willow grinned and felt some of the worry slide off her shoulders. She sent her a single heart and hovered over the messages. Then she tapped Jack's name and hovered over the empty screen. She hadn't heard from him at all since last night. What did you write to someone who had brought you the very phone you were messaging on and had come back to trouble for doing it? It was strange, but now that Jack had shared his side of things and she had shared hers, it made her worry about what to write when she never bothered about it before.

Well, come on, Sophie will be here soon, and the chance will be gone.

She tapped her fingers on the table and then typed.

Morning. Thanks again for yesterday, I really enjoyed it. I hope you didn't get into too much trouble. I Have something on with Sophie today, but I'll see you tomorrow. Thank you so much for this awesome bit of kit in my hands, I owe you one, I love it.

She pressed send and waited. It had taken him an hour to reply the last time she had messaged. She hoped he wouldn't take that long today, because she was nervous about his reaction for reasons she couldn't put her finger on.

The reply came back quickly and sounded more 'Jack' than he had for weeks.

Oh, I see how it is, princess, a bit of frost and you're running scared!

Wasn't too bad at home, and I really enjoyed yesterday too. Thanks for letting me offload, it led to a lot of thinking last night and I feel lots better about things today. You have a great day. Remember to lock up tight tonight and call me on your awesome bit of kit if you need anything. The only payment I want is your safety. I'll maybe see you tomorrow.

He followed with a winking emoji and Willow chewed her lip with a smile. It was a very positive message. She wondered what he had been thinking about and what he had decided that made him feel so much better. It made her feel stupidly out of a loop she had no reason to be a part of.

But I like him. A lot.

Doesn't mean he feels the same.

There was a knock at the door, and she was out of time for analysis. She rose to let Sophie and Frodo inside.

Frodo was as crazy as ever, jumping up her with a small whine, his tail wagging madly. She laughed as she scratched his back and behind his ears. Dogs were so unapologetically happy to see you, it was almost humbling.

Sophie was pulled in through the door, red faced behind him, her arms outstretched as she tried to hang onto the lead.

'Jesus Christ, Frodo,' she shouted, 'Wills, I swear he knew we were coming here, he practically dragged me up the hill. I'm thinking of making a small cart and letting him walk me in future.'

'He certainly has some energy, don't you, sweetie?' Willow scratched down to his belly as he stretched up to her shoulders with his paws. She was rewarded with a grunt of pleasure and a lick on the face.

'Okay, too far,' she said with a laugh, pushing him down as Sophie unhooked his lead.

'Is he going to be okay here?' Sophie said. 'He should calm down in a while and he's house trained.'

'It's fine, it'll be nice to have him around.'

'Get the kettle on then, it's bloody freezing out there.'

'It's dropped cold quick, hasn't it?'

'Ach, it'll probably be fifteen degrees again tomorrow. Left hand never knows what the right is doing up here. Half the time it thinks it's winter the year round. This year has been the best for a while.'

Willow put the kettle on as Sophie took off her coat and boots and came into the kitchen. Frodo was busy sniffing his way around the living area, and Willow was enjoying the bustle instead of the emptiness that this place usually felt.

'So, what are we investigating?' Sophie said.

'Martha Otis.' Willow said. Sophie frowned.

'Bit of a grim subject. Is this about your cupboard door again?'

Willow grinned. As much as Sophie was a chatterbox, and a second-hand information blabber, as Jack had called her, she was pretty perceptive.

'Kind of. It's a number of things, really. I emailed Mel about the cupboard after we last spoke about it, but she hasn't got back to me yet, and I also spoke to Maud the other day-'

'Aye, I heard about that one, but I wouldn't put too much stake on anything she says.'

There's a darkness coming.

Willow wished she could believe that it was drama, but after the last few days and the evidence beginning to build up, she thought Maud may have something to her abilities after all.

'Well, either way, I was still having trouble with the cupboard, and I need to figure out what the hell is going on here because I found something.'

'Well, I can sort one side of it for you. Where's the email? I can't understand why Mel hasn't mailed you back yet. She's usually pretty prompt.'

Willow pulled out her phone and searched her emails for the one she had sent to Mel. She showed it to Sophie.

Sophie took the phone and narrowed her eyes.

'Ah! I see. It's the wrong address. You have an extra 'a' in the name. See?' She handed the phone back to Willow and pulled out her own before beginning to type.

Willow looked at the address and rolled her eyes.

'I've messaged her for you,' Sophie said, as Frodo trotted into the kitchen, his nails clicking on the linoleum. 'So, Martha Otis? do you have a computer?'

'A laptop,' Willow said.

She took the cups through to the living area and pulled open the curtains. Light flooded the room, which looked tidy this morning now that the duvet was back where it belonged. When she looked back, Sophie was powering up the small machine on the table.

There was a small ping as Willow joined her at the table and entered her password.

'Ah,' Sophie said, 'here she is. Okay, so Mel says that the cupboard was always a little unruly. It usually opened by itself like there was pressure behind it. She says to buy a new catch if you like. Do whatever you need to secure it. She agrees it was annoying.'

'What about knocking the wall down?' Willow said with a grimace.

'I'm not sure she'd agree to you taking the cupboard out entirely for the sake of a loose door,' Sophie laughed. 'Get a latch. We can walk Frodo down to the store later.'

'Hmm,' Willow said, 'I think the problem may take a little more than a latch.'

Sophie sipped her coffee with raised eyebrows.

'You'd better come and see,' Willow said. 'Although let me give the context first. Ready?'

Sophie hugged her hands around her mug, her eyes alight with curiosity. She nodded.

'So, the cupboard door coming open was annoying the hell out of me, that I'll admit, but after a few nights, there were also noises coming from it.'

One of Sophie's eyebrows raised as Willow continued.

'And after a few nights of noises-'

'What sort of noises?' Sophie cut in.

'Well, like a...'

Series of thuds that sounded like a demon was trying to break in from the other side.

'...Scuffling kind of sound, I suppose. When I looked inside, there was a hole in the left-hand side of the wall.'

'I saw the hole, remember?'

Both of Sophie's eyebrows were almost in her hairline now. She was looking more than a little dubious.

'You did, and there was air coming from inside. Cold air.'

'From the walls,' Sophie said, deadpan.

'Not from the walls, that's the thing. So, the scrabbling around in there was freaking me out, and it seemed to be worse at night, or maybe it's just because I'm not in much during the day, but anyway, a couple of nights ago it got so bad that I called Jack up here to see what he thought of it.'

Sophie was nodding.

'You stayed at McGracken House a couple of nights ago, didn't you? Was that why?'

Willow almost baulked, it seemed there really wasn't a secret around these parts. Maybe Helena was right to have Jack keep his mouth shut if she didn't want everyone to know he was separated.

'Yes. He said that he thought it was an animal, and that we should let it out before it died.'

'Uh-huh. At midnight.' Sophie rolled her eyes.

Willow's mouth dropped open. 'I swear, Soph-'

Sophie began to laugh and held a hand up. 'No, no, I believe you, it stands to reason. I was just thinking about the time Jack had the hump with me for four days for picking up a butterfly by its wings. Getting an animal out of a cupboard at midnight? ... Aye that's Jack alright, there's no waiting until morning.'

'Well, as it happened when he cut a larger hole to get it out, the animal had gone.'

'If it's in the walls, you've got no chance, could be rats or mice.'

Willow wrinkled her nose. 'I hope not. I haven't seen any evidence though.'

'So, you went back to McGracken after that?'

'It freaked me out, Soph, I even admit I cried. I was terrified, so Jack took me back with him and showed me where I could sleep. It was the best night's sleep I've had in ages.'

'I think there was some chatting going on before bed,' Sophie laughed.

Willow reddened as she thought of their whispered conversation in the front room.

'Only a little. I was so freaked out that Jack made us a drink before bed, just to calm me down.'

Sophie grinned. 'You had him though, didn't you?'

Willow faltered. 'What do you mean?'

'About being married. He admitted it, didn't he?'

Willow felt her resolve crumble. How did Sophie know?

Jack's wife had been at the top of the stairs that night, maybe...

Except, no. Jack said he hadn't seen his wife for over three years.

'He did,' she said slowly. 'How do you know all of this?'

'Walls have ears,' she said. 'Helena was concerned about you being downstairs with him. That's why she called him up.'

Helena?

Willow felt an angry stab in her chest.

'She has no reason to be concerned about me.'

Sophie slapped Willow's arm. 'Not you, silly. Jack. He is an absolute sweetheart, but he gets too involved, and she's worried he's caring too much, which isn't what the house is about. His wife is in Edinburgh, you know, he's only back to help out because the House was getting too much for Helena and Mick. It needed repairs, and Jack has been helping with them. He'll be going back soon, and she knows how hard it is for him to separate from something he's committed to doing.'

'Like watching out for me.'

'Absolutely. She sees him going above and beyond for you, and she's worried.'

I bet she is.

Willow remembered how utterly dejected Jack had been as he had spoken about his marriage and his life. She forced back the defensiveness she felt before she snapped at Sophie and said something that she shouldn't.

'She needn't worry, Jack is a big boy. I'm sure he knows what he's doing,' she said.

'Hah, probably working out what he's missing,' Sophie said.

Willow frowned. 'What do you mean?'

'Between you and me, his wife is a right bitch, always wondered just what the hell he saw in her, anyway. He seems more at ease around you, more himself. Or maybe that should be more of his old self. I could never see him running some fancy company in the city, to be honest.'

Willow tried to keep her tone light. If she asked the right questions, Sophie would just talk, and that was all Willow wanted just now.

'You think he couldn't?'

'Ah, he can do anything he puts his mind to. But it's not Jack. Jack's a hard worker, but he's a sensitive soul. He's happiest around nature, he's never been bothered about money. That's why Helena and Mick always worried. A dreamer, they called him. Too much of a dreamer to get anything done with his life. They're glad he has to up his game. Me? I don't know whether he's the Jack I grew up knowing, you know? He doesn't seem to laugh as much. It's like the sparkle isn't in his eyes much anymore. He was always mischievous and witty, he liked to wind people up, but he loved to take care of them too. He was carefree, and I was pretty much infatuated through high school, but he was always with Jennifer. Then he got married, and he changed, anyway. Got moody, argumentative. I don't know...'

She trailed off and shrugged. Willow smiled.

'I don't know that he's changed that much. He winds me up something rotten,'

'Yes,' Sophie said. 'That's what I mean. He's more of himself with you, and he laughs more too.'

'I think we just bounce off each other, that's all.'

'And he gave you his number. I don't remember him ever giving someone at McGracken House his number for after-hours care. But that's why I said be careful, because as much as I love you, and as much as Jennifer is a cow, he's still married to her.'

Willow nodded and smiled, wondering just how much of this would go back to Helena.

Probably all of it.

'I know,' she said. 'Jack and I just get on really well, that's all. There's nothing going on, don't worry.'

'Good,' she said. 'Now what were you saying about that hole in your wall?'

Seventy-Four

C OOP WAS ABOUT TO smash the guy beside him who was snoring up a storm... until he realised it was himself.

Was that even possible?

He sat up, reluctant to go back to sleep, only to wake himself up again in twenty minutes.

It was still dark outside, but that didn't mean anything in October. He checked his phone. 6.30am, then he checked the GPS.

Still off.

The phone was probably dead, and she was charging it overnight, that was the likely scenario. He worked his jaw as he looked at the empty map and felt his stomach clench.

What if...

No, there was no way she knew. It was pretty much impossible to find out.

He stared at the screen.

Had Carlton looked at the phone since he'd had the app installed? Coop had come back and gone into a Tramadol sleep after Dez's firm handshake, so there was a chance.

Carlton wouldn't know about this app, though, and Coop hadn't added it to his home screen. There were seven pages of apps and games on the phone. Surely, he hadn't vigilantly looked at each of them.

This is Carlton. I wouldn't put it past him.

He wouldn't know what it was, though. The symbol was TT and Willow's name wasn't on it, only her number. If he looked hard enough, he may have connected the two, but...

What were the chances?

Slim to none, he thought.

The phone was just dead. He had to believe that for now or he would go batshit.

Coop swung his legs off the bed. He'd just follow his screen-shots. There were two places that he could check out, and action felt better than sitting around in the apartment or a hotel room waiting for her to show up again.

He washed in the bathroom, one handed washing no easier than it had been a few days ago, took some pills, packed his bag, and checked out.

He had a long drive today, and he didn't want to stop before he got to her.

His only focus now was Willow.

Seventy-Five

'**W**AKEY, WAKEY.'

Carlton felt a small push on his shoulder and woke to see Suzie smiling down at him with a cup of steaming coffee. The smell filtered into his nostrils as he sat up, his back resting against the headboard of the double bed.

'You may just be an angel,' he said. 'Thank you.'

'You'd better believe it. I don't make morning coffee for everyone.'

She shimmied off to the bathroom with a smile and the shower turned on. Carlton sipped at his coffee.

It would have been a pretty nice way to wake up if the events of yesterday hadn't filtered into his mind. He picked up his phone and looked at the app to find Coop on the move. Carlton sat up straighter. In fact, he'd been on the move for some time, he was already up by the Lake district and moving fast.

'Shit,' he mumbled, putting his coffee down and climbing into his rumpled suit and jacket. Suzie came out of the bathroom in the same clothes, but somehow looking and smelling fresher than yesterday. He smiled.

She was straightening out her skirt, and he wondered whether she had turned her knickers inside out, or whether she had removed them entirely.

He shook his head before he went down the rabbit hole.

'Coops on the move,' he said, certain he had coloured ten shades as he passed her to the bathroom.

'Which way is he headed?' she called through the door.

'North. Up in the Lakes already.'

'Ah. You know what that means, don't you?'

Carlton washed and patted his face dry.

'What's that?' he said.

'Number one, we're not going home today, and number two, the plan of action is more than likely being executed. What do you think he has up his sleeve?'

Carlton left the bathroom and faced her as she rummaged in her bag on the bed.

'Plan is being executed?'

Suzie rolled her eyes. 'Come on, hotshot, you're brighter than this. He has her location, right? Why else is he traveling all the way up here and still going? We're on our way to a crime scene about to happen.'

Carlton picked up his coffee and took a gulp. Hot liquid burned his throat.

'Ah.'

'Ah?' Suzie said, brows lifted in question.

'I guess I knew that somewhere in my brain, I just didn't equate it. She wouldn't be all the way up here though, would she? I feel that she would have been closer to home.'

'Why? Anywhere you don't know is as good as anywhere else, and she didn't want you to find her, did she?'

Carlton felt his stomach plummet through the floor.

'Oh shit. This is really it, isn't it?'

'It may be. Has he said anything of his plans?'

Panic surged in his chest.

'No. Revenge. I don't know. Oh, God, I'm not prepared. I didn't expect it so soon. His hand was supposed to put him off.'

He was babbling, but Suzie remained calm.

'More to the point, is Willow prepared? When did you last speak to her?'

'Ages ago. I told her what I thought about the plan, but I get the feeling she didn't believe me.'

'Why wouldn't she believe you? Even with what she learned about us, Coop is a different kettle of fish. She would be able to see that, surely?'

'Hmm, well, I put some other measures in place that broke her trust a little, shall we say.'

Suzie stared at him, her bag now on her lap, one hand inside.

'What measures?'

Carlton sat down on the chair opposite her with a sigh.

'I kept her on a higher dose of Prozac than she needed, to keep her docile and drowsy, and then I fed her a small lie that she may die if she had a panic attack. I told her that she had to keep herself in safe situations, basically stay inside, so that she could control them. She found out.'

Suzie put the bag on the bed and looked at him.

'Why would you do that?'

Carlton pursed his lips. 'Because I'm stupid?'

'Goes without saying.'

'I wanted to keep her inside, to keep her safe. I knew what Coop had planned, I just didn't know if he was going to carry out the threat or whether he would get someone else to do it while he was inside. If she was outside the apartment, she would be more vulnerable, and I didn't want anything to happen to her, so I tried to stop her from leaving at all.'

'Wow.' Suzie arched an eyebrow. 'As lovely as that is, you can't do that to people, hotshot.'

'You drugged your boyfriend to get into his phone.' Carlton pouted.

'You drugged your brother to get into his. If this is about who drugged who for what, Carlton, I have to say you're way ahead of the game, so don't try to twist this. Has this been going on since the attack?'

'Yes,' he said, putting his head into his hands.

'Fuck me,' Suzie murmured. 'There I was feeling sorry for you when you'd done all the hard work yourself. Willow was like that *because* of you, not despite your help.'

'I'm sorry,' he said, for lack of anything else to say.

'I don't think it's me you should be apologising to, is it?'

'I've apologised to Willow so many times, she won't listen.'

'I can't say I blame her.'

'No, I don't think she'll ever let me make it up to her now, either. I've lost her, Suzie. She's gone.'

Carlton felt the familiar rush of tears fill his eyes and Suzie sighed. She rose from the bed and sank into the chair next to him, putting an arm around his shoulders.

'We all make mistakes,' she said. 'The main thing is we put right what we can. You apologised, now you need to do the next best thing.'

'What's that?' he sniffed.

'For Christ's sake, message her and let her know he's on his way. Give her time to prepare herself in case we get there too late. Then we get in the car and go. We're faffing around here, and he could be there by now.'

Carlton felt a fresh surge of panic and checked his phone.

'He's still on the M6.'

'Right, so let's go.'

Carlton nodded and fired off a quick message to Willow before grabbing the bags and heading to the car. Suzie brought up the rear with an extra bag, which she threw into the back.

'Sandwiches and pop, in case we can't stop later.'

'Good thinking,' Carlton said, looking at his phone for the fiftieth time.

'This message won't send. It's just sitting here,' he said, climbing into the passenger seat.

'Then call her,' Suzie said, starting the car and turning back to the M6 North at a speed that would make a cheetah look like a tortoise.

Carlton tried and got the same message over and over.

This number is not available.

'Not answering?' Suzie said.

'I can't get through at all,' his voice squeaked, and he checked the tracking app. 'Coop is still on the road, so he's not with her yet.'

'You sure that's the right number?'

'Positive.'

'Maybe the phone is off. Keep trying. It's imperative that you get through.'

Seventy-Six

Willow stood by the door to the cupboard like she was waiting to show her friend an exciting gift, not a place of horrors.

'So, Jack came back up with me the day before yesterday and put an even bigger hole in the wall to try to find this animal. We found something else entirely.'

Sophie was looking at her expectantly as Willow opened the door. Before she could step inside, a black bolt charged past and clattered up the stairs with a series of barks.

Sophie looked inside the cupboard with a frown.

'Where'd he go? Narnia?'

'Up there,' Willow said, pointing to the ceiling as she listened to Frodo's claws click on the floor above.

Sophie stepped into the hole, put her head around the corner to look up the stairs, and then looked back at her, her mouth hanging open.

'It goes up,' she said, pointing.

Willow nodded. 'You can go up. It's safe.'

'Grab my phone, Wills,' she said from the bottom of the stairs. 'I need a light.'

Willow grabbed both of their phones from the table and went back into the hallway cupboard.

'Are these the spookiest stairs in history?' Sophie said as she climbed. Willow followed, feeling better about them when there was a large dog already scoping the room above.

'I think they are.'

'Why the heck are they boarded up?'

'I don't know. I was thinking it may have been something to do with what happened here.'

'Right, that's why you were looking it up! Makes sense. Ooh, we may be walking into a murder scene,' she said as she found the top of the stairs and turned into the room. 'Wow.'

Willow followed into the large dark space, which seemed unchanged.

Not that there was anything here to change.

Frodo trotted about, sniffing at the corners, as Sophie took a few pictures and one of the staircase.

'I'll send these to Mel. I wonder if she even knew?'

'I don't know, hard to tell at what point they were boarded up.'

'We need to investigate this. A secret room, Wills.' She turned to look back into the darkness, shining her light over the floor and the walls. 'A real secret room. How exciting!'

'You could see it like that. I think it's plain scary, to be honest.'

'It's just a set of stairs and an attic,' Sophie said with a laugh. 'Come on, let's see what we can find out. I want to know what Mel makes of this, too.'

Sophie clattered down the stairs, followed closely by Frodo. Not wanting to be up here alone, Willow shone her torch around one last time. The room was empty. And then there was an exclamation from downstairs.

'Oh, my God. I'm not sure Mel would agree to you writing murder across her walls, Wills. That may be a step too far.'

'It wasn't me,' she said.

'Has it been here all this time?'

'Yep,' Willow lied, 'since I moved in.'

'How did I never notice? That's creepy,' Sophie said as Willow shut the cupboard door.

'This whole place is creepy,' she replied. 'I try not to look when I come past this bit.'

Willow and Sophie spent the next hour going through the old news articles for Martha Otis's story on the small laptop. Most of the articles said the same and bore the same photograph – a woman with shoulder length dark hair, an eighties perm, and a wide smile as she posed in the garden of the cottage. The photo was taken just three days before the shootings, the caption said.

Willow stared. If Martha Otis was haunting this house, then she had taken on a form very unlike her own. Did spirits do that? She didn't think so.

Strange.

'Listen to this,' Sophie said, reading the article aloud. 'A small village was rocked last night after the brutal murder of two well-loved citizens, Martha Otis, and her partner Walter Ship-man. Otis and Shipman were said to have been at the Wild Pheasant pub in Clover Nook, appearing very much in love just hours before the shooting on the cold December afternoon. They left the pub at 6pm and walked back to Ivy Cottage alone.

It's thought that Henry Otis, Martha's recently divorced ex-husband, was lying in wait. At around 6.30pm on the evening of December 6th, 1989, Henry forced his way into the house in a fit of jealous rage and shot both his ex-wife and her new part-ner. Hearing the shots, concerned villagers called the police, who were on the scene within minutes.

The bodies of both Martha and Walter were found in the hallway of the small cottage. Walter had taken three shots, two to the abdomen and one to the chest. It is thought that he was in front of Martha and that he died instantly. Martha took seven shots in her arms, chest, and stomach, and one to the thigh. Henry Otis was found at the scene, staring at the bodies with a look of shock and horror on his face. He was arrested and has been remanded in police custody until a trial date can be set.'

'Gruesome.' Sophie continued with a shudder. 'In the hallway. Where murder is written on the walls. Jesus, I don't know how you sleep!'

'Not well, to be honest,' Willow replied.

Sophie scrolled down the screen.

'Most of these say the same. Later ones here say he was imprisoned for life. I'm not sure how long that was in those days. Maybe he's out now?' Sophie's face was a sheet of exaggerated horror.

'Nope, he died six years ago. Still in prison, apparently.'

Sophie swung to look at her. 'Hey, you didn't say you knew anything about this before we started. Where does it say that?'

'Maud told me when I saw her.'

'Ah. I suppose that's something she would keep track of.'

'Why?'

'Because she's a weirdo.'

'She seems okay, Soph. Maybe she does have some insightful ways? Some people can be highly intuitive, you know.'

'And maybe she's full of crap.'

'Maybe. But also, maybe not. Who really knows? I think she's just a lonely old lady.'

'Is that the impression you get?'

Willow nodded. 'Pretty much. She's lonely and likes the attention, whether that's good or bad.'

'You know what I think?'

Willow grinned. 'What?'

'I think you see the best in people that don't necessarily deserve it.'

'Is that a compliment or a put-down?'

'It's a bloody compliment. Christ, Wills, I only wish I had your ability not to judge. I can't help it.'

'You love the drama.'

'I love the gossip. It's bad, isn't it?'

'Not unless you say things about people that they wouldn't want you to repeat, or you repeat stories that you're not sure about. Stories are what's made the world go round for millions of years. It's how we learned - until we learned how to put things down on paper - you're a writer, you should know.'

Sophie wrinkled her nose.

'I really hate you.'

Willow giggled, and then Sophie began to laugh too.

'I love you, Wills. Let's have another drink.'

'I'll make,' Willow said, gathering the cups with a clink, 'you see if there is anything more to add to this story.'

Willow looked out over the frosty back garden in thought as the kettle boiled.

Martha's story was just that. She and her lover were killed in the hallway after her husband came through the front door.

Why does that equal a link to me - other than the blackness, I suppose, but this Cooper can't find me now, even Carlton doesn't have my new number. I think I'm pretty safe.

You can't outrun it. It will come.

The words bounced in her head. Maybe Maud is a crank too? She may have plucked that out of the air, and it just happens to match something else being said.

Frodo pottered into the kitchen and Willow filled a bowl of water for him. He lapped some and then stood by the back door.

'Shall I let Frodo out?' She called to Sophie.

'Yeah, just keep an eye on him. He's a comfort dog though, if you've got a door open in the cold, he'll be straight back inside. He shouldn't run in this weather.

In fact, he barely stepped outside the door, peed on the roses, and then strolled back inside. Willow shivered in the frigid air.

'It's bloody cold out there,' she said.

'You should have been out two hours ago,' Sophie laughed. 'There's nothing new here that we don't already know about the murders, and nothing mentions an upstairs room. Dead end with that. It wasn't the murder that closed it off.'

And yet Martha keeps drawing my attention to the cupboard. That is the area with the most activity, as Maud would call it.

Willow thought of the darkness that Maud had seen. She had said that it was coming either way, but now that Willow had intercepted the phone, there was no way that he would find her, surely. Carlton hadn't said that he knew where she was, and if he didn't, how the hell did his brother?

He may know other ways to find you, Jack had said.

She tried to dismiss it, but something clenched, sitting like lead in her stomach.

What if he found her out here, alone, and history repeated? What if Martha was trying to tell her something about upstairs because that's where it would happen?

I'm not sure spirits can do that, can they? They're in a world of their own pain, Maud had said.

She thought of the shadow at the back door yesterday, the way it moved past the window. Was that real, in her head, or part of Martha's attention grabbing?

Her heart stuttered and began to thump.

There was no way of knowing. Maybe he was already here and just biding his time. There were shadows everywhere around here that she couldn't see into.

I'm going to have to be ready if anything happens. I can't ignore it. Ignorance isn't bliss in this scenario, is it?

'Willow!' Sophie yelled from the dining table. Willow jumped and peered at her friend. 'Did you hear any of that?'

'Er, no, sorry.'

'No, because you disappeared off into dreamland, that's why. Mel just messaged back. She had no idea the cottage had an upstairs! You found a real secret room up there.'

Willow felt her stomach roll over as she took the coffee cups into the living area.

'Is she angry?'

'No, she just said that's where the air must have been coming from to keep opening the door. She says to keep her updated.'

'Okay, well, that's good news.'

'I wonder if Maud knew?'

'Maud?'

'Aye, it stood empty for many years after the murders, had a bit of a reputation of being haunted that stuck. As kids, we used to dare each other to peer through the windows. Some of the older kids used to jimmy the door and stay overnight as dares, you know? And then Maud rented it. She had it for about six or seven years before Mel bought the place and did it up. Maud was turfed out when it was sold. She wasn't happy at all. I mean, I wouldn't want to live here after what had gone on. But then, Maud is a wierdo, hey?'

Willow smiled.

'May be worth asking her,' she said, trying to force her attention onto anything other than the possible approaching disaster.

'Ooh, I should have asked Mel about the wall in the hallway too,' Sophie said, getting her phone out again.

'Don't bother,' Willow said quickly. 'I'll just paint over it. No point in worrying her. Do you think there's anything in Maud's abilities?' she said, changing the subject.

'Ha. I doubt it. Tam says she has the look of a psychic. I say she has the look of a lunatic. What did she say to you when you met with her the other day?'

There was a small creak above them. Willow swallowed a gulp of hot coffee, wondering how much to say. She noticed that Frodo, who was lying across the carpet on his side, had lifted his head to look toward the hallway.

Not now, Martha.

The air stirred around her arms.

'Quite a lot that seems to be right, as a matter of fact.'

'You believe then?'

'I don't know about that. I'm just saying that some things she predicted are coming true. One big thing in particular that she couldn't have known anything about.'

Sophie held her coffee cup before her, her eyes lighting up.

'Ooh, spill. What's going on? Did you ask her for a reading?'

'Not exactly. I fainted having a shower after yoga-'

'I heard about that. Maud found you, didn't she?'

'She did, and she got Tam really quickly, which was good of her. She walked back to the bottom of the lane with me afterward and said that she wanted to see me as she had some information. I didn't intend on going, but the next morning I decided to.'

'Did she give you the usual drivel about Martha Otis haunting the house?'

Willow forced a laugh. 'Oh yeah, that goes without saying, although with an unruly cupboard that had been forefront in my mind, anyway.'

'With that lot on the wall I can understand it, but if it's ghosts-'

Willow cut her off. This was one bit of gossip that she didn't want spread around. She didn't need to be known as the local lunatic, too.

'No, no. I'm not saying the place is haunted, and I know the air was coming from the room upstairs now, as Mel said. It's interesting, but now that I know the murders didn't take place up there, it's kind of lost its interest a little. I think it was probably boarded up to keep the cold out if I'm honest.'

'It *was* cold up there,' Sophie widened her eyes and a grin played around her lips. 'Maybe it's Martha,' she whispered.

Willow rolled her eyes.

'It's windy. Jack and I felt it when we opened the place up. There was a gale blowing outside that you could feel right across the room. It's like there's a gap somewhere, or lots of gaps.'

'So, someone blocked the stairs instead of fixing the roof?'

Willow shrugged. 'Maybe.'

Another creak from upstairs. Just faint.

Willow looked at Frodo. This time, he remained still as he lay flat out on the floor. Maybe she was imagining it with talk of the room and Martha.

Sophie gulped the last of her drink.

'So, what else did she say then?'

Willow looked at her. 'How much do you know about what happened to me in Bristol?'

'Next to nothing really, except about your idiot ex-boyfriend. Tam told me a little of what he was doing, and you told me the rest. If Jack knows anything, he's not spilling, and Helena would never say.'

'Helena doesn't know unless Jack has said anything to her.'

'I doubt it. I thought Jack was as clueless as me.'

'Okay, well, just briefly, I was caught up in an armed robbery at a pub four years ago. My dad was killed. That's why the panic attack outside the pub, the Prozac, etc, etc.'

'Oh wow,' Sophie put a hand over her mouth.

'There's more,' Willow said. If this got out, and it probably would, it could do no harm now. 'There were four attackers. Some of us took down two of them during the attack, but the other two got away. At the time they were running for the door I had a gun in my hand-'

'You what?' Sophie's eyes stretched wide.

'I didn't shoot anyone. I picked up the gun that had shot my dad and I was mad as hell, but a man took it off me and shot the second attacker on the floor. The other had already been killed.'

Willow was shaking but had none of the major flashbacks she'd had with Jack.

'Okay,' Sophie said, looking horrified and a little pale.

'So, back to Maud. She told me that something was coming for me. A blackness that I could try to outrun but I would have to deal with, eventually. This was something that I wouldn't be able to avoid, and that the energy was masculine.'

Sophie blinked and shook her head. 'Meaning?'

'Carlton drugged me to keep me inside and keep me safe he said. I didn't understand why, but it turns out one of the attackers that survived was his twin brother. Carlton knew about the attack but let me go on ahead with my family. He says that Cooper, his brother, is certain that I killed his friend as I had the gun when he ran, and he heard it go off. He wants revenge, apparently.'

Sophie shook her head.

'Nope, you lost me. What the heck are you on about?'

Willow pulled up the page about the attack on her laptop and turned the screen to Sophie.

There was a bang in the hallway. Both girls turned toward it, and Frodo jumped to his feet and stared at the door.

'What was that?' Sophie said.

'Probably the cupboard. This is what it does.'

'Okay, I take back the thinking you're mad with the ghosts. That's spooky.'

Willow raised her eyebrows and nodded. 'You should try being here with it at eleven o'clock at night.'

'No thanks.' Sophie got up and went into the hall, followed by Frodo. She shut the cupboard door with a bang, and they came back into the room, Frodo lay down by the door, his ears pricked.

Sophie read the article and Willow showed her the picture of the attackers with shaking hands.

'These two were killed. These two ran but were caught by police just outside. This one,' she said, swallowing hard as she pointed to Cooper Mathers, 'He is Carlton's twin brother.'

'That's fucked up,' Sophie whispered.

The creaking was back, Frodo's head lifted at the noise this time too.

'It is. But the point is, Carlton says Cooper is after me for killing his literal partner in crime.'

'But you didn't kill him?'

'No. But he thinks so, and now he's out of jail, so he's coming, anyway.'

'Fuck. Does he know where you are?'

'I don't know. I thought he was tracking my old phone after some weird messages, hence the new one.' She held it up. 'Other than that, I know nothing more.'

'Other than Maud's prediction? But she could be clutching at straws and getting it right by coincidence.'

'It's pretty accurate, though. Carlton says he's focused on find-ing me and she said the presence was masculine and that I would have to deal with it, eventually. I couldn't avoid it.'

'Did she say what the outcome would be?'

Willow tried to smile, but it was hard work. She was shaking like a leaf now.

'No. Of course not, just that he was coming.'

TH-UD

The cupboard door ricocheted off the hallway wall with a loud bang. Frodo got to his feet instantly with a volley of barks that made Sophie visibly jump and set Willow's nerves on edge. He disappeared into the cupboard even as Sophie called him back.

'Frodo!' she yelled as she ran into the hall. Willow followed with less speed. She really didn't want to follow him up the stairs where his barks were now echoing around the roof.

Even Sophie glanced back at her, pale, before disappearing up the stairs two at a time. Willow ran after her, not sure if she wanted to be up there or down in the hallway where Martha may be.

In the attic room, Willow saw Sophie run to the left, to where the roof sloped low, and where Frodo was barking like he had caught an intruder at the empty wall before him.

Willow felt the hair rise on the back of her neck as she backed into the stairway again.

'Frodo, what the hell is wrong with you? Get downstairs.'

Sophie pulled and tugged at the dog's collar and Willow felt a crawling up her arms in the darkness. Out of the corner of her eye, she thought something moved at the bottom of the stairs.

'No, Martha, please don't,' she whispered. She closed her eyes and then something large and furry bumped against her with a loud bark as Frodo skidded down the stairs again.

She screamed, unable to help herself, causing Sophie to scream with her.

'Get the hell out of here,' Sophie said, rushing past Willow, who was close on her tail. At the bottom of the stairs, Frodo's barking reverberated around the small cottage walls.

They shut the cupboard door with a bang and Willow followed Sophie to her front bedroom. The dog was in the middle of the room, hackles up, Barking toward the bookcase by the window.

'This is too fucking freaky,' Sophie said, grabbing his collar and pulling him out of the room. Willow shut the door behind him and then shut the living room door behind him too, locking him in.

In unspoken agreement, the girls had no intention of enabling the dog to get out into the hallway and up the stairs again today.

As Frodo finally calmed, Willow slumped in a dining room chair and Sophie sat in the one to the side of her.

'What in the hell was that?'

'That was the curse of the windy attic,' Willow said, thinking she must look as shaken as Sophie did next to her. Then Sophie began to laugh.

'I don't blame you for calling Jack, actually. That's some spooky crap.'

Willow grinned.

'It was worse the night I called Jack. There was rapping and scraping from inside the cupboard, too.'

'Did you ever find the animal?'

'No, but Jack said that if there were holes in the roof, it could come and go that way, so we may never find it.'

Willow's mind conjured up a memory of the thing on the roof, and she shuddered.

'I don't know how you've slept here, Wills.'

'It's only the wind and animals,' she said, playing down the terror that she felt, and omitting the smiley faces and the twitching figure that appeared now and again... and not always here, but now attached to her because of Cooper, apparently. 'But I've barely slept a wink between that cupboard, Cooper, and Maud's premonition, I must admit.'

'What are you going to do about Cooper?'

'I don't know. What can I do? I don't know how to defend myself. I feel like a sitting duck,' Willow said.

Sophie nodded, and then her eyes snapped back to Willow's.

'Well, actually, it seems obvious to me. The next step is to call Carlton, isn't it? This man is his twin brother. If there's anyone that knows how you may be able to stop this, it's him.'

Willow felt a small light of hope.

Carlton had told her of Cooper's plan and had said his behaviour was about keeping her safe from him. He would help her this time, wouldn't he?

Of course he will, he was devastated on the phone. Sophie is right. Ask him what can be done.

Sophie touched her arm.

'Willow?'

'You're right. I'm going to call him. He may be the only one who can help me right now.'

She pulled out the paper that she had written all the mobile numbers down on to, transferred Carlton's to the phone and saved it before she pressed call.

Seventy-Seven

T HE PHONE RANG WITH a number that Carlton didn't recognise. He stared at the phone dumbly.

'You answering that, hotshot?'

They were past the Lakes now, heading for the border of Scotland and Carlton didn't know what the hell Willow would be doing all up here. She had never been to the country in her life.

The phone rang off, and he shook his head.

'Unknown number,' he said, as the phone rang again.

'Unknown to you, but someone wants to talk. Maybe it's someone to tip you off about Coop?'

Carlton raised his eyebrows. 'I doubt it.'

'Just bloody answer it, before I do.'

Carlton pressed the green phone icon just before the answer machine cut in again.

'Hello, who is this?'

'It's me.'

Relief flooded through Carlton. He put his head into his hand and blinked away the tears that immediately filled his eyes.

'Willow? Babe, is it really you? Oh, thank God. How did you know I was trying to reach you?'

'What?'

'I was trying to call you, but the number was unavailable.'

There was a small laugh.

'I chucked the phone,' she said. 'That number isn't available anymore.'

Carlton swallowed, confused, and looked out of the windscreen. The traffic was lighter up here, but the rain was heavy. Still, he thought it would slow Coop as much as it slowed them.

'Why would you do that?' he said.

'Because I was being tracked.'

Carlton blinked and stalled, wondering if he'd heard her right.

'You know you're being tracked?'

There was silence on the other end of the phone, and then she spoke again. Her voice had hardened.

'Did *you* know I was being tracked?'

'No! No, of course not. I suspected that was the way he may go, but I didn't know he had got that far. I mean, I do now, but I didn't. That's why I was trying to call you.'

'Right.'

'If I'd have suspected anything, I'd have called you, like I was trying to. Straight away, I promise babe.' Then he blinked, and the thought stung, 'Except I'd never have got through anyway, would I?'

He heard Willow swallow, and her voice softened again.

'Pretty stupid decision on my part, really. I just presumed that if you were close to him, he would have more access to me the more I gave to you.'

Carlton winced and rubbed his head.

'Willow, he may be my brother, but we're not sharing information, babe. All he's doing at the apartment is sleeping, and the only reason I'm letting him do that is because then I know exactly where he is ninety-nine percent of the time. If I know where he is, I know he's not with you. I'm trying as hard as you to figure out what he's up to. I'm not just letting him run with this, you know.'

There was a period of quiet.

'Could you stop with the 'babe'?'

'Sorry,' he said, his stomach clenching with hurt.

'It's okay. Thank you for keeping an eye on him, but it didn't work if you don't know he's tracking me, did it?'

'Well, I kind of had an idea it was coming, so I was on alert. How the heck did you find out?'

'Your brother sent photos to me, did you know that?'

Carlton felt himself reel back in the seat. Out of the corner of his eye, he saw Suzie look his way with a frown.

'How did you find out?'

'Educated guess. He was at my apartment and I didn't know the number. Who else could it have been? He tried to pretend he was a woman at first, but when he posed as Kelly, called me the wrong nickname, and asked to meet up, I got suspicious.'

Carlton felt his cheeks burn. He had got their nicknames the wrong way round? And made her suspicious into the bargain. And he thought he had done so well. He almost told her it was him but thought better of it. If she asked how Coop had got the nicknames, he'd make up some story.

'You didn't give him your address then?' he said, knowing the answer already.

'I'm not stupid, Carlton.'

'I know you're not, ba... sorry, Willow.'

'I was speaking to someone up here who said that phones could be tracked through messages. He told me to get rid of it in case it was linked.'

He? Willow was speaking to a man up there about what was going on? Carlton's gut swirled, and yet, so what if she was? Look at what he had done.

'Good, that's good.'

Unless you were never going to let me know.

Willow seemed to calm at his reaction.

'It is? You know that he's tracking me, then?'

Carlton swallowed.

'I didn't, but yesterday he took my car. I was with Suzie at the time, so we're on his tail in hers.'

'Suzie? Suzanne? It's getting serious now, then?'

'No! No, it's not even-' He cut off, looking at Suzie as his cheeks reddened, and he wanted the car to swallow him up. '-on. It's not even on. I promise you.'

Suzie dropped her gaze and then looked back out of the windscreen with a flick of her eyebrows.

Carlton wanted to kick himself for even mentioning her.

'I'm not bothered, Carlton, we're not together anymore. You can do what you like,' Willow said, her voice edged. 'So, he took your car?'

'Yes, we're up in the Lake District now, on the M6 and he's still headed north. Are you in Scotland?'

There was a brief silence.

'How are you following him? Surely, he'll notice?'

'I hacked into his phone and added the GPS tracker to mine.'

'Like you did with me?' she said quietly.

'Yes,' he said, closing his eyes.

'Well, at least you're using it for good this time.' She paused. 'Are you telling me the truth?'

Carlton frowned.

'Are you serious? I've been through hell, babe. I'm trying my best to keep you safe. That's all I want. All I know is he's heading to the Scottish border. All we can do is tail him with the tracker. I know no more than that at the moment.' He shook his head and then added, 'Oh, and he stopped at the marina first to collect something. I don't know what it was. It could have been drugs, a firearm, or anything in between. All I know is that he stopped there, then headed towards you - if you're in Scotland, anyway.'

'Right. You're tailing him for me?'

'I don't want him anywhere near you, babe... sorry, Willow, but I don't know where you are to get there first, so we'll hopefully get there as he does. I can't sit in Bristol and do nothing, can I?'

'You did with the robbery.'

Carlton clenched his jaw as the virtual punch landed right in his gut.

'I was wrong, and very stupid. I know I've lost you, I understand that, but I won't sit back and watch him hurt you again. I couldn't live with myself.'

There was another brief silence that seemed to Carlton to drag on for eternity.

'Have you got a pen?' she said finally.

Carlton frowned and turned to Suzie.

'Pen?'

'Glove box, and some paper, too. Use the book,' she said.

He rummaged around in the small storage compartment and came out with both.

'I have now,' he said to Willow.

'Okay, here's my address.' She reeled off the address and the village and gave him the postcode. 'There aren't many main roads up here, but if you can get ahead of him, you could make it here first. At least then we can get our heads together and work out what to do. You know him better than me.'

Carlton wept with relief.

'Yes. Perfect. Thank you. Thank you. You don't know how much it means to me that you trust me. It means the world. We'll stop him together, babe. I won't let you down again.'

'If I wasn't backed into a corner, Carlton, I wouldn't do it, but honestly, I'm over it. Let's just figure this out the way we should have figured out the first attack. Okay?'

'Okay,' he said with a sniff. 'Okay, yes, I won't abuse your trust again. We'll be there as soon as we can.'

Seventy-Eight

'W HAT'S THE OUTCOME? CARLTON is coming up here, I take it.'
Sophie said as Willow put down the phone with a sigh
and a sinking feeling in her stomach.

'Yes, he's with Suzanne. Cooper's coming for me.'

Sophie laughed. 'So dramatic...,' then her face fell serious, 'What,
right now?'

Her laughter trailed away as Willow's face must have said the
rest for her. Willow nodded slowly.

'They're nearly in Scotland, both of them, luckily. I didn't tell
Carlton my change of number, did I? He's been trying to call
me. If you hadn't said to call, I would have been none the wiser.
Sometimes I'm so stupid.'

'Pride before a fall, my mum always says.' Sophie paused and
then shook her head with a roll of her eyes. 'Sorry, I didn't mean
that like it sounded.'

Willow shrugged. It was true either way.

'So, what do I do now, Soph?'

Sophie scrunched her face into a worried look.

'Well, I don't think you should stay here alone. What if Cooper
gets here first? I for one, don't need more murder in the hallway.
If you want my opinion, you should stay at McGracken House
until Carlton arrives. If this Cooper is still tracking you, he must
have your location. How is he doing that without GPS?'

'Impossible.'

'And yet he is.'

'Right. I need to get out of here.'

'Until Carlton and his floozy arrive anyway because it seems to me if he has your location, but it's not live - because it can't be live - then he has the cottage. Not where you actually are. It's small, but it gives you an advantage.'

Willow's heart thumped. Going to McGracken House was almost worse than staying here right now. She didn't know what Helena was thinking, and no longer knew what Jack was thinking either.

He did say to call him if you needed him, though.

'Wills? What are you still thinking about? Go pack a few things.'

'Well, he's nowhere near yet. He must have another few hours to go, and it's after two now. What if he stops overnight?'

'He may be driving at eighty and not stopping until he gets here. What then? It's still an unknown.'

'Okay, but Carlton has his location, and my address now, he can say-'

'No, Wills, he's not glued to it. Get out of here. Grab your things, I'll walk down with you.'

Willow nodded and sipped her tea. It didn't sit right, but Sophie was right. It was suicide to stay here.

'Wills?'

'Okay, can I drink my tea first?'

Sophie banged her head onto the table gently with a laugh.

'There's just no rush with you, is there?'

'He's hours away,' Willow said with a forced nonchalance, but her insides thought hours felt like seconds, and she had to admit that she was terrified.

After checking what she had packed three times over and deciding that it was all she needed, she locked up the cottage, double checked her car, and heaved a sigh of resignation.

Whether Sophie thought the lady was weird or not, there was definitely some proof of Maud's capabilities. This *was* coming, whether she wanted it or not, and whether she had been through enough or not. Now she had to deal with whatever awkwardness would sit at McGracken House for a few days until he got here, too.

'You could take the car and high tail it out of here instead?' Sophie said. 'Is that what you're thinking?'

'No. If he's tracking me, he's tracking me. I have friends here. I may as well see it out.'

There's a darkness. You can delay it, but it will come, and you will have to face it.

'Let's go then,' Sophie said. 'I'll walk down to the house with you.'

Willow would have described it more of a quick half jog as Frodo smelled the air and went loopy.

I would have preferred a slower walk, she thought, as they crossed the bridge and almost ran to the side gate of the house.

Sophie opened the catch and went through, the dog pulling her forward in his excitement.

'Goddamn it, Frodo, you're a pain in the arse!' She shouted, as he lunged at Duncan and Jack who were discussing something by the barn, and almost pulled her over in his effort to get to them. Willow couldn't help grinning as his claws scrabbled on the concrete and Sophie was dragged behind.

At the commotion, both men turned, and Jack caught Willow's eye, his face spreading into a grin, just before he was demolished by the large black dog. Willow winced, but Jack was larger, stronger, and more stable than she was. He caught the dog around the waist with a laugh as Frodo literally tried to jump into his arms, his back legs scrabbling for traction before hitting the ground and trying again.

'Woah,' he said, 'That's some greeting.'

Sophie, still on the end of Frodo's lead, ran headlong into both of them as the momentum pulled her forward. Willow couldn't help laughing.

'Fuck's sake, Frodo,' Sophie said, tugging on his lead. 'Stupid dog.'

Willow reached them just in time to hear Jack reply.

'There are no stupid dogs, are there Frodo? Just stupid owners.'

He scrubbed behind Frodo's ears and then pushed the dog back off him, and Frodo turned to Duncan.

Sophie was red-faced and panting.

'You did not just call me stupid, Jack McGracken.'

'You're not his owner, are you, Soph?' Willow said with a grin.

'Ha, exactly. I'm not his bloody owner, and thank God.'

Jack grinned as Duncan fussed Frodo.

'I didn't expect to see you today,' he said, turning to Willow.

'Unexpected turn of events,' she said, feeling herself flush. His smile was easy. He looked calm, fresh, more relaxed than he had for a good few weeks.

'I told her she needs to stay here, Jack, don't let her leave under any circumstances,' Sophie said as Frodo pulled at the lead again.

Jack's smile slipped, and Willow shrugged.

'Sounds like we need a brew,' he said, pursing his lips. 'You want one, stupid?'

Sophie whirled round, her mouth dropping open.

'No, thank you,' she said indignantly. 'I'll carry on walking the mutt before I end up murdering him. Nice of you to offer, though, and with an insult too? I'm honoured.'

'You're welcome,' he said with a laugh.

'I'll carry on stacking,' Duncan said, sensing the need for privacy and going back to the forklift.

Jack took Willow's bag from her shoulder and put it over his own. 'Come on then, princess, let's sort you out.'

Sophie turned and headed for the back gate.

'Keep me updated, Wills, I'll come and see you tomorrow. Good luck batting away the razor-sharp insults. You'll need to be on your toes by the looks of it.'

Willow smiled as Jack hitched her bag higher.

'I can handle him, don't worry. Thanks for your help today, Soph.'

'Aye,' was all she managed before she was dragged out of the gate.

Willow smiled at Jack, who nodded his head to the kitchen.

'Let's get inside before my back breaks. You didn't need to bring the kitchen sink with you. We can provide the necessary amenities.'

'Well, I was a little disappointed with the depth of the basin when I last stayed. Little luxuries matter if I'm staying a while.'

Jack laughed and swung an arm briefly and tightly around her shoulders. It sent tingles round her body and then she laughed with him.

Seventy-Nine

B Y 2PM, COOP WAS pissed off. His four-hour journey had already taken him seven and a half, and he hadn't got to Glasgow yet.

Everything was conspiring against him. Three accidents, one which stopped the motorway at Lockerbie for a good hour and a half, the other two he crawled past at a soul crushingly slow speed. The weather was the culprit.

The Wind battered the car, along with driving rain which almost flooded his windscreen so that he couldn't see the road. It had been manageable in the light, although the traffic had stuck to around 40mph, but the light was fading earlier than usual due to the stormy weather, and he was struggling.

Driving wasn't his forte, especially when he hadn't driven for almost four and a half years and now had a broken hand to deal with too.

The only thing he had eaten was tramadol, and even that wasn't doing much to numb the dull throb that pulsed up his arm each time his hand had been in one spot for too long.

As he stared out of the rain-soaked windscreen at the line of brake lights ahead, he decided to call it a day.

He was braking too late, and horns had blared at him more than once in the last half an hour. He was in pain, getting agitated, and getting rash. He had to stop.

At Abington, he left the motorway for the services and pulled round to a Days Inn.

He checked in, threw the bag into his room, ate some extra tramadol, and made his way to the restaurant.

He ate steak and chips, savouring each full and juicy mouthful, and then he went back to his room.

He yawned as he lay on the bed with the television and a can of beer from the car.

His eyes hurt, his hand hurt, and his head hurt.

He was tired.

Outside, the wind battered the window and the grey clouds drove rain up the glass in harsh splatters.

Absolutely not going out there again until tomorrow. She can wait.

He checked his phone.

Still no sign of her on the app, but that didn't mean anything now. He had a feeling that she had turned the phone off, maybe because she was stationary? He would find out either way.

The last place she had been tracked was Fort William. He would try the house there first and then come back down to where she had been in Clover Nook. Maybe someone there would be willing to tell him the truth if she wasn't around.

As his eyes dropped closed to the drone of the television, and the warmth of the room comforted his bones, and the effect of the pills numbed his pain, he thought of something else.

Carlton hadn't messaged or called.

And yet Coop had taken his car. He couldn't miss it.

Maybe Carlton had stayed out with the secretary. He hadn't seen her for a while, he had been too busy moping.

Oh well, it got Coop even further away before he was found out, and that was a good thing.

He threw the phone down beside him as his eyes closed and sleep claimed him.

Carlton had punched the postcode into Suzie's sat nav hours ago now, but the traffic and the weather seemed to be holding them up more and more. If he got out of the car and walked to Willow's, he would probably get there faster.

He stared silently out of the window as they hit Lockerbie and came to an almost complete standstill.

The Sat Nav got them off the motorway and took them around on the A76.

Suzie yawned.

'We need to stop for dinner or something, hotshot, I'm almost done. The traffic is driving me nuts.'

A gust of wind buffeted the car and rain hit the windscreen with a hiss.

'That's driving me mad, too.'

'Pull over, we'll eat the sandwiches and then I'll drive for a while if you like,' Carlton said.

He knew it was bad when Suzie agreed. Suzie never let anyone drive her pride and joy. Under any circumstances.

Except this one.

They pulled over in a layby, letting the engine run for warmth as they ate the sandwiches that Suzie had brought from the Holiday Inn. It was after 4pm and Carlton thought he had never been so famished.

'I hope this is worth it, hotshot,' Suzie said between mouthfuls of food.

'Of course it is. I didn't get to protect Willow the first time around. I ran. I was a coward. At least this time I get to see her straight. Coop may be my twin, but he's an arsehole, and Willow doesn't deserve this.'

'Did she do it, do you think?' Suzie said through another yawn.

'No. Her trauma was severe, but there were no side effects for killing somebody, just for going through the attack.'

'How do you mean?'

'The nightmares that she had and the flashbacks that gave her panic attacks were always about the closeness of the area, the volume of people, and her dad being shot. There was never anything about shooting somebody else or taking a life.'

'Would there have been?'

'More than likely. She's a good soul. To have murdered would have played on her conscience. She wouldn't have let the rest of the attack scrub over that, however bad it was.'

Suzie threw her empty packet back into the back of the car and retrieved a can of Coke from the bag. She opened it with a hiss and a pop.

'Why don't you tell him that?' She said before taking a long drink.

'I have,' he said. 'Coop is all but certain, just because she had a gun in her hand when he left. He heard the shot as he got out of the doorway. To be fair, the shot could have been anybody's bullet, or nobody's, but he is adamant that it killed Ben, or Bugs.'

'What did Willow say?'

'She said that a man grabbed the gun and shot one of them. She had nothing to do with it.'

'You believe her?'

Carlton nodded as he finished his sandwich.

'Like I said, there's been no evidence to suggest otherwise, and she didn't seem to be hiding anything when I told her what was going on. She was indignant.'

Suzie took a deep breath and sighed long and hard. She looked at Carlton.

'I'm sorry,' she said.

Carlton looked at her in surprise. 'For what?'

'Ruining your relationship for my own gain.'

Carlton looked at the last corner of the sandwich in his hand.

'You weren't the only party in this,' he said, 'and you aren't the only one to blame.'

'I started it. I shouldn't have said what I did.'

Carlton looked at her. She was biting on the side of a manicured nail as she stared out of the window at the blowing trees. A swirl of affection landed in his stomach, and he grabbed her hand.

'You have every right to say whatever you want, just as I can respond however I want. I kissed you, and I took you home. It was me.'

Suzie looked at him.

'No. I played you. Maybe she is coming back, or maybe she was, but I guess she's not now, is she? I played you on purpose, and the dice rolled in my favour. I don't feel good about that.'

'You were angry.'

'I was. I still am, but I understand a little better now. I see how much she means to you, how you interact with her, how you want to keep her safe. I also understand that you did some of this to her, too. It wasn't her choice. I just... well, what I thought I knew wasn't exactly the truth, was it?'

'No. I was selfish and cowardly. I still am.'

Suzie looked at him.

'No, you're not. Even after all she's found out, and her giving you the lashing you rightly deserved? Even after telling you that the relationship is over, and knowing that there's no chance she will come back? You're still here, you're still looking out for her. Still going the extra mile.'

'I have to. I let her down too badly. My behaviour was out of order. I can't control people, it was all wrong. I deserved to lose her. I'm a sad excuse for a human being.'

Suzie smiled sadly and placed a hand on his face.

'No. You know you did wrong, and you've been punished. Now you're putting it right - or trying to. I think that's an admirable human being. You're not a bad person, Carlton. You don't have a nasty bone in your body.'

'I feel like I do,' he said. 'Me and Coop shared the same womb. Surely there must be some bad blood in me.'

Suzie dipped her head with a slow nod.

'Maybe. You know what that means?'

Carlton shook his head.

'That there's good in Coop. Somewhere, somehow, there's a chink in the armour. We need to find that chink and stop him, because if this means a lot to you, then it means a lot to me too, and three heads are better than two, or one.'

She stroked Carlton's cheek, and he realised he was crying.

'Could you ever love me like you love her?' She murmured.

'I can try,' he said, pressing his lips quickly to her cheek.

'That's all I can ask,' she said. 'Come on, hotshot. If this means so much to you, then let's get to Willow ahead of Coop and see if we can work out a plan.'

Carlton nodded and with a new sense of resolve they swapped seats and continued up the road toward Glasgow.

He kept his fingers crossed that there was good in Coop, and asked for guidance finding it, because in the last thirty-five years he had never seen an ounce of good in his brother.

Eighty

T HEY SAT IN THE large rustic living room as Willow filled Jack and Helena in on the conversation with Carlton, and Sophie's suggestion that she stay for a while.

Far from being offish with her, Helena was very welcoming, her manner as mild as ever as she told her she was welcome to stay for as long as she liked.

The light was dimming in the sky outside and the living room was growing darker. Light from the kitchen outlined Helena in a halo that made her look like an angel, and right now, Willow thought she may just be.

'Of course, you must stay, as long as you need,' she said, holding onto Willow's hands warmly. 'You've done so well, darling, I'm very proud of you.'

Willow hoped the low light didn't show off too much of her red cheeks.

'Thank you, I'm so grateful to have somewhere else to be with people that I trust. I'm just worried about bringing trouble to your door now.'

'From what you just said, he may know where the cottage is, but he won't know you're here.'

'Yes, I'm almost certain. It just worries me that Carlton says he's still tearing up here. He has to be following something, doesn't he?'

'The phone is gone, sweetheart,' Jack said. 'there's no way he has direct access to you now. He could have checked out the place beforehand if he saw your position, for sure, that's probably what he's following.'

Willow nodded, but the unsettled feeling sat in her stomach. 'I hope so,' she said, biting on the nail of her forefinger.

'Listen, darling, whatever is meant to happen, will happen. There is nothing much we can do to turn a tide that is flowing, is there?' She shifted her eyes to Jack. 'From what Jack has said, you've had a rough ride, and that isn't over yet. If McGracken House is about anything, it's about help and support. We are all here for you, but I'm sure this man will head to the cottage first. We have the advantage here, not him.'

'Duncan is working on the pointing at the front of the house for the next week, too. He'll see any car going over the bridge,' Jack added.

'I know what the car is,' Willow said. 'A silver Astra, with a sports pack. It's Carlton's car he's taken. I know the number plate.'

'That's good.' Helena's eyes shifted to Jack again. 'We should give the number plate to Duncan too.'

Jack nodded. 'I'll get that sorted.'

'And you say this Carlton is also coming up here?'

'He was trailing him up here when I called.' Willow swallowed hard, thinking of the consequences right now if Sophie hadn't suggested she call him. 'I gave him the cottage's address so that he could try to get here first. Carlton is his twin. Hopefully, he'll have some idea how to stop him, or maybe if Carlton is here, he can talk him down.'

Although I don't hold out much hope of that after the last one.

Helena smiled and stepped forward to place a warm hand on Willow's cheek.

'It's a credit to your healing that you can put aside your differences and get along with him. That was good thinking,'

'I don't really have a choice,' Willow said.

'No, but pride is not something that is easily pushed aside.'

'It is if you're possibly in danger,' Jack said.

Helena raised her eyebrows at him and something unspoken passed between them. Helena drew her hand away from Willow's cheek and smiled.

'Well, I'll leave you to get settled. Let us know of any developments. Forewarned is forearmed.'

'I will, thank you.'

Helena turned from the room and went out into the yard with her usual glide.

The atmosphere later that evening was relaxed and chilled. It was almost like the calm before the storm. Willow felt relaxed but couldn't focus. Her mind kept drawing back to the day's events.

After she had spoken to Helena, she had gone with Jack to help clean out the chicken houses and collect any eggs. Then they had prepared dinner for everyone. Willow supposed that was an overstatement. Jack prepared dinner. He merely told her what to do at each stage. It made her want to cook more. In fact, growing the vegetables made her want to cook more too, although what she had planted were mere shoots at the moment, and what she had pulled up were planted months ago. She had to admit there was something satisfying about working the land and eating what you had grown and prepared.

She had been quiet as she worked, and Jack must have felt it too, although he had chatted as normal, raising a couple of laughs from her as the afternoon wore on. She had been half absorbed and half fretful, but worrying here, with all of these generous people, was certainly far better than worrying at the cottage with only Martha for company.

After dinner, with the wind and rain lashing down outside, they had gathered around the fire in the living area. Tilly, Duncan, and Warren were the only people here at the moment, but with Helena and Mick, there were seven people huddled in the lounge. Tilly pulled two bean bags from the corner and sat strumming her guitar as the rest of them chatted about the day, the weather, the work, and the animals. They were amicable, soft laughter and the strumming of music, adding to the warmth of the house.

It was nice to sit watching the flames dance, but only when Carlton called to say they were stopping for the night just below Glasgow, and telling her that Cooper had also stopped, did she finally let herself relax completely.

She was half asleep fallen onto Jack's shoulder, listening to his deep tones and laughter rumble next to her soothingly when Helena stooped before her with a smile.

'You don't have to stay down here with us, darling. If you're sleepy you can go on up whenever you like.'

'I may go up now, actually,' Tilly said with a yawn, putting the guitar back in the corner and standing to a stretch, her over-sized jumper rising to reveal her skinny frame. 'Night all.'

There were murmurs of goodnight as she raised her hand and went up the stairs, and Willow moved herself off Jack.

'I think I'll go up too, now I'm free,' he said with a chuckle as he stood. 'Come on, I'll take you to your room.'

He held his hand out to Willow and pulled her off the chair.

Willow hadn't the heart to say that she wanted to stay down-stairs with the quiet chatter and the warm fire. The last place she wanted to be right now was in her own room on her own.

After saying their goodnights to the remaining four, Jack followed Willow up the stairs.

Her room was to the left, the same one she had been in before. She turned to say goodnight to Jack, but he pushed her gently forward, on down the landing.

'Jack-'

'Shhh,' he said behind her, hand on her shoulder as he opened a door further down the landing on the right. Willow walked into a neat, warm room with a double bed, a chair, and a wardrobe. Just inside, through a door to the left, was an en-suite bath-room.

'What are we doing?' she said, confused as he shut the door quietly.

'Do you want to be on your own?'

Willow stared at him and then she shook her head. 'Not really.'

He nodded. 'Aye, I thought so, but there's no way Helena would have left you lying against me down there. Too close.'

'Sorry,' Willow said, feeling her cheeks go red.

'It didn't bother me, you don't need to apologise,' he said with a smile. 'Obviously you're welcome to go to your room, I just wanted to give you the opportunity to stay up a bit longer with company if you want to.'

Willow nodded and felt herself relax.

'I'd like that. I was enjoying listening to everyone. It was comforting.'

'I know. Helena's rules, or sorry... non-rules. There are no rules here... or are there?' His eyes twinkled in the low light as he wrinkled his nose. 'I can never quite fathom it out.'

Willow grinned and let out a low laugh.

'She would say none.'

'Except falling asleep on Jack's arm.'

'And quite possibly being in Jack's room?'

Jack grimaced.

'That's a biggie. That may get us both expelled from the house of no rules for breaking the rule that doesn't exist.'

Willow felt the titters rise from her stomach as Jack shook his head, and then he chuckled with her.

'Have a seat, chair or bed, wherever.'

Willow eyed the bed. Was it wrong that she wanted to lie where he had?

She decided she would take the chair, the bed seemed wrong, but Jack had followed her gaze and was already puffing the pillow against the headboard.

'Come on,' he said, patting the covers.

'I don't want to mess up the bed.'

'If you don't, I will later. Sit down.'

She sat, and he took the chair by the bed. She kicked off her shoes and put her feet up, turning to face him with her shoulder to the headboard.

Jack took off his own shoes and settled back into the chair, watching her with a sigh.

'What?' She said with a laugh.

'I can't believe what's going on with you,' he said. 'We've had some people through these doors over my lifetime. They all have baggage, but you brought a bloody truckload with you.'

Willow felt her smile slip, and Jack grabbed her hand.

'I'm only playing, princess. Hopefully, it'll be over soon, eh?'

'I hope so,' she whispered, as her stomach tensed with dread.

Jack dropped his gaze and began to massage her hand with his fingers. 'Are you okay with seeing him tomorrow?' he said quietly.

Willow felt her eyes dropping closed as the firm pressure eased her joints.

'Not really. I want to knock his head clean off. I suppose I have to see what he says first, though. He may be a slither of help.'

'I can help you knock it off if you like. I wouldn't mind seeing a few heads roll after all he's put you through.'

Willow smiled.

'You know what's worse? I didn't tell you this bit before.'

'Go on,' he said, lifting his eyes to hers.

'He's not only in her car, but she's with him.'

Jack stopped massaging.

'The secretary?'

'Yep.' Willow heaved a long sigh.

'Ah, sweetheart, that's tough.' Jack ran a hand over his jaw. 'That's really tough.'

Willow nodded and felt the tears gather behind her eyes. It was bad enough that he had cheated and that she had seen them together in an intimate position, but to have to face them tomorrow was something she hadn't planned for and didn't want.

'Odge over,' Jack said, getting up.

She moved to the other side of the bed and Jack eased himself down, mirroring her, his shoulder against the headboard. He wiped her tears and took her hands in his. There was about a foot between their curled knees, but Willow trembled, anyway.

She wondered whether she had ever wanted anyone as much as Jack, and yet the timing was unbelievably wrong. He had other things to tend to as much as she did.

'I'm won't leave you when they're here. One foot out of line and his head will roll, hers too if she's not careful.'

'You need to keep your temper, Jack,' she whispered.

'I didn't say I wouldn't. I'm just saying he'd better be respectful. I don't think he realises how much damage he's done.'

'He does. He cries every time he speaks to me.'

Jack assessed her.

'He should,' he said. 'Having any second thoughts?'

Willow frowned with a sniff as her tears dried. 'About what?'

'Breaking things off with him? It's a lot, losing your home and a long-term partner, I know. It's not nice.'

'Absolutely not. I can't be with someone who's done all of that and can live with himself or even attempt to justify it like he has. Carlton is generally a good person, but I'm not sure I can forgive him, and I certainly won't forget in a hurry.' She half smiled; half frowned at him. 'Why would you even ask that?'

Jack shrugged.

'He's remorseful. I just wondered if that changed the standpoint.'

'It doesn't.'

Jack looked down at her hands and then let them go gently. He flipped over to lie down on his back, placing the hand furthest from her behind his head on the pillow. Willow scooted down until her head was propped on her hand just above him.

He looked at her, his eyes soft.

'What about you?' she said quietly.

'What about me?'

'You said you'd thought some things through and that you felt better today?'

Jack smiled.

'I did, and I do. You were right yesterday. I avoid things because I don't like confrontation. The daft thing is it makes me angry, and I end up in arguments I don't want to have. I didn't realise how much that was holding me back. So, I had a word with Helena and Mick before what you'd said wore off. We discussed a lot actually, they made me see their side more clearly, and they listened. Talked me through some stuff. Ultimately, I decided I need to speak to Jennifer about how we can move forward.'

Willow forced herself to smile as her stomach plummeted.

'That's great news,' she said.

Jack's eyes shone with genuine happiness as he looked at her with a grin, and the heaviness seemed to leave his shoulders. The heaviness that had only descended when she had arrived at the gate.

'It is,' he said. 'It's pretty pointless me up here ignoring her when she's tried to talk things over more than a handful of times.'

'I thought you said you hadn't spoken to her in years?' Willow said, trying to swallow the lump in her throat.

'I haven't. She tries to speak to me though, she wants to work through this, it's more than a little unfair really, isn't it?'

'I suppose it is.'

'I need to get life back on track, princess. I'm going nowhere here, am I? I don't have a job, I don't even have a house, and I'm not getting any younger. Something you said about having a family really hit home too actually, because I really do want bairns, I don't want to be hanging around here with an estranged wife over in Edinburgh when we could both be getting what we want now, do I?'

'No,' Willow said. She lay her head down on the pillow as a tear slipped from her eye that she didn't want him to see.

Oh, grow up, Willow. It's time you learned to articulate feelings as well. If that's what Jack is here to teach you, then that's what you need to do to grow.

She thought back to a podcast that she used to listen to what felt like light years ago now. The pain that you go through, it had said, will lead to growth that you can only achieve by going through it. The way you respond is the only thing that matters.

How do you want to respond?

She had a while to think, it seemed, as Jack was still talking excitedly beside her.

'Sometimes life is about learning to comprise to move forward, isn't it?' he said, 'much like you're having to do with Carlton and this woman. What do you think?'

Willow turned onto her back, feeling the tear roll into her hair as she blinked away those waiting behind her eyes and forced down the lead weight that sat in her stomach. She took a breath.

I think that's very different.

'I think if you want a family that badly then you need to do it Jack, we only live once. Time is short. Too short for this crap. I've learned that much.'

Jack turned toward her with a grin.

'I knew you'd understand. You always do,' he said. 'I'm so glad you came here, princess, it's almost like fate.'

Willow couldn't help but smile as she turned to face him.

'I'm glad I could help you,' she said, looking into his bright, happy gaze.

Unable to help herself, she reached to trail her fingers over his cheek. He turned to kiss her fingers, and she closed her eyes. Her heart physically ached, filling her chest with thick, heavy lead.

'Am I keeping you up?' he murmured as he moved his hands back down to holds hers.

'I'm tired,' she said, keeping her eyes closed, so that she didn't have to see the happiness on his face again.

'Go to sleep then, sweetheart.'

She didn't answer. She was trying to keep back the emotion enough to get up and go back to her own room, but if she moved now and he asked why, she was afraid she would bawl.

Instead, she lay, breathing in his scent, feeling him close by, his warm hands around hers, hearing him breathe, and thought her heart may actually break in two.

Eighty-One

C OOP AWOKE TO DARKNESS and pain that rocked through his hand as he rolled over. He smothered a scream, rolled back, and turned on the bedside light. He picked up the tramadol, popping two in his mouth, then he grabbed the open beer from yesterday and swirled the can. There was a little left.

He tipped it to his lips and swallowed. The warm bitter taste made his lips curl but did the job.

Sitting up on the bed, he looked at the packet in front of him and gritted his teeth. There were only two pills left.

Because luck is on your side after all, so why the fuck wouldn't you run out of pills?

He lay his head back on the pillow and wished he wasn't alone. This vengeance plan wasn't half as much fun as planning a robbery with three of your best mates. He felt like he hadn't spoken for the last three days.

He picked up his phone and lit the screen.

4.05am.

Coop raised his eyebrows. He had fallen asleep just after three yesterday afternoon.

Thirteen hours? No wonder you're awake.

And still no messages from Carlton?

Strange.

In fact, it was more than strange. He'd expected at least a message, if not a ranting phone call, by now.

He checked the GPS for Willow. Still no signal.

He shrugged. He'd half expected it, it hadn't come on all day yesterday either. Coop decided he would follow his plan, anyway. If she wasn't there, he would have to reassess how he located her.

But he *would* locate her. He had to finish this.

Then maybe he would finish things himself and go back to dealing. It wasn't as lucrative as the big stuff, but alone it was what he could manage, what he was good at, and he had the means to access the pills.

He pulled the gun from his bag. It was weighty in his left hand and felt wrong. Being right-handed was bad enough, but with one hand?

How the fuck are you going to wield this and shoot a girl one on one?

In the pub had been different. He had opened fire on anyone, and it had felt good with the backup of his friends. Like they had levelled up.

On his own, with the girl looking straight at him? Coop shoved the gun back in his bag with a grunt.

Now is not the time to get all wet about it. Get this over with and then you can do a Radar and lie low for the rest of your damn life if you want to.

He put his focus back on Carlton and picked up the phone again with a frown.

Why had he not been in contact?

Had he stayed with the secretary for a few days? Maybe he'd had enough of being at home with him. The feeling was mutual.

Considering he was a twin, Carlton barely felt like a brother, and they looked nothing alike either. He had a feeling someone at the hospital either had a baby spare or swapped his real brother for this one.

With the familiar feeling of guilt that sat among the admonishment of his only brother, he flicked the phone on again, and then he remembered.

You fucking idiot! You linked his phone.

Coop realized he could see exactly where his brother was... and maybe he should have been doing just that.

Coop looked at the blue dot, frowned, and refreshed the screen.

He turned the phone upside down, thinking the screen had shifted because for some reason Carlton was above him on the map.

Above?

He shook the remaining sleep from his eyes and pinched the screen closer.

Just below Glasgow.

Glasgow?

He tried to get his head around what this could mean and came up with one solution.

Willow's phone was off because she had been tipped off about the tracking.

Theoretically, he had known that Carlton could have been the only person to do it. Now this showed him he was absolutely right.

The only reason Carlton was in Scotland was for Willow. He'd put his life on it. Carlton hadn't stepped a foot in this country before now, and he certainly wasn't on holiday.

And he hasn't contacted you about his car, which means he's hired one or is in someone else's and he doesn't want you to know what he's up to.

'Guilty as charged,' he whispered.

This gave him a new dilemma - which could be a new blessing.

If Carlton is on his way to Willow, he'll lead me straight there without the tracker.

But if he's not, I've wasted time.

What's the worst that can happen? I still have the saved locations and we're not a million miles from where she was last traced.

Then he had another thought.

Carlton's blue dot was stationary. At 4am, that was to be expected, but what if he had reached Willow already?

He pinched into the blue dot and a little research showed a hotel.

His shoulders relaxed, and then he tensed again.

If Willow was on the move because she knew, then she could be at the hotel, too.

Not ideal with what he planned to do, but maybe he could track them elsewhere. There must be a plan. They couldn't keep running forever.

They'll also be a little less on the ball now because they'll think you have no link to her.

Coop locked the phone screen and threw it into his bag. He had fallen asleep in his clothes and his coat yesterday, which helped his cause now.

He used the toilet, splashed water on his face and ran his good hand through his greasy hair.

Then he picked up his bag, dropped off the door card at reception, and got in the car.

Carlton's dot was still stationary for now.

It was 4.35am.

Which gave him a couple of hours to catch up, and according to the Sat Nav he would only need around half an hour.

Perfect.

He used the fuel station at the services to top the car up and headed back on to the motorway.

He would need to stay a fair way back from Carlton, but at least now the drive would be leisurely; if Willow wasn't with him, he would simply lead Coop straight to her.

Eighty-Two

W HEN WILLOW WOKE, FULLY dressed, and with a heavy blanket over her, the room was empty. Rain lashed at the window and outside the sky was grey and thundery. Wind roared past the house with a ferocity that she'd never witnessed before.

Today was the day she would see Carlton and Suzie. He was literally just an hour away... if they hadn't begun the journey already. She felt the uneasy knots in her stomach as she watched the rain slide down the window.

I don't want to do this day, she thought.

It was warm and cozy on the bed. She pulled the blanket up to her chin and buried her head in Jack's scent, listening to the rain battering the window and wishing she didn't have to get up at all.

She was almost asleep when the door clicked open and Jack came through backwards, turning to kick the door shut with two mugs in his hands.

He smiled, and she could have cried as she remembered the conversation from the night before. He was going back to his wife, and as for her... who knew after the next few days? Even if she survived, it looked like she may lose a good friend if he went back to Edinburgh.

'I'd say good morning,' he said, with a nod to the window, 'but it's as crappy as they come out there.'

Willow sighed and sat up, pulling the blanket up with her.

'I'm not so sure it's going to be a good day, either.'

She took the cup that he held out for her and he sat on the bed just below her feet.

'How did you sleep?' he said.

'Like a log, actually. I didn't think I'd sleep at all, but I couldn't keep my eyes open. I'm sorry I'm still here, I must have ruined your night. I was intending to go back to my own room.'

'I had half a bed, and that's all I need. It was nice to wake up and not have to wonder how you were. I think I spent half the night watching you.'

Willow grinned. 'Jack, that's plain creepy.'

'I didn't know you'd crash,' he said with a laugh. 'I was worried you'd wake and not know where you were, or know where you were and panic, or just be anxious about what was coming.'

'None of the above,' she said. 'I haven't slept so well for ages. I can't say I'm happy about it being today, though.'

'Aye, me neither. I'm thinking we should do away with phones.'

Willow sipped her tea and wrinkled her nose in puzzlement.

'Why phones?'

'Think how much less stress and trouble we'd have today without them. This Cooper wouldn't have been able to track you, and you wouldn't have had the pictures from him. You wouldn't have to spend it worrying about Carlton's call now, and I wouldn't be antsy as hell about ringing Jennifer.'

Think about how you respond. You can't control him, his feelings, or his actions. What would you say to your best friend?

Willow took a breath and swallowed the pain of her jealousy.

'I'm sure she'll be fine. What time is it?'

Jack frowned and looked at his watch. 'Nine forty. Why?'

'I read something once. It said, if you have to eat a frog in your day, do it first, then you can forget about it.'

'Ah,' Jack said, looking uncertain.

'Meaning, if you have something to do that you're not looking forward to, do it first and then you can enjoy the day without it hanging over you. So, if Jennifer is up, ring her now, get it over with.'

Jack gave a nervous laugh and ran a hand over his face.

'Sometimes you sound just like Helena.'

'Sometimes she's right. Go Jack. I have to get up anyway, and I need to get my stuff so I can get changed.'

Jack nodded.

'Okay, let me just check the coast is clear first. I'm not sure anyone clicked you were in here last night, thankfully.'

Willow put her feet into her boots and followed him to the door. He opened it and nodded.

'Off you go, then. I'll see you downstairs.'

'Call her, get things sorted out. You'll feel better,' Willow said as she passed him and stepped into the corridor.

'Aye, I will.'

Willow didn't look back as she made her way to her own room, slipping inside without seeing a soul and pressing her back to the shut door.

Why are you telling him to go back to his wife?

He has to do what makes him happy, and I like Jack enough to let him go.

Absolute bullshit.

She took a long hot shower, changed, and went to the window. From here, she could see the rain driving down the road almost horizontally. The trees were bending and swaying like they were dancing to the roar of the wind. Willow looked down toward the shop, which was just in view from up here, and then she looked back up the road toward the bridge and what she now knew was Maud's house.

At the side of the bridge, looking right up at her, was Martha.

Completely still except for the wind, which blew her hair around her face like a fan, as her dress flapped around her bare feet.

Willow's heart skipped, and she stumbled back from the window with a gasp, hitting the bed behind her and sitting down hard.

She caught her breath, and then she stood to peer back outside.

Martha had gone. If she had ever been there at all.

She moved back to the window. No Martha.

Nowhere.

I must have imagined her. I'm actually cracking up with the pressure.

Willow swallowed hard, moved away from the window, and went downstairs.

'It may be coincidence,' Carlton was saying as Willow paced the kitchen half an hour later, 'We came off the motorway yesterday and have been following the A road up. Coop was on the motorway, got off this morning around half an hour after we left and is now tailing us up the A road alongside the motorway.'

'Well, is there trouble on the motorway?' Willow said, glancing at Jack, who was propped up the kitchen doorway, arms folded, his face set in a frown.

'Hang on. I'll check.'

Willow waited as Carlton checked the traffic. She knew him well enough to know he would be pulling up Google maps and checking the colour of the thin traffic lines. Zooming in just to make sure.

She held herself back from yelling at him to hurry the hell up.

'No hold ups. We're on a small A road from Strathaven, heading toward East Kilbride. This road follows alongside the motorway, almost. There would be no reason to get off if you were heading this way. The motorway is clear. I think he's tailing us for some reason.'

'That makes sense. He no longer has the link to me, so if he has a link to you and you're up here, he's going to know that's for one reason only.'

'He can't have a link to me. That's what I don't understand.'

'Well, of course he can. How did you link to him? I'm pretty sure he knows many more illegal ways than you, right?'

Carlton seemed to stall with a small 'Ah.'

'What?'

'He had my phone to get your number, didn't he? He could have done it then.'

'Right.'

'Willow, babe, that means we're bringing him straight to you.'

Willow swallowed hard. Her heart was pounding. She looked at Jack, and now Duncan, in the doorway. Everyone here had been told a rough outline of what was going on at this point. Nothing was secret, and it was good to be able to talk about it.

'What's going on?' Jack said.

Willow moved the phone from her ear.

'Carlton says he's pretty sure Cooper is tailing them now. They moved ahead of him, and he left the motorway and is following them up an A road.'

'One way to find out,' Duncan said, rain dripping from his soggy curls. 'Tell him to pull over. See what happens.'

Jack was nodding.

'Couldn't he just turn off the phone?' she said.

'No,' Jack said, 'Then you'll not know either way. It's a good idea. Tell him to pull over first and check if Cooper stops. If he does, then turn off the phone.'

Willow felt her mind raging with the ridiculousness of all the tracking and trying to keep up with who was tracking who.

'Well, couldn't that be coincidence, too?'

'Not if they stop somewhere obscure for half an hour. They've only been on the road for twenty minutes. Why would he need to stop too?' Jack said.

Now Duncan was nodding. Willow's nerves were shot but her stomach settled a little. She wished she could tell Carlton to turn around. To go home, to lead him away. But she knew that Cooper wouldn't follow.

'Okay,' she said, putting the phone back to her ear and relaying the plan.

Carlton agreed until the turning off of the phone.

'No, if the phone is off, I don't know where he is,' he said.

'If the phone is off, he doesn't know where *you* are.'

'We can move much faster than he can. He's doped up with an injured hand. If he's tailing us, we can put our foot down.'

Willow huffed.

'And risk an accident, which leaves me alone with him, great plan.'

'I need to be in contact with you, babe, and I need to know where he is.'

'Use my phone to contact Willow. If Coop is tailing us, then he doesn't have an exact location. We can go straight there while he flounders and goes back to plan A.'

Willow froze at the sound of Suzie's familiar voice. Her skin prickled, wanting her to be wrong, to have said something stupid. To not be on her side, but it wasn't the case.

'Suzie's right,' she said. 'Turn the phone off and just get here. You can't be more than half an hour away now, an hour with the stop.'

She heard Carlton sigh.

'Okay, have it your way. He's keeping a fair distance behind at the moment, but then he knows I'll know the car. We'll pull over in the next layby and give it half an hour. We missed breakfast anyway. If he doesn't pass us, I'll message you, turn the phone off, and we'll come straight up to you.'

Well done, what a plan, Willow thought, rolling her eyes at the window.

'Willow, is that okay, babe?'

'Perfect, and please stop with the babe. Not only is it insulting to me, but it's insulting to the woman next to you.'

She heard him swallow.

'Sorry, I hear you.'

'Get here in one piece. Please.'

Eighty-Three

COOP DRUMMED HIS GOOD fingers against the wheel with growing frustration. Why in the hell had Carlton needed to stop when he'd only just got going?

He pressed his phone, which was balanced on his knee, lighting the screen.

The blue dot was still stationary. He thought it had been stationary more than it had been moving since he had thought to check the GPS. He wished he could be close enough to see what was going on, but he couldn't risk the car being seen.

It sucked. It made him want to shoot his brother in the head and carry on up to Willow alone.

Except you're not sure where she is, and Carlton knows.

He pulled a cigarette from his pocket, clamped it between his lips and lit it with the lighter on the dashboard.

He rolled down the window a little, blowing smoke, but quickly retracted it after the wind and rain battered his face, and a fast-moving lorry gave him a buffet and spray like an extra in a pamper session.

He was tired, even after all the sleep. His hand ached like a bugger, and he wanted to get this whole thing over with. It was getting annoying.

When I see her, I'll just pull the trigger, blow her away and leave. I can't even be bothered introducing myself.

The fog of smoke in the car increased, and he leaned to open the passenger window a little.

He had wanted to play with her, though, to make her understand the depth of what she had done. It was beyond annoying that he was having to wait around and get so pissed off. It was annoying that he had done his good hand in, too. If it had been his left there would have been no problem, but his right?

You fucking idiot.

The blue dot was still stationary. Had been now for five minutes, which felt like an hour. Maybe he had a flat.

Coop turned on the radio, found a rock station and blared some tunes. Psyching himself out while calming himself down. He would get there when he got there. She was going nowhere. The only bind was his fucking hand.

He reached into the bag, pulled out a can of beer and took the last of the tramadol.

Eighty-Four

W ILLOW HAD JUST FINISHED a small bowl of porridge at the kitchen table, and Jack was making drinks when the door opened, and Helena came in with a waft of freezing air and rain.

'Pigs are out again. The storm has frightened them, and they're bolting across the field. Blasted animals. How do you get a terrified, large, wet, and slippery animal back inside without a leash?'

She shook off her wet coat and moved to the sink, running the water to wash her hands.

Jack stirred the drinks.

'Well, this storm is a biggie, it's no wonder they're scared,' he said, 'Willow, make sure you drink up, I'll go and help out.'

He placed the tea in front of her and gave her shoulder a squeeze before moving away.

Helena turned from the sink with a smile. 'Thank you, Jack, that would be perfect. Willow, I'll speak to you now, darling, you can fill me in.'

'Okay.'

Helena turned back to the sink and Willow turned to Jack. He smiled gave her a wink as he grabbed his coat and stepped outside, pulling his hood up against the roar of the weather.

The message came through as Willow finished speaking to Helena about what was happening. It was from a number she didn't know, which made her wary at first, but the message was from

Carlton, who said it was Suzie's phone and that his phone was now off.

Cooper had stopped just down the road from them and hadn't moved the whole forty minutes they had sat in the layby. He was certain. He had switched off his phone and would use Suzie's to keep in touch from now on.

The main thing was that they were on their way, and hopefully Cooper wasn't still behind them. Carlton said that they would weave thorough Glasgow which would take them longer, but it would be easier to lose him if he was tailing by sight.

'Ah,' Helena said. 'There you go, he has nothing on you. When Carlton gets here, we'll get the full story and work out the next step. In fact, tell him to come here. If this Cooper has the cottage, it's better that no one is there when he arrives, isn't it? I think maybe the police would be a good idea too.'

'He hasn't done anything yet.'

'There has to be something they can do, and he's a known criminal. They have to take it seriously.'

Willow nodded as Helena squeezed her hand.

'Would you like another drink, darling?'

'I'm good, thank you. I could help with the animals, too, while we wait?'

'It's awful out there, darling, leave it to the men. While I've got you, I wouldn't mind a small chat, about Jack actually.'

Willow felt her stomach flip and her face redden.

'Okay,' she said, clearing her throat as her voice cracked.

Helena looked out of the window with a sigh before looking back at her.

'I know he likes you, Willow, I've known for a while, not much gets past a mother's intuition. You're a sweet girl, and if I'm honest, much more his type than Jennifer became as she grew up. False nails and fake tan were never his style really, and the city was more her thing, of course that's where the family tile firm was, too. Jack was always happy in the hills, in the lochs, and up trees. He was always a physical lad, always investigating something outdoors. He was so laid back he was horizontal, and we always joked that he'd just float through life. He never seemed to want to achieve anything more. He didn't seem to need it; his happiness has always been rooted in the earth and the animals. I never saw him as part of Jennifer's world, to be perfectly honest, but he seemed happy, so we went with it.'

Helena looked at Willow with a smile that didn't reach her eyes, and Willow thought of Jack's admission that he went along with the wedding for everyone else.

What a mess up. A twelve-year mess up.

'When he came home three years ago, he was different. Sullen, angry, and argumentative. He said he'd had enough, walked out, and we told him to sort things out.' Helena flicked her hand. 'He has a penchant for not dealing with problems, for letting things slide, it's part of his laid-back nature, but this was a marriage. He couldn't just walk away and pretend it never happened. We tried to get him to take responsibility, but he wouldn't talk to her. When Betsy came, I knew there'd be trouble, of course, and I thought it may jolt Jack out of his nonchalance. What I didn't expect was for him to explode. It's just not like him.'

Helena looked wistfully to the window again.

'It's been a strange time. I've tried to talk to him, to cajole him, to fight with him, anything to get my Jack back. I'm afraid we came to quite a stalemate. He was being stubborn, and so were we, I suppose. It's taken you to break that, darling.'

'Nothing has happened between us,' Willow felt the need to say, but Helena waved a hand to silence her.

'I'm not worried about that. What I really wanted to say was thank you.'

Willow blinked.

'Thank you?' she echoed.

'Thank you. Because whatever you've said to him while you've been here, especially over the last week or so, he finally seems to be taking responsibility. He sat us both down yesterday and had a very clear and comprehensive conversation about what things had been like in Edinburgh. He also listened when we told him a few things from our perspective here. I misunderstood how much courage it had taken to leave, or just how mortified he had been at having to come home. I'm afraid we only made him feel worse, well I did at least. I misunderstood the enormous responsibility he had taken for his own life by uprooting what he wasn't happy with. This is also a different

Jack, you know, one not content to go with the flow. One who will fight for his own happiness. It's a more grown-up version if you understand me?'

Willow nodded.

'You probably already know that he rang Jennifer this morning and asked for a divorce. Three months ago, there's no way he would have entertained speaking to her at all, and I can only put that down to you. You're the only thing that's changed around here. I don't know what you said, but it's got him moving, and I know it's not only about the words, darling, it's about you.'

Willow blinked.

A *divorce*?

She didn't know what she was supposed to say, didn't know what she *could* say, so she kept quiet.

'I say this so that you understand just how much we want to keep you safe, darling. Jack will fight for you, and with the way his temper flares these days, I'm not sure he'll keep his head. And as someone that he thinks enough of to change his ways, to do what's right, however hard, we will do everything we can for you too. We've all enjoyed having you here, Willow. You work hard, you're personable, and you've been quite an inspiration to the others, both here and in the village.'

Willow felt her cheeks redden further as Helena reached for her hand again.

'I've enjoyed being here. It's helped a lot,' she said.

'And that's not just the place, is it?'

Ah, she's fishing.

'Well, of course, Jack has been a rock. He's helped me through some tough times, not least this one coming. For all you say that he's laid back and doesn't really face up to things, he's been paramount in me doing exactly that to get to the bottom of this with Carlton and Cooper.'

'And afterwards? When this is over?'

Willow struggled for what Helena wanted to know, and why.

'After this? I don't know. I like Jack a lot, but he has things to sort out, and I have a mess to deal with, too. I have wondered whether to move on, whether to go back to Bristol, whether to travel.'

Helena's face fell a little.

'Ah. I had hoped that you'd stay around as one of our senior helpers, much like Jack, you have a lot to offer. You wouldn't have to move in here. You could stay in the cottage, and obviously we could pay you an allowance. Not much but, if you stayed here at the house, you would have no mortgage, no bills, no worries. You would be looked after completely. What do you say?'

Willow thought over the offer, which didn't seem to involve staying at the cottage at all, really. There she'd have rent and bills to pay, an allowance didn't sound much, and she couldn't keep using Mum's money. She'd need another job.

She's hoping you'll just stay here, and she's hoping Jack will just stay here if you do.

And what would Jack think of that?

He'd go absolutely insane. He wants a life. A family.

'I don't know what to say,' she said.

'Think about it. You'd be a great asset, and you're well liked.'

Willow thought about what Jack had said about feeling like he was trapped, feeling like he had to be on the job 24/7, having pocket money that he could never spend. Wouldn't this put her there with him? They'd both be trapped, and maybe not even together as Helena was clearly working on a hunch.

Was this really about having her here to help?

I don't think it is.

'I'm not sure,' she said. 'I think I'd like to see a little more of Scotland. It's a beautiful country, and I don't think I want to tie myself down just yet.'

Helena's calm façade slipped a little more and Willow knew she had it right.

'That doesn't mean I wouldn't love to come back often. This place will always be like a home to me, and I'm fond of the people I've met. But this isn't about me, is it? You're worried Jack will leave.'

Helena pursed her lips.

'I've enjoyed having him home immensely. He understands this place better than most, obviously, and he works tirelessly. This place has come on such a lot in the last three years, and Mick and I aren't getting any younger. I was hoping he'd stay around now.'

'Have you asked him if he wants to?'

'I'm scared to, but I see you, Willow, and if you go, he will follow.'

Willow shook her head, thinking about what Jack had said to her earlier.

'He won't follow me, Helena, I think he's through following anyone. I will say that he's already told me he wants to travel more, that he wants to see places, and he's more than ready to move. Possibly because he doesn't feel tied to Jennifer anymore if his plan was to ask for a divorce. He wants to move on, and he wants to live his own life. He adores it here, owes a lot of his fond memories to this place, but this isn't his dream. It's yours.'

Willow wondered whether she had said too much, and then Helena turned to her, eyes sad.

'He's told you that?'

Willow nodded. 'All of it, over time.'

Helena looked back to the storm raging against the window.

'After he came back, I was hoping Jack would be the one to settle here. His sister wants nothing to do with the place. She's living her life with no intention of coming home. I get video calls and messages, but I haven't seen her in person for years. Jack is different, though. He seems to get what he needs from this house, the animals, and working the land.'

'He's also spent twelve years in a loveless marriage, feeling trapped, doing a job he didn't want to do, and living in a city he didn't want to live in. I'm not saying he'll never come home, but Helena, he needs to live, he needs space to grow, to find out who he is, he needs to breathe a little. For the record I agree with you, I think he does get everything he needs from here, and I'm almost certain he'll be back, but for now he needs to do things his way and if that involves leaving for a while, I think... I think you should let him go.'

There was a shuffle in the doorway and Willow turned to see Mick, his soaked flat cap held close to his chest. Water dripped on the stone floor from his jacket like a tap.

'I think that's the most sense I've heard spoken for a number of years. I keep telling you not to push so hard, Helena, and here you are again, grilling the girl for what you need to hear.'

'I didn't need to hear this.'

'Aye, you did, and fair play to the lass for telling it straight. I told you before, let the lad go, stop trying to tell him what he needs, stop trying to hold so tight.'

Helena was staring at the table now, her hands wringing over each other, and Willow felt sorry for her.

'He'll be back. I'm certain. I don't even think he'll need persuading. This will always be his home.'

'You really think so?' she said.

Mick gave a sharp 'pah' and hung his hat and coat on the rack.

Willow smiled. 'He's as happy as a pig in muck out there,' she said, gesturing to the window and the storm.

'Course he is,' Mick said.

Helena looked at Willow with a small smile. 'You'll look after him, won't you?'

Mick gave a raucous laugh and Willow grinned.

'Jack is more than capable of looking after himself, but if he wants me around, I'll be there for him.'

Helena put a hand over Willow's on the table.

'He's a good man, isn't he?'

'You raised one of the best,' she said.

'She'd have raised a pansy left to her,' Mick laughed. 'She wrapped him in cotton wool, but he kept escaping. He's a good lad thanks to no one but himself and what mother nature taught him.'

The door to the kitchen swung open and Jack, Warren and Duncan stomped in, along with a gust of freezing air and rain.

They were head to toe in mud that streaked down them with the rainwater.

'Place will be the bloody death of me,' Jack said with a wide smile, his cheeks ruddy. 'But they're in.'

Willow rose from the table and caught Helena's eye with a smile.

'Pig in muck, I told you,' she said. 'I'll go and call Carlton with the new plan.'

Helena smiled - her warm smile. The one willow had seen when she first arrived. The one she had given Willow when she didn't think she would lead Jack astray.

It gave her a warm glow, like a seal of acceptance.

She went to call Carlton and tell him to come to the house instead of the cottage.

Eighty-Five

B Y THE THIRD SONG, Coop was getting bored and frustrated. Whether she would be there or not, the waiting around was doing his brain a disservice, and the pills were making him nod off under the drum of the rain as the pain eased a little.

What the fuck are you playing at, little brother?

He glanced at the phone again, pulling up the tracker.

The dot was gone.

He blinked, his heart plummeting. He turned the phone off and back on.

There was no mistake. The dot that had been Carlton was gone, which could only mean that he knew he was being tracked and had turned the phone off. Cut the connection.

'What the fuck?' Coop roared. He dropped the phone and banged his left hand onto the steering wheel.

This was getting beyond a joke, and he was getting pissed off with the whole thing.

He looked at his phone, checking the two places that the bitch had been recorded at.

Clover Nook was lower down than Fort William. He would stop there first. Check it out and then carry on.

If she wasn't at either of those two, he would start over, because right now she was becoming the biggest pain in his ass, and his brother wasn't far behind.

'How hard can this fucking be, Coop? Get your act together,' he whispered, imagining Bug's voice in his mind.

I am Bugs. I'm done. I'm going to this Clover Nook place, setting light to the fucking house, and doing the same to the one in Fort William. If she's in there, she can fucking burn!

That's more like it, brother, Bugs answered in his mind.

Coop gritted his teeth, started the car, punched Clover Nook into the sat nav and pulled out, wheels screeching on the wet tarmac.

One thing is a bloody mercy. You have a full tank of fuel. Straight there. No stopping.

Being on the road felt better. He turned the car back toward the motorway, blinking away the tiredness of the pills as he squinted through the windscreen at the rain.

Eighty-Six

T HE PHONE NUMBER ON the screen was unknown, but Willow was beyond knowing who was who anymore. She let the call ring off, wondering if it was someone she should speak to.

I'm losing my mind sitting here waiting for calls and people.

At least she felt like there was a solid plan and people around her to help. Duncan, Warren, and Jack had all told her that this man was coming nowhere near her. Mick and Helena were calm. Tilly was to stay with Willow in the event of Cooper arriving.

Helena had already informed the police and told them what was going on. They weren't able to send someone straight away; they hadn't the resources, but they had agreed to be on emergency alert for when Cooper turned up. If he turned up. They were doubtful with the storm due to hit its peak within the next couple of hours.

Willow had been almost sure that Cooper would follow Carlton here, but Carlton had called five minutes ago saying they hadn't seen any sign of him and were now heading toward the M8 as quickly as they could in the weather heavy traffic.

They would be around another hour the Sat Nav said, and with Cooper behind them, and now, hopefully in a quandary and wasting time making new decisions, willow was beginning to relax a little.

There were seven people here, and two more to join them soon. How much damage could one man do with so many people around and the police on alert?

Hopefully not a lot.

The phone rang again, the same number, and Willow stared with a sigh, wishing there was something more to do. No one would let her *move*.

The three men were still getting warm and cleaned up after the pigs. Helena was in the kitchen with Tilly, and Mick was out in the barn hammering at a side panel that was coming loose in the prevailing wind.

That left Willow alone in the living room. Staring at the walls, waiting for an hour that seemed like a week away.

She answered the phone just before it rang off.

'Hi,' she said, going to the front window and realising for the first time that the roof of Ivy Cottage could actually be seen from this position. For the first time, she wondered if sitting here was any better than sitting up there. She wondered what Martha was up to. If ghosts got up to anything at all whilst there was no one around to scare.

'I have a problem, Wills,' Sophie said on the other end of the line, an edge of regret in her voice.

'Soph? What's going on? You're lucky I answered an unknown number.'

'I'm lucky I wrote your number down before transferring it to my phone, that's what I am. How are things there?'

'Not bad. Still waiting. A good half an hour at least before the real fun begins, I would say, with what we've put into place this morning.'

'Thank God, because you won't believe what I've done.'

'Surprise me.'

'I've left my bloody phone on your worktop in the kitchen. I have to drive into Glasgow this morning, and I wanted to be away by now, but Mum is flat out refusing that I take her car without a mobile in case of trouble in this weather, especially as I rarely drive. I was thinking I'd come up and meet you. We could go to the cottage together and then I'd drop you back? I've just had a shower, so I can be with you in ten if that's any good?'

Willow stared at the Cottage roof. ten minutes was a long time, and a whole lot closer to Cooper arriving. She could be there in minutes from here and the physical exertion would probably do her good.

She would probably be there and back before Sophie even got in her car. Carlton wasn't here yet, and he was more than likely going to be here before Cooper. For the moment, she was safe.

She felt the pull, the adrenaline.

It wasn't like there would be anyone there but Martha.

'Okay,' she said. 'I'll be ready.'

She narrowed her eyes at the cottage roof.

Wait for Sophie? Or shall I just go? Surely the quicker the better?

The front door to the house was directly ahead of her, its large brass key sitting in the lock where it always did. Jack said that they rarely used it, because it was easier to go through the side gate, but she could use it now. No one would be any the wiser, and she'd be back before they knew she had gone.

'Thank you so much, Wills, you're a life saver. Won't be long.'

Willow cut the call. She listened to Helena and Tilly talking in the kitchen, heard the showers from upstairs and grabbed her coat. The keys for the cottage were inside.

She pulled it on, pulled the hood up, and looked out of the window again. Her heart was pounding, her body flooded with adrenaline.

Easy, doable.

She turned the key in the front door and left with barely a sound.

Turning from McGracken House, she began to run. As she turned over the bridge up to the Cottage, the full force of the storm became apparent. The wind almost forced her back down the hill in heavy gusts, and the rain pummelled her face.

Helena was right. It was vile out here, but rarely had she ever felt so alive. Especially for the last four years.

The rain physically hurt and fell in sheets so dense she could barely see a foot in front of her when the big gusts came. The wind raged, pushing her back, and she almost screamed in glee and raged with it.

She felt strong, and able and free. Alive and alert, and ready to tackle whatever the day brought with the same ferociousness as the storm was doing right now.

Things were going to work out just fine, she could feel it, there were too many people around her for it not to.

Eighty-Seven

W ILLOW KNEW SOMETHING WAS wrong when she stepped inside the front door. Through the glass, the cupboard
door swung as though in a breeze. It was a moment of hesitation
that she could do without as the fear and reality of living with
an apparition seized her.

She opened the door, and an icy breeze met her, clouding her
breath as her hair swirled into her face. The cupboard door
creaked and bumped gently off the wall.

Willow felt every nerve in her body fire.

It was like a vortex. Her own hallway was like a vortex, like this
was where the storm originated.

And where was the eye?

The door creaked and swung again, setting her nerves on edge,
and she moved to shut it. Her fingers barely touched the wood
before it slammed home with a loud bang and she yelped,
snatching her hand away.

*Calm down. You know the roof isn't fully enclosed. The wind blows
through the attic room when there isn't a storm, so it must be
raging up there now. This could have nothing to do with Martha.*

And probably doesn't.

'Get the damn phone and get out of here,' she whispered to
herself, trying to make her dumb feet move to the living room.

There were small thumps in the cupboard next to her, like
footsteps on the stairs. Willow's heart thumped in her chest,

and she finally moved, almost running to the living area, as the cupboard door clicked open again behind her.

'Get the phone and go.'

She skidded into the kitchen doorway as the back door shook and wobbled in its frame. She pocketed Sophie's phone and turned to leave the kitchen, but another noise stopped her above the roar of the wind and rain outside.

The small, familiar squeak almost made her scream, and she felt her head turn in slow motion as she looked at the back door.

The handle was turning. Slowly, and then it turned faster, almost shaking itself loose from its housing.

Everything is on repeat. I'm in a loop. I'm going insane.

The door fell silent, and Willow backed out of the kitchen, waiting for the shadow to pass the window.

Except that this time, it didn't.

It stopped, blocking what little light entered the cottage through the tiny pane of glass. Willow threw herself back against the edge of the dining area wall, facing the large front windows, her heart thumping wildly in her chest.

'It's okay, it's just part of the cottage. You've seen it before. Get out of here Wills,' she said quietly.

The door banged and Willow snuck a glance around at the window. It was clear, but the door handle was rattling again.

A gust of wind boomed around the cottage, and upstairs something creaked and groaned.

Willow wondered briefly if the roof would actually stay in place, and then she was skidding into the hallway. She turned to the front door and her heart gave a jolt as all the breath was sucked from her lungs.

Martha stood between the open cupboard and the glass door. There was a beat of silence, and then she twitched as Willow found her voice and screamed.

Martha stepped forward, her hands outstretched. A gust of wind blew her lank and dirty hair back from her face for a moment that revealed pale skin and red-rimmed eyes as black as coals. Willow's scream ran itself out, and she turned and ran for the bedroom.

A darkness followed on her heels, lowering the dim light of the corridor as she found the bedroom door and stumbled through it, slamming it shut with a loud bang. Wind battered the front window, seeming to rattle the glass in its frame, and a large gust seemed to shake the entire cottage.

Willow felt her stomach flip and threw herself down at the side of the bed, hands over her head. This room was worse, her nerves jangling as the wind seemed to moan through it.

'Fuck, fuck, fuck. What did you do Willow, what did you do? You should have waited for Sophie.'

She felt her chest constrict and tried to blow out a few shaky breaths that only sent tears of frustration and anger down her cheeks.

If Martha keeps you penned in here, you'll be stuck until Cooper arrives. Not only stuck, but alone.

'Is that what you wanted, Martha? Murder?' Willow whispered. 'It wasn't to protect me, to warn me or anything else, was it? You're bloodthirsty. This cottage is bloodthirsty.'

The room darkened as the wind died a little. Willow sat up slowly, peering at the window. She saw the shape that was blocking the light and pressed herself back to the floor.

Shit!

Was that a person?

Was it?

Someone looking inside?

Why would anyone want to look inside the cottage?

Carlton, it had to be, although she had given him the details of McGracken House. He must have got confused. She peered up over the side of the bed as the shadow disappeared from view.

Carlton, surely. Or maybe Sophie got to the house, and it's Jack, although it looked too large to be Jack, maybe Warren. Why would Warren come alone?

Willow crawled to the window on shaking hands and knees and peered out of the bay.

At the front door of the cottage was one person. Alone, as far as she could see, and they weren't dressed for the stormy weather.

Shoulder length dark blonde hair stuck to the side of their face and jacket.

She ducked back out of sight.

Size and shape would suggest a male…

The room seemed to fall still and silent as she remembered where she had last seen a male with shoulder length hair.

The photograph.

Cooper?

Willow's heart raced, her breath coming fast.

No.

Not yet. It hadn't been half an hour since Carlton had called. Cooper was behind them.

She peered back out of the window to see the bulk of his form walking to the opposite bay.

Trying all the windows.

Seeing who's inside.

Seeing if you're inside.

Willow scrabbled back around the side of the bed, but the only place that seemed safe right now was the hallway. The one section of the corridor without windows at all.

She would have to take her chances with Martha.

She rose and ran for the doorway, pulling the door shut behind her and tugging the others shut too, encasing the corridor in a dark cloak.

She eased down toward the front door.

If Cooper was heading back to the rear of the house, it would be now or never. If Martha was at the front door, she would have to close her eyes and run right through her.

Hopefully, Sophie was already at McGracken House, she would alert everyone where Willow had gone. Help was literally two minutes away. Almost close enough to touch.

Maybe they would meet in the middle.

Willow slid her back across the wall, keeping her eyes on the living room doorway.

As the side window of the living room came into view, she noticed it was empty and realized that Cooper must have gone back to the rear of the house.

Will he break in? Will he try?

If he does, he'll probably go for the back entrance. It's more concealed.

He's probably around there now.

Willow felt her shaking body banging her off the hallway wall as the front doors came into view.

Empty.

Martha was no longer there.

Maybe she was helping her after all. If Willow had run the first time, she would have been caught going down the road.

Her stomach plummeted as she thought of something else and realised what a close call she had just had.

The front door was open. Unlocked. She had intended to come in and go straight out again. He had missed it.

Divine intervention.

The hallway was cold. Pensive. Watching.

Would she take the opportunity or sit trapped like a scared rabbit?

Willow stared at the doorway, which seemed to pulse in her vision, as an all-encompassing inability to move overcame her.

He's at the back.

Go.

GO.

GO!

It was the cupboard that did it.

The doorway clicked open with a long, slow creak.

In the darkness of the cupboard, there was a form. Willow ran.

Imagining Martha behind her, knowing it was now or never, she hit the privacy glass and yanked open the door just as the solid front door swung open.

Willow staggered to a halt as the face from the photograph, now wetter and a lot scarier in the flesh, stared at her from dark blue eyes that seemed full of hatred.

The face grinned.

'Greetings little lady. It seems someone's at home after all. Can I come inside? The weather is not the most accommodating for the drive up to see you now, is it?'

Rabbit in headlights, Willow stared at him.

'Where are your manners?' he said, pulling out a gun and pointing it at her. 'Are you going to let me in, or do I force the issue?'

In a heartbeat, she was back in the pub. Chaos around her. This man, pointing a gun, firing randomly.

The terror didn't climb up Willow as much as swoosh over her whole body at once.

The walls closed in around her. She gasped and struggled to get any air, to get any hold on a grip of reality.

Not now. No. Not now.

It was her last thought as blackness took her vision and she felt herself topple backward.

Eighty-Eight

C ARLTON WISHED THE TRAFFIC would go away, wished the storm would go away, and most of all, wished Coop would go away. In fact, he wished Coop had never been born.

He tapped on the dashboard as the traffic crawled to a stop.

'What now?' he growled.

'Traffic, we're in the middle of a storm in case you hadn't noticed,' Suzie said with a small sigh. She leaned an elbow on the driver's side door and tapped the plastic trim around the window.

'Is there no way around this?' he said. He had mistakenly thought that the motorways would be their biggest problem, but here they were, stuck on the main roads instead. The traffic and the incessant worry about where Coop was, and how Willow was, were beginning to grind him down.

'Lanes, but I'm not sure how much faster we'd get there, and we risk turning round if there's flooding or fallen trees. I can try it if you like?'

Carlton looked and Suzie. Saw the tired rings around her eyes, and the pale pallor of her skin. They had eaten a meagre amount since getting up this morning and Carlton's own headache was testament to the lack of drink they had both had, too. And he hadn't had the traffic and driving to contend with, he had simply been communicating with Willow.

He had offered to drive again, but Suzie had refused. His mind wouldn't be on the job, and it was hard enough to drive in this weather without trying to sort Willow and how they were getting to her as well. Driving was something that she could do, and Carlton could figure the rest.

Carlton heaved a breath. 'No, you're right, that will probably cause more problems. We can only hope that Coop is stuck, too.'

He placed a hand on Suzie's thigh, feeling the warmth of her skin through her skirt, which had ridden well above her knee as she drove.

He dragged his gaze away.

'If I put my phone on for a second, I can check Coop-'

'No,' Suzie said, 'This is not a game, hotshot. You're not keeping it off for fun. In the time it takes for you to power it up and check him, he could be checking you too.'

'Well, it's not like we're anywhere bloody near anyway, is it?' Carlton said, feeling his cheeks flush as he waved a hand at the brake lights ahead. Suzie glanced at him before looking back to the road.

'Yes, I know, but any general information is still information. Keep it off. We keep going and hope we get there first. I can't see any reason why we wouldn't. We just need to keep calm.'

'We've gone the long way round, though. All that pissing about through Glasgow to lose him. What if he was never following us in the first place? What if he doubled back? From there it's pretty much straight, isn't it?'

'It's probably around the same, Carlton. It's out of our control now, we just have to do what we can. Calm down.'

Carlton clenched his jaw, biting back the anger he felt. It wasn't Suzie's fault they were stuck here. In fact, if it wasn't for Suzie, he wouldn't be here at all.

'What if that way is free flowing, though, Suzie? Maybe we should turn back.'

Carlton pulled his hand from her thigh and twisted his hands over each other on his lap. Suzie looked at him calmly.

'What into? The traffic that's blocked the other way too? We'd just be wasting time.' She looked ahead as the brake lights flicked off. 'Ah, here we go, we're moving again now, looks like there's an accident on the island.'

Carlton ground his teeth together.

'For Christ's sake. Just half an hour more. Please. I don't need this to take seven hours. Just for half an hour, can you all just drive like normal human beings and not idiots in a storm?'

Suzie navigated the accident and turned right around the island.

'Most of them *are* idiots in a storm, hotshot. To be fair, I'm beginning to think we're two of them. If this wasn't an emergency, I'd pull over and not drive again until this was over. It's horrendous.'

'I know,' he said with a sigh, 'I'm sorry I'm antsy, I'm not angry at you, just the situation.'

'Careful who you take it out on,' She answered, keeping her eyes straight ahead.

The road ahead was clear again and Carlton relaxed a little, although his stomach swirled with nerves and the car still couldn't get above forty without feeling like they were out of control with the lack of visibility.

'Sorry,' he murmured, letting his hand find its way back to her thigh.

He lay his head back against the headrest and stared ahead, hoping against hope that Coop was stuck in the traffic or had at least had the sense to pull over and wait it out.

Eighty-Nine

C OOP STARED AT THE girl's form.

He hadn't seen much of her over the years they had been together - or Carlton, let's be honest - but he knew it was her. He had studied the photographs, although she looked prettier somehow now, even in her collapsed state. Slimmer, her freckled skin dewy. Her eyes had been a deeper brown than he remembered too.

Willow.

It had taken so long to get here, and he hadn't thought it would be so easy to find her, but here she was.

Out cold on the floor.

Weeping Willow Carlton had called her once, but Coop was thinking it should be wimpy Willow. The way she had fainted before he even got through the door was just pitiful.

A stab of annoyance ran through him.

He had wanted to do the job and leave before anyone knew he was here, but this was pure anti-climax. What was the point of shooting a girl who wouldn't know any different? Who didn't show the terror that had been on her face just now, and who didn't understand the consequences of her actions?

Coop glanced back at the empty track.

He had left his car in a layby down the road and scaled up through the trees; it was unlikely anyone would know he was here for a while.

She at least ought to know what she had done, and just how much she had changed his life.

A gust of wind and driving rain almost forced him inside, making the decision for him.

He stepped around her feet and pulled the door shut, then with his only good hand, thanking the lord for the shape he had kept himself in, he dragged her back into the hallway and kicked the glass door shut.

A cupboard bumped open behind him, bashing into his backside as he bent to drag her up the carpet.

He kicked it back into its housing, but he had barely passed it before it swung open again.

'For fuck's sake, like this isn't hard enough with one hand,' he shouted.

He stood panting by the living room doorway as Willow stirred.

Not good.

Not right now.

He entered the living room and looked around for something to tie her with. Behind the door was a strip of material that he supposed was some sort of curtain.

Willow moaned on the floor.

He had to move faster.

He tugged the curtain three times before the material ripped down from the wall. Dragging the length behind him, he opened the door to find Willow on the move, crawling back down toward the doorway on her hands and knees.

'No you don't, sunshine,' he said, placing a foot firmly on her back and forcing her down to the floor. 'Stay right there and I won't blow you away.'

He dropped the material, fetched the gun from the waistband of his jeans, and cocked the hammer.

It felt good. He felt in control. Like he had come home.

'There it is,' Bugs said in his mind. 'Now you're back.'

Hell, yeah, I'm back.

A shiver of anticipation and adrenaline ran up his spine.

He placed the cold barrel against her neck, making sure she could feel the weight of the steel.

'Do exactly as I say, and you won't die. Not yet anyway.'

Ninety

WILLOW HEARD THE COCK of the hammer and felt the gun press against her skin.

Here, right in the hallway where Martha Otis and her boyfriend had met their fate some thirty years before.

She closed her eyes and shook under the weight of his impossibly heavy foot. Sweat covered her face, which felt cool in the breeze, especially down here on the floor.

'Are you going to comply, sunshine?'

Willow tried to nod, but the gun was held too firmly at her neck.

'Yes,' she said. 'Yes. I will.'

'Good girl. Get up.'

Willow rose shakily to her feet. Cooper followed with the gun, keeping it pressed against her.

'Lock the door,' he said, gesturing to the front door.

Willow felt her stomach sink.

She kicked herself for not saying anything to anyone before she left as she pulled the keys from her pocket and locked the solid front door.

Cooper held out a bandaged hand, and Willow's heart sank as he took them from her with a hiss and a grimace.

'Phone,' he said, keeping his hand raised. 'Put it on fucking silent.'

Willow pulled her phone from her pocket and put it on silent with shaking hands. Cooper pocketed the keys and then the phone with a curse.

'Into the living room,' he hissed. He seemed to have paled ten shades, his teeth clenched behind his jaw, but the gun was still held steadily against her skin.

Willow turned and made her way slowly into the room.

'Curtains,' he said, motioning to the windows. Willow glanced out of the living room window before she pulled the material closed, back down the road, where safety had been not ten minutes before.

Stupid Willow, utterly stupid, and not only that, but you didn't tell anyone. Someone would have come with you. You would have help now.

She pulled the side curtain shut too, and then he moved her back up to the table.

'Sit,' he said, motioning to the chairs. Willow sat at the side of the table facing the living room door. Cooper pulled a chair his to sit with his back to the hallway, blocking her escape. Resting his elbow on the table, the gun still trained on her, he smiled.

'Ah, a little reunion, finally. You don't know how hard you are to track down little Willow. Isn't this nice?'

He held his right hand down by his side and she looked at the bandage.

She remembered Carlton saying something about a damaged hand when she had spoken to him before, and although it had caused him obvious pain when he took her keys and phone, it didn't seem to be bothering him now.

'Well?' he said, a grin exposing yellow teeth.

'I don't know,' she said quietly, 'is it?'

His hair was wet, but she could see it was lank and greasy, and his face was pale with dark circles drawn under his sharp eyes.

'Of course it is,' he said, 'we have a lot to catch up on, you and me. I hear you've been having a hard time coping after the robbery. Carlton told me you've needed pills to get by. He was happy to supply, I suppose, as he's been happy to for me since

I got out. The money I've made in just a few short weeks! If the law knew what he was up to, eh? With both of us.'

Willow ignored Carlton's name. Cooper could be trying to get a rise from her, and who knew how much Carlton had or hadn't said? She eyed the gun, which was listing off to the side now, like the weight was too much for his hand.

'Are you here to apologise for making my life hell?'

'No,' he said. 'But I am here for your apology for making mine hell.'

Willow narrowed her eyes as he continued.

'After all, while you've been eating your pills, I've been in a prison of my own, haven't I?'

'If you hadn't committed the robbery, you'd have been free. You killed people. I saw you shoot at least two.'

'That wasn't proven. You killed, but you didn't get the time I did, did you? Why is that? Society is so unfair if your face doesn't fit, isn't it? Who says I should be the criminal in jail, and you should get out of jail free?'

'I didn't do anything wrong.'

Cooper raised the gun to her face, his own face squashed into a scowl, teeth clenched.

'The fuck you didn't,' he growled. 'I should just blow you away right now, be fucking done with it. I don't know why I'm wasting my time here.'

Willow's breath caught in her throat as she raised a hand to him.

'I didn't shoot him, but I can tell you what happened,' she said, trying to keep the fear out of her voice as her heart thundered. 'Do you want to talk about it?'

Cooper began to laugh.

'Talk? You'd like that, wouldn't you? Buy some time before someone knows something is wrong. Let poor Cooper spill the beans and then get arrested again. Is that how these things work? In a crime drama I guess it is. In reality, we don't do that. You know why?'

Willow shook her head as the gun wavered in front of her face. Out in the hallway, there was a small thud.

Willow swallowed hard, and an idea began to form.

'Because we're the more intelligent end of society, that's why, sunshine. We're the alternatives. We realise that life is freedom. There are no rules, no path, no right or wrong. We tread off the path and become filthy rich, while you fuckers are still dragging your arses to a nine to five, and earning fuck all while your boss treats you like a moron. You're the idiots.'

He thrust the gun closer to her face, and Willow jerked back with a whimper. Cooper grinned, but he didn't pull the trigger.

If you're going to act you need to do it now Wills, or it will be all over.

Willow clutched her chest and gasped for air, forcing the constriction in her chest, her breath coming in small whines as her eyes rolled.

Cooper stared at her.

'What's this?' he said with a frown.

'Panic... attack,' Willow gasped, trying hard to stop it from spilling over into a real full-blown one. 'I need... my pills.'

Ninety-One

C OOP COCKED HIS MOUTH at the pathetic mess before him. She had been stronger in the pub, that was for sure. He had seen the fight in her eyes, heard her pull the trigger after daddy-dear was shot.

He had thought she was a fighter, but she had changed.

As she struggled for breath, he lowered the gun to the table. It was heavy and awkward in his left hand, and his arm was screaming from trying to hold it up.

It was nothing compared to his right hand, which was just about screaming all it had after taking the keys and then the phone's weight in it.

The pain was rolling right up his arm and into his shoulder.

'Please...' she gasped in front of him, her eyes rolling. 'Pills.'

He rolled his eyes and raised the gun. If she was going to be this pathetic, then he may as well get it over with. She hadn't been as much fun as he thought. She slumped on the table, one eye pleading, and a thought hit him with the force of a sledgehammer.

Pills.

She may just be his saviour.

She has pills. Carlton gives her pills.

Maybe they were for a different kind of pain, but he thought anything would numb the pain in his hand if he had enough. He could try anyway. He had driven high before.

High was better than feeling this. High, he would forget every-thing, but if he blew her away, he wouldn't know where they were, and he didn't have time to search after the gun went off with no silencer.

'Where are the fucking pills?' he said.

She gasped and pointed with a shaky hand. He looked toward the kitchen.

Could be anywhere.

He cocked the gun and pressed it to her cheek. She whimpered and his soul soared. That was more like it. Maybe he wouldn't give her the pills after all, maybe he would just keep them to himself.

Her eyes rolled again.

'Where the fuck are they?' he said, clenching his jaw as her eyes closed. 'Open your fucking eyes, bitch. Where are they?'

For a minute he thought she was out, and he almost screamed with raw frustration and need.

'Where are the fucking pills?' he screamed at her, pressing the gun harder into her face, squashing her mouth into a kiss shape between the gun and the table.

Her eyes fluttered open.

'Bath... room,' she whispered.

He almost asked her to repeat it, but her eyes had closed again, and it couldn't be hard to find a bathroom in a one-storey cottage. He got up from the table where she was now lying still with her eyes closed. He nudged her head with the gun, but she didn't respond.

Fucking fainted again? This is boring, man.

He stepped into the kitchen and saw a door by the external door. He kicked it open.

There we go Coop, house layout extraordinaire. Of course, you'd put a bathroom next to the kitchen and crap where you cook. Perfect.

He grinned as he saw that there were two cabinets. A small one over the bath, and one next to the window.

He opened the one over the bath and threw out bottles of shampoo and shower gel. No pills.

Obvious, Coop, they'd be fucking mush by now.

This was absolutely not how he had seen this going off. He had expected action. A chase, some fire, and he had been looking forward to putting it out.

His hand throbbed as he searched.

Sometimes karma does things for a reason, you wouldn't have managed a chase.

He moved to the other cupboard and opened it up.

There was some medication in here, but Paracetamol and Ibuprofen were as hard as it got. The rest were creams and a small bag of makeup. A hairbrush and some bobbles.

He ran his hand across the two shelves, pulling the contents onto the floor.

No pills.

He stared, his eyes wild in the mirror ahead.

No fucking pills.

And then realisation hit him. In his need for pain relief, he had left her unattended.

She fucking hasn't.

He spun out of the room and into the kitchen in three strides before he realised she had.

The table was empty.

The bitch had gone.

Ninety-Two

WILLOW HEARD THE COMMOTION in the bathroom. A beat pulsed behind her eyes with the beat of her heart, but her brain was sharp with adrenaline.

There was no way she would make it all the way down the road. He didn't even have to chase her; he would simply shoot. She had to hide, but where?

She hesitated until her mind was screaming at her to MOVE.

Hearing the bottles clatter into the bath, she half rose from the table and then bolted across the room and out into the empty hallway. She slipped into the cupboard and pulled the door shut.

Seconds. She would have mere seconds before he knew she had gone, and when that happened, she didn't want to think about what would happen if she was found.

Her shaky hand found sharp chipboard and she stepped over the small lip that had once been the wall.

She pressed her hand back out to find the ironing board and lifted it as carefully as she could.

She pulled it shakily over the hole, trying to place the legs on either side of the large opening, although in the dark it was nigh on impossible.

She was beginning to sweat as the legs glanced off the opening twice, three times, and then they found something firm.

Willow blinked into the darkness and slowly released her hands.

Was that right? Had he heard? There was no way to know.

Was it enough?

She jumped as a crash came from the living room, followed by what could only be described as a growl.

'Where are you, bitch? You're going to pay for this. You jumped up, little shit.'

Willow's heart slammed into her throat.

She wanted to flee, to run right up the stairs, but she knew what was up there.

Nothing at all.

Besides, it was pitch black and with no phone, Willow was going to have to feel her way up. If he heard her, things would turn nasty pretty quickly.

Well, you can't stay here. He'll find you in seconds.

Willow's heart almost stopped as she thought about what she had done.

I'm an idiot! If I go up, I'm trapped. At least in a bedroom, I could have found a window key, or at least broken a window.

Up here I'm completely stuck. Not only that, but stuck with Martha.

She swallowed hard as the sounds of a search came from the living room. Rough grunts and the odd curse.

Willow looked up the dark stairway into nothingness.

No choice now.

There was one thing about going up in the dark. At least she couldn't see anything. Seeing Martha right now may just send her skipping straight back down to Cooper.

She climbed the steps carefully, slowly, trying not to make them creak as she held a palm to each wall.

Ninety-Three

T HERE WAS ALREADY A car at the gate where Willow had told them to park. Suzie pulled up behind it and Carlton was out of the car as it was still rolling and running through the side gate, as he'd been told. Disorientated, he headed toward shouting that seemed to come from the main house where an open door was swinging in the wind.

The scene in the kitchen of the large house was chaos. There was a blonde girl screaming, an older lady trying to calm everyone, and a handful of men shouting as they grabbed coats, all with worry written on their faces.

'Hi, everyone,' Carlton said pitifully, 'We're here.'

The older lady saw him and swung to him with a half-smile.

'We're not working today, darling. I'm sorry, you have to leave. Emergency.'

'No, I'm-'

'You heard her,' an older man with a cap said. 'We have an emergency. McGracken House is shut. Someone is missing.'

Boots thumped on the floor and the rustle and zips of coats rang in his ears.

'Willow?' he said, as Suzie joined him in the doorway, a burgundy hoodie over her head to stave off the driving rain.

Carlton would have laughed, but there was nothing funny about the feeling in his stomach right now.

The kitchen seemed to still, the faces of the four men and three women turned to him. The blonde girl hitched back a sob.

'Are you Carlton?' a man asked, his accent thick, voice deep. He was twice the size of Carlton, and twice as fit by the look of him. His cheeks were almost as red as his hair, and his gaze was hard. The fury radiating from him was almost palpable.

Carlton nodded, and the fury and worry on the man's features momentarily gave way to curiosity. He looked Carlton up and down and Carlton shifted uncomfortably in his creased grey suit, which looked suitably worse for wear after two nights on the road.

'Yes,' he said, still nodding, and then waved a hand to the side of him. 'This is Suzie.'

The man nodded and then pushed them both back out of the door with a sharp glance at the blonde girl.

'Willow is at the cottage. Who knows how long she's been up there. She was picking up a phone apparently, but that could have been as much as a quarter of an hour ago. She shouldn't be up there alone.'

Carlton half jogged at the man's side, but Suzie kept an easy stride next to him, as the other men followed them out.

'Is he there?' Carlton asked, his heart drumming at the unexpected activity.

'I bloody hope not, or you have some serious talking down to do.' He turned to Suzie. 'This your car?'

'Yes,' Suzie said, pressing the key fob to unlock it. 'Squeeze in, how far is it?'

'Up the road,' the man said, getting in the front and leaving Carlton to squash in the back with the other three. Suzie was moving before the doors were fully shut. 'Over the bridge. About two hundred yards,' he said, pointing as Suzie turned the car and headed for the bridge with a roar.

Ninety-Four

W ILLOW WAS ALMOST AT the top of the stairs when the cupboard door opened in the hall, spreading a shaft of light across the bottom steps. She gasped and flattened herself against the wall.

'Are you in here?' he said. 'Ah Willow, I'm so going to make you pay for this, sunshine. I have one fucking hand, one. All I want is a chat. Come out now, stop making things fucking awkward.'

Her heart thumped. She froze in place, not wanting him to hear her moving while he was so close.

There was a shuffling and then the ironing board clattered and fell, hitting the wall at the side of her with a loud thump. She jumped and stifled a cry.

'Ah, interesting.'

He's found you; you need to move. Now!

Willow stood one step from the top, shaking. She couldn't seem to force her legs to work.

Move Willow!

There was a step on the bottom stair and then a curse and a fumbling. And then his form was silhouetted against the light from the hallway.

He's got me!

He can't see you.

MOVE.

The terror moved Willow up and into the room as a light tracked up the stairs. She stood just beyond the doorway, holding her breath, trying to get her bearings in the darkness.

'Interesting how you've gone up. I was thinking you were cleverer than that, but thanks for helping me out.'

He began to climb the stairs.

Quickly.

Willow ran blindly. There was a darker bulk on the floor to her right, which she hoped were the blankets. They were the only place up here to hide.

She dropped to her knees next to the pile and crawled underneath, hoping no part of her stuck out.

There was a musty smell, stale, mixed with dirt. She tried not to breathe too hard, although terror was pushing her breaths faster and faster, the blood beating in her ears.

'Willow?' he said calmly, and then, 'Oh wow. So many places to hide. Why did you come up here?'

Under the blankets was complete darkness, but she could hear his footsteps. When he stopped next to her by the pile, she held her breath.

'I'm impressed,' he said.

She froze, hoping he was playing a game to get her out, and then a foot kicked at her leg, and she knew the game was up.

'I'm impressed that-'

He yelled and gave a grunt of disgust as Willow jumped up with the blankets and threw them in the direction she thought he was.

She floundered, trying to get back to the stairs, but he was in the way. She had to go round. The light followed her as she moved across the roof space.

'Well, I was going to say I was impressed with your hiding skills, but not so much. Were you any good at hide and seek?'

Willow ran. Heading toward the stairs without answering, but he caught on. He was closer, and Willow felt her soul shrink as he cut off the opening.

'I don't think so, do you?'

Light from the phone flashed in her eyes. She swallowed and shrunk back to the eaves.

'There's no escape, little Willow.' he said. A disembodied voice in the darkness behind the light.

'What do you want from me?' she said, her voice wavering as she pressed herself back against the wall.

There was a low laugh.

The light went off. There was a fumbling, and then the gun cocked, and Willow came to a realisation that almost made her cry with relief.

If the light was on, he had the phone, but with one hand he couldn't hold the gun. If the light was on, she was safe, but if he wanted to shoot, he would have to shoot into the darkness.

'Don't move, sunshine, or I'll blow you away.'

He's bluffing, Willow thought, swallowing hard.

It was black as night in here now that the light had gone off. Willow had the advantage of feeling the eaves next to her. She began to move.

Slowly.

'Let's have a small chat,' he said.

Why would he want to chat?

To find out if you've moved, dummy. He can't see you.

Which put paid to her plan of sneaking toward the stairs. She would be right next to him.

Fuck.

'What do you want?' she repeated quietly, hoping the softness of her voice wouldn't give too much away.

'What I want is for you to understand what the fuck you did.'

Willow shook in the darkness as she heard him change position. Where was he now?

You have to keep moving as he's talking. Quietly. If you stay still, you'll be a sitting duck.

'Okay. I'll listen, tell me.'

She took a few paces right, toward the wall of the stairway.

There was a clatter and a thud and then Cooper cursed.

'Fuck,' he hissed.

'What have you done?' Willow said, moving a few paces further.

'None of your business.'

She remembered his bandaged hand and wondered if she could play on it.

'I have painkillers if you need them?'

Cooper seemed to stall in the quiet, and then he said. 'I'm good. I don't need your help. Besides, you won't be capable of helping soon.'

Willow shifted further toward the wall as he spoke, trying to mask her footfalls, as something else occurred to her.

It couldn't be long until someone came now, Sophie must have got to the house at least. If she could keep calm and keep Cooper talking, she would have a chance up here in the dark. A better chance than downstairs.

Not so silly, after all.

'Why are you here? What do you need me to understand?' she said.

'Why?' Cooper began to laugh. 'Let me tell you a story.'

He seemed to step toward her, but she couldn't tell. The dark-ness was disorientating. She felt a bead of sweat run down her back as she crept back to the left.

She licked her lips and swallowed hard, waiting for him to continue.

'You have friends, don't you, Willow? Good friends?'

Willow didn't know whether he required a response, but she stayed quiet. Hopefully, one of those friends was at McGracken

House right now and they had found out what a stupid thing she'd done.

'Well, I had a good friend once,' he continued. 'We met at primary school and just clicked. Did everything together, we did. Everything. From pissing up the headteachers car, to graduating with no qualifications, to our first job together. We were entrepreneurs. We designed and planned all of our jobs, finally we let two more friends into the business. It was going great. We were earning a decent amount, and it was much better than a boring desk job. No taxes too. It was a win-win.'

Willow felt a chill creep over her as he spoke about what he and his friends had done over the years, all those people that they had hurt, physically and mentally.

'You mean the robberies?' she said.

'Crime pays, and let's face it, honey, it's all money. It doesn't matter which way it comes to you, but if you deserve it and you work for it, it will come.'

Willow gave a small huff.

'What?' he said. 'You think that a robbery isn't work? Do you know how much planning goes into something like that?'

'Can't say that I do,' she said, continuing to move back and to the right again now.

'A lot, sunshine. A lot. Do you know who the mastermind of all our planning was?'

Willow shook her head, although he couldn't see in the blackness either way.

There was a creak from what sounded like the hallway and the familiar surge of adrenaline and fear compounded the terror she was already feeling. She tried to focus on Cooper and his voice. From what she could tell, he hadn't moved from the direction of the stairway yet.

'Bugs. Bugs was the genius,' he said. 'He had all the contacts, all the ideas, and he always came up with the goods. You know where Bugs is now? Where my best friend is now?'

Willow bumped the stairway wall, at the corner now between the back wall of the house and the stairs up.

She shook her head, although she knew he wouldn't see, and that he didn't need it.

'Dead,' he said.

Sweat trickled down Willow's face as her mind replayed the gun taken from her hands and the bullets pumped into the mans back.

That's one less fucked up fucker...

'Oh,' she said, her voice wobbling.

'You killed him,'

His voice was rising. He was getting angry again, and anger would make him do stupid things, like try to rush her, or shoot the gun.

Would he know her place now?

He would be close.

Willow pressed herself against the wall.

'I didn't, I promise. A man took the gun from me. He shot him. I saw him,' she said.

'Bullshit,' Cooper spat. 'You killed him, you bitch, I saw you spraying bullets, and now you're not even giving me the courtesy of the truth. It's pathetic!'

Willow swallowed hard, and then something magical happened.

Above the roar of the rain, and the chill of the battering wind, there was an unmistakable sound outside.

A car.

There was a car. The relief dropped through Willow like a stone.

I'm okay. I'm going to be okay.

But as the doors banged shut, Cooper gave a roar of frustration.

'That's it, bitch. We're fucking through.'

A series of loud bangs ricocheted around the attic as he fired the gun.

Ninety-Five

'**M**Y CAR ISN'T HERE,' Carlton said. 'He can't be here yet.'

The man in the front seemed to relax a little as the car stopped and he threw open the door.

'Let's get her safe first and presume afterwards.'

The rest of them piled out of the car and shut the doors.

If it wasn't for the fact that all of the car doors were shut, the bangs could have been mistaken for that. As it was, the sharp cracks came after, stopping them all in their tracks.

The red-haired man swung to Carlton, colour flushing his cheeks.

'You so sure he's not here?' he said, 'because that sounded like a fucking gun to me.'

Carlton felt a whimper come up into his throat. He wished he could say the man was wrong, but he had thought the same.

There was a beat where he only felt the wind, and Carlton felt like he was in a dream as the scene played out around him. Willow was in the house, so was Cooper, and shots had been fired. It had made his blood run cold and sent a sheen of sweat to his face in the chill of the air.

The men ran to the front of the house, shouting and banging on the door. Carlton stood by the car, wind and rain combining to soak his clothes, but he barely felt it.

'There must be another way in,' the older man with the cap said. Carlton had picked up that his name was Mick. 'I'll try round the back.'

The two other guys were banging at the front windows and one disappeared round to the side at a jog as the other came back to thud on the door. The man who had known Carlton's name was almost frantic with fury that he couldn't get inside.

'The curtains have been drawn in the living room. The bastard has her in there.'

The man strode from the window back to the door and pummelled his fists at it, knocking another man out of the way in his haste. 'Why the fuck isn't it open? She only just came through it.'

'Jack, calm down, son,' Mick said, striding back from the side of the house. 'It's not helping.'

'We need to find something to ram the door or break a window,' one of the younger men said.

Mick nodded. 'Aye, maybe. The police are on their way.'

'The police could mean the difference between life and death,' Jack shouted into the wind.

Mick pursed his lips and nodded. 'Okay, I agree, let's do it. We try the door first though.' He looked at Carlton and Suzie. 'You aren't best dressed for log carrying. Keep trying the door until we get back. We'll check in the woods behind, won't be long.'

The three men had run on ahead and Mick turned to follow them without an answer.

Carlton blinked, feeling that this was all still a dream. It was Suzie pulling at him that finally got him moving.

'Try the door, I'll keep trying the windows. If she can get to us, she will.'

Carlton stared at her, dark hair slicked against her head under the soaked hoodie. Suzie was always so well put together. What was going on?

'Carlton!' she said more sternly as a gust of wind battered them.

'He wasn't supposed to be here yet,' he said.

'Well, he is. Get on the door.'

Carlton moved to the door and began to pound it, calling her name. It all felt so surreal.

It was even more surreal when a lady appeared behind him; her grey hair streaked with the odd cluster of brown. Wrinkles pulled her skin into deep pockets, which hung in jowls around her mouth. One brown eye, one milky, sat in deep sockets. He almost yelled as she stared at him from the side of the car, and then she moved forward, oblivious to the wind and rain around her.

Just before him, she stopped and tilted her head to one side.

'You,' she said. 'It's you.'

She scanned a dark eye over Suzie, who had stopped banging the window and was staring at the lady.

'Yeeess,' she said, nodding. 'Yes. The darkness has come.'

Ninety-Six

WILLOW FELT A SEARING pain in the top of her left arm as she stumbled backwards into the darkness, but pain was good, right?

The world was silent. There was no sound after the explosion of gunshots, but she could see the darkness, and she could feel. Was that enough to be alive?

Or was she dead?

Then there was a curse somewhere next to her, banging low and far away and a shrill ringing in her ears. She shook her head and rolled onto her hands and knees. She didn't know which direction the stairs were after the flare of the shots, but she crawled anyway. Anything to get downstairs and into some light.

Something warm trickled down her arm inside her coat, onto her hand underneath the cuff, and down onto the wood below. Something ominous that she was glad she couldn't see.

Willow clamped a shaking hand to her arm, and her fingers came away wet, a dark patch staining the palm. Under her coat, more ominous trickling took its place.

Blood. It had to be.

How deep?

She began to breathe heavily and felt the panic rise.

No. No. If I'm still here, alive on my hands and knees, then it's not bad. I'm not going to die. Not today.

Concentrate, she thought as she controlled her breaths in and out, steadying her breathing. She rocked back onto her heels, clamping the hand back over her arm to stop the anonymous tickle of warmth which sent terror racing through her.

She spun her head, trying to make sense of her surroundings. Cooper was somewhere here she knew, but for the moment she had lost all sense of direction and her hearing was all bells and ringing from the shots.

Pain throbbed in her arm, and her heart pounded faster as she thought about the bullet coming just a few inches more to her right.

Dead.

She would have been dead.

Gasping for air, she blinked and looked around. There was only darkness, and then a footstep. A rustle of clothing.

She held her breath, feeling the thump of her pulse in her neck.

Could he see her?

She stood, hugging herself back against the wall, trying not to whimper, and then there was a tug on her shoulder. She opened her mouth to shriek, and an icy hand covered it.

She couldn't catch her breath behind the firm grip as she heard heavy footsteps cross the other side of the room. Willow smelled the musty smell of the blankets. This wasn't Cooper, she knew that instinctively, but at the moment she thought it may be worse.

Martha?

Martha, who was dragging her backward as her arm screamed, dragging her against the wall, and then *through* the wall.

Willow felt dizzying disorientation and pain cloak her again as she seemed to fall, like Alice, down the rabbit hole.

Deeper and deeper, she thought.

Definitely dead. This is the strangest dream I ever had.

And yet the fingers felt real, and the smell permeated her nose.

There was a small shuffle, the hands left her, and Willow noticed it was light.

Not the brightness of an electric light, but the dull grey of daylight.

She blinked.

She was sitting on the floor, but as she lifted her head to the light, she saw a small window in the roof.

That's weird. The roof windows have been blocked over.

Am I in the same house?

She gazed at her surroundings.

The room wasn't as big as the attic room, but it was cozy, almost like a house contained in one space.

A small mattress sat in the corner of the room, complete with sheets and a duvet. There was a rug and a dirty bean bag next to her, and over the other side of the space, a small bookshelf, and a table with a child's chair. Books were crammed into the shelves, and a small torch sat on the table.

Willow blinked and shook her head.

Where am I?

Her arm stung and pulsed, and she used the light to look at her coat. The left sleeve was soaked with blood, and further investigation with shaking hands saw the material of both her coat and her jumper slashed from one side of her bicep to the other.

Sweating and shaking, she gently pulled the material apart with her fingers to see a deep slicing wound, but across her bicep, not through.

She closed her eyes with relief. The bullet had missed entering her arm by millimeters, but the wound was still oozing and still hurt like a bastard. She let the material fall back together with a grimace and clamped her hand back over the wound. If she could stop the bleeding, it certainly wouldn't be life threatening – she hoped, anyway.

Willow wiped the sweat which was running down her brow and scooted back against the wall.

And that was when she saw her, in the corner, huddled against the wall, watching through limp strands of hair.

She twitched.

Martha.

Ninety-Seven

'W'HAT ARE YOU TALKING about, lady?' Suzie said, leaving the window to approach her. Carlton stayed exactly where he was. He didn't know why he was the darkness, but he didn't want to find out what this creepy lady would do if he got any nearer.

She continued to point at him, her lips curling.

'He's not the bad guy here,' Suzie shouted above the wind. Rain battering her face. 'The bad guy is inside. How do we get in, do you know?'

'She's in trouble,' the lady said.

Suzie nodded. 'Yes. How do we get in to help her? Do you know this place?'

The lady frowned and put a hand to her head, waving away Suzie's voice.

'Ah,' she said, opening her eyes again.

There was a bustle from the corner, shouting, and then the men appeared, a large log between the three of them, the auburn man, Jack, up front.

'To the door,' he shouted.

Martha's eyes widened, and she moved forward.

'No!' she yelled, with more strength than Carlton had thought she would possess. She moved with agility around the men and to the doorway, placing herself across the solid wood.

'Out of the way, Maud,' Jack shouted.

'No. Do not enter the house. The darkness is here. She is not safe. He must not get in,' Maud said, pointing to Carlton.

Carlton blinked as he watched the show. Today was one of the strangest and most terrifying days he had ever encountered, but there was no way this crazy little old woman was going to stop these men from getting inside and getting to Willow.

'Move,' Carlton said. He was almost beside her now that she was at the door. 'There have been shots fired. Willow could be dead or dying, get out of the damn way.'

Maud stared. It was like she was staring through him, and then she blinked.

'You have a link,' she said.

Jack was still shouting, and Carlton was getting as frustrated as the other men.

'Get out of the way,' he shouted, pulling her toward him.

She stumbled, looking confused as the men lined up the battering ram and aimed for the door.

The lady, Maud, put a hand to his cheek. This close Carlton almost convulsed with disgust. The lady's eyes were unnerving, unblinking. Behind her, there was a thud that seemed to shake the whole cottage as the wood hit the door.

'Back up,' the older man shouted, counting down for another shot.

'It's not you.'

Carlton shook his head with a frown, wondering what the hell she was on about.

'Of course it's not me, it's my brother. He's inside, lady, shots have been fired. We need to get inside.'

There was a second thud as the wood hit. The cottage shook on its foundations, but the door sat solid, with a minor dent and a crack in the red paint.

Maud moved back to the door, and the men skidded to a stop as they began their run up. The log dropped at the rear and the frustration was etched on their faces.

Mick was shouting at her to move, but she merely shook her head.

'There is no need for this violence,' she said as the men shouted over her, and Mick tried to pull her away this time.

The lady stood firm, much stronger than she looked, and then she placed a hand in her pocket and pulled out a set of keys.

'There is no need,' she said, holding them high, 'we can use these.'

Ninety-Eight

C OOP FELT HIMSELF REEL from the shots. His left hand not as strong to hold the gun stable when it kicked. The flashes had turned his eyesight to bright dots, and his left hand hurt almost as much as his right as he staggered to his knees in the dark.

Get up.

Get up and finish the job. You don't know whether you've got her, and those people won't be able to bring her back if you've finished.

He felt his will slip.

He had messed up.

He was almost certainly going back to jail, and that was the one thing he had wanted to avoid.

Bugs. It was all for you. I'm sorry. I'm not cut out for this without you.

There was a loud bang, and the house seemed to rock on its foundations. His heart catapulted in his chest.

What the fuck was that?

Where was she? Had she got past him while he was down?

He felt his adrenaline and anger surge.

Did you come all this way just to fall at the last fucking hurdle? Get up and find her.

Coop placed the warm gun into the waistband of his jeans and pulled out the phone as another crash came from below.

Fuck, is the storm tearing down the house?

He unlocked the torch on his phone and spun around the open attic room.

She wasn't here.

He checked again, moving to the corners quickly and checking the pile of material she had hidden in before.

She was nowhere to be found.

At the wall across the stairs, he found evidence of not only what he thought was true, but that he had hit his target after all. She was injured but not down.

He sank down next to the bloody handprint and touched his fingers to the liquid. Still wet in places, but cool. She had been here precious seconds ago.

He used the phone light to look around but saw no other signs of her being there at all, so she must have got to her feet. There wasn't a lot of blood, but enough to know he had done damage.

And enough to know where she had gone. The hand had been facing toward the stairs.

He stood and lurched to the stairs, lunging down into the bright light of the hall.

Ninety-Nine

MAUD UNLOCKED THE DOOR. Jack moved to step inside but Mick put a hand on his shoulder, stopping him and gestured to Carlton.

'As the only person who knows this man well enough, I think that he should go first. If we all descend like lunatics and he has her, we could do more harm than good.'

Jack huffed, brushing away the man's hand and gesturing to Carlton.

'Go ahead. Best get inside or I won't be waiting much longer. I couldn't give a fuck who he is.'

Carlton nodded, stuffed down his terror and entered. He didn't want to go in first, heck, he didn't even want to go in last. He didn't want to see Willow injured, and he didn't want to talk to his brother.

He didn't want to be here, doing this at all. He wished it was all a dream and that he would wake up.

Feeling Suzie behind him, and hearing her murmurs of 'careful', he took courage from the fact that she was right there with him. She was a warrior, and he knew he would be indebted to her for a long time.

There was a second door ahead of him, made of glass. He pulled it open as a figure appeared on the other side. An outline he knew well.

Coop swung round as Carlton entered and ground to a halt. His brother was disheveled, and his face looked almost grey. His hair was hanging in strings around his face, which was set in a grimace.

He was alone.

No Willow.

Where the hell is Willow?

His heart was thudding against his ribs harder than he'd ever felt it.

'Coop?' he said.

Coop blinked at him. He didn't look all there, like he had just emerged from a dark tunnel and walked squinting into the light on the other side. Either that or he was stoned.

Then surprise replaced the grimace, and finally annoyance.

'Oh, fucking fabulous, look what the fucking cat dragged up here. What the hell are you two doing here already?' he said with a sneer.

'Where is she, Coop?' Carlton said, his heart banging.

He was dealing with a man he knew extraordinarily well, and yet a man who was so wild and unpredictable that he had no idea what his next move would be in this predicament.

'I don't fucking know, Carlton,' he said, sarcasm exuded his words. 'It went a bit like this. I shot her, then she disappeared. Poof.' He brought his closed left fist to his face and then opened it fully. 'Just like that.'

Carlton felt his stomach lurch at the sight of blood on Coop's hand. Willow's blood? Or his? What the hell had gone on here? Where had she gone?

Carlton blinked rapidly and swallowed the lump in his throat.

'She can't just disappear, Coop.'

Coop shook his head with another sneer.

'No, of course she can't, that's why I'm trying to find out where the fuck she is.' He raised his eyes to the roof. 'Fucking idiot,' he muttered.

'You don't need to. We can do that. The police are on their way. It's time to stop this, Coop.'

Coop's eyes flicked to the side of Carlton, and for the first time he seemed to notice the bustle of people behind him and Suzie. He squinted, his eyebrows pulled together, and Carlton saw his face change from a sneer to panic.

They had to act fast if they were to get hold of him now, or he wouldn't think twice about shooting, not that Carlton could see where the gun was.

'Oh, no. I'm not going back to jail, Carlton,' he said, shaking his head, eyes wide.

'You broke into this house and sh...' Carlton's voice caught as his breath hitched nervously. 'Shots were fired. Is Willow hurt?'

Coop was backing up the hallway.

'I don't fucking know,' he said. 'I can't find the bitch. If I were you, I'd get the hell out of here before I kill the fucking lot of you.'

He was eyeing the corridor both ways now that his back had hit the wall.

Trying to make his escape.

You need to calm him a little, make him think there's a chance.

'Well, let's go find where she is, and maybe the whole jail thing can be averted?'

There was a huff from behind.

'Over my dead body,' a voice said, and Carlton almost rolled his eyes. He was pushed and jostled as there was collective agreement from the back and Jack pushed his way froward and out up the hallway.

'What the fuck have you done with her?' he said, pointing a finger, his face red as he strode up to Coop.

Coop smiled and tucked his hand behind his coat to pull out a pistol. He pointed it straight at Jack, who stalled and seemed to be weighing up whether he was angry enough to ignore it.

'Oi, oi, I'm sure there's no need for that. Let's calm down now. We can talk this through I'm sure, no need to be rash,' Mick said, pushing his way into the hall, past Carlton who seemed to be frozen to the spot. Coop trained the gun on Mick instead and he also came to a stop, his face skipping through a cluster of emotions from smiling and authoritative, to apprehensive and fearful. Coop smiled as the hallway fell silent.

'I'll tell you what's going to happen,' he said, flicking the gun at the group, who shrank back to the walls. 'You're going to come inside, and you can look for your precious little Willow all you like, but I am walking out of that door before the police come. Right now.

'No chance,' Jack said, standing firm, and Carlton saw the other men nodding as they stood by Mick.

Coop's mouth drew a straight line as he swung the gun back to Jack, who didn't move an inch. He stared Coop in the eyes. 'I cannot let you walk away after this. Even if you haven't hurt her, and I think you have, she's been terrorized by the pair of you for the last two months.'

Coop raised an eyebrow and looked at Carlton.

'One for you too there, bro, oh, and shagfest Suzie at the back there. Say hi, Suzie.'

Carlton clenched his jaw as his face began to burn. He didn't dare to look at Suzie as Coop turned back to Jack.

'You're really going to be a pain in my fucking arse when I have a gun? Fuck me, move out of the way.'

He moved to step around Jack who stepped with him, blocking his way.

'No you don't.' Jack was shaking his head, eyes on Coop's as Mick edged nearer.

'Jack...' the older man warned, but Coop cut him off, his cheeks flushing red with anger.

'Are you fucking stupid? Move.'

Jack took a step toward Coop so that there was only around a foot between them. Carlton felt the tension in the hallway press against him as the two men squared up to each other.

'No,' Jack said.

Coop looked like he was about to lose steam from his ears. He was furious, and that set Carlton on edge. His heart was pounding, his hands shaking.

A furious Coop was a loose cannon.

'Move, or I'll make you and step over your bleeding carcass! Last chance,' Coop said through clenched teeth.

Carlton saw Coop flick off the safety, but he also saw the shake of his hand. He didn't know what that meant, but he knew he had to act quickly if he was to stop any more bloodshed. While Coop's attention was fully on Jack, Carlton reached his brother's side and grabbed his broken hand, squeezing as hard as he could.

By some weird coincidence, at that very moment, Jack shot out a hand and pushed Coop's left hand down hard without taking his eyes from Coop's. A shot rang out in the hallway, making Carlton's ears ring as a small hole and a dispensed bullet appeared on the carpet.

Coop howled in pain.

Jack shook the gun from his left hand easily and kicked it down the corridor toward the door. It landed at Suzie's feet, and she bent to pick it up.

'No,' Jack yelled, making her jump and look up at him. Carlton noticed she was pale. Possibly more out of control and out of her depth than she had been so far, maybe ever in her life. 'Leave it,' he said. 'It's live, and the safety is off, don't touch it. His fingerprints are the only ones we need on it.'

Coop dropped to his knees with a scream as Carlton squeezed harder. 'Fuck! You bastard, you fucking bastard,' Coop screamed, ten octaves higher than usual.

Jack turned back to Cooper and forced the hand he was still holding up Coop's back, hard.

'AARRGGGHH. Okay!' Coop yelled, 'Okay I'll talk. I know where she is. I know, just please let my hand go, let my fucking hand go!'

Carlton met Jack's eyes, and the man nodded. He let go of Coop's hand, feeling the room spin as he stepped away toward a living area, glad to leave the manhandling to the other men, who were now stepping forward to help Jack.

He was shaking hard now. All this commotion and Willow hadn't turned up? Where was she? Was she hurt? Dead?

'Carlton?' He turned back and saw Jack gesturing to a long piece of material that lay on the hall floor. 'Get the material. We can keep him contained until the police get here.'

Carlton nodded and picked up the length, passing it to jack and watching the group of men tie Coop's hands behind his back and usher him to his feet.

'Okay, let's sit him down, make sure he can't go anywhere,' Jack said as he pushed Coop through the door. Carlton took a dining chair from the table and turned it round, catching Coop's eyes as he did so. The look of pure hatred made his heart jump as the group jostled him to the chair.

He caught himself about to say sorry and turned away. That was the problem, wasn't it? It had always been the problem, and it had been the entire problem with the robbery Willow was caught up in. He never took responsibility for what he knew of his brother's actions, and he never made his brother take responsibility, either. He glossed over them, protected him, covered for him, and mainly ignored the wrongs he had done. He had known that Coop would come after Willow, he had told him as much, but Carlton had done nothing. In fact, he had done worse than nothing. He had offered his brother illegal pills and a place to stay.

Why are you such a wimp, Carlton? Even now, you should be helping these people, not sitting back.

He clenched his jaw as he watched the men tie Coop to the chair.

'We've got this, Jack,' Mick said, his hand on Jack's arm. 'Go and find her. She can't be far. Duncan, you go too.'

Jack nodded and got up from his knees where he had been securing Coop's feet to the chair.

The funny-looking lady was just inside the hall, staring at the ceiling as Suzie came into the living room and moved out of the way to stand by Carlton.

That was how it was, and how he was being treated.

Like a spare part.

More than likely they didn't know he felt that way, and there wasn't time to ask about poor Carlton's feelings, but he felt like a spare part next to these capable men. Jack had the kind of physique and forthright courage and manner Carlton could only dream about. He felt positively lousy in his puny creased suit.

He should look for Willow, but as he heard Duncan calling for her, he knew he would be surplus to requirements in this small house. In the hallway, he saw the strange lady point to the ceiling, and he saw Jack glance up and then nod before he stepped out of view.

Carlton's eyes fell back to the men who were finishing tying Coop up for the third time after he kicked both men and the material tie from his legs.

There were sirens in the distance. His brother was going back to jail.

Suzie grabbed his hand and gave a gentle squeeze, but it did Carlton no good.

He hadn't been courageous enough to help Willow the first time round, he hadn't helped her with her recovery, he hadn't helped her avoid Coop now, and he wouldn't be helping if she was hurt either.

Whichever way he looked at it, he didn't deserve her, and he absolutely deserved this now.

He may be a big-shot psychiatrist to outsiders, he may hold all the answers to everyone else, but inside he was nothing. He was weak and scared, and he had none of the answers.

He was nothing.

One Hundred

W ILLOW HEARD THE THUDS, which seemed to shake the house, and then heard bangs and the sounds of people downstairs. She knew they were probably here for her, but until she could discern a voice she knew, she wasn't about to leave the safety of this small room and entertain the possibility of meeting Cooper again.

She sat by the doorway, listening, wondering if they were police that had battered their way inside after a tip-off. But there had been no accompanying shouts as they had come in.

She hoped it was Jack and the others from McGracken House who had finally realised where she was, but another voice nudged at the edge of her thoughts. Up here in the roof, she was blind. What if Cooper had called for backup?

She strained her ears to see if she could recognise any voices, but everything was mumbled up here.

Where is Cooper - is he down there?

Icy fingers crawled down her back. Were these his friends? How many did he need?

Willow's breathing quickened and heart banged against her ribs. She looked at the girl, half hidden in shadow under the eaves opposite, and the girl stared back at her.

Willow said nothing. She had already tried to speak to the girl, who had scuttled back further into the darkness.

She swallowed hard.

And then there was noise from downstairs. A gunshot, and shouting.

There was more scuffling and shouting, and then the sounds became a little quieter. More muffled. As if they had moved from underneath her and into another room instead.

She looked at her arm. Her fingers were covered in blood now, but the bleeding from the wound seemed to be slowing.

Willow moved the material around the painful wound, and then a shout made her pause.

'Willow?' There was a pause. 'Willow? Are you up here? We have him restrained. It's okay, you're safe.'

Jack. That was Jack.

Shaking with fear and relief, she scrambled to her feet, setting off an explosion of pain in her arm. She winced and took a last look at the girl in the corner.

'Thank you,' she said, and then she turned the small handle that was on this side of the door and stepped out into the darkness.

'She's not up there you fucking wet, I told you.'

Cooper's voice stopped her in her tracks as the door clicked softly shut behind her.

She looked back. It was as though it had never been there, no way back inside now.

There was a counter downstairs from a voice she couldn't discern and then Jack's voice from the stairs at the side of her.

'I don't need your fucking help. You've done enough today.'

Willow felt disorientated in the blackness. She clamped a hand over her arm, wincing at the pain, and kept the top of her good arm against the wall, for support and direction toward what she hoped was the stairway.

Then a light appeared ahead, and Willow choked back a sob.

'Jack,' she said.

The light bobbed and shone into the room. Jack's shape followed it through, and then the light was on her.

'Willow!' he said, lowering the light as he stepped toward her. 'You're hurt. How bad is it? Let me take a look.'

Her breath hitched as she blinked back tears, and he brought the light up to the arm of her coat. Blood shone bright red in the light and Willow wondered how she could have bled so much and still be standing. The fingers of her right hand were streaked where she had been holding it against the wound. She knew that inside her coat her jumper was soggy with more, and her arm was beginning to itch where it was drying around the edges.

'Fuck,' Jack mumbled.

'I'm okay. He shot, but he couldn't see me. I think it was the car. He caught my arm, but barely. It's almost stopped bleeding already, I think.'

'That's a lot of blood, sweetheart. Let me have a look,' he said. 'You may need an ambulance.'

He lifted the torch, following the bloodstains from her wrist, and up to the more ominous part above her elbow and to the wound itself where the material of the coat and jumper were shredded in a neat slash.

'Fuck,' Jack muttered again. He reached out his free hand.

'Be careful, Jack. It hurts.'

She winced as he pulled some of the coat away from the wound gently and hissed through his teeth.

'It could need a stitch or two, but it's not bleeding too badly now.'

Willow nodded and then flinched in pain as Jack gently edged the coat out further, pulling it against the wound. He let the material go, gently folding it back down.

'Sorry,' he muttered. 'You were bloody lucky. So lucky. Fuck...'

He broke off, lowered the flashlight, and cupped his left hand behind her neck, fingers in her hair, palm and thumb on her cheek, then he lowered his forehead to hers. His breath was warm and sweet on her face.

'I'm so sorry, sweetheart, I said I'd always find you. I promised myself I'd keep you safe. What a shit job I've done so far, eh?'

He was being careful and tentative with her wound, but all Willow wanted was to feel his arms around her. She reached for him with her right arm, her hand on his waist pulling him closer. He lifted his head and placed a kiss on her forehead, before wrapping her gently in his arms, keeping his body to her right side and his arms above her wound. She could feel his heart pounding as much as her own as she lay her head on his chest and the familiar sensations of safety and security flooded over her.

'This was all my fault, Jack. I should have just waited for Sophie. I didn't even say where I was going. I was stupid, and still you found me.'

'Not quick enough. You could have been killed,' he whispered. She felt his jaw clench against her head.

'It's not your fault, Jack, it was me. The clock was ticking, and I thought I'd just be a minute. That it was better to just go rather than wait around. Ten minutes waiting for Sophie seemed such a long time, I didn't think.'

Jack brought his right hand back to her face, keeping his left around her back and pressing his forehead back to hers, closer this time. He was shaking, and Willow knew she was shaking too, trembling not only at what she had been through, and that she was finally safe, but at the sheer closeness of him.

'It doesn't matter,' he whispered. 'You're okay, that's what matters. You're here, and you're okay. You're okay...' He trailed off. Her heart clattered, and for a moment, there was nothing but the two of them in the darkness.

He moved closer and his lips grazed the side of her mouth, barely there before they had gone. Tentative, as though he wasn't sure he should. A butterfly kiss, she thought, closing her eyes.

She wanted more, but Mick called from downstairs, breaking the spell.

'Jack? She's not down here. Any luck up there?' Jack stepped back with a small sigh.

'Aye, I've got her,' he yelled back, then he turned back to her, taking her right hand in his. 'Carlton is down there, sweetheart. Are you ready for this?'

Willow felt herself wobble.

'Brilliant, she's safe everyone,' she heard Mick say downstairs. 'Jack has her.'

'Where the fuck...?' She heard Cooper begin, and then his voice faded into the background as anger wound its way up from her stomach.

'Ready as I'll ever be,' she said.

Jack nodded and led her back to the stairs. At the top, he moved her in front of him.

'You go down at your own pace. Take whatever time you need. I'm right behind you, princess, always.'

Willow turned to face the light and began to descend the steps.

☺☺☺☺☺☺

The Living room was packed with more people than Willow had ever seen in her own house, but it was the sight of Carlton that threw her as she walked slowly into the living room, with Jack behind her.

He was usually composed, uncreased, calm and in control, but now he was looking more than a little worried, dishevelled, and worse for wear.

He looked smaller, and somehow meeker. His grey suit was creased and his hair, for all it was short, had been blown into an unbrushed mess. His eyes were baggy and heavy, but when he saw her, a little weight seemed to slide off his shoulders.

'Willow,' he almost breathed, and then his face dropped. 'You're hurt.'

'Are you okay, lass? That looks nasty,' Mick said, moving to inspect the wound. His eyes met Jacks. 'Do we need an ambulance here?'

'No,' Jack said behind her. 'It'll need dressing, stitching at most. Maybe Tam could take a look and give her opinion, but it's not too deep.'

'I'm fine,' Willow said, keeping her eyes on Carlton.

'Thank God,' he said. 'I came as quickly as I could, babe... I mean... I... you know. Sorry. This is Suzie.'

He flapped a hand behind him as though introducing his pet dog. Like it wouldn't crush her soul to meet the woman from the pictures. The woman she had seen more of than she wanted to, and those images were seared into her brain.

Willow stared at Carlton. A familiarity that sat uncomfortable now. His eyes were full of pain, but she knew he had been harbouring Cooper as much as he had been feeding her pills and lies and sleeping with his secretary.

He was a people pleaser, trying to help and be friends with everyone. Even at the expense of her life, it seemed.

'Willow?' Carlton said again as the room fell quiet.

Willow felt Jack move closer and place a gentle hand at the small of her back, giving her the strength and confidence she needed to gather herself together.

'Yes, Carlton, I know. I recognise her,' she said, wondering if it was rude not to say hello as Suzie looked down to her feet with a flush spreading across her face.

Cooper hooted a laugh, drawing her attention to him. He was tied to a dining room chair with the makeshift curtain that he had pulled down just minutes earlier. With all of the people around her and sirens in the distance, his presence seemed much less terrifying now.

'Oof, that hurts, doesn't it, little brother?' Cooper said. 'You fucking deserved that.'

Ignoring him, Carlton's eyes travelled to Willow's hand, clamped over the wound which throbbed ceaselessly under her fingers. His eyes met hers and he tried to say something, but then shut his mouth and dropped his gaze.

'I'm sorry,' he said.

'Sorry for which part? For bedding your secretary in *my* apartment? Or for letting your brother think I'd done something I hadn't? For letting him come after me? Or for drugging me and keeping me locked away for the best part of four years?'

'Okay, these folks need a little space,' Mick said, rising from the chair. 'Into the back boys.' He turned to Willow. 'We'll be in a bedroom, Willow, pet. If you need us, just yell. We'll hang around for the police, they'll not be far off now.'

The men left the room. Willow thanked each of them as they went and frowned as Maud followed them out.

'Maud?'

The lady's lines moved her saggy skin into a smile that didn't reach her eyes. She placed a hand on Willow's cheek.

'There is little time for recompense and closure, child. I will speak to you afterward. Do as you need. The darkness will pass.'

For all it sounded like a riddle, Willow thought she grasped the nature of what Maud was telling her, and was comforted by it, although she couldn't understand why the lady was here.

She sees.

A flicker of knowing lit in the back of her mind as Maud followed the men.

'Jack? Get in here,' Mick shouted.

'I'm not going anywhere,' Jack said behind her.

'Give the girl some space, lad. It's courtesy.'

Willow turned to meet Mick's eyes. 'He already knows all there is, it's fine. I'd like him to stay. I feel a little outnumbered, to be honest.'

Mick dipped his head and pursed his lips. 'Okay, lass, if he starts to lose his head and get in the way, kick him back up here.'

Willow smiled.

'He won't.' She looked at Jack pointedly because it was important to her that he didn't interfere in the conversation, even if she wanted him with her. 'Absolutely no heads will be rolling today, will they?'

It was more a statement than a question. Jack's pale hazel eyes gazed back at her with understanding.

'Not if you don't want them to,' he said.

She nodded, knowing that Jack was a protector, and that Helena was right. He would fight for her, and after Carlton's lack of protection over the last few years, and as his brother had stalked her, she liked that side of him, but it wasn't needed right here and now. He respected her decision. He possibly didn't like it but understood that it was non-negotiable. She nodded to Mick, who disappeared behind the door of the furthest spare room where they had all gone.

Willow moved further into the room, as Jack leaned himself against the back of the settee, his eyes on Cooper.

Willow looked between Carlton and Cooper.

'So, do either of you want to help me understand what the hell is going on? What the hell has been going on for too many years by the sound of it?'

'No, Willow, don't misunderstand the situation. I was only trying to help. I'm not the bad guy here,' Carlton began.

Willow flicked her eyes to Suzie, who was staring at the floor. Carlton began to stutter. 'No, no. Don't. It was a mistake. It hasn't happened again,' he stammered. 'Has it Suzie?'

Suzie raised her eyes to his, looking a little dejected that he had brought her into it at all. Her cheeks were red. 'No,' she said, looking at him with disdain, 'Only the once.'

Willow shrugged. 'I'm not bothered, really. I wasn't asking about that-'

'It was one night, sure, but four times actually, if we're being pedantic,' Cooper said from the chair, a large smile playing across his mouth. 'Four times, was it, brother? Without protection, did you say?'

'No, Coop, no. It wasn't like that, you know it wasn't,' Carlton ran a hand over his face which wore an expression like he was in actual physical pain.

Jack shifted at the back of the settee with a huff, arms folded across his chest, his mouth a sharp line. Willow could almost *feel* him holding back, feel his coiled energy.

'It makes no difference,' she said, brushing the comment off.

It hurt. A lot. But if she showed weakness, it would make Carlton think she still had feelings for him, Cooper think he had the upper hand, and Jack want to knock both of their heads off. 'I don't care about that anymore. It's old news.'

Cooper's smile slid from his face as Carlton frowned and shook his head.

'I'm sorry, babe, I am. You don't know how much.'

Willow ignored him.

'I want to understand what's going on here. The build up to this. Why, Carlton? Why the pills, and why the monitoring, sure, but why are you still protecting him? Why give him a home, in *my* apartment, and why supply him with pills?'

The colour drained from Carlton's face as he shook his head and Cooper snorted.

'Oh, fuck off, little brother. You know how much I've made off your little stash since I got out? Almost a grand. She's not fucking stupid. She knows they come from you, and she probably knows you were supplying me before prison, too.'

'To fund your own habit. I was helping you out,' Carlton whined. Willow narrowed her eyes as Cooper began to laugh. She hadn't known he was supplying for Cooper before the attack, she hadn't even known they were in contact. Another revelation. Another lie.

'As if I needed that many pills, I'd have wiped myself off the earth if I had chewed on that lot myself. Of course I sold it all.'

'You said-' Carlton began.

'Of course I fucking said, I wanted the cash. Why do you think we got into the pub rounds? Because pills were no longer making us enough.'

'You got greedy,' Willow said.

'If you can take it, why not?' Cooper said with a smile.

Willow felt a stab of anger cut through her stomach as she thought of her dad.

'If you can take a life in the process, why not?' she said.

'I didn't ask you to be in the pub. Carlton knew. I told him most of our plans all the way through. Brotherly bond. I gave him a heads up. If he didn't pass the info on, I can't be held responsible. I didn't know you'd be there, more's the pity.'

'That's not fair,' Carlton said and Willow saw Suzie's hand slip to his arm and squeeze.

There was something still there then, whether they had only had one night or not. Willow was glad that she hadn't believed him when he said he had made a mistake. He may believe that, but Suzie would always be around, and if he had slipped once, how could he be trusted again?

Doesn't matter. You're through anyway.

'What's not fair is that you allowed her to be there, and she shot my fucking best friend.' Cooper's face was flushed as he thrashed his arms and legs against the secure binds. Willow's heart skipped, but Jack stood and Cooper stilled as he eyed him. His reaction gave Willow the confidence to challenge him.

'You shot my dad, and I shot no one. I told you that.'

Cooper sneered.

'If that's the truth, then why didn't Carlton say anything about it? I mentioned it more than once. He never backed you up, he just told me to leave it.'

'I didn't know,' Carlton said. 'I don't know.'

'Because you never asked,' Willow said, swinging back to Carlton. 'Every time I brought that night up, you told me to take more pills and stop distressing myself.'

'Of course. I didn't want you to go through any more trauma.'

'You listen to people for a goddamn living, and yet you couldn't listen to me. You couldn't let me make my own decisions. You couldn't let me figure this out for myself, and do you know why?'

Carlton's mouth opened and shut again. His pleading eyes made her sick as a realisation hit her.

'Because you thought it was true. You thought I'd done it and you wanted to bury it under the carpet. Didn't have to deal with it then, did you? I had no idea you were in contact with Cooper. I didn't even know he was involved!'

Carlton shifted under her gaze, fiddling with the neck of his shirt under his jacket.

'I didn't know,' he said as Willow's anger spilled over.

'No, you didn't know,' she spat. 'And you didn't bother to find out. I was terrified of speaking about it because you told me if I breathed too fast, I would die. I was so doped up I didn't even have the faculties to check out whether you were right, and I didn't think I needed to. Do you know why that was?'

Carlton gave a loud swallow and shook his head.

'Because I trusted you. Fully. I trusted you to help me out of this, not only as someone who loved me, but as a professional who knew what he was doing.'

'I'm sorry,' he whispered.

She swung back to Cooper as the sirens got louder. Almost here now, almost safe.

'And you? You know what I think your problem is?'

'I suppose you'll fucking tell me while I'm tied up,' he said. He tried for sarcasm, but his voice and face were tinged with worry from the sirens, and he was straining against the material rope.

'If I didn't kill your friend – and I didn't – then you have nowhere to go from here, do you? No one to blame, and nowhere to look but to yourself. This is more about you, your guilt. You knew what you were doing was fraught with risk. If you cared so much about your friend, then I think your real problem is guilt. Why did you abandon him?'

Cooper bared his teeth and strained as blue flashes pulsed through the curtains.

'I didn't abandon him.'

'You left him on the floor of the pub, injured. You ran out!'

Cooper's face reddened, and a vein bulged in his neck, but the ties held firm.

'You goddamn bitch, I had no choice. A few seconds later the place was crawling with police.'

'You got caught anyway. What difference does it make if you're caught outside, or caught tending to your dying friend?'

Cooper strained against the ties and Jack moved to the table, pulling a chair to sit next to him. Cooper seemed to lose a little steam.

'The point is, why did I even get caught? Who called the police, huh?' He said, eyeing Jack, before turning to Willow.

'You know who,' she said. 'I was in the damn pub. If I knew enough to call the police, why was even in there?'

Cooper stalled. He was beaded with sweat and his body odour was strong, even from where she was standing a good six feet away. He pulled against the restraints, veins bulging as he bared his teeth.

'So, who the fuck called them?'

'Who do you think?' she said.

'No,' Carlton whispered beside her.

Cooper wrinkled his nose, pulling his face into a scowl.

'I don't know,' he spat, 'that's why I'm fucking asking.'

Spittle landed on her lip, and she fought the urge to bring up a hand and wipe it away.

'Of course, you do. Who else knew about this? Who tried to stop me from going? Who tried to get you to pull out? If what he told me is correct, anyway.'

Cooper's eyes narrowed, and he shook his head as his eyes swung to Carlton.

'You're a fucking liar. Carlton may be a do-gooder, but he's my brother. My twin. We stick together. He's already back on board supplying me. He's a partner. My buddy. My fucking brother.'

'I can believe it knowing what I know now, yes,' Willow said, cocking her lip. She looked at Carlton, who was squirming and shaking his head. 'Tell him,' she said.

Carlton looked back down at the floor.

'You'd better fucking tell me she's wrong, brother,' Cooper said, his anger now directed at Carlton.

'She was in the pub, Coop. What did you want me to do? I was stuck. I didn't know how it would play out. I thought an anonymous call would be the best thing.'

'You fucking bastard. You got me locked up. I thought we were close, and you put me away. I trusted you, and you locked me up.'

Willow nodded. 'Ditto, I could say exactly the same. You fucked us both over, Carlton. The difference is that I didn't deserve it,' Willow said as Carlton bent into his hands.

Then he nodded and looked up with a sniff, although Willow couldn't see any tears. Suzie fed an arm around his shoulders. Shoulders that Willow would have hugged not three months ago and called her own.

A stab of hurt ran through her and she fought the urge to tell her to fuck off, get off her boyfriend, and get the fuck out of her cottage.

But it would make no difference. She would never take him back now, not in a million years.

Carlton looked at her, pain etched in his eyes and his face. Carlton didn't get upset often and for the last few months he had been upset at the end of a phone, so she hadn't had to see. But she knew this look well and knew it was genuine. He was like a transparent sheet when he was upset, and it upset Willow to see.

She knew that if she said she forgave him now and that she would take him back, he would brush Suzie away and fall at her feet.

But she couldn't do that. She was a different person three months ago, and she could never go back. Besides, she didn't want to.

The faint kiss in the dark (was it a kiss?) pulled back into her mind and her whole being pulled toward Jack. She liked his confidence, humour, warmth and even his hot-tempered fire better than Carlton's weak caring.

Even in his apology, Carlton was limp, almost too pleading.

'Willow, I can't apologise enough, babe. I should have spoken to you, should have formulated a better plan. I was scared, scared of what he would do to you. Everything I did was to keep him on-side, to keep the information feeding through. Even letting him stay when he got out, that's all it was. I was trying to protect you, and I did what I thought was right. I'm sorry. I never meant to hurt you. I would never hurt you.'

He looked at her, choking back a sob, and tears stabbed at her eyes. She blinked them away with a breath as he turned his gaze to Cooper. 'And we've never been close, Coop. You've always had the upper hand. Always. When you get out next time, if you get out, don't bother knocking. I don't have a brother anymore. I won't supply you, and I won't help you. You've wrecked my life in more ways than one since that attack, the ripples of the life you lead affect more than just you and what you want. It hurts, and it breaks people. I don't want to hear from you again, ever.'

Cooper's face was stone as the door banged three times and Willow nodded at Jack to let the police inside.

Coop stared at Carlton as the police came inside and the house became a hive of activity. He stared as a policewoman went through what had happened with everyone here at the house and advised Willow to get her wound looked at as soon as possible. He stared as the policeman untied and cuffed him, and he stared as he was read his rights.

He only looked away when he was finally escorted outside, put in the police car, and taken away.

One Hundred and One

W ILLOW WINCED AS JACK wound the bandage over the gauze that he had placed on the wound. He worked gently, but kept the pressure tight as Suzie cut and secured the bandage.

'That okay?' Suzie asked.

Carlton was slumped in a dining chair, looking grey and a little useless in an emergency. Willow supposed emergencies weren't something he ever had to attend to, and it was nice to know that Jack could step up, even if Carlton couldn't.

Jack nodded.

'Aye that's fine, that should keep it clean until we can get to Tam. She was a paramedic until a few years ago, she'll know what's needed.'

The burn and throb now that the wound had been cleaned and messed with was intense. Willow took the paracetamol that Jack had put on the table, and swallowed the pills with water.

There had been enough evidence and witnesses to arrest Cooper on the spot and hopefully he wouldn't be getting out for a while after he had fired with intent to kill. The throb in Willow's arm had almost been welcome at that point, and she welcomed it now. If he hadn't got her, he may have got away with purely having a weapon on his person, which was much less of an offence. For now, the pain was her friend.

'You're a little pale, sweetheart, shall I put the kettle on? A sweet tea might pick you up,' Jack said placing the first aid box back under the kitchen sink where he had found it.

Willow nodded and warmed as he asked Carlton and Suzie what they wanted. Whatever he felt, he was courteous, and Willow would thank him for it later. Her energy was flagging now that the pain and reality of what had happened hit her and the shock was wearing off, but there was still one more person she needed to talk to before they left.

Mick, Warren, and Duncan left soon after Cooper had been taken away. Mick was keen to get back to Helena and let her know they were okay. Jack had opted to stay as had Carlton and Suzie, possibly feeling they had nowhere else to go, and now there was only Maud that Willow couldn't comprehend. She turned to the lady who was watching from the living room doorway.

'Maud? What on earth are you doing here?'

'You'd better ask her why she has keys to your cottage too?' Jack said as he moved around them and into the kitchen.

'I can explain, child,' Maud said. She paused and held Willow's eyes. 'But I think you already know, don't you?'

Martha.

The name passed unsaid between them like a hot stone. 'What is going on here, Maud?'

'Come with me, child. I need to show you something.'

'Is Martha her name, or is that what you call her?' Willow said in the small attic room.

Maud had taken her straight upstairs to the small door and knocked four times. Martha had opened it to let her inside, creeping back from them at the sight of Willow, although she was visibly pleased to see Maud.

'It is a strange coincidence, but yes, Martha is her name. She is eighteen, barely a child. She is mute, but not deaf. The twitch seems to be left over from the violent and abusive childhood that she escaped. She has been living here undetected for many years. When I found her here five years ago, she could only communicate by pointing and gesturing. I know sign language well, my own daughter is deaf, so after I had gained Martha's trust, I taught her. She uses it fluently now, using the mirror to practice.' Maud gestured to the mirror on a table next to a small bookcase crammed with books and a small chair. 'It made it much easier for us to communicate and when she goes out into the world, she will know a universal language.'

Willow looked at the girl, who looked back at her with haunted brown eyes. Now she knew was only eighteen – and not a scary ghost - she suddenly seemed a lot smaller and far less threatening than she had before.

You made her bigger in your mind. Fear does that.

'When I lived here, she was able to come in and out of her space, obviously, but she felt safe up here. This was her side of the attic. If she didn't want to come down, then all I could do was furnish it for her. That's why she has the mattress, bedding, and the rest of the furniture here. I fed her, I've brought her new clothes, shoes, tried to bath her and tame her hair. She doesn't want it. All she seems to be interested in is knowledge. I taught her to read, taught her to communicate, and then I was taken from her life when Mel brought the cottage. The rest she has taught herself. She's feral by rights. She likes to be unseen.'

Maud looked at Martha, a kind, soft look, and Martha stretched out a hand to place in Maud's.

Willow frowned.

'But wait, I saw her at the community centre, at the bridge, and down at your house.'

Martha began gesturing, her hands flowing between each other in synchronicity as Maud nodded.

'I know, Martha. I know. She says she was trying to warn you but didn't know how. She comes down to my house sometimes at night. She can get in the back; I leave her a key. My food is her food, and my home is hers, too. Normally, that is the only place she goes. When I saw she was at the community centre, I knew I had to speak with you. Before now, she has never shown herself to anyone but me, especially in the daytime. Mel didn't know that she was here at all, as far as I'm aware. Martha was almost frantic at what you didn't know.'

'No, Mel knew nothing, other than the air from upstairs kept opening the cupboard door. But you knew? And Martha was scaring me to death? You knew what I thought, and you reinforced it.'

'I did, I was trying to protect Martha, but I also tried to make you less afraid, didn't I? I tried to make you see she wouldn't hurt you. That she wanted to help.'

Willow huffed. 'You try living with all the commotion, mostly in the evenings after dark. It was terrifying. Why didn't you just tell me?'

'That there was a child living in your attic? And all the complications that would bring as you interfered? No, it was easier to leave it be, especially as I knew you wouldn't be here long.'

Martha tucked a cold hand into Willow's and tugged. Willow looked at the girl, her heart-shaped face visible as her hair fell back. She began moving her hands rapidly and finished by pointing at her.

'She says she's sorry. She wanted to warn you, not scare you, but she was getting desperate,' Maud said.

Willow smiled at the girl.

'You don't need to apologise, but there was all the commotion with the cupboard every night?'

There was more hand movement from Martha, and more translation from Maud.

'She wanted you to be aware of this space upstairs, she knew that you would need it, and need her. She is a light worker, like I am. She sees, but her visions are stronger, clearer. She is more adept. When I lived here and I could work with her, she would often fall into trances and then tell me what she would see. Mostly it was about me at first, and those things would come true. I admit I used her a few times when I had clients to see. She doesn't need the physical connection as I do. I wanted to get a feel for these people beforehand. Martha can connect through a mere photograph of a person.'

'So, your entire business is fake?'

'No, child. I see too, just not as well as Martha does.' She placed a hand on the child's head and for the first time Willow saw a smile cross Martha's face. 'I have worked hard to develop my skills with a lifelong learning. Martha is eighteen. She has a gift.

She sees naturally. Which is why she ran away from the violence at home and ended up here when the cottage was empty.'

'When was that?'

'She was seven. Terrified, but resourceful. She got inside to keep warm and safe. The downstairs was often open back then, you see, the upstairs rooms were her salvation from intruders. She ate very little from the forest and bins each night. A habit I couldn't get her out of after I caught her at my own fridge here one night. That's how I found her, you see? I knew that food was going missing, so I set up a watch and caught her. Anyway, she remains a night owl.'

Martha signed, and Maud nodded.

'She says the night is safer. It is dark, and she likes to hide. There are not many people out at night.'

Willow nodded. 'I get that. I don't even know how you got out, though. I saw you downstairs way before the stairs were revealed, didn't I?'

Martha's hands flashed, and Maud picked up the translation baton.

'There are many ways she can get in and out. There is a back door key that is hidden outside for getting into the lower areas of the house. She can also get inside the front bedroom window from the outside and re-lock it from the inside. There's a knack, apparently.'

Willow shook her head.

'Yes, I suppose that goes without saying, but how does she get up here? The entrance was blocked?'

Maud smiled. 'The window.'

Willow frowned, and Martha pointed to the small skylight.

'There's ivy at the side of the house. Over the years, she's pulled bits away. She scales it easily now and climbs over the roof to the window here, at the back.'

'Ivy?'

'It's old and strong. If it was taken away, the brickwork of the house would possibly be compromised now, child. It's plenty strong enough for a child's weight.'

Willow had a sudden vision. A primate spider crawling across the roof one dark evening.

That was Martha?

She blinked.

'That makes sense,' she muttered. 'I didn't see the door when we first came up here, but I suppose if she doesn't need it...'

Maud watched Martha as she signed.

'Yes, that's right, Martha. The door here can only be opened from the inside. We fixed it together before I left after Mel brought the place. If Mel, or anyone else, found her, she would be carted off to the authorities. Neither of us wanted that. This is her home, and I was only over the road. I could see her, still teach her, still loan her my books. We had a system, but she knew she couldn't be found for it to continue. Another reason she stuck to being active at night when Mel was asleep.' Maud shrugged as Martha nodded. 'We removed the light from up here and boarded and tiled over the other skylights, reducing the likelihood of anyone seeing the small door here. We plastered that over the outside so that it looked like a wall at a glance. I hired in a firm with no connections to come and seal up the stairway, making the cupboard simply a cupboard and not an entrance to the upstairs.'

'Wouldn't house plans have shown the rooms, though? When Mel bought the place?'

'The house had been derelict for a number of years when I rented it directly from Martha Otis's extended family. They weren't interested in anything official as long as their house was put right by somebody else and it gave them an income. They knew nobody was interested in living in a house where brutal murders had taken place. When Mel brought it, they were equally happy to let it go, which rocked everything for me and Martha. I showed Mel around myself and told her nothing about the upstairs. She was a cash buyer, and again the Otis family let it go easily with a self signed agreement. I tried to sway Mel, to tell her the place was haunted, to tell her of the damp, of the house's cold. She was so excited about being here, I don't think she even looked through any official plans. We just hoped that she wouldn't go investigating. As it turns out, she was completely unaware.'

'But there was a lot of work went on here apparently,' Willow said.

'At ground level, aye. It was an enormous relief when Mel ran out of money before the roof.'

'The rent contract said that it had been done through and insulated completely. Top to bottom.'

'Well, lies can be told now, can't they? To get a higher price. Martha will tell you they never entered upstairs. The cupboard was blocked and there is no other attic hatch to get inside.'

Martha shook her head.

Willow looked at the girl. Silent, stealthy, and able. How many times had she appeared in the kitchen out of nowhere? How many times had she been in the hall?

It was obvious now that Maud had told her about the bedroom and the back door, but at the time, it had been terrifying.

She tried to take it all in.

'Wow. So I saw you because you wanted me to, but you couldn't speak to warn me.'

Martha signed with a small smile.

'And you were too scared for her to approach you,' Maud said. 'She says she left messages, though.'

'Faces. Yes. And that was you scratching in the hall just before Cooper came up here.'

Martha nodded and cast her gaze down.

'It doesn't matter, Martha. As long as I know I'm not living with a ghost, I'm happy enough. It can be painted over.'

'Are you going to stay?' Maud said, the hope in her voice unmistakable.

Willow remembered Helena's words about Jack and the divorce. She remembered the light kiss a mere hour ago in the darkness as he held her.

Cooper was back in jail, and there was no way she was getting back with Carlton. There was no point leaving now when she was enjoying herself and there was such a huge opportunity here. She was enjoying herself and the people she was getting to know.

'I think I am. This is my home now. I want to stay on for as long as Mel lets me.'

Maud cried. Actually cried, and the grin on Martha's face spoke volumes as she moved to hug her friend and teacher. Willow smiled.

'You can stay, Martha. This is your home too, but don't you dare start scratching the walls and bumping open the doors at midnight again. If you want to sleep up here, fine, and I'll leave the stairs open, but there's a bed downstairs.'

Martha grinned and stepped over to Willow. She grabbed her hands with a smile.

'I do have a condition,' Willow said, and Martha's smile slipped. 'You can't live like this forever, and someone with your skill and dexterity and love of learning should be out in the world. There's so much to see out there.'

Martha shrank back, and Willow grabbed her hands again.

'I'm not talking about uprooting you completely right now. Over time, slowly. Maud and I will both help you, and we'll always be with you. You deserve to shine, not to live up here in the darkness. You didn't escape one prison to be held in another. Let us help you. That's my condition.'

Martha looked to Maud, whose tears had spilled over again. Maud nodded with a sob.

'Yes, Martha. You're a bright girl. I'll never leave you alone, and you don't have to move any faster than you want to. Let us help you. Maybe one day you could even come and live with me, at my house.'

Martha still looked unsure, but a small smile formed on her lips. Willow could tell that it was more about pleasing Maud than wanting to change anything, but she hoped that would change with time.

As Maud and Martha hugged next to her Willow felt something she hadn't felt in a long time. Genuine excitement and happiness about what lay ahead.

She had a plan for the future now, a purpose, not just hiding from Carlton and Cooper, and that felt good.

The old Willow was gone, her shackles were gone, and the future felt vast and bright in front of her.

Epilogue

6 MONTHS LATER.

The roar of water accompanied Willow as she climbed up the mountain's sloping side. Steps carved from the rock at the bottom had worn her legs to shaking pins of jelly, but now they were on a flatter path, less of an incline. It was gentler on the calves than the steps, but out of the trees the sun beat down unbearably warm in the late spring sunshine, and the higher they got, the hotter it seemed.

If Jack's face was red - and it was - she dreaded to think what colour hers was.

Probably a fetching purple.

She placed a hand on a jutting bit of rock as the terrain steepened again, literally following in Jack's footsteps as he climbed ahead of her.

'Just a little way more now,' Jack urged as Willow gasped for breath. He turned and held out a hand, pulling her up onto the small rock ledge he stood on.

With a burst of effort, and Jack's help, she climbed up and placed her hands on her thighs, breathing heavily as cool water sprayed her face, wetting her T-shirt and bare legs.

She closed her eyes.

'That spray is heaven,' she panted. 'Are we here?'

Jack laughed. 'No, but it's only a small way further. I'll let you choose - the long way or the short way up?'

Willow opened her eyes as Jack put a hand under the fast spray of the waterfall and threw the cold water over his face and neck.

'Up?' she said, looking toward the top of the waterfall. 'Up there?'

'It's not far.' Jack grinned. 'I promise you.'

She stood now that she was getting her breath back and placed her hands on her hips as she eyed the water. It wasn't particularly steep at the side of the waterfall except in places where the rock was higher. It did look unforgiving if she slipped, though. She chewed her lip and glanced down the falls as they trundled downwards with a roar.

'What's short and what's long?' she said as Jack pulled the pack from his back and handed her a bottle of water. She took a drink as he turned her away from the falls to the left.

'See where the path cuts around to the left of the water here? It climbs to the top from there, but it's a fairly meandering path. Takes a while.'

Willow looked to the dirt path at the side of the waterfall and saw that it did indeed lead away from the falls before disappearing up and out of view.

'Uh huh, and the other path?'

Jack grinned, his eyes glinting mischievously, and Willow raised an eyebrow. 'You want me to climb the bloody waterfall, don't you?'

He shrugged. 'It's not that bad. I used to do it when I was just a wee bairn.'

'Good for you,' Willow grumbled, wiping the sweat from her brow, the water bottle still in her hand.

'It's literally about thirty steps and you'll be at the top, but you'll have to climb some of it. I'll be right behind you, though.'

Willow looked up at the falls and the rocks at the side. It wasn't far to the top, she thought, as Jack pointed out the route up and the rocks to use and to stand on.

Willow sighed. 'What do you think we should do?' she said, already knowing the answer.

Today, she was going to climb a waterfall.

Every hike with Jack had her testing and pushing herself to the limit at some point. He never went faster than she could go, and never pushed her beyond what she could do, but he was a better hiker, better climber, fitter, more agile. He'd spent a lifetime up in these hills. He knew them backwards, he said.

'If I didn't think you could do it, I'd take you round. Last year when I was going to bring you, I'd have taken you round without question. I think you can do this. In fact, I know you can.'

Willow looked at him. His eyes were alive, as only nature could achieve, and he looked beyond happy. He loved the outdoors, he loved the physical exertion, and he loved the scenery, it was unrivalled, he said.

Willow was beginning to love it just as much, although she would sometimes rather take a short, non-sweaty stroll through the forest, while chatting without having to gasp for the breath to speak.

She looked back at the top and huffed a breath.

'What if I get stuck?'

'You won't.' Jack put their bottles away, swung the pack back onto his back and fastened the waist and chest straps. 'You hiked further up the second sister at Glencoe in fashion boots. You can absolutely do this, it's easier than it looks.'

Willow laughed.

'At least I have proper boots now,' she said, looking down at the brown ankle height boots with thick tread and waterproof uppers that were the most comfortable things she had ever put on her feet. Her legs were bare and tanned up to her denim shorts. In truth, she felt fitter and more able than she had ever felt in her life. She looked back up at the falls, and Jack slipped his arms around her waist from behind.

'I'll be right behind you, I won't steer you wrong. We'll be up the top in two minutes,' he murmured, 'I won't let anything happen to you, just listen to what I tell you as we go.'

Willow's heart thumped as she turned to face him. She put her hands on his firm chest. He circled his arms around her back.

'If you really don't want to, princess, we can go round. It's not an issue.'

'No, I'll do it. If I slip and die, can you tell my mum-'

'That you love her, and she's to bury you here. Aye,' he grinned and raised an eyebrow. 'I got it the last fifty times you told me.'

'Well, that's because you keep taking me to treacherous places. I've only been hiking for the last two months, Jack, and already I've scaled vertical slopes, scree, rockfalls, dense cloud banks, and now waterfalls.'

'What haven't you managed to do?' he said.

'Well, hopefully not this,' she said. 'Can I ask you a favour?'

'Anything,' he said, and her heart flipped as he looked softly into her eyes. He pushed, but he cared, and she knew he would happily walk round if she felt this was too much. The truth was, she enjoyed the pushes. They were teaching her more about herself than she would ever have discovered alone.

'Next time we get out, can we go for a small stroll on a flat beach somewhere?'

'Of course,' he said, 'I know... we'll take the kayak, or better than that, I know somewhere you can jump from the cliffs into-'

'Jack!' Willow said, cutting him off. 'A walk. Just a small walk and a picnic, somewhere I don't need an hour-long shower to remove an inch of sweat and dirt afterwards.'

Jack laughed and pulled her into a hug. 'I know, I'm only playing. Aye, we'll go somewhere flat. Let's get up this waterfall. I've got a surprise for you at the top, but it won't be good for much if we take much longer.'

'Will I like it?'

He pulled away and looked down at her.

'The surprise? I bloody hope so. It took me ages to sort without you knowing. Let's get up there.'

Willow nodded, her heart beginning to thump again as she turned to the rocks ahead.

It was an easier climb than she thought, made easier by the fact that Jack knew where she should step and what she could hold on to at the steeper parts. He stayed directly behind her most of the way up, enveloping her between his arms as he guided her. At the top, she pulled herself over a small, steep ledge, her mouth dropping open before she'd even got to her feet.

Ahead of her was a deep and clear body of water. A small loch that had been forged over the years by the stream that ran down into it. As the mountain rose beyond, a waterfall fell into this loch before falling over the edge and down the waterfall that she had just climbed.

All around the green mountainside looked lush with grass and heather, and a small cluster of trees sat just beside the water.

'Jack, oh my God, this is beautiful.'

'It is, isn't it? Worth the climb?'

She grinned as he climbed up next to her.

'It really was. I think it's the most beautiful place we've been yet.'

'Told you it was pretty special. You never know what you're going to be rewarded with around any corner. This was somewhere I liked to be a lot when I was younger.' He dropped the backpack onto the ledge, and pulled Willow further toward the loch, away from the edge.

'Wait here,' he said, not waiting for an answer before disappearing around the side of the hill.

Willow watched him go with a small frown.

He was a different man to the one she had met last year, although his care, patience and attention stayed the same. He was funnier, more energetic, more enthusiastic, and if he could be, even more beautiful - or maybe that's because he was still holding back, despite the small kiss in the attic. In front of her was a man that she very much wanted to be in the life of, and for a long time, but he was anxious, and she thought she could understand that. He'd been effectively trapped for a long time.

His divorce was slow going. He was apparently entitled to much more than Jennifer wanted to give, but Jack had nothing to lose by waiting it out. His solicitor's fees were paid by Mick and Helena, who he would pay back when it was settled, he assured them, although they had said they didn't want it back. Meanwhile, he was enjoying recapturing his life as Helena loosened the reins a little.

With a smile, Willow turned to look over the top of the waterfall and saw Clover Nook from a dizzying height. From up here the road was small, the line of houses and shops tiny, as was the community centre, and McGracken House and farmland. She saw the river running through the village. The river that this water joined, after travelling through the bracken and grass into a man-made tunnel that ran underneath the road.

Just above McGracken House, amongst the trees, sat Ivy Cottage. Small and squat from here, looking tiny next to the big house at the bottom of the road.

Willow felt a warmth flood through her that was nothing to do with the sun that was beating down. She loved Clover Nook, loved the people here, and had made some lifelong friends.

She continued to go to yoga, loved the sessions with Tam and the chats with Sophie. Tam was also helping her through a course to become a yoga instructor herself and agreed that she would split the sessions at the centre with a view to retiring in a year or so. Tam was old, she said, but if Willow could carry on the sessions, she would be thrilled, as would the villagers.

For now, Willow practiced teaching two classes a week and earned half pay as Tam supervised her. She had also taken on two shifts a week at the shop, and spent the rest of her time at McGracken House, helping with the house and the animals, and the people who came and went. McGracken House felt more like home than Ivy Cottage did now, especially as Helena was back to her warm, accepting self and all of the mess with Jack had been smoothed over.

Willow's eyes travelled to Ivy Cottage, sitting innocently in the sunshine, with a ripple of heat rising from the slate roof like a mirage. She thought of Martha.

She was like a different girl now, too, her blonde hair clean and shiny. Gone was the filthy grey dress, the straggly hair, the bare feet. In its place were new clothes and shoes and a young girl that was shining through her new found life. She spent her life between the cottage, where she slept downstairs now, and Maud's where she also had a bedroom. She slept where she felt like sleeping. Neither Maud nor Willow was opposed to having her, especially as she had saved Willow's life. But Maud was becoming a more regular choice now. Maud and Martha seemed to feed each other's need for company and companionship, and obviously Maud could chat to Martha easily, and her shelves held the books.

Some villagers knew of her now, and Maud made up a story of her being a long-lost niece. A half-brother with no other family had died. The child had come to live with her as there was nowhere else. A few villagers seemed skeptical. Maud had lived in the village her entire life, but they couldn't deny that her father had walked out when she was young, and that he could have fathered another child.

Maud seemed happy to let the gossip feed itself until the rumours ran in circles and finally fizzled out.

The only thing that continued in Ivy Cottage was the drawing of faces and the messages that accompanied them. Martha's faces were mostly happy these days, and mostly on a pad of paper that she and Willow kept especially for the purpose of communication until she could learn more sign language herself. They had a system, and Willow was growing to like the girl a lot, but she was happy for Maud to take over. She had no intention of taking on a child when her life was just getting back on track. The mess on the hallway wall had been refilled and smoothed before painting, but the hole had been left in the cupboard for the stairway in the cottage to be used. At some point she would get the roof fixed, maybe open up the skylights, and install a door to keep out any chill, but there were no longer any noises from the cupboard, and it no longer blew open in the breeze now that a lock held the door shut. Martha carried one key, and Willow kept the spare in the kitchen drawer.

The cottage was the same safe and homely place that she thought it had been when she first moved in ten months ago, and after conversations with Mel she was seriously thinking about buying the place with the money that she had got from the sale of her apartment and furniture in Bristol.

Carlton had wanted to sign the apartment back over to her after the fiasco with Cooper, but she had told him to sell it and they would go halves. He was mostly at Suzie's now, and there was no way she was ever going back to live there. The apartment had sold quickly, and Willow had ended up with more money than she had ever seen in a savings account. She was well able to live on the small income she acquired at the moment, so she let the bulk earn interest while she decided. She loved Clover Nook, and wanted to stay as long as she could, that she was certain of.

Carlton managed to keep his clinic running, although he lost some good clients over the madness that was last winter. He was happy with Suzie, or so she thought. He was evasive when she spoke to him, but she was no longer concerned. She wished him well but didn't wish to be in his life any more than she had to be. She wanted to put the last five years to bed and start over.

As for Cooper, he was apparently going to jail for a long time, although his trial had yet to begin. Willow was just happy that he was locked up without bail and couldn't track anybody else down. Helena's Karma got him after all.

Willow turned to look for Jack but saw no sign of him yet, so she sat down, hanging her feet over the ledge, letting the spray cool her legs and the sun wash away her cares. She smiled and closed her eyes, turning her face up to the sun.

Was there anything better than this moment, right here and now?

She thought it may just be perfect.

There was a scuffle beside her, and then Jack was back. She felt his movement with every fibre of her being until he was still, and so close that his left leg touched her right and their shoulders bumped gently.

'Here you go, princess,' he said.

She turned, opening her eyes to two small glasses with long stems. A strawberry was placed on each rim, and more cut strawberries were inside, accompanying the pale fizzy liquid.

'Where did you get that?' she said, her jaw dropping open.

'You said you wanted a picnic.'

He flicked his head to the pond behind them. On the grass under the shade of the trees was a picnic blanket with a wicker basket and a cool box sat in the middle.

Willow felt a grin spread across her face.

'Oh my god, Jack, what have you done?' Willow felt the grin spread further as she looked at him. 'Are you for real?'

Jack raised his eyebrows. 'Your wish is my command. It's getting warm fast though, here, have this.'

She took the glass from him and took a sip. It was cold and bubbly and slid down her throat like liquid ice.

'It's-'

'-Prosecco,' she finished with him.

Jack nodded with a grin and held his glass up. She clinked it with hers.

'Cheers,' she said, upending the small glass and finishing it in two mouthfuls, relishing the cold that ran all the way to her stomach.

Jack's glass was still full when she looked back at him. His nose wrinkled as he peered at the liquid.

'What's the matter?' she laughed.

He handed her his glass.

'Aye, as romantic as this is, Prosecco tastes like crap. You have the fizz, I'll have the strawberries.'

'You just crushed my perfect moment,' she said, laughing. 'I hope you're not going to make me climb down that waterfall after this.'

'There's a whole bottle over there yet. I'll carry you back if I have to.'

Willow grimaced, and they both laughed.

'What are we celebrating?' she said, sipping from Jacks glass.

Jack looked out over the waterfall toward the village with a small frown that accompanied his smile, and then he looked back into her eyes making her stomach flip. He rarely sat so close, and she could see every amber fleck in his eyes, every freckle on his skin, a small scar on his chin that he said he got climbing as a child.

He's just perfect.

'You,' he finally said.

'Me?'

'I wanted to thank you, for everything. For understanding, for letting me get my head together, and for letting me take some time alone. I'm an idiot, I know. Truth be told, I was scared. Terrified of getting into something else where I'm trapped. As soon as I knew we had free rein, I wanted to run for the hills. I know I've messed you about, messed with your feelings, and I'm sorry for that. I don't want to hurt you.'

'I know. You've explained this, Jack,' she said with a small smile. 'It's fine. I needed space to process everything that went on, too. I'm lots more settled now than I was. I don't mind, as long as you keep pushing me up waterfalls. You're my best friend here and I adore you, but you've been through a lot, too. I want whatever makes you happy.'

Until that involves a woman, she thought, but until now he hadn't shown any interest in anyone else. He was still tactile, still caring, still attentive. It was just the relationship he couldn't handle, and she hoped that was short term, but until he said otherwise, she would just continue to give him, and herself, space.

Jack smiled at her.

'Aye, I know, and that's why I can't let you go.'

'I'm not going anywhere,' she said.

'But you could. That's the point. This works both ways, I'm not tied to you, but you're not tied to me either. I don't know what scares me more.'

Willow shook her head. 'You're not making much sense.'

'I know,' he said, swallowing hard. He looked nervous. Willow drank the prosecco, put the glass next to her own and took his hand in hers. 'I'm struggling. It's pathetic. I hate this.'

'Don't you always tell me the longer you think about what's in front of you, the harder it seems?'

He nodded.

'So how is this any different?' she said. 'Do you want to take the long route or the short route?'

'Which do you prefer?' he said.

She grinned. 'As if you need to ask. The short one. Push yourself, get over the fear, challenge yourself. You taught me it's the best side of life to be on.'

'The short one,' he murmured, dropping his eyes to their inter-twined hands on his knees.

Willow nodded. Her heart was drumming. This was very unlike confident, chatty, laid-back Jack. She didn't know what was so important that he could barely speak to her. He'd always said he liked that they could talk openly about anything.

She felt her cheeks flush in the sun and thought maybe she should have taken it easier with the prosecco. Her head was a little light.

'Start climbing, don't think,' she whispered, wondering why she had said it out loud.

He raised his eyes back to hers and she felt a connection so strong that she couldn't look away.

'I can't help but think,' he said. 'I think about you all the time. I think you're wise and beautiful, and I love how easy you are to talk to. I love the highlights that the sun catches in your hair, the deep brown of your eyes, the way your freckles come out in the sun. You're funny, smart, brave, and kind. I love how you look after me, and look out for me, and how you humour me when I try to push you up waterfalls or tell you it's just another ten minutes when it's an hour. I love the way you look at me, the way you build me up when I'm feeling low.' He smiled down at their hands. 'I don't know, Willow, but I... I think I'm falling in love with you.'

Willow blinked at him.

Yep, definitely too much Prosecco.

I'm in dreamland.

Did he really just say that?

'Oh... er... wow. I didn't expect that,' she stuttered, and mentally kicked herself.

Jeez, Willow, that took so much effort, and that's all you can say?

'Neither did I,' he said with a frown, his face red. 'I don't know where that came from. I know we're not even together. I just... I can't imagine being with anyone else, and I don't want to spend any time with anyone else. All I think about is you, and what will make you happy, and where to take you next. I don't want to waste any more time being scared of what that means.'

Willow's heart was pounding as she looked at him. If she was honest, he looked almost ready to throw up, and by being quiet she was doing him no favours, but she couldn't think of a thing to say. This was something she had dreamed of in a far-off distant future, not today, not right now. It caught her off guard and took her breath away.

'Jack...' she tried.

'I don't expect you to feel the same, I know that's strong. I can't just expect you to feel the same way after all this time, and after I've messed you about. I said too much, I'm sorry. I don't know what I hoped to achieve by it. I just... forget it... forget I said anything.'

He trailed off and Willow's heart went out to him. He was so utterly nervous, and this wasn't Jack at all. Ever.

'Jack,' she said gently, 'You know what you could have said?'

He looked at her and shook his head so quickly it almost looked like Martha's twitch.

'You could have said. Willow, I like you. Can I take you to the top of this perilous waterfall - because that's the kind of guy I am - kiss you, and just see where things go from there? Maybe a stroll along a seventeen-mile disused railway to the coast? Maybe a night camping on a red ant hill? Maybe a short walk up Ben Nevis? What do you think?'

A grin was starting to spread across Jack's face as he shook his head.

'You enjoyed all of those things, right? Because we don't have to go so crazy all the time, I'm just letting off steam. It's nice to have someone to do it with, that's all.'

'Loved them,' Willow said without cracking a smile. 'Especially the ant bites.'

He chuckled and nudged her shoulder, and she grinned.

'It was more fun than a night stuck in a Bristol apartment, by a long way.'

'So, what you're saying is, I've got to work on asking a woman out, eh?'

'It's painful, Jack, really,' she said, squeezing his hand with a grin.

He smiled, looking over the village below, and rubbed a hand over his mouth.

'Hypothetically, what would you say? To your own question, not mine?' he said.

'About ant bites and seventeen-mile walks?'

'Maybe picnics and moonlit walks by the sea?'

'Ah, now you're talking.'

He chuckled. She smiled and leaned to kiss him gently, a butterfly kiss, at the corner of his mouth much like the one he had teased her with in the attic. He turned into her, their heads almost together as his lips brushed hers gently.

She felt his need and wanted to respond, but she held back, playing with him for just a while longer.

'I don't know,' she whispered against his cheek. 'It would depend on the kiss.'

She felt him grin as he pulled back to look at her.

'You don't make it easy, do you, princess?' he said tucking a strand of hair back behind her ear.

'Nothing worthwhile is ever easy,' Willow said, leaning her face into his hand. 'Some guy told me that once trying to get me up the tallest mountain in Britain.'

'I knew that would come back to bite me,' he said, leaning closer, his hand running back into her hair.

Willow closed her eyes, and then his lips were back on hers, and amongst the explosions in her stomach and the giddiness she felt, she had only one overriding feeling as he kissed her gently.

She was home.

THE END

Review

If you enjoyed this book it would be fantastic if you could leave a review.

Reviews help to bring my books to the attention of other readers who may enjoy them too.

Help spread the joy... or indeed, the fear!

Thank you!

IN A CABIN, IN A WOOD... SOMETHING IS LURKING, BATHED IN BLOOD.

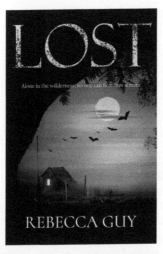

Is something sinister sharing the isolated cabin with Mac? or has the 'mind guy' lost his mind?

Visit www.rebeccaguy.co.uk for more information.

TURN THE PAGE FOR A PEEK AT CHAPTER ONE.

Lost Chapter One

'**Y**OU LOOK LIKE HELL, Mac.'

Mac Macauley looked up at his older brother; the *only* person from whom he would take such a statement. Tom gazed at him across the table, his eyes narrowed and scrutinizing. Finally, seeming to accept Mac's state of hell, he gave a small nod and flipped open the paper. Mac felt his stomach sink.

'Want me to make you feel worse?' Tom said, eyebrows raised over the paper's edge.

'Sure, why not?' Mac said with a sigh, leaning back into the chair and bringing a hand up to scratch the back of his head.

Tom placed the paper - 'The Times' of all things - down onto the table between them, spinning the writing to face Mac. He placed a finger on the article as if it didn't already have a screaming headline that may as well be emblazoned in red and roaring with flames.

HAS THE MIND MAN LOST HIS MIND?

After another embarrassing send-off, you have to wonder if the guy who says you can have it all, Mac Macauley, really has lost it all. The motivational sensation who once filled the Royal Albert Hall with his astoundingly fool proof plan to hack the mind, and access the subconscious to create the perfect life, regardless of circumstance, once again left us with a lack lustre feel at his latest talk in Islington yesterday. Seemingly a theme after the loss of his wife six months ago, the media mind-hacker can't seem to get it together, forcing us to wonder if there really is a mind-hack after all, or whether his framework is built on less solid foundations when faced with real tragedy...

No. Not today.

Mac dragged his eyes away from the article and back to Tom's, hoping his brother wouldn't see the thud of his heart under his worn jumper.

'It's a good point,' he said with a shrug as he reached for his cigarettes from his jacket pocket. He pulled one free and put it between his lips.

'What?' he said, catching Tom's frown.

'Sula hated that. You'd given up.'

'For all the good it did me. Sula's dead.' His heart gave a small jolt. A lot less of a shock at saying the words out loud now than he'd had in the beginning. The effects of true love and companionship already fading.

No, not fading. *Suppressed.* He closed his eyes.

'What happened?' Tom said gently.

Mac opened his eyes, confused.

'The talk?' Tom gestured to the paper, which accused innocently from the tabletop. Ignoring Tom's disapproving look, Mac lit the cigarette as he thought.

What happened? That's a good question, Mac. What the hell happened?

He'd lost it. That's what happened, just as the paper said. Lost his wife, lost his life. And now his career was busy getting lost, too. Why not? When life shit on you, it really took a dump, and then it added some more to the pile for good measure.

'You read the article,' he said with a mirthless laugh. 'I lost my wife. Lost her, like we were strolling around Sainsbury's, and she wandered down the wrong aisle. Like an odd sock, she just got...' he threw his hands in the air, '...lost. As if she can be found. Like she'll just turn back up with a smile and say 'gotcha! Had you going for a minute there, didn't I?'

Tom raised his hands. 'Okay, okay. I get it, and I know it hurts. Listen, Mac, maybe it's time for a break, you know?'

Mac took a drag of his cigarette, his face flushing under a week and a half of dark stubble. Heck, the one thing he hadn't lost was the ability to grow a beard. How about that?

'Why would I need a break?'

Tom's mouth bobbed open as he fished for the right words to say. 'Well, you haven't stopped, Mac. All the booked engagements, all the talks, the shows, the interviews. You've just kept steamrollering right through.'

'That's how we get through these things, right? We carry on, Tom, because there's nothing else to fucking do is there? What do I have left? You think I want a mini break in the Maldives? Work. My work is all I have. I want to help people-'

'You're wrecking it, Mac. You need a break. You can't keep going-'

'I *have* to keep going, I have no choice. It's okay for you, Tom. You're not in the public eye. There's no escape for me. Ever since Sula died, people with cameras have been camped on my lawn. My fucking lawn, Tom. And do you know why? Not because they care, not because they want to wish me well, oh no, because they want to see me collapse. They want me to crumble. They want pictures of me looking wasted and beaten. They want to be there to capture it all, to laugh, to write their stupid stories. Because they want headlines like this-' he waved a hand at the paper, which fluttered and crackled under the force of the air thrown at it. 'This sells, Tom. It sells.'

Tom was nodding. 'Yes-' he said, as Mac barrelled right on over him.

'Tragedy sells, shock sells, bereavement sells, falling apart sells. No one wants to listen to the good news anymore. They're all baying for blood. My wife died, Tom, she *died*, and they love it, they...' Mac felt his voice quiver, felt the depth of emotion cut him short, and felt the hot tears threaten to burst forth. He jabbed his thumbs into his eyes, removing them before they arrived.

Mac heard the scrape of a chair and felt a hand squeeze his shoulder.

'Yes,' Tom said, closer to him now, 'that's exactly what they want, because they don't know you. They don't care. It's so easy to de-humanise these days. So easy to tear people apart on social media, in the paper, on the news. But Mac, you're giving them exactly what they want.'

Mac looked into the crow-lined eyes of his brother. His best friend. He cared, Mac knew that, could see the depth of emotion running behind his eyes too. He had known and loved Sula like a sister, as had Tom's wife - who was still here. Flesh and blood.

A stab of unfairness ran through him at the aneurysm that had taken his perfectly healthy wife with a ferocious disregard for the lack of her years.

Tom placed a hand on his arm.

'Look at you, Mac. Have you looked in the mirror? Seen your clothes, your hair, your face? When did you last have a shower? You have to stop because you're giving them fuel. Your career will be over if you keep going. Is that what you want?'

'No, of course not. Being able to help people reach their potential isn't a career, Tom, it's a calling. I have to do this. There are people that need my help...'

'You are one of them,' Tom said. 'Take a break. In six months, a year, you'll be-'

'A year?' Mac spluttered. 'I can't take a year off. Don't be ridiculous.'

'Call it development. You've barely had time for yourself for the last ten years. Read up, learn, look at new theories, rejig the framework. Think of it as a working break. One where you don't need to take a shower and look the part. One where you don't need to worry about getting lost when giving a talk because you think you see her in the audience. Take books, get researching, write a whole new fucking formula, but take a break, Mac, please. We're worried about you.'

Mac swallowed. Tom was forgetting the one problem with his little theory.

'Tom, the other reason I can't take a break is a little more obvious. They won't let me. Wherever I go, Whatever I do at the moment, they're there. Always. Sometimes just one, sometimes a dozen. Do you think I'm going to get off the plane in Gibraltar to find not one person has discovered where I'm going and on what flight? To find not one of them has followed me? I'm stuck. From all angles. I've tried to ask for privacy, I've tried the 'leave me alone', it's not working.'

'Because you look like hell when you're asking. You look broken. It's what they want.'

'So, what's the solution, Tom, because from where I am, it seems you're enjoying this discussion a little too much. Pointing out how dirty and slovenly I am-'

'No, Mac. No. That's not it. Not at all, and yes, I do have a solution. One that I think will work. Just hear me out.'

'I'm all ears.'

'Good,' Tom said, then he took a breath. 'Do you ever watch Bear Grylls?'

LOST IS AVAILABLE AT ALL MAJOR RETAILERS NOW!

SOMETIMES THEY COME BACK...

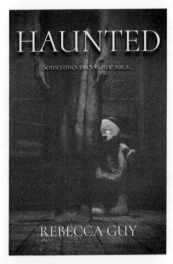

Sixteen years ago her sister died, now she's back. Haunted, terrified and alone, will the truth set Meredith free, or take her soul?

Visit www.rebeccaguy.co.uk for more information.

TURN THE PAGE TO GET THE FIRST SIX CHAPTERS FREE!

Want six free chapters of **HAUNTED?**

Sign up to my mailing list to read the first six chapters for FREE!

You also get access to exclusive behind the scenes content and extra's, and you'll be the first to hear about promotions, discounts, forthcoming titles and competitions!

Signing up is completely free and you will never receive spam from me.

To sign up visit - www.rebeccaguy.co.uk

You can opt out easily at any time.

DECEPTION. GREED. VENGEANCE. BETRAYAL.

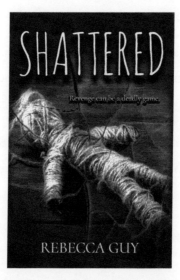

A secret envelopes Fortwind House, years old, covered in dust and locked up tight. Rumours surround the formidible woman who lives there, rumours that terrify Charley, but it is the secret that will blow her life apart.

Visit www.rebeccaguy.co.uk for more information.

ENJOYED THIS BOOK? CHECK OUT A PREVIOUS RELEASE FROM REBECCA GUY

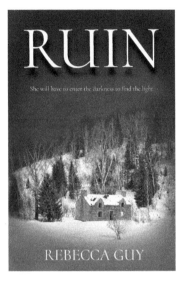

What do you do when your dream home becomes your worst nightmare? Emmie Landers is about to find out!

Visit www.rebeccaguy.co.uk for more information.

Milton Keynes UK
Ingram Content Group UK Ltd.
UKHW010254221123
432980UK00005B/313